MW01593917

ALEJANDRA'S QUEST

BETTINA A. DEYNES &
ROBERT F. WIEDEFELD

iUniverse, Inc.
Bloomington

ALEJANDRA'S QUEST

Copyright © 2013 Bettina A. Deynes & Robert F. Wiedefeld.

All rights reserved. No part of this book may be used or reproduced by any means, graphic, electronic, or mechanical, including photocopying, recording, taping or by any information storage retrieval system without the written permission of the publisher except in the case of brief quotations embodied in critical articles and reviews.

iUniverse books may be ordered through booksellers or by contacting:

iUniverse
1663 Liberty Drive
Bloomington, IN 47403
www.iuniverse.com
1-800-Authors (1-800-288-4677)

Because of the dynamic nature of the Internet, any web addresses or links contained in this book may have changed since publication and may no longer be valid. The views expressed in this work are solely those of the author and do not necessarily reflect the views of the publisher, and the publisher hereby disclaims any responsibility for them.

Any people depicted in stock imagery provided by Thinkstock are models, and such images are being used for illustrative purposes only.

Certain stock imagery © Thinkstock.

ISBN: 978-1-4759-8760-7 (sc)
ISBN: 978-1-4759-8761-4 (hc)
ISBN: 978-1-4759-8762-1 (e)

Library of Congress Control Number: 2013907422

Printed in the United States of America.

iUniverse rev. date: 5/13/13

To:

Johan Deynes

Stefan Deynes

Christian Deynes

Jonathan Wiedefeld

Kristopher Wiedefeld

Keith Wiedefeld

Build me a son, oh Lord,
who will be strong enough to know when he is weak,
and brave enough to face himself when he is afraid.
One who will be proud and unbending in honest defeat,
and humble and gentle in victory.

Douglas MacArthur

This novel, though based on real events, is fictionalized, and any resemblance to actual persons or entities is coincidental.

ONE

Alejandra German, known to most as Ale, was a remarkable young woman. At just seventeen, she immigrated to the United States from Uruguay with her mother, to join her older brother, who had arrived two years earlier. She initially spoke no English and had nothing of value other than an unusually strong will and a collection of dreams. Much of her enthusiasm about her future was fueled by her belief that life could not possibly be any worse in America than it was in Uruguay.

Her parents had divorced when she was four years old, and her single mom did her best raising two children in Uruguay under extremely dire financial circumstances. At age thirteen, Alejandra was shipped off to a boarding school in Argentina, where she took a job in the school library to pay for her tuition and other expenses and later graduated with a solid grade point average. Despite strong family ties, Alejandra's experiences during the first seventeen years of her life contributed heavily to her intense spirit of independence and self-reliance. These personality traits would most likely stay with her for the rest of her life.

During her first three years in the United States, she earned a paltry wage cleaning office buildings, usually being assigned all of the restrooms. She and her mother were living in an old, dilapidated apartment building infested by rats, mice, and roaches, even in the sleeping quarters. The only requirement for Alejandra and her mother to call this place home was that one of them had to be gainfully employed with a steady income, further pressuring the young girl. Each day when she got home from work, she dutifully listened to a tape of *The Eagles*, a popular American musical group.

The tape and the tape recorder were given to her as a present by a coworker. Alejandra listened to the songs, over and over again late into each night, and this provided her with the foundation she needed to learn English. She looked up the words to all of the songs in an English-Spanish dictionary, wrote them down, and then memorized the songs with the English lyrics. When at work, she would sing the songs to herself, and at the end of each part of every song, she would repeat the English words and their definitions in both Spanish and English. She did this until she finally understood enough English to start learning words from other sources, thus building her vocabulary.

After three years of backbreaking manual labor, she was offered a promotion into a newly created human resources position. The rapidly growing company had not previously employed anyone in this capacity and the duties would be almost overwhelming. Alejandra's understanding of the English language had improved markedly, and her bilingual skills would be indispensable in her new job, because the majority of the company's employees were Hispanic and spoke little English. But not all was pleasant with her new management career. Although growing, the company was still small and struggling. She worked in a cramped, dingy, and dirty office for eight to ten hours a day. The place didn't even have a restroom!

The next two years passed slowly. Her professional skills and ability to speak English grew steadily during this time. She was making business contacts outside of the company that she knew would be invaluable later in her career. Earning a little more money in this role than she had previously, she was able to get a better place for her and her mother to live shortly after being promoted. Alejandra soon realized that she was transitioning into a world of job opportunities that she'd never even known existed. Before long she applied for and was hired into the position of Director of Human Resources at a slightly larger company in the same area. When she arrived for her first day of work, she was delighted to learn that there was actually an employee restroom.

Over the next few years, Alejandra continued to grow, both personally and professionally as she settled into her new job and her new life. It was during this time that she met Franco German, a charismatic full-time student from Spain attending a Washington area nursing school not far from where Ale and her mother lived. She had not been experienced in the rituals of courtship during her high school years in Argentina and was hesitant at first. She often wondered why it was that whenever she developed a crush on a boy back home she would enjoy an uneasy level of excitement and suspense, right up until he would seem to be smitten with her. Then, as soon as he seemed to be on the verge of asking her out, she would almost immediately lose interest in him. She later quipped to herself that the excitement of the fantasy made the reality of a catch anticlimactic. But Franco was different. He was highly religious, as was she, and he was both kind and sincere. He was a few years older than she, and he seemed to be in a better place in his life, with a consistently positive attitude that served to lift Ale's spirits when they most needed it. He pursued her differently than she had ever imagined in a potential courtship. Franco was interested but aloof, supportive but noncommittal, generous at times, but apparently a bit selfish at others. He supplied her with a sense of hope that she'd never before enjoyed, but there was a mystique about him that always left her wondering if, after all, he would satisfy her needs on a long-term basis.

After an eighteen-month courtship, Ale married Franco in a simple civil ceremony. His relatives back in Madrid did not attend, as they made no secret of their disapproval of a simple girl of no means marrying into their wealthy family of doctors and lawyers. The first year of the marriage was a struggle, with him in school and almost always studying and her working long hours in an attempt to kick-start her career. Moreover, the fact that neither of them had any prior experience in the bedroom often left her with unresolved expectations. After a year of financial sacrifice, they moved into an apartment that was much nicer than she had ever dreamed of, but another source of tension in the relationship soon surfaced because she alone was the breadwinner and any improvement in their meager lifestyle was entirely her accomplishment. Two years later they started a family.

Unrelenting hard work, patience, and a never faltering confidence in her own ability to overcome adversity had paid off for her. But she knew that this was no time to rest on her laurels. She was becoming increasingly aware every day that if she were to continue to grow and succeed there would be yet another crucial challenge to be conquered. Her life consisted of a never ending juggling of responsibilities at home and at the office, but she would have to find a way to squeeze a significant commitment of time into this already hectic lifestyle. She would have to earn her Bachelor's degree in business if she wanted to continue to grow.

Not long after the birth of her second child she found herself sitting in her first college class at Loyola University in Baltimore. She had somehow found a way to rearrange her entire life—family, work, and babysitters—in order to take a step that would certainly improve that life permanently.

Although it was a small class she was still extremely nervous. At 6:00 p.m., just when the class was scheduled to begin, her first college professor walked into the room. His name was Terry Longbow.

The first thing that Longbow did was to go around the room asking each student one question, "Tell me one thing that will sustain you and will cause you to succeed in your college career, which you are beginning this evening." Ale was the last to answer because the instructor had started around the room from his left and she was to his right. One student said that he would succeed because he was smart, another claimed that her strong faith would keep her going. When it was Ale's turn, she said, "My family is not supportive of this at all. They are upset with me because they think that too many things are already distracting me from spending time with my sons. I don't know if I can do it or not, I just know that I have to." As she spoke a single tear rolled down her cheek.

Despite her initial lack of confidence, Ale succeeded in her undergraduate work, graduating with honors with a degree in management four years later. All of the nights of class and the many hours that she sacrificed away from her family had paid off. She had been a student in five of

Longbow's courses during those four years and her obvious intelligence and determination impressed him so profoundly that he offered her a part-time job with his firm, Orion Resource Management, Inc., as an intern shortly after her graduation.

Her performance in this position was stellar in Longbow's eyes, but he always felt that her confidence in her own abilities needed reinforcement, just like that first night when she sat in front of him in class. Later she was hired into the full-time role of project manager, and still later she was promoted to managing partner. Her pursuit of education did not end with an undergraduate degree. Immediately after graduation from Loyola she studied everything possible in the discipline of human resources, and within six months she passed a grueling industry examination which earned her certification as a Senior Professional in Human Resources, a much coveted credential. To say that Alejandra German was a compulsive overachiever would certainly be a gross understatement.

❋ ❋ ❋ ❋ ❋

Delta flight 1920, a sleek new version of Boeing's popular 737 was slicing its way through the cloudless sky on a routine morning flight from Los Angeles to Memphis and was just an hour from its 1:30 arrival. Ale German occupied seat number 21E, and she was not at all happy about having to change her original itinerary, an aisle seat on a non-stop flight from LAX to Baltimore, to this cramped center seat vexation bound for Memphis. The only thing worse than the body odor of the three-hundred pound man sitting nearby was the incessant screeching of a cat squeezed into a cloth carry-on bag stuffed under an elderly woman's seat. This three-and-one-half hour flight would surely be recorded in Ale's personal journal as the most uncomfortable she had experienced in years, which would be saying a lot for a woman who hated to fly even under the best of circumstances. Her hands were folded neatly in her lap, and her elbows were tight into her sides since the armrests to either side of her were monopolized by her fellow passengers in row 21. She had discovered a few hours earlier that losing herself in thought enabled her to ignore her surroundings and the constant fears of flying that haunted her on every trip.

It's two days before New Year's Eve, she thought, *I've been away from home for four days, and suddenly Terry asks me to change my travel plans so that I can meet him and his son, Michael, in Memphis. He said something about Michael's boss wanting some business advice. Why couldn't we meet in Baltimore after the first of the year? After all, Terry, Michael, and I all live in Baltimore, and from what I understand the business that we are to be discussing is in Baltimore as well. Terry has pulled some last-minute stunts in the four years that I have been working with him, but this one is going straight into the record book!*

Ale allowed her mind to drift away from the inconvenience of this unplanned stop-over as she focused on her family back in Maryland.

I haven't seen my sons since the day after Christmas. I guess they have been so busy playing with their new toys that they haven't even noticed that I've been gone. And I know that Franco hasn't cared much about my absence since my mom is there to take care of everyone. I'm sure that he's been absorbed in his own life —as always!

A small jolt of turbulence briefly interrupted Ale's thoughts and her stomach ached from nervous anxiety. *God, I hate flying,* she thought.

I wonder if I'll ever be happy! I mean, I wonder what true happiness is. Maybe I'm as happy as anyone can be in life, but I just don't know it. Does that make me selfish? All I want—all I've ever wanted-is to be a highly successful businesswoman, with a truly happy marriage to a man who is extremely attentive to me and the children. That's the standard that I have set. And I have just answered my own question. No, I can't possibly be as happy as anyone can be in life because I'm not a successful businesswoman—yet—and I have a husband who is so wrapped up in his work and his own life that he barely knows that I'm alive. Well, maybe that's a little harsh, but he certainly is far from attentive to his wife and his two young sons. Boy—I sure wish this bucket was landing at BWI instead of Memphis!

TWO

THE FIVE MULTI-COLORED ducks ceremoniously marched single file out of the elevator onto a bright red carpet that stretched before them to the large, circular fountain in the center of the hotel lobby. The ducks seemed to waddle in unison, all leaning to the left and then to the right at the same time, as though their actions had been meticulously choreographed. The scores of people in the lobby, who had just minutes earlier been talking and laughing loudly, were quickly silenced as soon as the elevator doors opened, revealing the stars of this twice-daily parade. One by one each duck reached the end of the red carpet and hopped up onto the rim of the masonry wall containing the sparkling pool on top of which the ducks would swim in a circle around the tall, gushing fountain in the center. The spectators began talking and laughing again while the ducks swam for fifteen minutes. And then, on the signal from their keeper, an elderly gentleman neatly dressed in a Bell Captain's uniform and eerily resembling George Burns, the spectators once again fell silent, and the ducks retreated in single file across the carpet and back into the elevator.

If it is 5:00 p.m. in Memphis, Tennessee, and you are witnessing this traditional parade of the ducks, then you know that you are in the lobby of the grand old Peabody Hotel, one of the South's finest.

It was two days before New Year's Eve, 2006. Terry Longbow, his son Michael, and his business partner Alejandra German were sitting in the lobby, with front row seats for the duck parade, awaiting the arrival of Greg Holland. Terry and Ale were the only two owners of Orion Management Resources, Inc., a strategic management consulting and corporate turn-around firm. During their relatively short but exceptionally busy partnership, they had been involved with companies, both large and small that were facing the brink of extinction if someone didn't move in and take control of all of the firm's business operations. As seasoned turn-around specialists, Terry and Ale were accustomed to initial meetings with prospective clients that were punctuated with high levels of stress and an emotional sense of urgency. But this meeting would be different.

"I still don't know why we're meeting with Holland," Ale stated assertively.

With their recent hectic schedules and the demands of their current clients, Terry hadn't taken the time to lay the foundation for this meeting with her. He had simply placed the appointment on their Blackberry calendars simultaneously and then forgotten about it until now.

"I apologize, Ale! I should have briefed you earlier on this. We're going to have to do a better job of coordinating things like this now that we're getting so swamped with work. That's what we would advise clients to do, isn't it?"

Michael had been sitting quietly and listening to the brief exchange. He didn't know Ale well at all in spite of the amount of time that she and his father had been in business together. He had only met her on two occasions, and for only a few moments each time, during the past half-decade. His father believed strongly in keeping business separated from his personal life, and knowing that he was an essential part of the latter, Michael hadn't expected to be close to Ale in any way over the years.

Michael had arranged the meeting in Memphis so that his friend and boss, Greg Holland might be able to get some business counseling from his father. Although Terry and Ale worked out of offices in Baltimore, Memphis was the most convenient place that all four could meet on such short notice during the holidays.

"Can I try to shed some light on this for Ale, Dad?"

"Sure, son—you're the one who requested the meeting in the first place," said Terry.

Michael Longbow had wanted to pursue a career as a commercial pilot for as long as he could remember. Terry had been a commercial charter pilot and flight instructor in the late 1960s and early 1970s, and Michael treasured pictures of his father in and around aircraft while he was growing up. Some of his favorite pictures were of his dad when he was a civilian flight instructor for the United States Naval Academy. Michael was now a certified flight instructor, and he worked part-time at a flight school on the eastern edge of the Baltimore-Washington International Airport, formerly Friendship Airport (where his father had once taught).

"I asked my dad to meet with Greg," Michael said, "because he owns the flight school where I work, and he asked me if I would ask Dad to give him some business advice."

Greg Holland knew of Terry's background both in aviation and business from his close association with Michael, and he was hoping to parlay the relationship into free advice regarding some troubling aspects of his investment in the flight school. Greg had hoped that Michael could convince Terry to take some time to help him, and, so far, it had worked out just as he had wanted.

"Is Holland a potential client or is this going to be a spiritual meeting?" Ale asked, looking as though she wasn't sure who would be providing the answer.

Terry had accepted that Ale was all business, and when it came to asking her to give up her personal time for a meeting like this one he acknowledged that she had every right to be. But, at some twenty-five years his junior, she was still an apprentice in a highly technical and complicated business environment, and he felt that she could benefit from this informal advisory session with a struggling entrepreneur.

"We never know do we, Ale?" said Terry. "Let's just get a bite to eat and have a pleasant conversation, and we'll end a very hectic and busy year with no stress for a change." Terry rose and motioned for them to move into the hotel restaurant on the far side of the lobby.

Terry and Ale were both aware that she still had a long way to go before he would be able to confidently assign to her an entire major project, which was one of the reasons that he had her participate in meetings like this one. As talented and bright as Ale was she was also acutely aware of how much experience she had yet to gain, and welcomed every opportunity for more exposure to the real world. For this, she relied solely on Terry's judgment as her partner and mentor, although at times his timing could prove irritating to her.

As Michael began to explain that Greg started the flight school from scratch a few years earlier on the Eastern Shore of Maryland, he was distracted by something at the entrance of the restaurant, and he quickly interrupted himself. As a slim and casually dressed man approached their table Michael stood and held out his hand to shake.

"Dad, Alejandra German, I would like for you to meet Greg Holland," said Michael in a formal, yet somewhat enthusiastic tone.

Terry and Ale simultaneously stood and reached over the table extending their hands for the obligatory introductory handshake. Greg Holland turned first toward Ale, shook her hand firmly but slowly, and said, "It's a pleasure to meet you, Ms. German." He could not seem to help being struck by her disarming allure. Ale, in her early thirties with strikingly exquisite, yet subtle physical features, had a way of directly capturing a man's attention and making him self-conscious. Greg's first impression of her was apparently disbelief. He must have been thinking, *how can a woman so young and so naturally attractive also be smart enough to be the co-owner of a corporation that specializes in such a tough business?*

"Please call me Alejandra, Greg," said Ale with a little more formality than he might have wanted. Greg then turned to Terry and shook his hand with a greeting and a smile, and all sat down at the table.

"Perhaps we should look at the menu and order before getting down to business," Greg suggested. Everyone agreed, and all were prepared to place their orders when the server arrived a few minutes later.

"I guess the best place to start is at the beginning," said Greg. "I was a stockbroker for a large national brokerage firm for about twelve years after I graduated with my Bachelor's degree in business from James Madison University. I had built an extremely strong book over those years, and my income rose to nearly seven figures annually for my last five years with them. But I found that I was increasingly unhappy with the brokerage business, mostly because of the selling tactics that are customary. I finally decided to leave the business and find a new career and, fortunately, I got out just before the tech stock bubble burst at the turn of the century. I was able to enjoy a nest egg of several million dollars that clearly would have disappeared if I had waited just six more months to make that decision."

"You were very lucky," said Ale.

"And that's just what it was, Alejandra—luck. Literally all of the brokers I worked with who told me I was crazy for leaving wound up losing everything just weeks after I left."

Greg went on. "So after I left I was faced with the decision of what I wanted to do when I grow up. I didn't have any interests, but I did have plenty of money. I soon decided to pursue a passion that I had as a teenager to learn how to fly. I took some private pilot lessons in a Cessna 172 out of a small airport outside of Baltimore."

"Did you like it?" Ale asked.

"I loved it," Greg said enthusiastically, "so much so that I invested a million dollars in starting a flight school at Easton Airport, on the Eastern Shore of Maryland."

"Why did you ask to meet with Terry?" Ale asked and then looked at Terry as if to say, *Why am I asking all of the questions here?* Terry remained silent. This was always his plan with Ale in meetings like this. He wanted her to take the lead so that she was benefiting from the experience as much as possible.

"Right to the point – I guess it is time," said Greg. "I now own a flight school that has moved three times to and from airports on the Eastern Shore, and is currently located at the Baltimore-Washington International Airport. Over ninety percent of our business comes from a contract that we have with The United States Naval Academy to train Midshipmen before they graduate and move on to Pensacola for their formal career flight training. We're having problems with cash flow due to the low margins on the Navy contract and the seasonal nature of that training.

I am considering closing the doors, taking my financial lumps, and just walking away."

Greg finished the last bite of his steak and took a sip of his Coke before continuing. "Here's what I'd like to know from you."

Finally! Ale thought as she sat back in her chair having finished her meal nearly twenty minutes earlier.

"Terry, you have decades of experience with both aviation and business. My question is, can a flight school make it at BWI? Should I keep pluggin' at it or should I wash my hands of it now and cut my losses?" Greg was now more serious and sullen than he had been since his arrival. Michael stopped chewing and just stared at Terry waiting for an answer, obviously surprised by the dire nature of Greg's question.

Terry sat quietly for a few moments. He looked at Michael, then at Ale, and then straight at Greg. "Greg," he said, "you're not asking an aviation question, you're asking a business question." Terry waited as long as he could for effect before he continued. "And the business question you are asking doesn't require decades of experience to answer. That's why I'm going to defer to my partner. Ale will answer your question."

Ale shot a look at Terry that he hadn't seen from anyone since the days before his divorce some fifteen years earlier. But she never lost her composure. No one at the table knew that she was actually steaming under the surface for being placed in this position of having to deliver a professional opinion without the benefit of any research or preparation. No one else could tell that she was wondering why Terry would try to embarrass her like this, even if the meeting was only a favor that he was doing for his son.

"I can answer it for you, Greg," Ale said, "but you are going to have to answer some very penetrating management and finance questions about the business first."

Terry noticed the PDA sitting just a few inches from Michael's left hand. He caught Michael's attention and formed a wry smile while glancing at the unit. He then sent an infrared message to Michael's PDA that read, "Watch her handle this!"

Terry knew that Ale was annoyed with him for putting her into what she considered an awkward situation, but not because she let it show. He knew it because he knew her. Despite a bit of discomfort on his part for having surprised her with center stage with a stranger, Terry decided to sit back and watch Ale handle the remainder of the meeting with little help from him. At this point, Michael looked as if he had resigned himself to the role of passive observer, sitting quietly and staring at Ale as though her every sentence had him hanging in the balance.

"Greg, what's the name of the flight school?" inquired Ale.

"Camber Flight Training, Inc."

"Who is 'Camber'?"

"It's not a who," Greg replied politely. "Camber is a technical aviation term that is used to describe the difference between the distance over the top of an airfoil compared to…"

Ale interrupted at this point. "Sorry Greg, it doesn't sound like this explanation is going to be something I need to know right now, so let's get back to attempting to answer your question."

Ale shot another glance at Terry while still speaking directly to Greg. "Maybe it would help if I briefly explained how we work when we are considering a new client for our turn-around services."

"Please do, I think I would find that interesting," said Greg attempting to not sound condescending.

Ale began her explanation. "The initial stage of working with a company that is in trouble is like the process that a doctor would use with an unconscious patient who has just been brought into an Emergency Room. So much so that we use the same word used by the medical profession in that situation, 'triage,' and we also use the term 'vital signs' to describe the primary key indicators of the health of our own business 'patient.' Just as doctors will use vital signs, among other indicators, to give them insight into the current condition of a patient, we will use revenue levels, cash balance, cash flow, amount of debt, and other measures to give us an initial idea of the status of our 'patient'."

"I understand," Greg said, "go on."

"So what I am going to do here rather quickly is to get an idea of the current health of Camber Flight Training, Inc.," said Ale, "before I can even attempt to give you a general answer to your question of whether the company can succeed at BWI."

"That makes sense!" Greg stated as he sought some form of expression of approval from Terry. There was none.

"And what makes even more sense, Greg," she said, "is the question of whether the flight school can continue to exist regardless of where it operates. So we'll try to answer that question first, and if the answers that we end up with support a conclusion that the business is viable, then we'll try to address the issue of where it is located and whether it will survive there. Does this also make sense?"

Greg smiled at her and said, "More sense than anything has made to me for a long while!"

THREE

ALE LOOKED AT Terry and said with just the slightest hint of sarcasm, "Feel free to jump in here at any time, Terry!" Once again she did not reveal any level of frustration via facial expression or the tone of her voice. In fact, she was now feeling extremely comfortable going solo. Ale was operating without having to use Terry's presence as a crutch, which was exactly what he had in mind when he'd turned this meeting over to her.

"I'm listening, Ale! Go on," said Terry.

"Greg, what is Camber's current annual revenue?" she asked.

"A little over a million dollars a year."

"And the company's profit or loss on that level of revenue?"

Greg replied sheepishly, "We've lost about fifty-thousand dollars this year on that revenue level–but there's a good reason for that …"

Ale interrupted him again. "Not yet. We'll talk about contributing factors in a few minutes. Let's just get the details out of the way right now." She continued, "So, you're generating a million dollars and losing about five percent. How much money do you have personally invested in the business at this point?"

"Roughly a million dollars," he said looking even more uncomfortable.

"Any other investors at risk?" she inquired.

"No," he said, "I have bought everyone else out. I own 100% of the business myself right now."

"And how much debt does the firm have on its balance sheet?"

"None," Greg said sternly, "I don't like debt!"

"Describe your customer base to me."

"Ninety-five percent of our revenue now comes directly from the training contract that we have with the Naval Academy. We provide up to twenty-five hours of flight instruction to each Academy senior who is assigned to our school."

Ale followed up. "So it is safe to say that your entire business is dependent upon this one contract with the Navy for its survival?"

"Yes, that's one of the reasons that I don't sleep very well at night!"

"You mentioned earlier that you are fairly well off financially. How much more are you willing to invest in the business if you decide that it would be worthwhile to keep it open?"

"Obviously, there must be a limit."

"That's what I'm asking you to do, Greg—set the limit."

"Another hundred thousand—max!" he said, again sheepishly.

"OK, Greg, let's recap." Ale emphasized her words with a rhythmic use of her outstretched hands. "We're trying to determine if you should keep Camber open or shut it down. You have about a million in sales this year, and you've lost fifty-thousand at that sales level. The company has no long-term debt, and its survival is entirely dependent upon one single customer. If you maintain the same annual revenue stream and the same level of expenses against that revenue, you would be able to continue operating for the next two years before you have reached your remaining personal cash investment threshold. Without considering anything else in our superficial analysis, what would you say if the tables were turned and you were advising us about the future prospects of this business right now?"

Having finished their dinner almost an hour earlier, Terry asked Ale if she was running short on time to get to the airport for her return trip to Baltimore. "No," she said. "I've stuck with this all afternoon, what's another hour or so?" *After all*, she thought, *I'm not even sure anyone at home will care if I'm gone an extra few hours, or even a day for that matter!*

After hearing her response Terry suggested that they continue the meeting at another Memphis landmark not far from the Peabody Hotel. The trio walked across the street to an alley and the entrance to the famous Charlie Vergo's Rendezvous Restaurant, home of the best dry-ribs on the planet. They sat at a table near the bar and continued the conversation.

Greg sat quietly, staring at Ale with a facial expression reflecting his deep thought in response to her question. Michael was obviously bored out of his mind with the conversation, and Ale was beginning to think that she might not see her young sons again until the next year, which was two days away. But she was determined to finish what Terry had her start, and it was to that end that she sat patiently awaiting Greg's response to her last question.

Greg stared out the window for a while longer. "It's funny," he finally said, "I came here thinking that Terry would give me the answer, and now you're asking me for the answer." It was apparent that the irony of the situation perplexed him a little.

"I guess the way things stand with Camber right now," Greg said, "I would be a fool to sink another hundred thousand dollars into it just to wind up two years down the road right where I am now."

Ale quickly replied, "OK, so you're saying that you should close the business."

"Not so fast! I'm not saying that just yet. I'm saying that I shouldn't keep it open if the only prospect that I have is to end up the next two years with no improvement in the business, but having lost another hundred thousand dollars."

Ale looked him straight in the eye and asked, "What other options do you see, Greg?"

"This is your game, so I have to play by your rules," said Greg. "You said earlier that we have to decide whether Camber can succeed as a business first and if we believe that it cannot, we won't even consider the location issue. Right?"

"That's what I suggested," she responded.

"But what if we can identify some things that pertain to the location and the markets of the business that could be improved upon and that would create a better chance for success? Wouldn't it be wise to explore those first instead of just ignoring them and pulling the plug prematurely?"

Terry knew all along that Ale was skillfully playing a hypothetical game of cat-and-mouse with Greg. She threw out the caveat in the beginning, which required a definitive answer from Greg one way or the other. But this approach was designed to find out whether Greg had come to Terry for help making an actual decision, or if he had come seeking support for a decision that had already been made. If Greg had jumped at the opportunity to use her logical analysis of the current situation to decide to close the business, Ale would know that this had been his intention all along and that the four of them would be able to finish quickly and go their separate ways. But that is not what happened.

"Yes Greg," Ale said, "that would be a wise tact. What do you suggest that we consider?"

Greg placed the index finger of his right hand vertically over the center of his lips and gently tapped. It was obvious to him that Ale was an unusually logical thinker and that any alternatives presented by him would have to be rational in order to be acceptable. He was approaching this challenge as though she were the decision-maker, not him.

"In order for Camber Flight Training, Inc. to be eligible for the Naval Academy contract, it had to first achieve a formal status with the Federal Aviation Administration as a Part 141 flight school. This certification required the development of a highly regimented training program and navigation through a dense federal bureaucracy for over two years," explained Greg.

"So what?" asked Ale, so as to encourage him to continue.

"Well, the Part 141 certification is not only required for the Navy contract, but it is necessary to operate a federally approved civilian career flight school as well. We have never focused on that market because working with civilians can be a real pain in the butt!"

"How so?" inquired Ale.

"The Navy students mainly do what you tell them to do. They're not demanding. The twenty-five hours of flight training that we deliver to each of them is highly standardized, and so the expectations of the students are fairly consistent and we can handle them easily. Plus, they're not the ones writing the checks for their training. Civilians, on the other hand, can be difficult. They are paying out of their own pockets, and there can be as many different expectations of the experience as there are different personalities. You have to manage civilians with kid gloves all the time."

"So where are you going with this, Greg?"

"We've already established," Greg explained, "that if we just service the Navy contract for the next two years it will cost me another hundred thousand dollars, and the business is likely to remain stagnant. But what if we expand into the civilian career market? We might then have a lot more flexibility with our pricing. We could at least double the size of our revenues, and this should allow us to make a profit instead of continuing to lose money. What do you think?"

"I have two reactions, Greg," replied Ale. "First, doubling the customer base while maintaining the same pricing and margins will just create larger losses faster. This is a mistake made by many neophyte entrepreneurs. The pricing of the civilian program must be increased as you suggested, but it will have to increase dramatically in order to not only make the civilian program profitable, but to make up for the losses in the Navy program as well. Will a civilian market in that region sustain that kind of premium pricing structure? Also, what about civilians being a pain to work with?"

Greg smiled and said, "Well, I guess we'll have to do some research on the effect of the pricing, and we'll have to accommodate the needs of the civilians if it means the survival of the company."

Ale was pleased with the direction that the conversation was taking. She didn't know if what Greg was suggesting would actually be feasible for the company, but she was at least causing him to think this thing through in a structured, business framework. And that, after all, was what Terry and Ale did for a living.

"Before we jump at this option, give me your assessment of the civilian market for career flight training in the Baltimore-Washington area," said Ale.

Greg smiled as he said, "OK, Ale, now we are finally getting to the location issue. The Baltimore Washington International Airport is located almost squarely in the middle of the corridor that connects the two large cities. There are literally millions of people living in and between these two cities and most of them are within an hour's drive of the flight school. In addition, we have large federal facilities in the area like the National Security Agency, Goddard Space Flight Center, and immediately adjacent to the airport is the Northrup Grumman plant. All of these entities employ civilians and military personnel who receive veterans' benefits, which will at least help to pay the cost of career flight training. The market is rich with potential!" Greg insisted almost as though he was trying to convince himself more than her.

Now Ale was moving in for the kill. She would ask the final question which was designed to bring Greg to the point of decision, and at least a preliminary answer to the question that started all of this.

"What about competition?"

Greg thought for a moment. "Not a discouraging factor! We have the only fight school at the BWI location, and there are a few small flight schools within a half-hour drive of BWI, but none of them is equipped to capture, or even seems to be interested in the market. I think that if we were to expand our operation and market directly to the potential civilian career students in the area we could easily double the size of the company within the next two years. It is highly likely that this would create a business model that could sustain a profitable enterprise and turn what is now a loser into a thriving winner."

Ale stated emphatically, "So there you have it!"

"What do I have?" asked Greg.

"Your answer, which is the reason you asked to meet with us in the first place. You asked if a flight school business like Camber could survive at BWI airport, and it sounds like you have just made the case supporting that not only could it survive, but maybe it could even thrive there. You just have to make some radical changes in your business model and your product offering and pricing, at least according to the logic that you just used here with us today."

Greg looked pleased. Ale seemed to be quite proud of herself. Terry was smiling. And Michael was elated that he was obviously getting close to going home to Baltimore to prepare for New Year's Eve.

The four rose from the table at the same time. Greg shook everyone's hand, thanked each individually by name, and then left through the front exit of the restaurant. Terry, Ale, and Michael sat back down at the table.

"So what do you think?" asked Michael.

Ale replied, "Remember the questions I was asking Greg?"

"Yes, you began by asking him about revenues, profit or loss on those revenues, and debt," said Michael. "But you didn't ask him about the company's cash position. Why?"

Ale laughed. "Because he wouldn't have even requested the meeting if the business had a strong cash position. That's the trap that many entrepreneurs fall into. If there is enough cash on hand to pay the bills, regardless of the source, then they think that everything will be alright. Greg said that he did not want to invest any more than another hundred thousand dollars in the business. If he were to invest that amount it would just be a source of sorely needed cash, a blood transfusion if you will, to keep the business alive for a little while longer."

Michael scowled. "So Camber is on its last legs, right?"

Ale nodded. "Unless Greg can pull off one or all of the strategies he was talking about implementing when he left, Camber is just a money pit with little or no hope of a turn-around."

Michael looked at Ale, and then at Terry, and said, "Happy New Year!"

* * * * *

U.S. Airways flight 1751 was hurtling through the thin atmosphere at forty-one thousand feet on its way to San Diego with Terry and Ale in seats 17B and 17A respectively. It had been Terry's turn to sit in the cramped middle seat of the Boeing 757, and he was seriously dreading the remaining two-and-a-half-hours of the flight. Both of his legs were asleep, his neck had gotten stiff about four hundred miles back, and the grossly obese woman sitting to his right was sound asleep and was a lot less to his right than when the flight began. His hope that soon their company would be generating enough profit that they could afford to travel First Class had repeated itself in his head so many times that it had taken the form of a mantra.

Their trip to the West Coast on this mid-January day was a previously unplanned one, necessitated by the sudden death of the forty nine year old owner of Solotype Composition, Inc., located in Carlsbad, California, which is about an hour's drive north of San Diego. Saul Sherry's wife called the night before to break the news of her husband's massive heart attack, and asked Terry if he would travel to Carlsbad for the funeral and to help stabilize the family business after the loss of its patriarch.

Ale was the first to break the hour-long silence between them. "Saul was a good man," she said.

Terry was silent for a few more moments. "Yes he was," he finally said.

"What do you think will happen to the business now that he's gone?" Ale's question was more rhetorical because she so feared Terry's response that she hoped he would just ignore her.

His answer was prompt and pointed. "It's going to tank, and quickly!"

Solotype was a smaller business in the book publishing industry. At less than five million dollars in sales per year, the firm specialized in taking completed manuscripts from managing editors and turning them into the finished pages that would then be sent to printing companies for mass production. Saul's father had founded the company in 1962 when the craft was called "typesetting" and all of the work was tedious and performed by hand. It was a brutal way to make a living.

Saul inherited the business after his father died of a massive coronary at age fifty-two. The junior Mr. Sherry struggled with the business for years. For the first five, he had to play detective because his father was an extremely secretive business owner, keeping all of the details of how he operated the enterprise very close to his vest. There was little documentation to guide

Saul in his early attempts to take over, and the transition from his father's regime to one of his own was a frustrating and thankless undertaking. Solotype finally recovered from the loss of its founder under the leadership of a young and inexperienced Saul Sherry.

But no sooner had he regained control of the struggling firm when the industry underwent a drastic and rapid change. The advent of computer generated page composition caught everyone in the business by surprise. It seemed as though the laborious process of creating press-ready pages from manuscripts was transformed into a computer intensive one almost overnight. Saul was faced with the certain extinction of the business if he couldn't quickly retool it and retrain all of his employees in order to keep up with the competition. The new capital required for the transition into the computer age had to be borrowed, and for all of the years that followed Solotype's balance sheet was crushed under the strain of all of this debt.

Just a year before his death Saul learned from one of his few remaining client publishers about Terry and Ale and their ability to repair broken businesses. The years of intense competition and the price increases required to continue servicing Solotype's heavy debt had chased many of its customers away, and Saul knew that he would have to restructure the firm if it were to survive.

Orion Resource Management, Inc. was commissioned to painstakingly dismantle the entire company and then slowly put it back together again with a much leaner and more competitive foundation than had existed at any time during its history. The resulting five-year business plan had been implemented just a month before Saul's death, and even with that in place, Terry and Ale had cautioned him and his stockholders that survival would be an uphill battle in an ever changing industry.

"It's a real shame," said Ale in a sullen tone.

"What is?" said Terry.

"That Saul and his father before him would work so hard for so many years just to have the entire family business, and their entire livelihood wiped out by one stroke of fate," she lamented.

"There is a very fine line between fate and stupidity in business, Ale," said Terry.

"What do you mean?"

"Do you know anything about the history of steam locomotives and their manufacturers in America, Ale?"

"Nope—but I bet that I'm about to learn!"

Terry ignored her patronizing tone. "For over one hundred years the production of steam locomotives for the nation's railroads was concentrated in the hands of a few large manufacturers. But these giants of industry became extinct in the middle of the Twentieth Century. And do you know why?"

"Because the locomotive was replaced by the diesel engine?" she asked sheepishly.

"You're close," Terry said. "If the manufacturers of the locomotive had simply been replaced by the manufacturers of the diesel engine we could probably call that fate. But that's not why the former disappeared. The mission of the locomotive builders was nothing more than to build steam locomotives."

"What should their mission have been?" asked Ale.

"If they had seen themselves as builders of propulsion systems for the nation's railroads they might have been prepared to conduct research that would have led to the first diesel powered railroad engine. Had they been the first to invent the diesel locomotive, which, by the way, was actually an electric engine with the generator powered by the diesel engine, then they could have been the first to manufacture the advanced engine. Thus," Terry went on, "they might well have stayed in business. Instead, General Electric came along with the Diesel. And the crazy thing is that GE tested and perfected that engine for about thirty years, using it first only as a switch engine before it was commonplace as the primary railroad engine. The makers of the steam locomotives just continued to produce their model during those thirty years. They were fat, dumb and happy until they died. That's not fate, that's stupidity."

"So it's not fate that will tank Solotype, it is stupidity?" surmised Ale.

"Look Ale, I loved Saul Sherry and his family. But they failed to keep up with the times without having to add enormous levels of debt onto their balance sheet. Strike One. Saul never took care of himself. He never went to the doctor, exercised, or watched his diet, in spite of knowing full well what killed his father. Strike two."

Ale chimed in, "And strike three is that he left behind a business that has no trained and competent successor, just like his father did."

"That's right Ale. What we did for that business requires an experienced chief executive to execute the strategies that we helped to identify in order for the business to survive. Saul might have been able to pull it off, but they just can't afford the time and the cost of bringing someone new like that on board now."

Ale was deep in thought for awhile. "So, it's never fate—it's always stupidity?" she finally asked.

"Fate is the hunter, Ale," Terry instructed. "Fate will get you, and it may temporarily weaken you. Stupidity will always kill you!"

FOUR

Terry Longbow was born and raised in a small town just west of Baltimore. He was an only child which in all likelihood contributed significantly to his strong sense of independence as he was growing up. From as early as he could remember he'd had a love affair with flying and he never wanted to be anything other than an airline pilot.

When Terry was six years old, his parents joined a small country club within walking distance of his home. He was introduced at this early age to golf and swimming and spent all of his summers at the club. While he never excelled at golf he was a member of the club swimming team, and at the age of fourteen he won the statewide championship for the butterfly, an accomplishment that he never took seriously. At fifteen, he earned his credentials as a Red Cross certified lifeguard, and he took a job at a neighborhood pool, first as a junior guard and then when he was sixteen as a full lifeguard. As soon as he received his first paycheck he started taking flying lessons at Friendship Flying Service, located at Friendship Airport, which was much later to become BWI. On his sixteenth birthday, he soloed in an aircraft for the first time out of Lee Airport, located just to the west of Annapolis. He went on to obtain his Private Pilot's License on his seventeenth birthday and his Commercial Pilot's license on his eighteenth birthday. Each of these achievements came at the earliest age allowed by

Federal aviation regulations, and he was extremely proud that he had earned every penny that it cost to become a professional pilot.

By the time Terry graduated from high school, he was well on his way to becoming a Certified Flight Instructor. His grades were never particularly good in school mostly because he concentrated all of his time and effort on studying for his career in aviation. He flunked out of the local community college after his first year and went to work full-time as a flight instructor for Friendship Flying Service. Just as soon as Terry had built enough time in his logbook to be minimally qualified he got a job flying for United Airlines. But it would be six months before he could report to Denver for training, and around the middle of this waiting period he received a telegram from United informing him that he was being furloughed even before he started his training. Needless to say, he was devastated. The chief pilot who had hired Terry explained that the influx of high-time pilots returning from the Vietnam War, coupled with a glut of pilots from an earlier aggressive hiring campaign had bumped him from his dream career. When he asked the chief pilot for advice, the older man told him in no uncertain terms that he should get out of aviation and find a more stable life's work. The chief said that the airline industry would almost certainly experience a feast or famine existence for decades to come and that it would be a risky career at best. Terry reluctantly took the chief's advice and abandoned his quest for a career as an airline pilot.

The next ten years of Terry's life became a patchwork quilt of education and jobs. He returned to the community college and graduated with honors proving, he would say many times later in life, that success in college is not so much a matter of intelligence as it is a matter of will. He went on to graduate with a Bachelor's degree in Business from Michigan State with the same academic result. He would eventually complete his MBA at Wharton and all of his doctoral studies, except the dissertation, at Stanford.

Terry's first full-time job after graduating from Michigan State was back in aviation. He had spent the entire summer living with his parents and looking for a job. He decided, after two months of unsuccessful looking and totally out of desperation, to visit Friendship Flying Service to see if he could do some part-time flight instruction while he searched for something outside of the aviation industry.

Terry met with Cory Feldman, the general manager of the flying school, and learned that Cory was preparing a proposal for a contract to conduct flight training for all of the senior midshipmen of the United States Naval Academy. This would be before they graduated and moved on to the Naval Aviation program in Pensacola. Cory asked Terry if he would like to head-up the project if their bid was successful and Terry enthusiastically accepted.

He spent the next twelve months working for Friendship Flying Service as the chief flight instructor for the Naval Academy flight training program. When Corey Feldman notified him that Friendship had secured the contract to train midshipmen from the Academy the company had nothing in place to support a program of this magnitude. Terry's first responsibilities involved the buying and delivery of a dozen new aircraft, the hiring of twenty five new certified flight instructors, and the creation of a formal training course outline that would be submitted to the FAA as soon as possible for approval. He worked nonstop, seven days a week for the first three months while designing an effective training program for the midshipmen.

During the twelve months that Terri held this job he gained an enormous amount of experience in both aviation and small business management. Nearly one thousand midshipmen were trained successfully during the year that Terry was in charge of the program without any accidents or incidents to blemish his record. But the program was initially designed to last only nine months. Training halted after the senior midshipmen had graduated and the third-year midshipmen were off on their summer routines. Terry had to make a living even during the summer, so he decided to leave aviation altogether and once again to pursue a career outside of this field.

The ensuing thirty years were filled with fascinating and challenging positions in the field of management and finance. He served for nine years as the chief fiscal officer of a large community college in the Baltimore area immediately after leaving Friendship Flying Service. He left this job in higher education administration for an opportunity to serve as a regional director with the American Management Association, a job with high national visibility. While with the AMA, he was able to deliver over one hundred seminars and workshops, in the United States and in Canada, on topics ranging from the fundamentals of management and finance to designing and implementing corporate strategic plans. It was this position that served as the foundation for Terry's future endeavors in the corporate turnaround industry. And it was while he was on assignment delivering a program on strategic planning for company presidents in Florida that he met the chairman of the GSA Corp, headquartered in Memphis. This chance encounter led to an offer from GSA that resulted in Terry moving to Memphis and engaging in his first real-life company turnaround. He spent a year carefully dismantling one of the wholly-owned subsidiaries of GSA and strategically reassembling it for profitability. When he was finished with this assignment he was fully prepared to successfully take on much larger turnaround opportunities with companies in imminent danger of failing.

It was while he was working in Memphis that Terry started Orion Resource Management, Inc. It was his dream to build a company that would be national in stature and would serve the needs of businesses and other organizations that found themselves in financial or some other kind of trouble. Working alone he accepted turnaround assignments in Chicago, Minneapolis, Los Angeles and back in his hometown of Baltimore. It was during a project in Baltimore, and while he was teaching part-time at Loyola, that he discovered Ale in her first college course. After Ale graduated and accepted a part-time job offer with Orion, she and Terry worked diligently together on three corporate turnarounds before the meeting in Memphis with Greg in late 2006.

Ale and Terry worked closely together for four years prior to the Memphis meeting. While she profoundly admired and respected him, she also was acutely aware of his shortcomings, especially in his dealings with others. On occasion, they would discuss the strengths and weaknesses of each as perceived by the other. Terry would say that he liked the strength that Ale demonstrated in their business dealings with others but that he wished she were less conciliatory and compromising on the negotiating side of the business. Ale, in turn, would say that Terry was extremely dynamic, forceful, and analytical in his approach to the business but that she wished he wouldn't shoot himself in the foot so often when dealing with others. She explained to him more than once that his personality characteristics tend to manifest themselves in a way that is far more focused on results and forcefulness and much less concerned with the necessity to work with others in the achievement of lofty, and sometimes unrealistic goals. There had been occasions when Ale came to Terry's rescue when he'd unintentionally and abruptly speak to someone too strongly. As a gift she once gave him a tee shirt with, "Doesn't Play Well With Others" emblazoned across the front. He was far less amused than she'd anticipated. And she knew all too well that his personality type also tends to jump at a challenge that may be more than achievable, more for the sake of the competitive excitement than a realistic opportunity for success.

* * * * *

It was late on a March afternoon in 2007, and Terry and Ale were sitting across from each other at a conference table in a room that they regularly used for meetings at their Columbia, Maryland location. For over two years Orion Resource Management, Inc. had contracted with a national provider of "a la carte" office services for office and conference room space, as well as receptionist and secretarial services. Although expensive on an hourly, weekly, or monthly basis, leasing these services only as they are needed is the perfect way for a new or early stage business to make use of working and meeting space that is much more functional and professional than working out of the local Starbucks. The two business owners wanted to avoid the trend followed by most entrepreneurial startups where they would schedule meetings and conduct business in any local coffee shop or restaurant with free wi-fi and a convenient location.

Ale asked, "What time did Greg say that he would be here?" She knew very well that Greg Holland had requested this meeting with them at 4:00, but it was already 4:15 and she had to finish a proposal for a prospective client by the next morning.

"Let's just wait for him until 4:30. When he called me last night and requested this meeting it sounded as though he wanted to talk about something rather urgent," said Terry, after a brief look at Ale that conveyed his awareness of her impatience.

"Okay," said Ale after a quick glance at her watch. "You know Terry, I've been meaning to ask you something."

"What's that?"

"Do you remember that conversation we had on the way to San Diego a while back about fate and stupidity," she asked.

"Yes. What about it?"

"Well, you said that there is a fine line between fate and stupidity as a cause of a business failure. I've been thinking a lot about that lately, and it seems that the cause of just about every example of business failure that I can think of would actually fall under your category of stupidity rather than fate. So I was wondering, where do you draw that line? How do you classify a failure as the result of one or the other?"

Terry looked at his watch and then pressed a button on his Blackberry. "Greg, where are you?" he asked into the phone. "Okay, we'll wait for you." He glanced at Ale and said, "We've got some time, he's in traffic from Washington, and he'll be forty-five minutes late."

Ignoring the expression on Ale's face as she rolled her eyes in frustration Terry began to answer her question. "Let's talk first about fate," he said. "Fate is a crucial factor in people's lives as well as in business situations. First let me give you an example of the former that pops into my head. When I was a flight instructor way back in the early '70s, I was flying with a student early on a January morning. We were flying west out of Friendship Airport in a small, two-seat trainer at about two thousand feet, and we were headed for Montgomery Airpark, a small private airport about twenty miles ahead of us. The morning was cold and clear, and the air was extremely smooth. The student was doing the flying, and he had the aircraft 'trimmed' well, which means that it would essentially fly itself straight ahead on the same heading and at the same altitude even if he took his hands and feet fully off of the controls. Suddenly, and without any obvious reason, the nose of the aircraft pitched up slightly and we began gaining a little altitude. I looked at the student, and he looked back at me and then he proceeded to trim the plane again, and we thought little of it." Terry paused and waited for a wise crack from Ale about where all of this was going, which she politely withheld.

"When it was time to land at Montgomery Airpark the student was performing extremely well, so I told him to go ahead and land the aircraft himself. He had progressed during previous lessons to a point where he was ready to solo, and I had planned to let him do that on this scheduled flight. Just as he was doing a splendid job of touching down on the runway, with the main landing gear under the wings touching the runway first and the nose wheel still off the runway, I noticed that the nose of the plane was settling lower than normal. Something was wrong! So I took over the controls and pulled the mixture all the way out, which stopped the engine. The nose of the aircraft sank down all the way to the surface of the runway and skidded ahead on a bare nose wheel strut for a few hundred more yards. Somewhere between Friendship Airport and Montgomery Airpark we had lost the nose wheel off of the aircraft – it just fell off in mid-flight!"

"Was anybody hurt?" asked Ale with a look of concern.

"No, we both walked away without a scratch."

"Sooooo," inquired Ale, "fate caused the nose wheel of the plane to fall off in mid-flight?"

"No," said Terry. "That was stupidity! You see, a mechanic had failed to properly tighten a bolt securing the nose wheel to the strut during routine maintenance before our flight."

"But we were talking about fate, right?"

"Yes," said Terry, "I told you that story so that I could tell you this one. In the car after that incident I began to think about where that wheel might have fallen off. The best I could figure it was right over the town of Columbia, Maryland. And I envisioned some poor older fellow who had never flown in an airplane in his life because he didn't want to die in a crash, walking out of the front door of his home and getting hit in the head by this aircraft wheel falling out of the sky. Now that would have been fate!"

"That's terrible!" complained Ale. "How do you know that didn't really happen?"

"Because it would have been in all of the papers. I think the wheel wound up in the lake east of the town. The point is that I define fate as something incredibly bad, or incredibly good, that happens to someone or to a business without the one impacted by it having done anything whatsoever to initiate it. The poor guy walking out of his house as he does every day and getting flattened by an aircraft wheel falling out of the sky is fate. The neighborhood retail business that is totally destroyed by a tornado on a summer evening in Kansas, that's fate."

Ale thought for a moment, then said, "So you would define anything that would cause a business to fail that is not purely the result of some totally random phenomenon as stupidity, right?"

Terry said, "Yup, pretty much! But," he continued, "it's not quite as simple as that. Businesses that fail due to stupidity don't necessarily have to be managed by stupid people. Many times a rational and intelligent management team will make a decision, or a series of decisions that cause a business failure."

"So that's fate, right?" asked Ale with a look of satisfaction.

"Nope—still stupidity! But in this case we'll call it unintentional stupidity. This would be one of those occasions where the managers would strike their foreheads with the palm of their hands afterward and ask, 'what was I thinking?'"

Ale saw Greg walk in. Both Terry and Ale stood, shook hands with Greg, and then everyone sat at the table.

Greg apologized for being so late and then began the meeting by saying, "This won't take long. I have decided to shut down Camber, unless Orion wants to buy it."

Ale focused a look at Terry that clearly registered her surprise with him, and Terry responded with one that suggested that opportunity was knocking. Neither said a word for several quiet moments.

FIVE

GREG, TERRY, AND Ale sat and stared at each other for what seemed to Ale like several minutes.

She was the first to break the silence. "Greg, you are telling us that if we don't buy the flight school you will close it down?"

"That is exactly what I am saying, Ale!" said Greg.

"But I thought when we met a few months ago you had decided to stick with it and expand your customer base beyond the Navy into the civilian market."

"I did," said Greg, "but it has been a long winter! I have cut all of the overhead expenses back to almost nothing, so I am doing everything myself. I'm just simply tired of fooling with it."

Terry raised his right hand slightly off of the table and gestured with his fingers pointing at himself and Ale. "So why are you coming to us?"

"The two of you are in the business of saving companies," Greg began, "and I would like to see this company survive. In addition, Terry, you have a significant amount of experience in a flight school."

Terry interrupted Greg before he could begin his next sentence. "But that was over thirty years ago."

"Yes, but you do have the experience. It's a lot like riding a bike! Once you get involved you will begin to remember things that will help you to overcome the industry learning curve much faster than someone would if they had no earlier exposure to the field."

"Why don't you just cut your losses and shut it down now?" asked Ale.

Greg briefly looked down at the table where he was doodling on a pad of paper. He thought for a moment and then said, "I have about a half dozen good people working for me at Camber, and I just don't want to put them out of work if I don't absolutely have to. I think that if you were to come in and take over the operation it could be successful. I just don't have the interest, the energy, or the patience for it anymore."

Ale glanced at Terry as if she was looking for a nod of approval, but there was none. She then said, "Greg, we're not in the business of investing cash up front into an enterprise and then turning it around. Ordinarily we are paid in either cash or a share of the ownership of the company, or both, to deliver our services. How much were you thinking of selling it for?"

"It is totally open for negotiation. I have only one purpose in being here today – to hear you say either 'yes, we'll consider it,' or 'no, we're not interested.' If you are willing to give it some thought then we will sit down again real soon and hammer out the details."

Terry responded quickly and Ale gave him a look as though she was a bit startled at his remark. "Greg, we will certainly give it some thought. In fact, I would like to go ahead and perform our necessary research on the business, the industry, and the potential customer bases and we'll get back to you by the middle of April with either a proposal or a formal rejection of the opportunity. Can you hold out until then?"

"I guess I don't have any choice," said Greg, "If I want the business to continue then I'll just have to wait. But I will ask that if there is anything between now and then that you determine would cause you to decide that you are not interested in taking over the company, would you let me know right away?"

"Sure," said Terry, "and likewise, if anything should change on your end of the deal you'll let us know. Right?"

"Of course," said Greg.

Terry and Ale rose from the table and walked Greg to the door of the conference room. After they each shook hands with him and said their good-byes Terry closed the door, and he and Ale returned to the table.

"I'm sensing that you're not entirely happy with the way that ended," said Terry.

"I would be happier right now if you had told Greg that we would discuss this and get back to him in forty-eight hours with an answer as to whether we are even interested in doing the research," Ale stated firmly.

Terry thought for a moment, sensing that perhaps he had not given his partner the respect that she deserved in the meeting by postponing the decision to take this matter to the next step until after they had discussed it further. "Why are you annoyed with this outcome?" he asked.

"I have two concerns, Terry. The first is time. You have been an exceptionally good teacher and mentor to me for the past few years. If there is one thing that you have drilled into my head time and time again it is that our most precious resource is time. We have two clients that we are extremely active with right now, and I have a proposal sitting on my desk that is due tomorrow for a prospective client. If we are successful with this new client I just don't see how we will have the time to even begin researching the Camber project, let alone engaging it."

"And your second concern?" prompted Terry.

"If the importance of time as a resource is at the top of the list of lessons you have drilled into me, then the importance of not letting our emotions influence our business decisions is second on our list of operational priorities."

Terry looked surprised. "And you think that I am allowing my emotions to affect my thinking in this case?"

"I know you, Terry! You've always loved aviation. When we travel together on a plane, you stop right in the middle of our conversation when the plane is on its takeoff roll down the runway so that you can gaze out the window. You've always been like a kid when it comes to flying. I've often wondered why you didn't renew your pilot's licenses at some point during all of these years. You have plastic models of airplanes in your office. I think that you immediately saw an opportunity to become active in aviation as soon as Greg said that he wanted out. This looming emotional toy could be clouding your judgment with this project. I'm sorry, but at this moment I don't see that there is any more potential for us or Orion by getting involved with Camber than if we were to squander our time in a casino in Atlantic City."

Terry was both perturbed and proud. He did not like that Ale had been so blunt with him – mostly because she may be right. But he was proud that she felt comfortable speaking her mind in that way. After all, she was a full partner in this business, and she had every right to exercise control over a situation that she felt may be heading the firm in the wrong direction.

Ale wasn't sorry that she had directed her frustration at Terry the way she had, but she also had an enormous amount of respect for him and his role in the company. He had more often than not sacrificed in recent years so that Ale could learn as much as possible about business and, in many ways, about life in general. Finally she said, "Look Terry, let's move ahead with the research and a proposal for Greg. But let's also be extremely careful to respect the level of commitment that we have to our other projects. If we see anything with the Camber deal that just doesn't fit we'll dump it right away. Okay?"

"Absolutely Ale! You proceed with your proposal tonight, and I'll start working on the Camber data. We'll agree that I have a good feeling about Camber and you have a bad feeling about it. That will force us to proceed with caution. Right?"

"Right," said Ale, with just a touch of righteous indignation.

Ale arrived home that night at about ten o'clock as she had so many nights during the last few years. She unlocked the front door and entered the living room of the house she and her husband had bought in a suburb of Washington just a few years ago. The family's French Bulldog, Max, eagerly greeted her by jumping in the air repeatedly until she stopped to scratch him behind the ears and acknowledge his enthusiasm at her arrival. After taking her shoes off and leaving them by the sofa, she tip-toed upstairs and entered Stefan's room first, gave him a gentle kiss on his forehead as he slept soundly, then repeated the gesture of motherly love with her youngest son, Johan.

Immediately after Ale's graduation from Loyola, Franco confronted her with a decision he had made regarding his own career, and he presented his new goal to her as a quid-pro-quo for his perceived sacrifice while she was in undergraduate school and away from the family. She was proud of herself that she had not overreacted when he took this approach, given that he had done little out of his normal routine to accommodate the needs of their sons during the demanding pursuit of her degree. It was the selfless and time consuming dedication of her mother, arriving at the house early every morning and staying until late every night, that sustained the family while Franco worked different shifts as a nurse at a local hospital and Ale put in long hours for Orion and then attended evening classes at Loyola. But Ale never set the record straight with Franco that it was her mother and not he that had sacrificed dearly so that she could achieve her educational goals. It just wasn't worth the inevitable argument that would ensue if she had. So when Franco presented his career decision to her as repayment for his earlier dedication to her goals she sat quietly and listened. Franco's family was wealthy and influential in Madrid having distinguished itself with several generations of medical doctors and lawyers. When he traveled to America after graduating from high school to attend a prestigious medical school his relatives were all proud and supportive. But when he changed his mind and decided that nursing would be a more attainable career goal his family all but disowned him. Now, he had concluded, was the time to go back to medical school and to become the doctor that was everyone's expectation from the beginning. Upon hearing of her husband's intention to return to medical school Ale was at first angry, then she was worried about how the move would affect the family and their marriage, and then she was simply conciliatory. Franco entered medical school, Ale's mother continued to care for the family on a nearly full-time basis, and Franco and Ale saw little of each other after he started the program.

Ale knew that Franco was still awake and studying in the room in the basement that he had turned into an office a year earlier. She walked over to the door at the top of the stairs and opened it.

"I'm home," she said gently, but loud enough that he should have been able to hear her. There was no response. More and more often Franco would fall asleep in his downstairs office, and he would not be seen again upstairs until early the next morning just before he was due back at the university for class.

Even the dog acted as though he was glad to see me, she thought as she turned out the lights on the first floor and climbed the stairs to her bedroom for the night—alone once again.

* * * * *

The process of researching and investigating everything possible about a company before one becomes involved with it is called due diligence. It can take the form of a series of meetings between the parties interested in aligning themselves with the company and management of the firm, in which case those involved will just trust the accuracy of the information being exchanged. Or it can involve a painstaking and tedious physical examination of all company documents, as well as detailed interviews with all of the key company employees, with the goal of constructing a comprehensive snapshot of the exact condition of the firm in advance of any formal partnership arrangement. Terry and Ale had been strong advocates of the more structured and thorough approach to the due diligence process. On any number of occasions, Terry had pointed out to Ale after learning via the media of the details of a recent business collapse that the failure would probably not have occurred had the appropriate due diligence techniques been employed early-on. He also had preached for some time that the technology industry bubble and then crash in the late Twentieth, and early Twenty-first centuries would never have happened if the investors in that house-of-cards movement had properly executed structured due diligence regimens.

The comprehensive due diligence analysis of any small to medium-sized firm should take one or two seasoned professionals approximately thirty to ninety days to complete. Terry was acutely aware that he would be performing the tasks for Camber alone and that he only had about fourteen days to complete them. While he knew that he would be able to count on Ale's help if he actually needed it, he was inclined to do as much by himself as possible to avoid the risk of antagonizing her any further.

Early in the morning following their meeting Terry sent an e-mail to Greg requesting all of the documentation available from Camber, and he made sure to remind Greg of the condensed timeline within which they must complete the entire analysis. He specifically identified the need for copies of the Income Statements, Balance Sheets, and Cash Flow Statements for a period of at least the preceding two years. He also requested a copy of the current contract between Camber and The United States Navy depicting the conditions of the training to be provided to the midshipmen of the Academy, and a copy of all other contracts between the company and any entity doing business with it. Terry was particularly interested in leases for the building occupied by Camber, agreements with fuel suppliers, leases for the aircraft utilized by the school in the delivery of flight instruction, insurance policies, aircraft maintenance contracts, and a list of employees, their individual job titles, and their salary arrangements. He knew from prior experience that this document request would be only the first of many in his challenge to determine the exact status of the company. But with this information in hand he would be able to get a good start on the voluminous undertaking.

Terry was aware that Greg was extremely anxious to either shutdown the company or to dispose of it. But he was surprised when he received a call that same evening informing him that Greg would be delivering a package containing the requested documentation the next morning. So far, thought Terry, this project is moving along exactly as he had hoped it would.

During the next two weeks, Terry pored over hundreds of pages of documents that he had first requested from Greg, and others that he obtained after that initial e-mail. He met with Greg on three occasions evenly spaced through the two-week period and was able to listen to explanations of elements of the paperwork that were still unclear to him after he had examined it. And finally, late in the second week of his exhausting research, Terry felt confident that he had the entire snapshot of the company that he and Ale would be considering as their next turn-around project for Orion.

Terry learned during his research that Greg and another partner had started Camber in early 2000 at an airport just outside of Easton, Maryland, almost in the center of the state's Delmarva Peninsula. Both men had been interested in investing in the business because of their mutual desire to learn how to fly and their considerable personal financial portfolios. Their rationale was that it would be foolish to pay someone to teach them how to fly at an existing flight school in the area when they could own a school and the aircraft themselves and create a company at the same time.

The first two years of Camber's existence were tumultuous and characterized by challenges and changes. The customer base for a flight school in the Easton area of rural Maryland turned out to be far too meager to sustain the business so after only one year the entire operation was moved about twenty minutes west to the Bay Bridge Airport facility. Bay Bridge had only one runway as opposed to Easton's two. But it was located right on the eastern edge of the bay, and immediately adjacent to the Chesapeake Bay Bridge which carries vast numbers of commuters between the Annapolis, Baltimore, the Washington D.C. metroplex and the Eastern Shore of Maryland every day. At about the same time as the move to a potentially more fertile market for the school there was a parting of the ways between Greg and his first partner in the business. While the details of the split were not apparent in the materials that Terry was researching, it was obvious that the relocation of the company and the increase in business had placed an enormous amount of pressure on Greg operating as a sole owner.

It was during this second year of Camber's operation, and its first at Bay Bridge Airport, that Greg took on another partner in the firm. It was also during this time that the company successfully bid on and won the contract to train senior midshipmen from the United States Naval Academy. Winning this contract seemed at the time to be a feather in everyone's cap because it represented nearly five hundred new students for the school and a revenue base from this single source that could reach one million dollars annually. But it also created serious and significant challenges for the fledgling flight school. Greg and his new partner worked feverishly in an attempt to find and hire qualified flight instructors, and to locate and to lease or buy over a dozen aircraft suitable for the Navy's training needs. It wasn't long after they actually started training the midshipmen that it was obvious that the facility at Bay Bridge was much too small to comfortably and safely accommodate Camber's rapid growth and that they would have to once again relocate the operation.

The management team chose the Baltimore-Washington International Airport as the new home for Camber and its potentially prosperous future. Although a busy operational hub for several domestic and international airlines the facility had years before built a single runway, segregated on the eastern side of the field, dedicated to the exclusive use of general aviation aircraft. Adjacent to this runway were two small terminal buildings and two large maintenance hangars to accommodate the needs of the civilian general aviation population. And, best of all, there was no flight school operating at BWI at the time that Camber had to make a move. During the spring of 2002 Greg relocated the entire flight school into the small but adequate terminal building on the north side of the general aviation ramp at BWI airport, and began functioning as the only flight school in the densely populated corridor between Baltimore and Washington, D.C.

SIX

On Tuesday, April 13, 2007, Greg Holland had been on time for his 10:00 a.m. appointment with Terry, and was sitting alone at the table in the conference room in Camber's rented Columbia, Maryland offices. Terry had arranged this meeting with Greg the day before for the purpose of reviewing all of the data from his research on the company, prior to a final proposal document by Orion. Neither of these gentlemen had any preconceived notions that discussions in this initial meeting would include details of an offer, which would certainly have been premature.

Greg was growing impatient awaiting Terry's arrival when finally the latter walked into the room with hands raised in a gesture of apology. "I am so sorry for making you wait this long, Greg! Ale is in Cincinnati working with a client, and we're shorthanded on the phones with two people out with the flu."

"I don't mind, Terry," said Greg, as though he was trying to convince himself as well.

Terry sat down and proceeded to open several file folders on the table in front of him. Within moments, there were cascades of financial statements, spreadsheets, and background documents forming a semi-circle in front of him in a strategic arrangement that translated into an impressive presentation of thoroughness.

"Greg," Terry began, "as you can see I have completed a great deal of research in the past two weeks. I wanted to take this opportunity to confirm some details with you before I go ahead with Ale in a discussion as to whether or not we will be interested in actually proceeding with the project."

Greg said, "Okay, but I was hoping that all of the questions you've been asking me and all of the detail that you have been collecting meant that you have already decided to move forward with it."

"No, not yet, and I apologize if I said or did anything to give you that impression," Terry said rather sheepishly. "When it comes to the due diligence stage of any project we are extremely thorough and we never rush a decision to proceed until we feel comfortable with the data that we have reviewed."

Greg responded with an affirmative nod, although with a bit of a frown as well, and Terry continued. "I am going to make this meeting as quick and as painless as possible. Before I ask you each of a series of questions I will be explaining why the answer is important to us. By taking this approach, I will be making sure that you and I are on exactly the same page regarding the data upon which we will be basing our decision. But one of the possible shortcomings of this approach is that I risk insulting your intelligence. I know that you have been around for awhile, so please don't misinterpret the simplicity of my explanations or take them personally."

"I completely understand Terry."

"Ale and I use a series of factors in the analysis of any business, which we call vital signs, and these benchmarks allow us to determine the overall health of the firm in fairly short order. The first of these that I will cover today will come from Camber's balance sheet, specifically cash and net worth. Of course, you know that a company's balance sheet serves as a snapshot at any point in time of what is owned and what is owed by the business. The cash position demonstrates the ability of the entity to pay its obligations on time, and net worth signifies how much is left over after all of its liabilities, or obligations, are accounted for."

"I'm with you," said Greg.

"Camber's balance sheet as of March 31st, just about two weeks ago indicates a cash balance of a little over one-hundred thousand dollars, and, as of the same date, shows a negative net worth of one-hundred thirteen thousand dollars. How do you explain the negative net worth in spite of a pretty strong cash balance?"

Terry wasn't in any way attempting to trip Greg up with this apparent inconsistency on the balance sheet. He knew that this was comparable to a situation in the finances of an individual where there would be a large amount of debt sitting and waiting to gobble up a sizable amount of cash that the person had sitting in a savings account. In the case of Camber, this meant that the firm had, on March 31st, one hundred and thirteen thousand dollars more in financial obligations than it had in the bank and in other assets that it could use to pay off those obligations. That's usually not a good sign to business people like Terry and Ale.

Greg gestured toward a stack of papers sitting on the table just to the left of Terry. "Can I see that balance sheet?"

Terry was obviously immediately embarrassed. "Of course, Greg, I have copies of everything for you," he exclaimed hastily. "Here you are."

Greg took the pile of papers from Terry's hands and examined the two on the top of the pile. Camber's balance sheet filled those two pages.

After just a few moments of intense inspection, Greg said, "Terry you know how important it is to consider the balance sheet in its entirety, don't you? I mean you can't just separate one or two line items and draw any meaningful conclusions from them, right?"

"Yes and no," responded Terry quickly. "While it is essential to consider all of the entries on a balance sheet, in the final analysis it all comes down to cash available to cover obligations and the resulting net worth. But, let's go ahead and discuss your approach to Camber's balance sheet."

"What you have said about Camber's cash position and net worth is correct, but look at this." Greg pointed to a figure on the second page of the document labeled "Capital Loan."

"Okay," said Terry, "That's a large liability! Who does Camber owe that money to?"

"Me," said Greg. "Between the time that we moved to BWI and earlier this year the company went through some tough stretches. I had to invest a quarter of a million in cash in order to keep it afloat. I had intended to pay myself back in small amounts over the next few years until I get back to even. Now I'm not so sure that will happen."

Terry was quick to respond, "So when you told us there was no debt when we met a few weeks ago you meant none that was owed to anyone other than yourself. And if you were to forgive this loan to the company, then…"

"Whoa!" exclaimed Greg. "I never said anything about forgiving the loan!"

"Okay Greg, hypothetically then, if you were to forgive this loan it would remove about two hundred and fifty thousand from the liabilities on the balance sheet." There was a pause. "And so the net worth of the firm would become a positive one hundred and fifty thousand dollars instead of the negative one hundred and thirteen thousand dollars portrayed on the balance sheet now, right?"

"Yes," but Greg was quick to add, "but only hypothetically!"

Terry took what seemed to Greg to be several minutes writing notes in a spiral-ring notebook that he constantly used to document all of his daily business activities, but it actually only took about a minute. Greg knew that what Terry had written was going to be important to the future of any negotiations that may occur. He wished he knew what was going into the notebook.

Finally, Terry looked up from his notebook and said, "Alright Greg, let's talk about the income statement. I have some concerns about the operating results of the company over the past fifteen months."

The temperature in the conference room had risen to a point of borderline discomfort for both men. The building was notorious for being either too cold or too warm during the change of seasons in the spring and in the fall of each year, and this sunny day in mid-April was no exception. Terry left the room momentarily to see if he could find someone on the building's maintenance staff who could adjust a thermostat before one of the two men fell asleep.

"Okay, where were we?" asked Terry upon his return.

"The Income Statement," said Greg.

"Oh sure! Your copies of the 2006 and first-quarter 2007 Income Statements should be directly underneath the balance sheet on your pile there," said Terry pointing at the stack of papers sitting in front of Greg.

"Again Greg, I don't want to insult your intelligence, but it is essential that we are both on the same page with regard to the definitions that we are dealing with here. The balance sheet of a company depicts its position with regard to how much it owns, how much it owes, and how much is left over, also known as the net worth of the company. The income statement, also known as the profit and loss statement, portrays the company's revenues, expenses, and the difference, also known as the profit."

Greg was being patient with Terry's overly simplistic overview of the fundamentals of corporate financial statements for two reasons. First, he knew how important it was to make certain that both of them were speaking the same language so that there would be less of a chance of a disagreement later on. Second, he was extremely anxious to get this deal done and, therefore, he would accept just about any approach of Terry's in order to do so.

Terry continued, "The total revenue for Camber from January first, 2006, through December thirty-first, 2006, was just a little over a million dollars, and the source of virtually all of that was the Navy program. Am I correct on that?"

"Yes," said Greg.

"Okay and the costs directly associated with producing that revenue totaled a little over seven hundred and sixty two thousand dollars," said Terry with an inquisitive tone.

Greg looked closer at a paper before him. "Uh, let's go back for a moment, Terry, that sounds way too low to be our total expenses for the year."

"That's right," said Terry "let's review the mechanics of the income statement a little further and you'll see where that number fits."

Greg agreed and picked up his copy.

Terry pointed with the sharpened end of a pencil to a number on his copy that he was holding in front of Greg so that he could see it clearly.

"This number, just over a million dollars, represents the gross revenues of Camber for the 2006 year."

Greg said, "I understand that."

"This column of figures directly below the gross revenue itemizes all of the expenses that were directly related to producing that annual revenue. But it doesn't include expenses for the year that were not directly related to producing that revenue. So, for example, the cost of leasing the aircraft and also the fuel used by Camber in the training process are included because they are directly related to the generation of the revenues, but the costs of telephone and computer services are not directly related to the production of income and, therefore, are not included in this particular column."

"Okay," said Greg, "so what?"

"So we subtract the total of the column of direct expenses, labeled here as 'Cost of Revenue Production'," said Terry, "from the total revenues, and we arrive at what we call 'gross profit'."

"Boy, I should have paid a lot more attention to this stuff before now, right?" said Greg, more than a little embarrassed.

"The question I have, Greg is how did you manage this company for so long without being familiar with these simple fundamentals of finance?"

"Anita Giovetti is my bookkeeper, and she puts all of the numbers into the computer. There are also times when I enter data, like when she's off or busy with something else. But I've never paid much attention to details like we're going over today. I've been way too busy with the day-to-day challenges of running the flight school to take time to sit and learn how to read this stuff. Guess that's wrong, huh?"

Terry looked at Greg with a wry smile and said, "Greg, you would probably be amazed at how many business owners Ale and I come into contact with who know as little or less than you about actually managing a business. What these folks are interested in is being involved in the facets of the business that interest them the most."

Greg sat and stared out into space for a few moments. He wore a look of resignation on his face like he'd just somehow had an epiphany. And Terry was more than accustomed to seeing this look on the faces of less-than-successful business people who had suddenly realized how much their business had suffered as a result of their failure to learn and then apply the most fundamental elements required for success. Terry never ceased to be amazed as this same scene repeated itself over the years.

Greg gently shook his head as if he had just regained consciousness and said, "Okay, let me see if I can summarize what I have just learned here before we go on."

"Go for it," Terry urged.

"The primary purpose of the income statement is to portray, for any given period of time, the profit of the company, which is calculated by subtracting the total expenses from the total revenues for that time period. And the total expenses are divided into two categories, those directly related to the production of revenues and those that are not. And I'm going to take a guess here that you want to be able to control those two types of expenses separately, and that's why it is necessary to keep them apart on the income statement."

Terry smiled and said, "Greg, it's just that simple!"

Greg now showed a look of determination on his face as he continued, "So looking at Camber's income statement for 2006 I can see some problems. We generated revenues of a little over a million dollars, and it directly cost us a little over seven hundred and sixty thousand dollars, or about seventy-six percent, to produce that annual revenue. Therefore our gross profit, which is calculated by subtracting the direct production expenses from the total revenue, was a little more than a quarter of a million dollars, or twenty-five percent of the annual gross revenue."

"That's right," said Terry, "so where do you see the problem?"

"On the income statement," said Greg, "the expenses that are not directly related to the production of the revenue must be subtracted from the gross profit in order to calculate the actual profit for 2006. We had nearly four hundred thousand dollars in expenses not directly related to revenue production, and only two hundred and fifty thousand dollars in gross profit. We lost over one hundred and twenty two thousand dollars for the year."

"That's right, Greg, and what is probably the reason for that loss?"

Greg thought for a moment, and then said, "We probably lost that much because I didn't do a very good job of controlling the expenses that weren't in direct support of the revenues."

"Actually Greg," said Terry rather emphatically, "you lost a significant amount of money for the year because you did a poor job of controlling the business in general!"

The conference room had gotten even warmer as the meeting had been in progress for just over an hour. It had obviously been an eye opening experience for Greg so far and yet the two had barely scratched the surface. It had become obvious to Terry about halfway to this point in the meeting that it was going nowhere.

"Greg," said Terry after some reflection. "Camber's income statements for the 2006 year and for the first quarter of 2007 paint a rather vivid picture of a business that is poorly managed and is barely surviving on its own merits."

Greg did not look up at Terry from the papers sitting on the table in front of him. "I know," he admitted with the first detectable sign of discouragement since these discussions began months earlier. "That's why I came to you," he added, "you're a turn-around guy and this business doesn't just need a cash infusion or a new owner, it needs to be turned-around from top to bottom. And that's why I said that if you aren't interested in taking over the firm I'll just shut it down."

Terry did not say anything in response, he just looked at Greg and waited to see what would happen next. Finally, Greg uttered, "Well, I guess you are trying to tell me that you aren't interested in pursuing this any further. Is that right?"

"No," Terry immediately replied, "that's not right. Ale and I are partners in Orion, and I wouldn't make a decision like that without her full participation. But I am telling you that if we happen to decide to get involved you must be prepared to accept terms of a deal that will not in any way favor you until we can get the business back on its feet again. If you are expecting that we will be making an offer to you based on a cash purchase of some kind, then you should be the one walking away from the table even before Ale and I have a chance to discuss it again. I can tell you right now that just isn't going to happen."

Greg seemed to recognize that he was suddenly involved in the first phase of negotiating the survival of Camber, and he apparently hadn't expected that in this meeting. But he also must have recognized that he had little choice in the matter. "Let's continue to pursue this. I'll let you know if I want to walk away if that time comes," he said with a degree of resolve.

Terry had opened a door for Greg that would allow him to get out while the getting was good. But he was pretty sure that his motivation for doing so was more for the welfare of Orion than for Greg. He knew that the financials of Camber were going to be totally unacceptable to Ale and that if he pushed for a deal with her it would just seem that his emotions were getting the best of him. He was bothered by this apparent weakness on his part. If the deal looked bad he knew that he could have cancelled it without first sitting down with Ale and that she wouldn't mind at all. But something was just nagging at him, telling him to go ahead and to have the meeting with Ale anyway. He just had a feeling that this would turn out to be a surprisingly good company to own in spite of the primary obstacles that were evident as a result of the due diligence.

"Alright, Greg," said Terry, "if you are committed to proceeding knowing full well that the next phase of any deal that could result may not be favorable at all to you then I'll arrange to sit down with Ale."

"How long do you think that will take?" asked Greg.

"Give us five days. Ale will be back from Cincinnati tonight. We will meet for several hours tomorrow after she returns to the office. Then I am sure that she will need to think about this for a day or two before we make a final decision. You can expect that we will either have a rough draft of a proposal for you or we'll let you know that we're not interested within the next five days."

Greg agreed. Both men stood, shook hands, and Greg left the conference room. Terry remained behind and sat back down at the table staring intently at the papers in front of him.

For nearly thirty-five years, Terry had been actively involved in businesses usually in an extremely difficult time in the firm's life. There had been successful experiences and some not so. But the one thing that all of these challenges had in common was the high degree of uncertainty in the very beginning as to whether or not becoming involved with them would be a worthwhile undertaking. And now Terry found himself wrestling with that same question regarding the Camber project.

As he looked at each of the papers in front of him on the table, which summarized the research he had performed on Camber, questions kept nagging him about the thoroughness of his work. *What have I missed? Why do I keep getting this strong feeling that Camber would be a good deal for us if these numbers look so bad? Was a two-week period long enough to adequately research the company and its environment? Could Ale be right? Is it true that I am subconsciously so eager to get back into an aviation business that I genuinely can't see the forest for the trees here?* Terry sat with these thoughts and his papers for nearly two more hours and then he made a decision.

He knew that he would not be able to extend the amount of time for his research, and he wasn't sure that an extension would produce any different results. So he would send Ale all the material. Terry was sure that she would be able to digest all of this data and then bring to the table an extremely objective and candid opinion as to what to do.

Terry's final thought before beginning the task of delivering all of the due diligence materials to Ale's office was, *am I making the right call by relying so heavily on Ale's judgment with this one?*

* * * * *

Alejandra German possessed a number of qualities that would serve to ensure her success in the world of business and her work ethic was at the very top of the list. Over the years of her relatively short career, she had become accustomed to long, arduous hours every day of the work week and she ruthlessly guarded her weekends so that she could spend them uninterrupted with her children. Except for Friday evenings, which was the beginning of her Sabbath, she developed a habit of stopping by her office when returning from a trip regardless of the time of night. Terry had long since stopped trying to convince her that she should go straight home from the airport upon her return and that anything on her desk at that point would certainly wait until the next day. One of those qualities she possessed was obviously stubbornness, but it didn't always work in her favor.

Ale's flight from Cincinnati arrived at BWI at 9:00 that night as usual. She got off the plane and boarded a parking lot shuttle at the front curb of the terminal as usual. She drove straight to Orion's Columbia offices at about 10:00, picked up the pile of papers on the center of her desk as was her habit, and left for home. Upon her arrival, the house was dark with the exception of a light that she could see under the door to the basement. She started for the door to let Franco know that she was home but then she stopped and turned toward the stairs leading to her bedroom. After quietly kissing the boys goodnight in their rooms, she walked into her room and prepared for bed by herself—as usual.

SEVEN

THE MORNING AFTER Terry and Greg's meeting Ale fixed breakfast for her children, dropped them off at school, and she was in her office by 8:15. Having picked up the Camber due diligence package from her desk the night before, after her late arrival from Cincinnati, she studied it late into the night at home, and she was ready for Terry by the time she got to work.

When Terry arrived he saw that Ale was already in her office working at her computer. He went straight to his office, hit the power button on his computer, and began sorting the piles on his desk in anticipation of a busy morning. With the sound of a double beep from his computer signaling that he had e-mail waiting, he noticed one that stood out from the rest. It was from Ale, and she had sent it at 2:00 a.m. "Ready to discuss the Camber project whenever you are!" was all that it said. *How in the world did she come back late last night, stop by the office, go home and still have time to digest two week's worth of research?* he wondered. He thought for a moment and then replied to her e-mail. "10:00 a.m." was all that he wrote.

Terry proceeded to prepare himself for his meeting with Ale as though it was one with a client instead of with his partner. He was psyching himself for what he anticipated would be an extremely negative reaction to the due diligence materials and he focused on forming a strategy that would eventually be the best one for Orion. *I'm not going to sound in any way defensive*, he thought. *She will almost certainly recommend that we pass on this deal, and if she does, I am going to agree with her and that will be that. But I want to make sure that this is a good learning experience for her, so I will challenge her conclusions with that objective in mind. After all,* he thought, *how thoroughly could she have prepared for this in such a short period of time?*

At the scheduled meeting time Terry and Ale walked into the conference room together. Terry flipped the light switch, closed the door, and sat down. *Interesting*, he thought, *I can't remember many times when Ale and I have been sitting on opposite sides of the table. What did you expect?* he continued, as though he was having a conversation with himself. *Did you think maybe you would both be sitting on the same side even though no one else is in the room? You are taking this whole thing way too seriously!* Terry was becoming more comfortable with these conversations with himself that seemed to be occurring much more frequently. He chalked it up to his age and didn't afford it much importance.

"How was your trip to Cincinnati?" he asked with a warm smile.

Ale was all business in situations like this. She was always polite and cordial, but not what anyone would consider relaxed or overly-friendly.

"Very productive," she replied, "but you know me, it would have been half as long if the people with whom I was meeting had just kept quiet and listened. I swear," she continued, almost as though she was talking to herself, "the less people know the more they want to say! The 'BS' meter was running for at least a full day of the two-day meeting. I haven't quite mastered the technique of running meetings like you have."

Ah, it isn't like Ale to blow smoke at me, especially in a setting like this, Terry said to himself, *so I'll just assume that this was a sincere attempt at flattery and we'll get on with it.* "Don't sell yourself short, Ale, you can run an effective meeting with the best of us. It's just hard to do so with a client who is paying the tab. They can take it personally if we seem to be curt with them."

"And the irony with this company in Cincinnati, Terry, is that for all of their talk as though they are management experts they are managing that firm around and around, faster and faster in ever decreasing concentric circles until they lose themselves right up their own asses!"

The unusual nature of the silence in the room for what seemed to Terry like several minutes was matched only by how long his mouth remained open while he stared at her in disbelief of her vivid description of their client's incompetence.

"How about if I give you the long and the short of my opinion on Camber now and then we can discuss it?" she asked, very much as though she was gently directing Terry.

"You see," Terry said having recovered from his earlier shock, "right down to business! You're one of the best!" *Now who's blowing smoke?* he asked himself.

"Okay let's begin," she said, as though she didn't even hear that last remark. "Camber is bleeding badly! In 2006, they lost over one hundred and twenty two thousand dollars on gross revenues of a little over one million dollars. Their gross margin was over two hundred and fifty thousand dollars, or about 25%, which is quite strong. But that also means that they expended way more than their gross margin on non-revenue producing costs, and thus the large loss. During the first quarter of this year, they're showing a gross margin of close to eight thousand dollars on a gross revenue of nearly two hundred and fifty thousand dollars. That is extremely weak, and then you see that they expended nearly fifty thousand dollars on non-revenue producing costs. Now I ask you, how can a business continue to do that and survive? A gross revenue of two hundred and fifty thousand dollars and a gross margin of eight thousand? They lost forty two thousand dollars in the first quarter alone. This isn't a business, it's a hobby!"

Ale took a sip from the bottle of water sitting in front of her, and Terry took advantage of the break to ask her, "So what does that mean to you, Ale?"

"It means that in addition to Camber being an anemic performer, at best, we can't trust these numbers." She continued, "Terry, you have drilled it into my head that we must always pay close attention to consistencies and inconsistencies especially in the due diligence stage, right?"

"Right," said Terry.

"Well the income statements that Greg has provided are loaded with inconsistencies, and we can't ignore that!" Ale was on a roll. "In addition the balance sheet is nothing more than a pig with lipstick and a pretty dress!"

Terry took particular note of the colorful if not politically correct analogy. Although it was quite unusual for her to wander so close to the edge of a dangerous metaphor he acknowledged to himself the fact that it was just the two of them in the room and that she was using this opportunity to demonstrate her strength to him.

Ale never broke stride. "The balance sheet reflects a cash balance of close to one hundred and ten thousand dollars, which at first glance doesn't seem so bad. But it also shows that over sixty five thousand dollars of that cash has been placed on account by the Navy, which leaves only forty five thousand in cash that is actually an asset of Camber's. To make matters much worse, Terry, there is a capital loan due to someone in the amount of over two hundred and twenty thousand dollars. All of this boils down to a negative equity position for the company of about one hundred and thirteen thousand dollars."

Terry smiled ever so slightly at her sharp emphasis on the word *negative*.

"Okay then," he said, "financial summary, as though I can't predict exactly what you're going to say."

Ale picked up a random collection of papers and held them out toward Terry for emphasis and said, "The firm barely has any cash of its own and it has a significant operating loss over the past fifteen months. In addition, it has a negative net worth in excess of ten times its cash position. To make matters worse, it has no visible sustainable organic solvency for the foreseeable future. Those are four of our most significant vital signs that can only be summarized for this business as putrid."

"Awe come on, Ale," quipped Terry, "don't hold back, tell it as it is!" They both smiled and took a couple of deep breaths. Each sipped from water bottles on the table and then just kind of stared at the other for a few moments.

Terry thought hard about the concise summary that Ale had just delivered. He focused on her use of the term "sustainable organic solvency," a phrase that he'd developed years ago to describe a situation where a company can generate enough revenue, solely on its own, to cover its operating expenses without having to rely on investors' dollars in order to survive. He coined the term after watching entrepreneurs regularly scramble for investors' money to cover operating costs instead of concentrating on the creation of sustainable revenues to pay those expenses from cash generated internally. *She's right*, he thought, *there isn't any clear path to a sustainable organic solvency in Camber's current condition.*

"So you're saying that we should walk away from this now," suggested Terry.

"No," said Ale. "I think that we should develop a proposal for Greg that creates an opportunity for him to recoup his investment in Camber eventually, but which also leaves all of the risk of this project squarely on his shoulders. We should put in the time to turn it around without any cash investment on our part, and we design the proposal in such a way that we will own the company in its entirety after the successful turn-around. That's the way you make money in this business—you buy-in low with an opportunity to sell-off high. With you managing this project, Terry, I think there may be a chance of doing that."

Terry was speechless. *And I thought that she was going to come into this meeting less than fully prepared*, he said to himself. *Is it possible that the student is quickly turning into the teacher?* he wondered.

"Let me make sure I understand you," Terry said. "We're looking at a project that is desperately devoid of any present value whatsoever and you are suggesting that we go ahead and invest time in the development of a proposal to take it on for Orion?"

"That's what I'm suggesting," said Ale with a sort of Cheshire grin.

"Why?" asked Terry.

"A couple of reasons. First we can chalk it up to portfolio effect. You know, when you have a portfolio of investments you make sure that you have some risky, but potentially rewarding ones in addition to the less risky ones with a more reliable return on your investment. Camber will be our risky venture."

"Okay what else?" asked Terry.

"Look Terry, I have a tremendous amount of respect for you, always have and always will. If you have a gut feeling about this project, then I don't want to stand in the way. If we design the proposal correctly and if Greg is willing to go along with it, we can get out at any point with little more than our time invested in it. And Greg will probably not lose a whole lot more than what he would lose if he just walked away now. So I think that we should just get on with it and see what happens. But if it will require even the slightest bit more from us than our time over the next few months to a year then we get out—fast. Agreed?"

"Agreed," said Terry. "When do you want to get together to design the proposal?"

"Right now," said Ale. "We can get the critical points done in the next few hours, and then I'll write it up tonight. We'll go over the rough draft tomorrow afternoon, and we'll be able to meet with Greg to present it to him within twenty-four hours of when we finalize the document."

During the past couple of years Terry had worked with Ale to help her fine tune her "get it done now" approach to business. Both had observed and worked with numerous businesspeople who demonstrated less than a sense of urgency when it came to follow-through on projects, and Terry had been pleased with Ale's perfected impatience with the "mañana will be fine" philosophy of management practiced by so many. He was impressed that she was eager to move immediately on a project that didn't exactly thrill her in the first place.

"Okay let's go," said Terry, "you seem to have some ideas about how we structure this thing, so you take the lead."

Ale didn't even stop to take a breath. "Let's get the most crucial requirements out of the way first. As with every project we accept we will require absolute and unequivocal control of the company. We need to be able to go into this one, especially this one, without having to worry about anyone looking over our shoulders and second-guessing what we're implementing."

She took a sip of water and continued. "We will initially buy forty-nine percent of the stock in the company and Greg will retain the other fifty-one percent. There will, however, be a covenant in the agreement that the only way that he can actually exercise his majority vote is if he wants to terminate the project altogether. Otherwise, we have the unrestricted authority to do whatever we believe needs to be done."

"Okay," interrupted Terry, "I thought you said we wouldn't be investing any money. How much do you propose we pay for the forty-nine percent share of the ownership?"

"One dollar." Ale was all business. She showed no facial expression when she delivered the solution and Terry worked hard to hide his acceptance of what she was suggesting.

Ale continued as though she had scripted the whole thing in advance. "Greg is going to have to guarantee a line-of-credit of one hundred thousand dollars for Camber that we can draw on as needed for cash and for any projects that we believe are necessary for the operation and growth of the business. In addition, he leaves in place any and all credit agreements for the company, whether or not they are personally guaranteed by him. Fuel is the one that I am particularly concerned about."

"Wow!" exclaimed Terry, "do you think he'll go for this?"

"We don't care at this point, Terry. We're designing a proposal for the turn-around of a company that is for all intents and purposes dead. If Greg wants to salvage it he will have to invest in the infrastructure needed to keep it alive, and then to grow it into a profitable enterprise. If we succeed he will have a significant value-base from which to recoup his investment. Besides, look at what I'm proposing. He won't have to provide any cash up front, but he will be increasing his risk substantially – as it should be!"

"Anything else?" asked Terry almost sarcastically.

"Yes," said Ale. "He's been running this company for over five years. We've done our initial due diligence, but we won't know where all of the skeletons are until we actually get in there and get our hands dirty for awhile. We have to put a clause in the contract which states that Greg is personally responsible for the value of any decisions, mistakes, problems, etc. that may occur after we take over, but which are the direct result of his management prior to our involvement. There is a quarter of a million dollars in a note payable to him on the balance sheet that we can draw against if anything arises that falls into this category. Again, all of the risk has to rest on his shoulders, not ours!"

"Now that I think about it, Ale, he is really not putting himself at any more risk by agreeing to these conditions than he would have been assuming had he continued to run the business himself, right?"

"Right," she said, "and we're not going to ask for anything in return except expenses. Orion will be reimbursed for all out-of-pocket expenses but will not draw a fee for the management of Camber until the cash flow will support it. Strictly sweat equity! If we succeed then we get a piece of the pie, and if we don't we haven't cost Greg anything for our own efforts on Camber's behalf."

"Obviously you've given this a lot of thought, Ale."

"What, did you think I was going to walk in here unprepared?" she asked with a smile.

Now Terry felt a little more than embarrassed, but he didn't want to let on to Ale. He had made the mistake of assuming that she would not pay much attention to this potential project because of her initial impression that he would become emotionally involved in it. Not only would he have to keep these earlier doubts of his confidence in her a well protected secret in the future, but he would also have to pledge to himself that it will never happen again.

After a short period of silence, she said, "I'll work up the rough draft of the proposal tonight if you agree. The rest of it will be standard boilerplate from our master agreement format."

"Okay Ale," Terry said, "I really appreciate all of your effort on this!"

"Of course," she said, "we're partners, right?"

"Right!"

* * * * *

It was a sunny April afternoon at the Inner Harbor of Baltimore as Terry sat quietly on a public bench on the promenade of the northern side of Harborplace. It was still a little too chilly on this spring day for tourists and their children to be out on the water. So for now all of the rental boats were tied to the small dock waiting for the first warm day that will have them dotting the harbor like scores of small, colorful corks bobbing up and down on the glassy surface. Terry sat facing the rows of small, two-seat green, red, yellow, and blue paddle boats lined in two rows facing him and running from his left to his right. Behind the smaller paddle boats were larger ones, some a bright green and the rest a bright purple, shaped like six foot-high dinosaurs. He imagined the excitement of the children certain to be lining this dock in just a few weeks waiting with their parents for their turns to board these small vessels and paddle out to where the big boats were entering and leaving the harbor. In spite of the slight chill in the air, the direct rays of the late day sun warmed Terry's face as he thought about the meeting with Ale and Greg scheduled for a little later that afternoon at nearby Phillips Restaurant.

It was difficult for Terry to concentrate on the details of the proposal to be discussed at the meeting. Not just because of the sights and sounds of the harbor but because his mind kept wandering back a couple of years to a conversation that he and Ale had on a plane after their visit to the first company that they were evaluating together. That business was in serious trouble, much like Camber was now, with no free cash and a mountain of debt. They had spent two full days running the gamut of due diligence tests, and as they sat on the flight home together Ale was the first to break a long silence.

"You're unusually quiet. Is everything okay?"

"Yes, Ale," Terry remembered saying, "let me ask you a question. You spent the same two days looking at that company that I did. What is the very first thing that you would do if you were going in there alone to turn it around?"

Ale thought about the question for a few moments, and then she answered. "I'd roll up my sleeves and change the entire human resources function into the best anywhere!"

Terry recalled that he was silent as he stared out the window after her response.

"Obviously you're not thrilled with that answer," Ale finally said.

"You're fired," Terry said, without even turning toward her from the window.

Ale didn't seem to know whether to take him seriously or to laugh, but she decided that it would be better if she didn't laugh. "Please explain," she finally queried.

"Ale, you're a terrific human resources specialist, worth your weight in gold to any organization with critical personnel or HR problems. But this outfit is in the organizational emergency room hemorrhaging cash and unlikely to survive without life support for its balance sheet. And your immediate triage solution is to administer cosmetic surgery." Terry was warm but firm with this response.

Ale said, "So you don't think that what I do is very important?"

"Of course I think it's important! But that's not the point. We have to approach the business patient as though we're doctors, and we must get the life-threatening factors stabilized before we can even think about the ones that can wait. You're not a specialist anymore, at least in the narrowest sense, you save the lives of businesses and the livelihoods of their employees. Patients that bleed to death on a gurney in the Emergency Room don't do anyone any good!"

"I get it," said Ale. "Am I still fired?"

"Of course not, I just wanted to make sure I had your undivided attention!" he remembered replying.

Terry couldn't help thinking that she had come a long way in such a short time. She had been an extremely quick study and now it appeared that she was more than ready to attack some serious challenges on her own. He smiled ever-so-slightly when it occurred to him that he hoped she didn't get too independent with her newly acquired competencies. *I don't know what I would ever do without her*! he thought as the sun warmed his face.

Ale knew exactly where to find Terry at the appointed time. She joined him right in front of the paddle boats sitting on that bench next to Baltimore's World Trade Center where he once had maintained an office shortly after forming Orion, many years before. "Whatcha thinkin'?" she asked playfully as she approached him seemingly out of nowhere.

"What? Oh nothing, Ale, I was a thousand miles and years away there for a few moments. Are we ready to go?"

"Yup," she said.

"Good because you're handling the whole meeting!" Terry knew that this was what she actually wanted anyway, so he figured that this would be as good a time as any for her to solo.

"Great!" said Ale. "I sent the proposal to Greg last night by messenger. He should be prepared to discuss it in detail. We've got about ten minutes to get over to the restaurant."

Terry stood from the bench and issued a small moan as he did. He hadn't realized how long he had been sitting in the one place and how stiff his legs had become as a result. He glanced back over his left shoulder at the rows of paddle boats and at the World Trade Center towering over them. He then walked with Ale past the *USS Constellation* to their left and toward the food pavilion of Harborplace, where Phillips Seafood Restaurant has been a landmark for decades.

Greg was waiting for them at the entrance to the restaurant. He smiled and waved when he saw them enter the harbor-side door of the large pavilion about a hundred feet away from him. Ale noticed right away that he had in his hand the package she had sent to him the day before, but she couldn't tell from her vantage point whether or not the large envelope had been opened.

"Hello Greg," said Terry cheerfully as he extended his right hand.

Greg said his hellos to Ale and Terry, shook their hands, and then gestured into the restaurant. "I took the liberty of getting us a table over by the window," he explained as he led the way.

When all three were seated and had ordered two iced teas and a Diet Coke with a twist of lemon and very little ice for Ale, she began the meeting by asking Greg if he had been able to review the proposal.

"Yes I have," said Greg with a much more serious expression than they had seen to this point. "So what it all boils down to," he said, "is that you expect me to sell forty-nine percent of the business to you for just one dollar while I shoulder all of the guarantees for the liabilities including another hundred thousand dollars on a new line of credit. Oh, and I will have no say in the management of the firm."

"That's right," said Ale, "and don't forget, you will be responsible for the value of any and all financial events that arise after Orion takes over the company, but are the direct result of anything that occurred prior to that time."

The fact that Ale was carrying the ball for Orion in this meeting so far did not go unnoticed by Greg. "Who would be the direct project manager on site at Camber?" he asked.

Ale was quick to respond, "Terry, but I will be involved and on location as required."

Greg thought for a few moments as he looked at Terry, Ale, and then down at the proposal that he had opened in front of him. He then held the document in his left hand and gestured with it toward the two sitting across the table from him. "I've carefully read this thing over at least four times since I received it yesterday."

Ale assessed the expression on Greg's face as a negative one. She was fully expecting an outright rejection of their proposal as she restrained herself from looking at Terry to her left. *Frankly*, she thought, *I'm not going to be terribly disappointed if he turns us down flat!*

Greg continued, "I don't like the situation in which I find myself here today. And I don't like the terms of this proposal! There is nothing in this document that favors me except for the outside chance that you might be able to turn this thing around, and I might be able to recoup some or all of my investment. In all fairness, Terry, you prepared me well for what this proposal contains."

Greg stopped and stared at them once again, this time for about two extremely long minutes. Then he broke the silence. "Ale, give me a dollar, and you will be the owner of forty-nine percent of Camber Flight Training, Inc. Terry, I'll see you first thing in the morning at BWI."

EIGHT

TERRY LONGBOW DROVE onto the parking lot in front of the building housing the offices of Camber Flight Training, Inc. at exactly 6:00 a.m. on Thursday, April 15, 2007. The air was filled with the sound of jet engines as airliners and corporate jets were taxiing and taking off from the Baltimore Washington International Airport just a few hundred yards from where he chose a parking spot for his first day as chief operating officer of Camber. As Terry opened his car door, he couldn't help but notice the distinct odor of jet exhaust that permeated the air around him and he stopped momentarily as a flashback to his flying days some thirty years earlier overtook him. His eyes became transfixed on a Boeing 757 that had just appeared climbing into the air from behind the building after taking off from one of the runways, and he stood motionless and watched as its image became smaller and smaller and then eventually disappeared into the vast blue sky. He suddenly realized that the broad smile that had unconsciously appeared on his face was the result of an overwhelming feeling that he was finally back where he belonged. He thought about Ale's earlier suggestion that his motivation behind wanting this project was because of his passion for aviation. It was now clear to him that the indignation he had expressed at this suggestion was actually a form of denial. Every person who has ever experienced the thrill of flying knows that the feeling of excitement created within from just being near aircraft is in fact a passion that will remain inside for life. After more than three decades, this same love had once again made its way to the surface for Terry, and he could not have been happier to be walking back into the world of aviation.

Terry's business day when he was on the site of a client usually began at 6:00 a.m., so it was not out of the ordinary that he was standing in front of the Camber facility at that time of the morning. He did not know what time Greg had meant when he said the day before that they would meet first thing in the morning, but it was his intention to arrive early. He wanted to walk around so that he could get a feel for the location before becoming buried in detail with Greg. As he stood at his car and looked toward the front of the building, Terry noted some of the general exterior features of the flight school and its surroundings.

He was standing on the easternmost fringe of the BWI airport property directly in front of the building housing the Camber offices, which was a small, one-story structure that was once a general aviation terminal. It stood between him and the sprawling expanse containing runways, taxiways, ramps, and service roads typical on the acreage of an airport serving a large metropolitan area. To his right, and attached to the Camber building, was a large hangar which appeared to be constructed of some sort of gray fabricated metal. To the right of the hangar and extending for what seemed to be a mile was a series of fenced-in parking areas for airport patrons' cars. To the left of the Camber facility, detached from it by approximately twenty feet of open space, was an even larger hangar that was identical in appearance to the one on the right. And to the left of this larger hangar, and separated from it by a security fence and gate, was a larger, single story building serving as the current general aviation terminal for the BWI facility. As he walked toward the front door of the building, which housed the offices and the people associated with his newest business venture, he felt an energetic bounce in his step signifying the excitement that was characteristic of the first day of any new job.

Terry was surprised that both sets of double doors leading into the building were unlocked as he passed through them and into a large lobby area with two sets of four individual chairs. Each group was situated in a circle facing a low glass top table with magazines and newspapers on top. In front of the wall to his left, he noticed a reception counter about four feet tall and made of some sort of dark wood, perhaps mahogany. He walked farther into the lobby and looked for some sign of life. The masonry wall directly opposite from him was solid with the exception of a large, clear glass section on each side containing doors which appeared to lead into a hallway running parallel to the lobby and containing closed office doors. A small sign above the glass door to the left side of this wall read "Camber Flight Training, Inc." with the "n" missing from the word "training."

As Terry walked in he was startled by a loud voice coming from his immediate left in the hallway.

"Good morning," barked Greg in a tone that Terry thought was way too cheerful for this ungodly hour.

Terry pivoted quickly to his left and saw Greg standing about three feet from him with his right hand extended, a cup of coffee in his left, and a smile from ear-to-ear. "Good morning," he said, although quite a bit more reserved than Greg's greeting. "I'm surprised to see you here this early, Greg."

"Been here since five," said Greg. "I've been showing up at the butt-crack of dawn since things started to get tight on us. It's quiet at this time of the morning, and I can get stuff done before the instructors and students arrive for the first wave of flights to go out. Want some coffee?"

"Never touch the stuff, Greg," said Terry. "I'm a big hot tea drinker in the morning."

"Tea," said Greg, almost startled. "We don't have any tea!"

Terry realized that he was going to have to make some changes, or at least some minor adjustments, during these first few days on the job, and he quickly decided that the latter would be best for a smoother transition into the saddle for him. "That's okay, Greg, I can go down the street to the Seven Eleven if I need anything," he said rather pointedly.

"Okay," said Greg, almost obvious in his relief that he wouldn't have to provide Terry with his tea every morning. "Where's Ale?"

"You won't be seeing much of Ale," said Terry. "I'll be here every day, at least for several weeks, and I will be updating Ale regularly by phone each evening and occasionally in person a couple times a week. Once we get the board structure in place she will be here for every board meeting, however."

Greg looked at Terry for a moment, then he said, "Shouldn't it be the other way around? I mean, she's the junior partner. Right?"

"That's not the way it works, Greg. I am the lead on this project and she's the lead on other projects. We keep each other well informed about our own projects. She'll be around only if I need her here, or, of course if something happens to me then she'll take over."

"I get it," said Greg. "Why don't you come in here, I have some things set up that I want to teach you first."

Greg gestured with his left hand for Terry to enter an office down the hall and to the left.

"This is the brain center of the operation!" Greg exclaimed.

The office was extremely small, perhaps ten feet by ten feet. There was a workstation module against the wall to the left of the entrance and to the right was a four-drawer lateral filing cabinet. A computer monitor sat on top of the workstation with the CPU sitting on the floor below on the right side of the space provided for one's legs while sitting at the workstation. A large printer was crammed into a corner to the right of the entrance, between the lateral file and the opposite wall, and was precariously balanced on a table that appeared much too small to adequately support it. Greg brought a small chair into the office and positioned it directly behind the chair already in place at the workstation. He motioned to Terry to sit on the smaller chair as he sat at the larger one and logged onto the computer. Terry obliged, although grudgingly.

Greg began to show Terry each page of a stack of papers, which he described as flight tickets, and was giving step-by-step instructions for entering the data from each of the tickets into the computer in what was obvious to Terry to be a painfully tedious process.

"What are we doing, Greg?"

Greg stopped poking at the keyboard and said, "We have to enter the data from every flight from yesterday so that all of the information is properly recorded."

Terry attempted to disguise his early onset of frustration. "Why are we doing this and why is it the first thing that you are showing me?" It was obvious to Terry that he was about to learn a great deal that had not been discovered in his earlier attempt at due diligence.

Terry was a firm believer in the importance of senior management learning as much of the detail involved in the day-to-day operation of any enterprise as possible. But he also knew all too well that valuable time would be wasted if that were to be his immediate focus with this project. He had researched enough to know that Camber was dying, and not slowly. It was imperative that he invest every minute of his time in the development of an operating plan for the next one hundred days of this company's life. Moreover, he knew that sitting with Greg and learning how to type data into the computer would not contribute in any way to this critical survival phase. His challenge, at that moment, was to find a tactful way to communicate to Greg the necessity of moving in a direction different from his.

"Greg," Terry began, "are you in a hurry to move out of Camber and into something completely different?"

Greg turned away from the computer and swiveled around toward Terry on the wheels of his office chair. The look of puzzlement on Greg's face communicated a sense of frustration that apparently equaled Terry's and he stared at him for a few moments before speaking. "Why do you ask?" Greg finally said.

"Have you ever seen a professional juggler on the stage?" asked Terry.

"Sure, but what…?"

Terry interrupted and smiled. "Okay what about two jugglers working together?"

"Yes, of course," he said.

"In order for two jugglers separately juggling, uh, bowling pins let's say, to start passing pins to each other without dropping them they must continue to operate independently to get a rhythm going before they coordinate a transfer of pins." Terry continued, "We have to do the same thing here. I'm going to have to get my arms around a lot of different and general aspects of the operation of this business immediately. And if I sit here for a day or two trying to learn how to enter this data I will have lost those two days which should have been used to map out a recovery strategy for the business. Not to mention the extra time I would lose entering data once I've learned how to do it."

"So, what are you suggesting?" asked Greg as though he still didn't quite get it.

"If you're not in a hurry to get out of here then we should work together during this transition, but initially with different functions. I'm suggesting that you continue to do everything that you have been doing to this point to keep the business going, and I'll do what I need to do to get up to speed with the generalities of the operation. At some point, we'll each feel comfortable with where I am on the learning curve, and that's when we'll start involving me in the day-to-day details." Terry understood all too well the tendency of entrepreneurs to tackle projects like this one without a coordinated plan of attack, and he wasn't going to let that happen at Camber on his watch.

"I get it," Greg said after a few moments, "first things first!"

"Right," said Terry. "Now how about giving me a tour before I get started on my side of the equation?"

The two men stood and walked through the office door and made an immediate right turn into the narrow hallway separated from the lobby to their left by a floor-to-ceiling masonry wall. On this wall was a large collage of regional aeronautical maps all connected with masking tape to create a single map of the continental United States. It was crude in its appearance, but Terry assumed that it was helpful to students to get "the big picture" of the navigation process. Even though he knew that it would be highly unlikely that any student at Camber would be taking a trip from the East to the West Coast any time soon.

The next door to their right opened into a space which was about half the size of the office they had just vacated and was obviously being used as a storeroom. As they continued walking a short distance the hallway opened up on the right into a larger open space with a sizable conference table sitting in the middle and eight simulated leather, high-back executive chairs distributed uniformly around the table. Terry couldn't help but think that the formality of this space was out of place compared to the décor of the rest of the facility he had seen to this point. To their far right the longer wall of this three-sided room was comprised of floor-to-ceiling windows with an unattractive view of the outside wall of the detached hangar that Terry had noticed earlier before he entered the building. On the other two walls forming this space were wooden cabinets which appeared to be oak, which added further to the unusually formal "feel" of the room for Terry.

"We use this space for small ground school groups and for company meetings when we have them," said Greg.

Continuing to walk forward they came to a door that opened into a larger office area with three small, metal desks spaced evenly around three of the walls, with more floor-to-ceiling windows occupying the fourth wall. This room was obviously where more of the company employees worked.

"This is where you can work, Terry," said Greg rather abruptly pointing to the desk directly in front of them and facing back out of the door where they were standing. Terry's immediate reaction was that he was not crazy about the idea of sharing space with other employees, but he was quick to realize that he was soon to have much bigger problems to solve.

The total of all of the space rented by Camber was comprised of these three offices of varying sizes, the conference area, and the hallway. Although the lobby was a relatively larger area adjacent to Camber's facilities it was designated by the landlord for general use by the flight school and three other tenants occupying the building. Camber was exclusively using the eight-foot-long wooden counter, resembling a small airport terminal ticket counter. But Greg said that it had been purchased by another tenant and himself a year earlier with the intention that each company would use half for the purpose of greeting and otherwise accommodating its own customers. Terry made a mental note that one of the challenges lying ahead will surely have to be the acquisition of additional space for daily operations.

"Let's take a walk outside," said Greg.

"Okay," Terry responded as he followed his tour guide to a secure set of double-glass doors located on the opposite side of the lobby. They stopped just before the first door as Greg grasped a bright red badge attached to a lanyard hanging from his neck. Terry hadn't noticed the badge before now because it had occupied a pocket on Greg's shirt and was not in clear sight until he removed it. Greg quickly swiped the badge through an electronic security reader attached to a wall to the left of the door and just below eye level. After swiping the badge and entering a code into a keypad, Terry heard a distinct click at the door just before Greg pushed it open and signaled to follow him out of the building and onto the airport ramp area. The air was filled with the whine of aircraft engines, and the fumes of engine exhaust.

They next entered an expansive concrete parking and taxiing area the size of several football fields and occupied by dozens of corporate jets parked in parallel rows. Each row began close to the buildings and extended away from them on the ramp, and although the planes were of varying shapes and sizes, their noses formed a perfectly straight line in each row as though they had been placed there by some giant hand along an invisible straight-edge. Terry tried not to gawk at the massive acreage of the BWI airport, which extended for miles to the south, west, and north beyond the general aviation ramp where they were standing. He didn't want Greg to notice the excitement generated inside of him by just being close to this environment once again, but it was difficult for him to contain his enthusiasm.

As they walked Greg explained that the Camber fleet was tied down on the far south side of the ramp, away from all of the jet activity. Terry remembered that smaller aircraft had to be secured by ropes attached to metal loops protruding slightly from the pavement to keep them from moving about in the wind. As they approached the final two lines of planes, at least a half-mile from where their walk had begun, Terry thought about how tiny these planes seemed among the larger jet aircraft. It was hard to believe that each represented an investment of at least one hundred thousand dollars.

"And here is our fleet," said Greg, intruding upon Terry's wonderment amid his surroundings.

"Okay," said Terry, "give me the lowdown."

Greg didn't hesitate. "We have fifteen training aircraft: ten Diamond DA20s, a DA40, three Cessna 172s, and an old Piper Arrow. The DA20s are the smallest with two seats and these are used primarily for our Navy training program. The others each have four seats, and we rent these to certified pilots more than we use them for any training."

Terry walked over to the DA20 parked closest to them and stood in front of the leading edge of the wing. The aircraft was all white except for two thin red stripes running from nose to tail, and two sets of large, red identification numbers painted both on the fuselage and tail. It was a single engine plane with a propeller in the front and long wings extending from the lower portion of the fuselage, unlike many aircraft built by another manufacturer, Cessna, which have the wings located high on the fuselage. Terry had flown both low and high wing aircraft during his days as a flight instructor and was still familiar with the handling characteristics in flight of each type.

Greg reached into his pocket and found a set of keys that he used to unlock and open the canopy of the plane. The canopy was a clear, Plexiglas bubble which covered the entire cockpit and, when opened from the front on hinges in the rear, pointed itself to the sky at a sixty-degree angle providing the only access for pilots to the two seats inside. Terry placed his right foot onto a small step protruding from just behind the trailing edge of the wing, and then his left onto an area located on the top of the wing immediately adjacent to the fuselage and just under the cockpit. He pulled himself up onto this inboard area of the wing, which was coated with a black friction surface for this purpose, by using a silver handle on the fuselage that he grabbed with his right hand. With one simultaneous forward and upward thrust Terry's weight shifted from both feet on the ramp to his right foot on the step and then to his left foot on the wing. He seemed quite pleased with himself that he accomplished the climb without any help or instructions from Greg, especially considering his age and how long it had been since performing the maneuver during his flying days. Rather than easing himself into a seat in the cockpit he chose to place one knee on the friction strip on the wing and lean over the left seat to get a good view of the instrument panel. His reluctance to climb into the seat stemmed largely from a quiet fear that he wouldn't be able to get out again without assistance from Greg. The entire cockpit was an extremely small and confined space especially for his six-foot, two hundred pound torso.

"I'm surprised at how much I recognize from so long ago," he said to Greg.

"It's a lot like riding a bike, Terry. I bet you get the hang of flying again quickly once you get back up in the air."

"Thanks Greg, but that's not anywhere in the game plan. I guarantee I won't have any time to try to get back into that saddle."

Terry carefully descended from the wing in the opposite order from which he had mounted it and Greg closed and locked the canopy. The two walked parallel to the two lines of aircraft comprising the Camber fleet and toward the hangars and buildings, the smaller of which was coming alive with company flight instructors and students starting the walk to the flight line for the first flights of the day. As they continued their walk toward the oncoming groups of two Terry noticed that the building to his right, the larger of the two general aviation terminal facilities displayed a three dimensional sign across the top which said, "Elite Flight Support Services."

Gesturing toward the building Terry asked, "What's this?"

"That's the company that provides the support services for all of the corporate and transient aircraft that come through BWI every day. They are also our landlord," said Greg. "Do you want to go in and have a look?"

"Later," said Terry.

Greg waved as the first of the pairs of flight crews approached. When they stopped directly in front of them, Greg said, "Terry, I'd like for you to meet Joel Fadely," gesturing to the shorter of the two on the left. "Joel is our chief flight instructor for the Navy and civilian programs. And this is his student, Jonathan."

Terry reached out and shook hands with each in the order in which they were introduced to him. "It's a pleasure to meet you," he said. It was a particularly refreshing surprise to him that Joel's Navy student was in uniform. Although he assumed that it was one of the more relaxed uniforms assigned to Midshipmen, it stood in stark contrast to Joel's overly casual T-shirt, jeans, and an old pair of tennis shoes. He also noticed what appeared to be a look of puzzlement on Joel's face when introduced to him.

After Joel and his student continued to walk toward their plane, Terry asked Greg, "Have you briefed the employees on the change taking place?"

"No," said Greg, "I haven't had a chance."

"I think that should be a high priority. Can we call them all together anytime soon?" asked Terry.

"That's really difficult to do on short notice," Greg said. "I don't want to cancel any flights just for a meeting. How about doing it on the next day that the weather is lousy?"

"Okay," said Terry, "then at least get an e-mail out to all of them right away. It will cut down on the rumors!"

Greg agreed just as three more twosomes stopped in front of them. "Terry, this is Stacey McCoy, our chief flight instructor for instrument training, and Darryl Flint, our chief for commercial training, and Elmer Maurer, our chief of administrative services." Greg went on to introduce each of the students by first name, and as Terry shook hands with them he exchanged the appropriate pleasantries.

Once again each student was dressed in an informal Navy uniform, and each flight instructor looked as if he were attempting to outdo the others with clothing more in vogue for the homeless. Terry was beginning to wonder how many more surprises were in store for him on his first day at Camber.

As the two new business partners approached the door of the Camber lobby, a tall, young, and handsome man was exiting with two teenagers in tow. Greg stopped abruptly just short of colliding with trio and turned to Terry after briefly shaking hands with the group's leader. "Terry," said Greg, "meet Brother Toby McKinley and a couple of his students, Joe and Peter."

After shaking each of their hands, Terry asked Brother Toby if he was an instructor for Camber.

"Not yet," said the Marianist cleric. "I'm a private pilot and a computer science teacher at Mount St. Paul's High School just south of Baltimore. I have a flying club at the school, and Joe and Peter are two of about thirty of our club members. I rent planes from Camber and take the students over to the Eastern Shore for the learning experience."

Terry smiled broadly and said, "It's a pleasure meeting all of you. Have a great flight!"

Brother Toby and his two protégés walked briskly onto the airport ramp toward the flight line and a waiting Cessna 172 which they had scheduled for the early morning flight.

Greg and Terry continued into the Camber lobby and toward the offices of the flight school. Terry made a mental note of a nagging question that he wanted to ask Greg about Brother Toby and his flying activities as he decided that the question should wait until later.

NINE

ALE'S UNUSUAL MORNING began with a 6:00 fight with Franco, mainly over him once again "hiding" in his basement fortress the night before when she arrived home from work. Unfortunately, these fights were a rather routine occurrence lately. The unusual aspect of this particular argument was that they were both in the same room long enough for an altercation to actually get started. A little later she got the boys ready for school and dropped them off as she did every school-day morning and spent the rest of the ride into work fuming while thinking to herself over and over, *something has got to give soon! I can't go on living like this.* This was followed immediately by the injection of reality when she reminded herself that she had no options other than leaving Franco, which she had always adamantly refused to consider because of the potential effect that this life-changing move would have on Stefan and Johan. And, as always, her thought process ended with, *so I guess I'll just have to live with it* as she parked her Nissan Pathfinder in the lot in front of the building housing the Orion offices.

In the world of business turn-arounds first impressions are at best fickle indicators of organizational strengths or weaknesses. That is why strong turn-around managers spend as much time as possible watching and analyzing in the very beginning of projects instead of making quick and perhaps ill-informed changes. This is actually an excellent strategy for any manager entering a new position or confronting a new situation in an established one. Watch carefully, listen carefully, wait to form opinions of what is happening around you, and then execute the decision making process when all of the facts seem clear and devoid of emotion. Of course, Terry had found himself in many situations where he had to act swiftly to save an organization from demise. But these dire circumstances usually were restricted to actions involving cash and were surgically performed while attempting to leave other facets of the organization unchanged for as long as possible. In the case of Camber he could afford to wait and observe for at least a short period before he began to make significant changes. He decided not to say anything to Greg about the attire of the flight instructors until he prepared a list of changes that must be made, but he also decided that this would be a priority. Flight training is a precise and disciplined process and one can't help but wonder how precise and disciplined a flight instructor could possibly be when dressed for a day at the beach.

After returning to the Camber offices from his tour of the fleet Terry proceeded to the office that he would be sharing with the "chiefs" and sat down at the desk that Greg had assigned to him earlier. He removed a letter sized, leather spiral-ring notebook from his briefcase and turned to a page in the middle marked by a single paper clip protruding from the top of the page. For nearly twenty years he had been in the habit of writing all of his notes, about anything to which he might later want to refer, in a formal notebook just like this one. Prior to developing this habit he would write things on scraps of paper, post-it notes, restaurant paper napkins, around the edges of newspapers, and on the envelopes of mail that happened to be within his reach. When he later wanted to retrieve something he knew he had written he would have to find and assemble all of the various bits and pieces of paper, and finding what he was looking for became a time consuming and wasteful scavenger hunt. His notebook idea, while nothing more than common sense, came from an association he had with a senior manager at one of the first companies that he worked with. After Terry left that company for another assignment the manager with the notebook habit became a United States Congressman, and later the Governor of the State of Tennessee. He figured early on that this was a practice adopted from a more than worthy role model and one that would serve him well. On the first day of January of every year he began a new notebook and carefully filed away the one from the previous year. While younger managers around him, especially Ale, criticized his continued use of paper rather than a laptop for this purpose, he was extremely comfortable with his tried-and-true method and was rarely at a loss for the details of any event that he had recorded.

Terry learned how to use the telephone intercom system quickly and he used it repeatedly for hours to request from Greg stacks of files on various subjects. In reality the intercom was hardly necessary because of the proximity of their two offices, but he decided that the phone would be more professional than shouting down the hall beyond students and instructors conferring in the meeting area. He first digested the details in the records of each of the fifteen aircraft in the company's fleet, noting that all except two were leased from owners obviously hoping to make a profit from their asset under management to the flight school. The other two were owned by Camber and represented assets on its balance sheet free-and-clear. He then studied the personnel records of every employee and, although they were very sloppy in appearance and currency, he learned a great deal about the nature of employment in a flight school and the qualifications of the workforce, or the lack thereof.

Then came the financial records. Camber had been using Quickbooks, a commercial software product popular with small to medium-sized companies. The state of the financials was identical to that of several other struggling companies with which Terry had worked. The strength of Quickbooks is that it is easy to learn and operate by someone who knows little or nothing about company financial structures, but its greatest weakness is that it is easy to learn and operate by someone who knows little or nothing about company financial structures. Terry once asked a woman who had worked for five years as the "bookkeeper" for a small company he was involved with why she had made a particular entry to a balance sheet account rather than a more appropriate income statement account. Her response was, "What's an income statement?" He could tell without much effort that Camber's books had been handled in much the same way since they began keeping records. He recalled Ale's comment a week or so earlier about not being able to rely on the figures that they'd been presented for their due diligence work.

Terry worked intensely without paying much attention to the employees coming into the office past his desk to the other two located in opposite corners. He made an effort to not appear rude and introduced himself to those he hadn't already met but his attention was glued to the files in front of him. He occasionally got up to bring soft drinks back to his desk and to take bathroom breaks but otherwise he kept right on working and lost all track of time. At 8:00 p.m. he looked at his cell phone, which he had turned off to avoid interruptions, and he couldn't believe the time. He saw several missed calls from Ale and decided to check-in with her.

"Hey," he said when she answered.

Ale sounded very happy to hear from him. "Hey stranger, what's going on?"

"I thought I'd give you an update on Camber before it gets too late," he began. "I've been at it for fourteen hours and really haven't even scratched the surface of what we really need to know. But here's what I do have in a nutshell."

Ale knew that he was reading directly from his notebook and that she should just be quiet and let him go through his notes.

Terry continued, "Greg seems to be doing all of the accounting and data entry for the business himself although he did mention at one point a woman who comes in on a part-time basis to help with that. There are fifteen aircraft in the fleet and the files indicate that thirteen of them are leased which means that Camber is at the mercy of several other people for the assets used to generate all of its revenue. I have met several of the flight instructors, another key component in the generation of revenues for the company, and I am not at all impressed with any of them. And I have spent several hours with the financials, on Quickbooks by the way, and you were right on target with your earlier assessment. They are very sloppy and we can't rely on them until I have gone through them item-by-item. That chore alone will take months."

After a pause Ale said, "That's it? Sounds like you've had quite a day. What's your next step?"

Terry replied immediately, "I am going to start the hundred day planning process. If I can get that plan done within the next two weeks then I can direct my attention to the financials and other problems. I do, however, have to interview each of the employees to see how many time bombs are lurking just under the surface. But my assessment for now is that this 'little project' that we have gotten ourselves into is going to be significantly more work than we had originally bargained for."

Ale replied, with a snicker, "What do you mean we?"

* * * * *

Terry arrived on the Camber parking lot once again at 6:00 a.m. for his second day on the job. Like the day before there was only one other car on the lot and he assumed that it belonged to Greg. He made a mental note that Greg is obviously a morning person and if he wants to sit down to discuss anything with him it would probably be best to do so as early in the day as possible. And that is exactly what he intended to do on this sunny spring morning,

Between the time of his departure from Camber after 8:00 the evening before and his early arrival this morning Terry was busy formulating a strategy for dealing with Greg as an active participant in this project. It was a requirement of the proposal agreed upon by all that Greg would relinquish day-to-day authority to Terry so that necessary decisions could be made without excessive discussion and delay. However, Terry also recognized that Greg was presently the only investor with a tangible stake at risk in the business. By design, if their collective efforts to resuscitate the business should fail, Terry and Ale would only lose the time that they had dedicated to the project. Greg would lose all of the money he had invested in the business to that point. And probably the full amount of a one hundred-thousand-dollar line of credit and an operating credit card account to be guaranteed by him as a condition of the Orion/Camber agreement.

Terry decided that his strategy for working effectively with Greg must have him carefully walk a fine line between keeping Greg informed of activities and decisions executed on behalf of the firm while tactfully but strictly limiting involvement of the former owner in their development and execution. Accordingly, this morning's meeting between the two would focus on the need for and requirements of establishing a one hundred day plan for the business without expending any time and effort on the defense of this course of action, should Greg happen to disagree with it.

Terry walked through to the far end of the lobby toward the glass door that provided access to the Camber hallway and, upon opening the door, was greeted by Greg as he was leaving the small clerical office. Each man appeared to be slightly startled at the unexpected appearance of the other in the confined space of the hallway. Greg was the first to muster a greeting followed almost immediately by a reply of, "Good morning" from Terry.

"Once I get settled and you return how about we sit down and discuss where I think we are at the moment," suggested Terry.

"Fine," said Greg, "let's go down to Starbucks and meet over a cup of coffee."

"Sounds good, I'll drive."

Greg continued to walk across the lobby to the men's room down the hall and Terry turned and proceeded toward the glass doors of the office area. As he opened one of the two doors he heard a familiar voice. Terry turned in time to see Brother Toby and three more of his students enter the lobby.

"Good morning, Brother Toby," said Terry with a friendly wave in their direction. Flying again today?" he asked cheerfully.

"Yes indeed," came the reply. The foursome appeared to be in a hurry to get out onto the ramp so Terry continued on to his meeting with Greg.

Terry was pleased that Greg had suggested a meeting place away from the office, thinking that the less the employees see them conferring together the less fear might be generated among them regarding the implications of the change in management and ownership of the company. His experience in the turn-around business supported the theory that, just as nature abhors a vacuum, employees abhor any change, either perceived or real, in their working environment, and he had sensed an air of trepidation among the flight instructors the day before in their shared office.

At Starbucks the conversation was light with Greg commenting about his daughter's imminent return from college for the summer and Terry nodding politely with only an occasional superficial question about her summer plans at home. After getting their drinks from the counter they sat at a small table near the window and watched the steady traffic for a morning fix of caffeine and sugar that would cost them, on average, about seven bucks.

"Now this was a terrific idea," said Greg as he slowly blew through the little hole in the top of his cup of 'daily blend' in an attempt to cool it off.

"What's that?" asked Terry.

"Starbucks," said Greg. "Who would ever have thought twenty years ago that millions of people would make enough time to stand in line early each morning on their way to work for the privilege of spending seven bucks for a cup of coffee?"

"Do you know the story of Starbucks?" Terry inquired with a smile of enlightenment suggesting that the story was about to be told.

"No, all I know is that they have thousands of stores around the world and they are making tons of money."

"I'm not going to spend much time on it but the story is relevant to what we're trying to do." Terry saw this as an opportunity to connect the process that he and Ale would be employing at Camber with success stories having similar start-up experiences. "Howard Schultz is the founder of Starbucks—at least as we know it today. He started with very little of his own, struggled with ideas and concepts for his involvement in a business that he loved, and eventually bought the Starbucks concept from other owners with the dream of improving and growing it from its relatively humble beginnings. There are several books out there chronicling the details of Schultz's successes and failures, but the bottom line from his story, at least for me, is that his motto was 'luck is the residue of design,' which is a strong indication of the importance of planning in the creation and growth of a successful business."

"Planning," said Greg more than a little skeptically. "Okay, but he had to have a lot more going for him than just planning to have created an empire like this, right?"

"Sure," said Terry, "but it all had to start with a concrete and viable plan. And Schultz wasn't the only one. Fred Smith, the founder of Federal Express, and Ray Kroc, the founder of MacDonald's, had very rocky, nearly disastrous starts. But each succeeded beyond his wildest dreams after designing and implementing foundational business plans."

"So why do I get the feeling that you are going to suggest that we need a plan for Camber?" asked Greg appearing to move a step beyond skepticism.

"Probably because that is exactly what I came here this morning to tell you. Except we're not going to develop just one plan, we're going to develop two plans for the business. I am embarking today on the creation of a hundred-day plan that will clearly detail exactly the steps that we have to take in order to survive the next hundred days. It will identify deadlines and who is responsible for the completion of every step and it will estimate the cost of completing each of those steps. Upon its completion we will have a step-by-step blueprint for success in turning this thing around during the next three months plus a few days."

Greg sat for a moment and stared at Terry. Up until this point he had been sipping on his coffee but he wasn't even doing that anymore. Finally he said, "And the second plan, what is that for?"

There was no necessity to sell Greg on these fundamental moves with Camber, and Terry knew it. But he felt strongly that the turn-around process would be less cumbersome if Greg were on board and could be totally supportive of the efforts. "The second undertaking will be a comprehensive five year strategic plan establishing the direction in which the company will move over the long-haul and the resources it will require to move successfully in that direction."

"Other than the fact that one has a duration of one hundred days and the other a duration of five years, what's the difference between the two plans?" Greg's voice was betraying his calm exterior demeanor at this point. He was clearly not liking what he was hearing but Terry refused to be discouraged and used Greg's apparent lack of enthusiasm as more of a motivator.

"The hundred day plan is a tactical plan. It is composed of specific steps and time lines designed to get us out of the mess that we are in as quickly as possible. The strategic plan is a more general and comprehensive plan designed to move the company toward long-term success and it will not be as concerned with the day-to-day operations as will the shorter-term hundred day plan."

Greg sat quietly and stared once again. Terry sat just as quietly and stared right back matching Greg sip-for-sip. After at least three or four minutes of the visual showdown, Greg was the first to break the silence.

"Terry, I spent four years in an undergraduate business program at the university and, although I graduated with a Bachelor's degree in business, I believed then as I believe now that everything they were selling in that program was a pile of crap—and that includes wasting a lot of time and effort on planning. What we need at Camber right now is for people to roll up their sleeves and get to work, not for you and Ale to sit around and try to think about this stuff. What you are talking about is going to take a lot of precious time and, frankly, I just don't think we have the luxury of that kind of time. This is not the way to go!"

✳ ✳ ✳ ✳ ✳

Back at the Orion offices, Alejandra German sat quietly at the table in the conference room as she listened to Terry summarize the conversation between he and Greg at a Starbucks just two days before. It was another Sunday morning meeting for Ale, forcing her to miss yet another weekend day with her family. She found her mind wandering back to the kitchen in her home, where her sons were surely out of bed by now and eating some breakfast prepared by her mother. She stole a glance at her watch. Ale always wore the same one with the white band and little pretend diamonds to the left and right of the watch's face. Franco was either studying or at the university library and she knew that he would not be with the boys at all today, just as he had not been available the day before. It was 10:00

a.m., and from what she was hearing from Terry she was sure to be at the office at least until dinnertime. Terry was talking and she was looking at him and nodding every once-in-awhile, but she betrayed her lack of attentiveness when she turned her head to look out the window and then smiled, just a little. She was thinking about the day before, first with her mother and her sons at church, then at a local restaurant for a family lunch, and later at the park just walking and talking with the boys about anything and everything that had nothing to do with Orion. She thought about how this meeting with Terry certainly would have occurred on Saturday, the day before, had she not made it perfectly clear to Terry from the very beginning that she never works on her Sabbath. A devout Seventh Day Adventist since she was a child, she explained to him before she was hired that she serves everyone else six days a week, so the very least she can do is to devote Saturday to God and to her family. Though she missed her sons very much on this warm spring morning she was counting her blessings that they had been able to spend the entire day before together. That made her feel good inside. But she also could not help but wonder what life would be like for her if she and Franco enjoyed normal working schedules, leaving the weekends solely for family time. And she wondered just how happy she might be if she were not so taken for granted by her husband. The realization that her marriage had become more of a business relationship, seeing to it that the needs of the boys and the house were taken care of, than a supportive and loving one made her sad once again. *Something is going to have to give*, she thought. *After all, I just want to be happy, nothing more, just to be happy—and loved! Is it really so impossible to be professionally successful and at the same time personally happy? I am going to have both in my life,* she continued to think, *and I don't have anything like either right now!*

Ale hadn't noticed that Terry stopped talking.

"Is something wrong, Ale?" he asked.

"No Terry," she said. "So tell me exactly what we've now learned about Greg and the project after your meeting with him on Friday morning." She always was good at recovering from any kind of a misstep.

"As I was saying," he continued, "Greg strongly disagrees with taking the time to develop a hundred day plan. As a matter of fact he is convinced that any time spent on planning is a huge waste. I think he was expecting that we would come in and just continue doing what he had been doing all along."

Ale waited for a break in his delivery and then asked, "Is he going to be a problem?"

"No," said Terry, "not at all. After he made his point at Starbucks we got back in the car and he didn't say another word about it. Besides, he really doesn't have a choice now does he?"

Ale sat for a minute without saying anything. Then she said, "You know, Terry, I've been thinking. Maybe I should jump in here with you and help on the Camber project, at least for the next hundred days or so."

At first glance it would appear that Ale was contemplating a sacrifice by adding the project back onto her already full plate of client activity. But in reality it was more of a selfish move and she was well aware of what she was doing. She had three clients that were out-of-town start-ups and had fallen three months behind in their payments to Orion. Start-ups are time consuming to begin with but when they require overnight travel and they are on the deadbeat list for even a month it becomes time to reassess the value to Orion of continuing to work with them. Not to mention the fact that substituting Camber for the three out-of-towners would require Ale to stay in town, and home at night with the boys, for a full one hundred days. She briefed Terry on the proposed switch and he quickly agreed, telling her that he thought it made more sense to work on one local project that wasn't contributing to cash flow than three that require travel that weren't paying. And he did not let on to her that he knew full well that this move would allow her more time with her family.

"Okay then it's agreed, where do we start?" Ale asked.

Terry opened his notebook to the pages containing his notes from the previous three days of onsite work and began to brief Ale on the details of his findings. "This is going to be a pretty standard hundred day format," he said as he flipped through a few pages to find the one that started with the previous Thursday's observations.

A hundred-day plan for a turn-around project is more of a to-do list than an actual plan. The first step is to make a formal list of every move that must be made, of every action that must be implemented, and of any data that must be researched to ensure that the enterprise can continue to operate for at least the ensuing hundred calendar days. The plan uses a triage, or diagnostic approach to saving the company and although it focuses heavily on the financial aspects of corporate survival, it includes other critical management factors as well. One of these will certainly be the number and quality of the existing personnel at Camber, and Terry was especially pleased to have Ale's help with this dimension of the project since it was her specialty. He also mentally noted that this would be one more project to allow her to fine-tune her financial expertise, a discipline that was present but nowhere near as demanding with the start-up companies that she would now be leaving behind.

Terry and Ale discussed the fact that the hundred day planning process would in all likelihood require three times the effort of any other company of relatively the same size. There will be the routine triage effort inherent in any project of similar scale, but there will also be the completion of the detailed due diligence exercise that Terry was forced to abbreviate because of the severely restricted time available just a few short weeks earlier. In addition to these two challenges they were embarking on the turn-around of a firm in a highly regulated industry demanding that they both learn some rather complicated and comprehensive laws and guidelines. In retrospect, although he had not entered this meeting with the thought that Ale might take an active role in the Camber project, Terry was happy that it had indeed turned out that way.

At 1:00, three hours after the start of their meeting together, Terry felt as though he had thoroughly briefed Ale on his findings from three days of research and observation on site at the flight school. Ale volunteered to take the remainder of the afternoon and as much of the next day as necessary to compile all of Terry's findings into a coherent hundred-day plan. She suggested that the two of them meet again the next afternoon to review what she had accomplished to that point. Terry gratefully agreed and left the conference room bound for BWI airport for more onsite sleuthing.

❊ ❊ ❊ ❊ ❊

At about 2:30 that afternoon Terry felt the need to stretch his legs. He had not taken a walk out on the airport ramp since his hurried tour with Greg on the first day so he decided to try it again, but this time on his own. The entire BWI airport facility is a federally secured and restricted area allowing for access only to individuals who have been investigated and cleared by the Federal Aviation Administration, the Transportation Security Agency, and the Federal Bureau of Investigation. Terry knew that he would have to be escorted out onto the ramp by an employee of the Elite Flight Services operation next door, so he proceeded across the parking lot past the large hangar on his right to the front door of Elite. Once inside he introduced himself to the Elite employee at the counter in the lobby of the rather posh general aviation terminal. He produced a photo ID, and was escorted onto the ramp by a badged escort whose job actually was to provide the support services to corporate and general aviation aircraft visiting or based at BWI. He walked with the escort to the line area where Greg had shown him the Camber fleet a few days before, talking the entire time to the young man charged with the responsibility of never letting Terry out of his sight for security reasons.

Suddenly Terry was confronted with a realization that literally caused him to feel a little nauseated and forced him to wonder what he may have gotten himself and his partner into with this venture. It was a gorgeous spring day with a deep blue and cloudless sky. There was little wind to speak of and the aviation weather forecast called for more of the same for the remainder of the afternoon. And yet, there in front of him on the ramp on a perfect afternoon for flight instruction, was the entire Camber fleet of aircraft, all fifteen of them, securely tied down. His Elite Flight Services escort, responding to the look of stark amazement on Terry's face at the serene and motionless line of planes in front of him, informed Terry that not one Camber flight had departed the ramp since late on Friday.

TEN

ONE OF THE most critical disciplines required for the effective management of any business involves the efficient and productive utilization of all of the assets of that business. Terry's experience with this fundamental axiom evolved from decades of his research into the day-to-day operations of the airline industry. Although he had not been directly involved with any aspect of aviation for many years, he found it both informative and enjoyable to study everything that he could get his hands on about the trials and tribulations of this consistently troubled form of international transport. The prevailing rule that seemed to appear and reappear in his research of the airline business model was that when the assets, or in this case the aircraft, aren't flying the company is not making any money. Now Terry found himself confronting a blatant symptom of this fatal condition plaguing enterprises, especially flight schools, across the country. Lazy assets, those that are not constantly producing a continuous revenue stream to the income statement of a business, are in reality seriously draining the working capital of that business. He stood on the ramp with his escort by his side dumbfounded by the sight of approximately two million dollars worth of lazy assets, owned by Camber and its leasing partners, that hadn't earned a nickel for the company for nearly forty eight hours of superb flying weather.

Terry stared at the fifteen aircraft tied-down on the ramp in front of him. He had not yet produced any of the financial projections necessary for the proper planning required for the resurrection of Camber. But he knew that these assets would have to be tied-down without generating any revenue every night of the year and during many poor weather days. He also knew that the competition would prevent him from exercising any degree of flexibility in the pricing of the company's product to offset additional poor asset utilization. He was nearly overwhelmed by the stark realization that the scene in front of him represented yet another problem he hadn't counted on, one that clearly would have been obvious to him with the proper due diligence had he taken the time to perform it.

"Hello, Greg?" Terry caught himself shouting into his cell phone over the roar of the aircraft engines near him on the ramp. "Terry here," he continued. "Listen Greg, I'm standing on the ramp in front of our fleet. It's beautiful out here, perfect flying weather and every aircraft available to us is securely tied-down and hasn't moved since Friday afternoon. What's up?"

"Oh," replied Greg, "we don't fly on the weekends," he said without hesitating.

Terry paused in disbelief for several moments before he asked, "What do you mean we don't fly on weekends?"

Greg now seemed to discern a distinct annoyance in Terry's tone. "Listen Terry," he said, "we don't have any civilian students to speak of, the Midshipmen don't want to fly on weekends because they would rather spend this time with their girlfriends or boyfriends, and the flight instructors like to have their weekends off too. So," Greg inserted with some emphasis, "it's been a battle that I haven't wanted to fight."

"Well, Greg," said Terry with every bit of self-control he could muster, "I intend to fight that battle and I intend to win it!" Terry did not want Greg to think that he hung-up on him, but he also didn't wait for a response from Greg before he pressed the "End" button on his cell phone.

Terry turned his body on the ramp in almost a military fashion and began to walk briskly back to the Elite Flight Support facility. His escort, who found it difficult at first to keep up with him, heard him mutter to himself, "Un-fricken-believable!"

As the daylight turned to night on a particularly beautiful spring evening at BWI airport, Terry was sequestered in the office at Camber poring over the flight and financial records of the company. His initial fears from his afternoon walk on the ramp were confirmed by the documentation spread out in front of him in dozens of file folders. There had been little if any flight activity, and therefore little, if any revenue generated during the previous year on weekends at Camber. To make matters worse the files indicated that the company had been virtually closed during the prolonged Naval Academy Christmas vacation and spring break periods and with alarmingly little flight activity during the summer months as well.

One question kept haunting Terry through the night, *How do I describe this situation to Ale at our planning meeting tomorrow afternoon?* He acknowledged to himself that she had not been at all anxious to get involved with Camber in the first place. *And she has broken ties with her other clients so that she can work full-time on this project, only to find out now that this battle will be solidly uphill for both of us, and for much longer than either of us had ever anticipated.*

Before Terry nodded off to sleep well after midnight, he said to himself, *It's a glass half-empty, glass half-full situation. I'm just going to have to present it to her as the glass being half-full!*

* * * * *

Alejandra German began her Monday in the typical fashion by first dropping her sons off at school by 8:00 and then grabbing a grande cappuccino made with skim milk at a Starbucks. Also, as usual, she was at work at her desk by 9:00 after tolerating rush-hour traffic on I-95 North for close to forty minutes. Ale could be relied upon, even early on a Monday morning, to provide all those around her with a positive and motivating demeanor as she settled in for her first long day of another long week of demanding and seemingly relentless commitment to Orion. She felt particularly refreshed this morning because her meeting with Terry had ended early the day before allowing her to work at home with her sons nearby for the remainder of the day. Although she worked on the Camber plan well into the night, it was a treat for her to be able to tuck the boys into bed and to say goodnight to them in person, in spite of not having seen nor heard from Franco for the entire day. As she constructed spreadsheets on her laptop at the dining room table, she realized that she should not become accustomed to having this kind of time with her family often during this project. It was becoming apparent to her that, although she would be traveling far less, Camber would be consuming an enormous amount of her time during the months ahead.

At 1:00 Terry and Ale met in the Orion conference room to review Ale's work during the previous twenty-four hours on Camber's One Hundred-Day Plan. Neither of them was much on small talk, especially when there was a great deal of work to be done, but Terry began by asking Ale if she had been able to spend some time with her family the afternoon before. Ale knew that this initial question was uncharacteristic on Terry's part, and she instinctively replied with a question of her own.

"What's wrong?" she asked, almost as though she was teasing him.

"Nothing, why?" he said sheepishly.

She gazed at him with a much more serious expression for a moment and then said, "I can read you like a book, Terry. I know that you have a strong interest in my boys, and we frequently have our moments when we discuss things that are going on in our lives outside of Orion. But when you start a meeting like this with a question like that I know that something is bothering you and it has nothing to do with whether I was able to spend time with my sons yesterday. So spill it!"

Terry knew better than to patronize Ale with a comment about how perceptive she was. He decided that his best course of action under the circumstances would be to lay the facts out on the table without embellishment. And that's exactly what he did. He described in detail the walk that he had taken on the ramp at BWI. He knew that she had been in town the day before, so he didn't spend any time elaborating on how perfect the weather was for flight training. He went on to deliver the punch line to her, that all fifteen of their aircraft had been tied-down on the ramp for the entire weekend. He divulged that Greg informed him that this was a situation that he was not only aware of but one that he essentially supported. And Terry explained to Ale that a review of the company records for the previous year confirmed that asset utilization was indeed a serious problem that needed to be addressed immediately. Terry's initial calculations from his Sunday afternoon working session indicated that the aircraft assets of the company were actually working at a rate of approximately seventeen percent. He elaborated by stating that this utilization figure represents the number of revenue producing hours the planes actually flew as a percentage of the number of hours that they should have flown. He had subtracted hours reflecting night, estimated poor weather, and estimated down time while aircraft were in the shop for maintenance. Terry stopped and stared at Ale. He was waiting for the inevitable conclusion from her that they had committed to this project much too hastily and that they should reconsider now before more surprises were uncovered.

Ale stared back at him, expressionless, for several moments. Then she broke the silence.

"We got ourselves into this with the clear knowledge that Camber is only serving the Naval Academy market and that there are few, if any, civilian customers, right?" She was emphasizing her words just slightly with the tips of her extended fingers on her right hand touching a bare portion of the conference table in front of her in perfect time with the individual syllables in her question.

"Right," said Terry.

"Then," she continued, "unless I'm missing the point of your concern we've got no place to go but up—if you'll excuse the play on words. Listen, we have the assets sitting virtually unused on the ramp, a goal of building a civilian clientele, and a potential market of literally millions of people in the Baltimore-Washington metropolitan area to draw from. I think that this is extremely positive, why are you looking at it in any other way?"

Terry thought for a few moments, then he said, "I guess I am very sensitive to the fact that you were seriously opposed to our involvement in this project in the first place. I would be extremely embarrassed if it turned out that our commitment here is obviously a mistake, especially this early in the game."

Ale smiled at him and with a reassuring and emphatic tone she said,

"You and I are partners. If we succeed, we succeed together, as though we're one. If we fail, we fail together, as though we're one. Let's get past this silly preoccupation with whether we should have gotten involved in this project to begin with. Let's get it done, whatever it takes, and let's never look back, OK?

Terry smiled and said, "OK!" He reflected briefly on Ale's enormous growth since he'd first met her. *She is now every bit a full partner in this business and, in many ways, the student has become the teacher. What a terrific feeling*, he thought as he continued, "Now, let's see what kind of a Hundred Day Plan you've got for Camber."

Ale spent the next four hours briefing Terry on the financial, marketing, production, and management challenges that must be overcome during the next hundred days. Her presentation was based solidly on the use of Orion's primary benchmarks, which were known to their clients as vital signs, and on the use of only measurable outcomes for evaluation of their potential accomplishments. She outlined over two hundred critical steps that must be implemented in the process with the cost and the person responsible for the implementation of each step clearly identified in the documentation. She provided detailed and comprehensive spreadsheets for financial and production progress and outcomes, and each spreadsheet was accompanied by a thorough explanation. And at the conclusion of her briefing she emphasized that they only had until July 31st to accomplish all of it.

There was a silence in the room that lasted for about thirty seconds but seemed much longer. "Well?" said Ale finally breaking the quiet.

"Like I asked at the beginning of this meeting," said Terry with a smirk, "were you able to spend any time with your family yesterday?"

Ale laughed and then said, "Let the work begin!"

As they were cleaning the files and spreadsheets from the conference table and packing them into briefcases and labeled boxes Terry turned to Ale and said, "Call Greg and setup a meeting so that you can brief him on the interim plan. And then get in touch with Lieutenant Leo Forrester, the guy in charge of the Navy flight training program at the Academy, and set up a meeting with him to discuss the plan. But don't include Greg in that meeting, meet with Forrester alone, preferably here."

"OK, what does your schedule look like?"

"I'm not going to be there," he said. "You can do it by yourself."

"That's fine with me. But are you being efficient or are you taking the coward's way out?" Ale was chuckling and her inflection was light-hearted, but the words were more sincere than not. She knew that Greg was a disbeliever in the art of planning, and she fully expected to have her hands full trying to convince him of the critical nature of both the interim planning process and the changes necessary to the structure of the business in order to turn it around.

Terry said, "If one must be a coward it is best to be an efficient coward!"

Ale laughed and then asked, "No seriously, what if Greg doesn't buy it?"

"Doesn't matter! You're not selling it." Terry continued, "He doesn't have a choice. Be cordial but be firm. You're a full partner in this, and he will either go along with it or he will get out of the way. My money is on the latter option. You are taking the time to brief him on our strategies and plan as a courtesy. Get it done and then let me know how it goes. I'll be down at BWI, and you can join me on the site when you can. Remember, you are not looking for his blessing, or even his cooperation. We're moving ahead with or without him!"

"And Forrester," Ale continued, "what's the game plan with him?"

"Get the real skinny on the relationship between Camber and the Navy," replied Terry. "Find out how stable this foundation is since it represents the lion's share of the firm's revenues right now."

Ale nodded her approval, turned, and left the room. Terry watched her leave and donned a wry smile. *There's nobody better at potentially impressing a disbeliever with reality than Ale*, he thought. *She's got brains, and she's an excellent communicator. That's a one-two punch that will motivate Greg to either want to be a productive part of all of this or to want to vacate the effort. Either way,* Terry continued to surmise, *the result will be positive.*

Ale called Greg and informed him that she would like to schedule a meeting with him at his convenience. Since Greg had left the investment brokerage business his calendar was abundantly clear, and they agreed to meet at 9:00 the next morning. At first he a wanted a 7:00 starting time,

BETTINA A. DEYNES & ROBERT F. WIEDEFELD

being the morning person that he was, but Ale was able to maneuver him into the 9:00 slot which was more manageable for her.

"Okay Ale, I'll see you and Terry at your offices at nine in the morning," said Greg.

"Terry won't be joining us for this meeting, Greg," said Ale.

There was a brief silence then Greg asked, "Is there a problem?"

"Not at all," said Ale. "Terry and I are fully engaged in this project now, and he will be on-site at BWI while I brief you here at the office on our interim plan."

Again a short silence until Greg said, with a bit of concern apparent now in his voice, "Why don't we just meet at BWI so that Terry can be involved too?"

Ale knew that this was a pivotal moment in the developing relationship between Greg, Terry, and herself and that her answer to his question, which was phrased a bit more like a strong suggestion, would set the tone for her corner of this triangular affiliation. She contemplated an appropriate response for a moment. After searching for words that would convey strength yet not suggest arrogance, she replied, "Greg, you, Terry and I have met together on several occasions on this project, but you and I have never met one-on-one. I thought this would be a perfect time for us to do that and Terry agreed. I hope you don't have a problem with it."

Ale had constructed the wording of her response perfectly. She was professional and firm. She succeeded in disarming Greg by neutralizing any defensiveness that he might have used to pressure her into agreeing with him. And she communicated to Greg for the first time that she was a force to be reckoned with on this project. She also laid the foundation for the atmosphere of the meeting the next morning. She had wanted to respond in a fashion similar to Teddy Roosevelt's philosophy, "walk softly but carry a big stick." She achieved her objective.

"Alright Ale, I'll see you in the morning," said Greg.

Ale's first instinct was to reach for her phone to call Terry and tell him of her initial triumph. But a little voice inside of her head stopped her. *"You're a full partner in this business and with Terry,"* the voice said, *"he expects success so don't engage in a 'show-and-tell' session with him. Just get on with it."*

ELEVEN

At 9:00 A.M. sharp Ale was sitting at the large oval table in the Orion conference room awaiting Greg's arrival. Five minutes later the phone on the table in front of her rang. When she answered it, the Orion receptionist informed her that Greg was running about fifteen minutes late because of traffic. When he arrived a few minutes later his profuse apologies for his tardy arrival dispelled any notion of gamesmanship on his part, had she suspected it in the first place.

Ale's extensive human resources training and experience had conditioned her to evaluate people's personality styles almost immediately. From her initial assessment since their first meeting in Memphis, she knew that Greg was relatively steady and dependable in work and personal relationships, that he was conservative by nature and that he should not be expected to welcome change with open arms. She also knew that because of a submissive primary profile he would not be too difficult to control with regard to his eventual acceptance of the plan on which she was about to brief him.

After Greg got settled at the table Ale began the meeting. "Greg, we've been in the business of organizational turn-arounds for a long time now. The cornerstone of our success has always been the development and implementation of a comprehensive and detailed strategic plan, and that process begins with a shorter and more tactically oriented plan with a duration of one hundred days."

Greg sat motionless and expressionless as Ale talked. She made a mental note that his lack of any initial reaction made the meeting seem more like a poker game than a planning briefing. She also decided that a distinct lack of enthusiasm on his part for this meeting and its subject was much easier to deal with than an attitude of visceral revulsion. She was, however, aware that his silence could turn into a vocal disapproval at any moment, a turn of events that she hoped to avoid.

Ale was accustomed to working with business people who not only did not understand the fundamentals and importance of effective planning, but many strongly argued that the process was a waste of time. Her exposure to newbie entrepreneurs accounted for most of the anti-planning mindset. As she sat across from yet another disbeliever the faces of dozens of others before him flashed through her mind. She had long since learned that any attempt to convince these people early in a project that they were wrong would be fruitless. This was a concept, she thought, that must be demonstrated by using it successfully. There was no sense in attempting to preach the benefits to Greg at this point.

But then she had a thought that caused a chill to run down her spine. It was easy for Terry to say that Greg had no choice but to work with us or to get out of the way. But Greg had agreed to guarantee the line-of-credit for the business in the amount of one hundred thousand dollars, and if he decided to walk the line would walk with him. At that point, Ale decided that it was time for some ice water in her veins. If Greg were to pull the line it would be better now than at any time in the future. Ale forged ahead with her presentation undaunted by the reality that had just occurred to her.

"Greg," said Ale, "during the next hundred days we are going to have to make some pretty drastic changes to just about every aspect of Camber's business model if we are to succeed on a long-term basis. In fact, the biggest problem we face is that there is no business model in existence at the moment. Everything from financial record-keeping to the scheduling of students and aircraft, to the lack of a dress code for employees, to a serious general deficiency in compliance with federal regulations and laws must be addressed and changed as quickly as possible. How do you feel about that?"

Ale waited patiently while Greg sat before her with a distinct lack of facial expression. Finally, he spoke.

"Look Ale, I'm here because you asked me to be here. Frankly, I don't care what you and Terry do with this pig. I have made my decision to turn it over to you entirely, and I stand by that decision even if I don't agree with your approach. So let's just proceed and don't worry about whether you have my support or not."

There it was! Terry was right again. Greg had basically written this thing off in his mind, and she and Terry were free to implement any changes they saw fit without being concerned with a possible backlash from him. Ale was relieved to have this out in the open, and the little half-smile on her face betrayed her otherwise stoic reaction to what she had just heard.

"Okay," she said, "do you want me to continue?"

"Sure, don't confuse my desire not to interfere with a lack of interest. I would like to be kept informed of what you are doing but don't hesitate to do what needs to be done."

At this point, Ale's approach to the briefing changed rather dramatically. She no longer demonstrated any hesitation to present the hundred day plan in an affirmative, even aggressive manner. She suddenly had this feeling that she was in charge and no longer subservient to Terry or Greg in her prescription for corporate remedies to be initiated for the ailing Camber. Her presentation continued with deliberate candor and without interruption.

"We're going to have to reconstruct the financial system and all of the transactions that have been entered into it for at least the past year and maybe longer. We can continue to use Quickbooks as the platform, but the current formatting and presentation of financial data is not accurate, in fact it is misleading. The Profit and Loss Statement and The Balance Sheet comprise the backbone of any business for effective decision making and those financial statements for Camber do not reflect a realistic financial picture of this company. I don't believe that it is anything intentional, but the Quickbooks software must be used properly if the statements it produces are to be useful."

The young entrepreneur spent the better part of an hour-and-a-half drilling Greg on the shortcomings of the Camber accounting and scheduling systems. She demonstrated serious flaws in the Balance Sheet, Income Statement, and the Cash Flow Statement, and then she used the actual online scheduling system to point out its deficiencies to the beleaguered and slightly less than enthused former stockbroker.

Ale removed a bound copy of a document from her briefcase, which was sitting on a chair next to hers. She said, "Greg, this is a copy of our Hundred Day Plan for Camber. Take it home and read it if you like. It contains all of the specific steps we will be taking during the next three months, and it lays the foundation for the five-year strategic plan that we will be implementing for the business soon thereafter."

Greg accepted the document and extended his right hand to shake hers. "I've had about as much of this fun as I can stand for one day," he said as he smiled and walked to the conference room door. He added, "Good luck with all of this!".

Ale watched as he closed the door behind him. As she turned-off her laptop and placed the documents from the table into her briefcase, she thought, *He's not a convert, but he's also no longer an obstacle. Not a bad day's work – and it's only noon!*

* * * * *

Lieutenant Leo Forrester was a young, career Navy former combat pilot serving as a temporary coordinator of the Academy flight training program for a period of one year before he reported for an assignment as a combat flight instructor. In his Academy role, he was a surrogate for the real Naval authority for the program in Pensacola, Florida. Forrester was a likable young officer who clearly exhibited all of the most prominent characteristics of a highly dominant personality. But he managed to suppress his naturally forceful approach in his job at the Academy and was easy-going and friendly in his day-to-day encounters with people. He seemed to view his role with the Midshipmen more as a counselor than as one of authority and discipline. The young unmarried Lieutenant was a strikingly handsome man with short and neatly cropped dark hair and subtly inviting facial features perfectly balanced above a strong, square chin. His daily routine included a rigorous early morning workout, so his six-foot-two physique was lean and firm. He was never flashy or dramatic, and he exhibited a conservative air in both his behavior and dress when not in uniform.

The Lieutenant's penchant for reaching a compromise and his obvious dislike of direct confrontation in his current position made him an extremely unlikely candidate for a job where he routinely had to serve two masters. But he had made the conscious decision when he drew this assignment that he would not allow any potential problems arising from this temporary desk duty to interfere with his impending coveted stint as a Navy combat instructor. On the one hand, he had to satisfy his bosses at the Academy who wanted to ensure the ultimate success of every Midshipman selected for the flight training program. On the other hand, he served the officers in Pensacola who clearly viewed the Academy flight training program as necessary to eliminate those Midshipmen, soon to become Ensigns, who apparently did not have what it took to be successful at Pensacola.

Ale was sitting in the Orion conference room reflecting on her meeting with Greg which had ended about an hour earlier when she was notified by the receptionist that Lieutenant Forrester had arrived. She asked the receptionist to escort the officer to the conference room and awaited his arrival. Although she was unaccustomed to being surprised by the physical features of someone she was meeting for the first time, it was difficult for her to disguise her first impression of the captivatingly good looking uniformed officer who entered the door to her left. She stood and smiled as she extended her right hand to toward him.

"Lieutenant Forrester," she said as her voice cracked ever so slightly, "I'm Alejandra German. It is a pleasure to meet you!"

"Ms. German, please call me Leo and the pleasure is all mine, I assure you."

"Please have a seat," she said as she gestured to one of the three empty chairs on the opposite side of the table from her. "And do call me Ale."

With the pleasantries behind them, Ale returned to her all-business game face.

"Leo," she began, "as you already know from Greg, my partner and I are taking control of Camber in an attempt to turn the business around and make it a profitable one."

"I'm aware of that," responded Leo.

"So it is imperative that you share with me now any skeletons that may be in the closet that you think might be important for us to know about."

"What exactly are you interested in knowing?" Leo asked. At the risk of looking as though he was engaging in some sort of cat-and-mouse game with her, Leo was not about to begin telling tales out of school without some idea of where Ale was going with this meeting.

"We would like to know how stable the relationship between Camber and the Navy is, and if there are any problems with that relationship, either now or on the horizon, that might impede our progress with this turn-around." Ale looked Leo straight in the eyes while delivering this sentence to convey her sense of urgency.

"As you may know, Ale," Forrester began, "there are two entities which directly call the shots when it comes to the delivery of flight training to our Midshipmen. The Academy is responsible for the daily lives of these students and for their general well-being. But the flight training command in Pensacola is responsible for overseeing the quality and quantity of the instruction produced by each civilian training contractor."

"I understand that the people at the Academy and those at Pensacola don't always agree on how the program is to be delivered," said Ale.

"That's right, but it almost always comes down to the Pensacola crew having the final say when that happens," replied the Lieutenant. "To continue, Camber has been less than successful during the past two years in delivering all of the training necessary within the time limits prescribed in the contract, and that is going to have to improve dramatically and quickly."

Ale thought for a moment and then said, "But I have been told that there is a serious problem with large numbers of Midshipmen not being available for scheduling as well as not showing up for flights booked and confirmed on the schedule. How can we possibly meet the contractual time-line requirements when the students are not cooperating?" There was strength in her voice that seemed to impress Forrester immediately.

"That story cuts both ways, Ale. We have had numerous reports of Mids showing up for scheduled training only to find that neither the aircraft nor the instructor are available for the lesson."

"So we have a scheduling problem that must be solved," continued Ale. "Is there anything else that we must address right away?"

"Not right now," Forrester advised. "Why don't we each go back to our respective operations and do some research on the scheduling issue? We can meet again next week with the objective of solving the problem once and for all."

"Sounds good, Leo. By the way, I understand that Pensacola keeps stats on the success of each student in training down there sorted by the initial civilian flight schools they attended. Are you aware of how the students from Camber perform compared to those from other contractor schools?" asked Ale.

"Yes, I am."

"And how have the Camber graduates fared in Pensacola?" Ale asked coyly.

"Consistently the best by far," responded the Lieutenant with a broad smile.

"Let's not forget that, okay Leo?"

"Okay, Ale."

Forrester stood and extended his right hand toward Ale across the table. Ale shook his hand and escorted him from the conference room and through the lobby of Orion's offices.

"I'll call you in a few days, Ale," he said as he exited.

"Okay Leo. Take care," she replied. While her left hand was still grasping the door handle, she closed the door gently with her back and stood leaning against it for a few moments with a broad smile of contentment adorning her already glowing face.

Ale invested the remainder of the evening and night in the review of the interim plan that she had presented to Terry earlier that day, making certain that everything was in its proper place for the meeting the next morning.

TWELVE

THE SUN WAS hiding behind an overcast sky on that late Sunday afternoon in mid-May as Brother Toby McKinley and his three young students from Mount Saint Paul's High School in Baltimore worked on the final flight planning maps for their trip from Dayton, Ohio to the BWI airport. The ceiling over the Dayton Wright Brothers airport was reported at 5:00 p.m. as 8,000 feet with a ten-knot wind from the northeast and visibility of eight miles. Brother Toby watched carefully as the three members of his popular St. Paul's flying club meticulously plotted the compass heading of each of the six relatively short legs of the four hour trip home.

"Right turn after takeoff to 110 degrees until we intercept the 270 degree radial inbound to the Columbus VOR," barked Alan Harrison. Alan was a senior at St. Paul's as were the other two flight enthusiasts and the three were accustomed to working closely together. They were varsity track teammates as well as classmates, not only during their four years of high school, but also for the eight previous years at the St. Mark's Parish School.

"We'll climb to and maintain a cruising altitude of 5,500 feet," added Peter Weston, with his usual attention to detail. Peter, as the Editor-In-Chief of the school newspaper, spent many hours each week at a computer reviewing the submissions of his reporting staff and junior editors with a keen eye for the structure of the next edition of his pride and joy, "The Mount."

Joseph Bartow, the president of the school's Catholic Youth Organization and the class valedictorian for their graduation ceremony the following week interrupted the others' concentration when he cautioned, "I'm concerned about the weather along the route! The twelve-hour forecast calls for a gradual deterioration in the ceiling and the visibility at both Pittsburgh and BWI by midnight. I think we should…"

Alan didn't even give Joe a chance to finish his thought. "It's 5:30 p.m. Joe. The ceiling is 8,000 feet, and the visibility is eight miles or better all along the route. We'll be arriving at BWI by nine o'clock, which gives us a three-hour cushion on that forecast. We need to finish the planning and get on our horse. What do you think, Brother Toby?"

The thirty-one year old Marianist brother's love for flying was superseded on his list of life's priorities only by his love for God and his church. He had a passion for his religion, flying, and for teaching, and he decided early in life to combine all of them into one calling. His first assignment as a Marianist brother was in San Juan, Puerto Rico, where he befriended the owner of a local flying school and received a large discount on the flying lessons necessary to obtain his Private Pilot's license. The first thing he did even before unpacking his bags after a surprise transfer to the St. Paul's High School to teach in the Computer Science department was to secure a ride from the school to BWI airport and Camber Flight Training, Inc. He became a regular at Camber renting aircraft and taking students for rides over to the Eastern Shore of Maryland. The students would give him enough money to cover the rental in a win-win situation where they would learn more about flying, and he would be able to log the flight time and stay close to his second love in life. It wasn't long before he started a flying club for the students of St. Paul's where they could meet after school and on weekends and develop their own passions for the freedom and excitement of a world they had only read about before Brother Toby came to town.

During the previous winter, the flying brother sought and received donations for a flying club contest at the school which required a lengthy essay submitted by every club member on the topic of why they wanted to be a pilot after graduating from high school. The only prize in the contest was a round-trip in a Cessna 172, with Brother Toby at the controls, to the United States Air Force Museum in Dayton, Ohio the following spring. Alan, Peter, and Joseph unanimously won the contest which was judged by all of the senior class at St. Paul's at the end of March.

"We're not going to take any chances," said Brother Toby. "I may be flying the plane, but you three are an extremely essential part of this flight. Make a decision and make it now!" As always Brother Toby's voice was calm but firm. He knew that if these well-intentioned but neophyte student pilots failed to make the right decision he would take command immediately and do the right thing.

"We really do have to get home so that we can be in school tomorrow," said Joe. "My dad will really be mad if we miss another day of classes after taking Friday off to come on this trip. I missed a calculus test on Friday, and I can't afford not to make it up tomorrow morning."

"Joe, make up your mind!" exclaimed Alan. "First you complained that we aren't paying enough attention to the weather, and now you're suggesting that we shouldn't be cautious because we can't miss school tomorrow."

"Decision—now gentlemen!" The teacher could sense that a valuable learning experience was about to occur for each of the students.

Alan made a suggestion. "We should complete the flight planning. We have each of the airports along our route circled in case we need to duck into one of them if the weather suddenly turns against us. The forecast along the route supports this decision, and we have ample options to fall back on if the weather geeks turn out to be wrong. All in favor?" The other two students raised their hands as did Brother Toby, after a brief hesitation.

N9275W, the formal aircraft identification of the 1980 Cessna 172P with Brother Toby McKinley at the controls and three of his students in the remaining passenger seats taxied slowly away from the general aviation terminal at the Dayton Wright Brothers Airport. Joe Bartow sat in the seat immediately to the right of the pilot which was a privilege he won after a series of coin tosses on the ramp just prior to the four boarding the plane. Peter was sitting in the seat directly behind the copilot and Alan was strapped in behind the pilot.

The Cessna 172P is a single-engine aircraft with wings mounted into the fuselage above the cabin area as opposed to a Piper Cherokee, for example, with wings attached into the lower fuselage. The difference is negligible for most pilots and is more a matter of personal preference than one of safety or handling characteristics. Pilots trained in "high wing" aircraft tend to favor this aircraft structure over "low wing" aircraft, and vice-versa, throughout their general aviation flying days.

Although the "172," as it is abbreviated by fliers, is designed to be flown easily by a single pilot, Brother Toby had Joe performing the traditional duties of a copilot as a learning experience. Alan and Peter were paying close attention to every move being made in the front of the cabin. The aircraft was stopped with the parking brake locked in an area adjacent to the end of the active runway, and as Joe completed the reading of the "Takeoff Checklist," Brother Toby physically touched the appropriate instrument or control in the cockpit as it was identified.

"Cabin doors," barked Joe, reading from the checklist attached to a small clipboard strapped to his left knee.

"Closed and locked," said Brother Toby.

"Flight controls."

Brother Toby pulled the yoke, a control that looks similar to the steering wheel in a car, all the way toward his chest as far as it would extend and then turned it all the way to the right and did the same to the left. "Controls free and correct," he said after completing the exercise.

"Mixture," continued Joe.

"Rich," said the pilot.

After carefully completing the full pre-takeoff checklist, Brother Toby extended a thumbs-up to Joe, his signal to contact the airport control tower. Joe double-checked the tower radio frequency from his handwritten notes also attached to his kneeboard, made certain that the frequency set in communication radio number one was correct, and then pressed the switch on the right side of the yoke in front of him with his right index finger. The

Cessna 172 was equipped with dual flight controls so that either a pilot or a co-pilot could fly the plane independent of the other.

"Dayton tower November 9275 Whiskey is holding short of Runway 2, and we're ready for takeoff."

The response from the tower was quick and crisp. "November 9275 Whiskey taxi into position and hold on Runway 2."

Brother Toby eased the throttle toward the console just enough to increase the power of the engine which caused the aircraft to move forward slowly in the direction of the runway. He steered the plane by pushing on the left or right rudder pedals at his feet, which turned the nose wheel in the desired direction. Using a combination of power and steering he positioned the plane with the nose pointing directly down the center-line of the runway. Alan and Peter each stretched toward the center of the cabin so that they could see around the pilot and copilot sitting in front of them.

"I love that sight," said Peter, almost in a whisper, as he gazed at the runway extending for over a mile in front of them.

"November 9275 Whiskey you are cleared for takeoff on Runway 2. Good evening, gentlemen!"

The words from the tower pierced the tranquility that had settled in the cabin while the pilot and his passengers were awaiting the takeoff clearance. As Joe acknowledged the clearance through the microphone by repeating the words verbatim back to the tower, Brother Toby deliberately moved the throttle forward into the lower section of the console with his right hand. Finally, the large knob at the end of the throttle shaft would no longer move forward. At the pilot's fingertips, just on the inside of the throttle knob and surrounding the throttle casing, was a round locking mechanism. Brother Toby firmly turned it clockwise until the throttle was locked so that the vibration from the engine would not cause the throttle to move inadvertently out of the full power position. He made this adjustment without ever taking his eyes from the centerline of the runway.

The plane was accelerating down the runway, and while the pilot was focused on keeping the nose wheel on the centerline with left and right movements of the rudder pedals, Joe was calling out numbers from the airspeed indicator located on the instrument panel. Two airspeeds were critical for a safe and successful takeoff and climb out. At 55 knots, the pilot eases the yoke back slightly to lift the nose wheel from the runway. Once the plane is clear of the runway, however, the pilot gently lowers the nose by relieving back pressure on the yoke ever so slightly until the airspeed increases to the required climb speed of 70 knots.

"30 knots," Joe announced.

"40 knots."

"50 knots."

"55 knots."

"Roger, rotating," said Brother Toby as he eased the yoke slightly toward himself with his left hand while his right hand was still resting on the throttle as a safety precaution even though it was locked. First the nose wheel and then the two main wheels smoothly left the ground. He instinctively eased some of the back pressure he had applied to the yoke and waited for the airspeed to increase to 70 knots. Once it did he adjusted trim mechanisms located to his right between the pilot and copilot seats, placing the aircraft in an aerodynamic configuration where it continued to climb straight ahead at 70 knots without any pressure necessary on the controls.

"Flaps up," called Joe. "Actual time of departure was 6:02 p.m.," he added.

Reaching over with his right hand Brother Toby placed his index finger below the flap switch and applied pressure to it from below. "Flaps up," he confirmed.

With the aircraft safely off the ground and climbing at approximately 650 feet per minute, Brother Toby wanted to make sure that his student passengers were not nodding off. "Alan," he said without turning his head. "What is our first intercept and heading?"

"Turn right to a heading of 110 degrees and intercept the 270 degree radial of the Columbus VOR. Proceed direct to Columbus, sir."

The pilot placed the aircraft into a thirty-degree bank to the right and then rolled out of the bank on a heading of 110 degrees. "Confirm 5,500 cruising altitude, Peter," he commanded with authority.

"Cruise at 5,500 feet, sir," came Peter's reply.

As the plane climbed through 5,200 feet Brother Toby began to apply a slight forward pressure on the yoke. At 5,400 feet, he eased it forward a little more, and when the altimeter indicated 5,500 feet he placed enough forward pressure on the yoke to reduce the rate of climb of the aircraft to zero, leveling off at their planned cruising altitude. He simultaneously eased the throttle back to a cruise engine RPM of 2200, and he leaned the fuel mixture to a cruise setting as well. His final act in the process of maintaining the cruise altitude was to trim the plane once again so that little if any pressure would be required on the controls to continue to fly straight-and-level at 5,500 feet and on a 090 degree heading toward Columbus.

Each of the occupants in the cabin was wearing an aviation headset equipped with an extension reaching from the left ear to just in front of the mouth. On the end of this extension was a small microphone and the wearer could easily adjust the microphone extension up or down, and in or out, so that the voice-activated microphone would sit just in front of the mouth. Communicating in a noisy aircraft cabin was far more effective with the use of this equipment.

"Ladies and gentlemen this is your Captain speaking from the flight deck," quipped Brother Toby. "Everybody okay back there? You're mighty quiet!"

Alan was the first to reply, "Okay here," with Peter immediately duplicating the reply.

"Alan, what is our ETA over Columbus?"

"Two seven, sir," said Alan. When the Captain asks a crew member for an estimated time of arrival at an airport or over an en route aeronautical navigation fix, it is customary to omit the hour. Instead, the crew member responds with the number to which the minute hand of the clock will be pointing at the time of arrival. Of course, that only works if the time of arrival at the selected site will be within an hour of the requested ETA.

Alan continued, "And that should put us into BWI at about 10:20, sir."

"Peter," said Brother Toby, "give me a fuel report."

There was silence for several moments and then Peter responded, "We had 53 gallons of usable fuel on board at engine start and at this cruise altitude, power and mixture settings I estimate that we will be burning approximately 9 gallons per hour. With Alan's ETA for BWI, we should be burning about 40 gallons for the trip leaving us a reserve of 13 gallons, or close to twenty-five percent of our total usable fuel capacity, sir."

"We have more than enough fuel to make the trip without stopping along the way," the Captain stated. "Everybody okay with a non-stop to BWI?" Each of the three students responded in turn and in the affirmative.

The air was smooth at 5,500 feet, and the aircraft was cruising at 120 knots on a heading of 090 degrees. This heading appeared to be adequate to maintain a course direct to the Columbus VOR facility. A VOR, or very high frequency omni range, is an aviation navigation device on the ground that emits specific radio signals extending out from it on each of 360 radials. On the ground, the actual unit looks like the top half of a bowling pin pointing straight up to the sky and located on the top of a small round, red and white checkered building. The VOR is usually located on the property of an airport but can sometimes be found in an open field that is owned and maintained by the FAA. In the cockpit, there is a round instrument that is designed to intercept the radio signals transmitted by the VOR unit on the ground. It can also distinguish between each of the 360 radials so that a pilot can select the one radial that represents a straight line from his aircraft's position directly to or from the VOR facility. The background of the instrument consists of a small white circle and extending down from the top and in front of the circle is a white needle. The needle is designed to pivot vertically from the top of the dial to its far left and right. The pilot adjusts the heading of the plane to the left if the needle is positioned to the left of the circle, and vice-versa. When the needle is centered in the circle, the aircraft is on course and proceeding directly to the VOR unit on the previously selected radial.

"Joe, take the controls," commanded the Captain. Brother Toby was not a licensed flight instructor, but it is legal to allow someone to manipulate the controls of an aircraft in flight under the supervision of a licensed pilot. "Just maintain 5,500 feet and keep the needle centered," he added. Joe complied and seemed to find it impossible to hide the broad smile on his face.

The smooth flight and the quiet drone and vibration of the engine made it easy for Brother Toby to drift away in deep thought. He found himself back in Dayton at his parents' home where he and his students had spent the previous two nights. It was one of the main reasons he had chosen the Air Force Museum for this trip, eliminating the cost of a hotel room and rental car. Although generous contributions from supporters at St. Paul's had made the trip possible, the cost of the aircraft rental, fuel, and the overnight tie-down at the Dayton airport depleted the cash available for any luxuries such as restaurant food and commercial lodging. He closed his eyes and could see the smiling faces of his mother and father as they waved to him when he'd departed just a few hours earlier. He smiled back at them and almost waved when he realized that he was daydreaming and that the boys in the plane would think he was crazy if they saw him wave toward the windshield in the front of the cabin. He awoke from his short diversion to inspect the instrument panel with Joe still at the controls. All was well as he gave Joe a smile and a "thumbs-up" for his performance.

Two hours had passed, nearly half the trip. Brother Toby had taken the controls back from Joe awhile earlier sensing that the young student was tiring and after noticing that the palms of the boy's hands had turned red and were sweaty from the tight grip he had maintained on the yoke. They were losing daylight rapidly, and the ceiling had gradually lowered from its previous level of 8,000 feet to approximately 6,500 feet. The cabin grew silent, the fatigue of three days of traveling and little sleep catching up with them.

"I'm going to descend and maintain 3,500 feet." Brother Toby's voice seemed a little startling to the others as they suddenly realized they had been half-asleep. "We'll give ourselves some breathing room with that lower ceiling," he added.

As the Captain eased the throttle back and lowered the nose with some forward pressure on the yoke he asked, "Alan, where are we?"

Brother Toby was a licensed Private Pilot, but he had not yet obtained an instrument rating. As a Private Pilot, his flying was restricted to Visual

Flight Rules requiring that he maintain visual contact with the ground and that his forward visibility remain at least three miles at all times, day or night. While a Private Pilot without an instrument rating is permitted to use navigation instruments, during a VFR flight the primary reference for navigation is always the visual confirmation of landmarks on the ground.

"We're coming up on Morgantown, sir," was Alan's reply.

It was almost dark, and the Captain could easily see the lights of a medium-sized town just ahead. He rotated a knob just above his left knee on the instrument panel, which created a red illumination on the instruments. It is much easier to see inside the cabin at night with red lighting than with the glare and harshness of white lights. As his eyes adjusted to the new lighting inside he noticed that small beads of water had begun to form on the outside of the windshield. As quickly as the tiny beads of rain developed they combined to form larger ones, and then just as quickly they were eased off of the glass surface to his left by the force of the 120-knot air flowing over the aircraft. The disappearing beads were immediately replaced by more beads which repeated the same pattern.

"I hadn't expected rain this early," said Brother Toby without directing the comment to anyone in particular. "Joe," he continued, "tune-in the Morgantown weather information."

The Morgantown airport AWAS, a recorded aviation weather announcement for the airport which was updated frequently, was reporting a ceiling of 5,300 feet with a visibility of 5 miles and winds out of the east north-east at ten knots. It also reported a barometric pressure of 29.48, which, when entered into a small window of the altimeter by rotating a knob located just under and to the right of the instrument, adjusts the altimeter to read an accurate aircraft altitude above sea level.

"Joe, adjust the altimeter setting to 29.98. Alan, how far to our next checkpoint and what is it?"

There was a hint of concern in Brother Toby's voice as he involved his students in the events unfolding inside the cockpit. But it was the events beginning to confront him on the outside that were of greatest concern to him.

Alan responded, "Hagerstown will be on our left in six minutes, sir."

The minutes passed, and the rain increased in intensity. Larger streams of water now hitting the windshield and rapidly moving off again to the left. The total darkness outside added to the obscurity of the navigation process, but the Captain could still see the lights of tiny towns passing below to both their left and right. His concern was steadily increasing as seven minutes had passed and a cluster of lights representing a town the size of Hagerstown had not yet appeared. His palms were becoming moist and uncomfortable around the vertical sections of the yoke as his grip tightened. *Had he become distracted and missed Hagerstown*, he thought, *or had they drifted off course?*

Brother Toby was working hard to hide his anguish over a rapidly deteriorating situation. Figuring that they had drifted off course to the right because of a wind from the left he altered his heading a full fifteen degrees to the left. The rain was now pelting the windshield with a sound that reminded him of the bacon his mother was frying earlier that morning in her warm and safe kitchen. And the stark silence of everyone else in the aircraft during the previous fifteen-minutes contributed to an increasingly ominous atmosphere.

"Alan, what is the elevation of the tallest obstacle on our remaining course to BWI?"

Alan used a small flashlight to check the Washington Sectional map spread out across his lap in the back seat. If the worsening weather outside hadn't alerted the three students of a serious problem, Brother Toby's question more than confirmed it.

"One thousand six hundred feet about ten miles due west of Frederick, Maryland," said Alan.

Brother Toby eased the throttle back slightly and applied a small amount of forward pressure on the yoke. The ceiling was dropping, and he managed to stay just below the clouds as he descended through 3,000 feet. He could still see small isolated pockets of lights on the ground, but there appeared to be patches of fog or low-lying clouds intermittently obscuring his view.

Do I go down to 2,600 feet which will allow me to clear that 1,600 foot obstacle by 1,000 feet, he thought now in a near panic, *or do I turn around and go back to Hagerstown and land?* He continued to descend through 2,900 feet, and then through 2,800 feet. *I don't have enough money for a hotel room or food if I turn back,* he thought, still considering his options.

At 2,600 feet indicated on the altimeter he announced, "Guys, we're turning back."

The Captain shoved the throttle swiftly into the panel and began a turn to the right. The aircraft was fully engulfed in the clouds. A loud thud shook the bottom of the fuselage both feeling and sounding as though they were in a fast moving car that had hit a speed bump.

Inside the cabin, there was barely enough time for the three students to begin to scream, and Brother Toby could only begin to utter the sounds, "Oh God have mer…!"

The serenity that had existed that night on the 2,145 foot western ridge of Quirauk Mountain was suddenly and mercilessly shattered by the piercing shrill of twisting and shredding metal as November 9275 Whiskey was torn apart as it crashed through a cluster of tall pine trees. The wreckage of the plane came to rest in pieces scattered over an area of approximately 1,000 square yards and as suddenly as the night air had been filled with the sound of tragedy it just as suddenly returned to an eerie, motionless silence.

When rescue crews reached the mountaintop the next morning, the effort was quickly declared one of recovery rather than rescue. Because of the proximity of the crash site to Washington, DC, it did not take long for representatives of the National Transportation Safety Board to arrive. One of the inspectors on the scene looked up at the left wing of the Cessna precariously balanced in the top of a large stand of pine trees and then she looked down at a portion of the aircraft's instrument panel lying on the ground in front of her. She knelt down to get a closer look at the altimeter, and through the broken glass she noticed that it was still registering an altitude of 2,600 feet on this 2,145 foot mountaintop. It was immediately obvious to her that the altimeter had been mistakenly set sometime prior to the crash causing it to read 455 feet higher than the actual aircraft altitude.

It later was determined that the plane crashed a full fifteen miles north of its planned route.

Later that afternoon a reporter from *The Washington Post* was interviewing representatives of the FAA and NTSB at the site of the accident. He was leaving the scene when he stopped to talk with a man who said that he had lived on the mountain for nearly fifty years, and he knew it like the back of his hand. The article in the next day's edition of the *Post* quoted the man as saying, "It's really too bad—twenty feet higher and it would have cleared."

THIRTEEN

THE MOOD IN Terry's car could best be described as morose. Neither Ale nor Terry said a word to each other for several minutes as they drove from the second of two funeral services conducted for Brother Toby and his three young students on this otherwise bright and sunny Tuesday morning. The two entrepreneurs had traveled together to the West Coast earlier in the year for the funeral of their client, Saul Sherry, which was a particularly difficult experience under the circumstances. But nothing could have adequately prepared them for the grief-stricken scene they had just witnessed in the auditorium of St. Paul's High School that morning. The four caskets, each raised from the floor by a four foot metal support base were lined in a row next to each other between the front row of auditorium seats, and the stage and on top of each was an eight-by-ten picture of its occupant. The three pictures of the students had been taken only a few weeks earlier for their yearbook, which was to have been distributed at a graduation ceremony scheduled for later in the week. The photo of a smiling Brother Toby standing arm-in-arm with his parents was about a year old but striking in the reality of his sudden loss nonetheless. The sounds of parents, teachers, fellow students, and friends crying and wailing, were much too upsetting for Terry and Ale to forget anytime soon regardless of how hard they would try. This tragedy would serve as a loud wake-up call for each of them, not only as a realization of their own mortality, but as a gripping awareness that they had entered a dimension of this new business venture that had not been apparent before now.

Ale was the first to break the somber silence in the car. "What are we doing, Terry?"

Terry did not take his eyes from the road to look at the expression on Ale's face when she asked that question, but he could tell from the inflection in her voice that something more than what they had just experienced together was bothering her. He decided that answering her with another question would be the best response. "What do you mean?"

"For five years now we've worked with printing companies, computer manufacturers, software firms, furniture manufacturers, and one national pizza chain." Her voice was beginning to crack as though under the strain of what was to come next. Terry sat quietly and stared ahead as she continued. "Frankly, the biggest challenge that we've faced so far is how to ensure that a high quality color printing product is produced or that pizzas are consistently delivered hot and on time."

"What's your point, Ale?"

"My point is that we're not delivering pizzas any longer. Suddenly we're in a business that demands a level of quality that people's lives will depend on every day and that's downright scary to me! And it doesn't help that I don't know the first damned thing about flying or flight training. Hell, I don't even like to fly in an airliner, and suddenly I'm an owner of a company that sends people up in these little two-seat tin cigar boxes every day. I don't know if I'm ready for that kind of responsibility. I'm thinking that maybe now would be the right time to take our marbles and move on to a better opportunity, one without as many risks."

"Listen Ale, I know you're upset about what has happened, and God knows I am too. But we can't allow ourselves to over-react to this situation. It is clear to me that Brother Toby made a mistake."

"Yeah," interrupted Ale, "a mistake that was fatal not only to him but to three young and innocent boys!"

"Be-that-as-it-may, Ale, we're not going to be able to control the judgment that our students, instructors, and graduates use in the cockpit.

But we will be able to have an extraordinarily strong influence on the judgment and the professional performance of everyone who comes into contact with Camber if we set this thing up and run it the right way."

Ale thought for a minute or two. "So you are saying that you know how to structure the training programs so that there won't be any more accidents?"

"No, I'm not saying that at all. I am saying that we must not only take the business side of this enterprise apart and restructure it, but we have to do the same thing with every element of the flight training side of it as well. If we can do that, Camber's product will be thoroughly trained and prepared pilots who will be far less likely to get themselves into the kind of predicament that Brother Toby experienced."

"So you're saying that Brother Toby was not a good pilot and that he wasn't properly trained?"

Terry was now focused on the conversation and at the same time attempting to pay attention to the road and other drivers. "Ale," he said, pointing toward the windshield, "how many fatal auto accidents occur in this country every day?" he asked firmly.

"I don't know," she said with a shrug, "hundreds, maybe thousands."

"And how many of those accidents do you think are caused by drivers that were poorly trained before they even got their driver's licenses versus those that are the result of good drivers who become distracted or complacent behind the wheel, at some point after they've been licensed drivers perhaps for years?"

"Okay," said Ale, "now it's my turn—what's your point?" She emphasized the word "your" in a tone of voice that seemed to be just a little less stressful than the conversation that preceded this question.

"My point is that we are right back to a discussion of risks. You make it sound as if there are no risks associated with owning and managing a pizza business. You know as well as I that if we hadn't exercised strong control over the quality and freshness of the ingredients used in the pizzas someone could have gotten sick, perhaps even died from some of them. Or, God forbid, one of the drivers might have gotten into a fatal car accident on a delivery run. We couldn't have controlled that potential outcome.

There are risks associated with every business on this planet, large or small. The fundamental goal of what we do every day is to identify and then to minimize every single risk as much as humanly possible, not just on the business side but on the technical side of every business we own or manage. There are two basic rules in business. Rule number one is that we'll never be able to eliminate risk altogether, and that means there will always be the chance that something will go wrong. And rule number two is that we'll never be able to change rule number one."

"Once again, Terry, I don't know a thing about flying or flight training. How can I be useful on the quality side of Camber's business?"

Terry's tone was now more comforting and less defensive. "You can learn as much about flying and flight training as possible while you are working your magic with the business side on the ground."

"You don't expect me to go up in one of things with you do you?"

"No, but that's not exactly the spirit of learning that I had hoped you would embrace!" said Terry. "How much on the technical side of the printing business did you know when we first got involved in that industry? Or the computer manufacturing or pizza businesses? How much did you know about producing the actual products in those businesses at first?"

"Not much," said Ale. "I understand what you are saying, and I'll do my best with this one as well. But we have to make a pact right now that nothing, absolutely nothing will interfere with our new mission at Camber."

"What's our new mission?" asked Terry.

"That nothing will be more important to us every day, not profit, not value, not even our own happiness, than will be our dedication to the highest quality flight training experience on the face of this earth for every one of our customers. I won't move ahead with this project unless safety and quality are our two highest priorities!"

"I totally agree, Ale."

Halfway through Terry's brief response Ale's cell phone rang and she quickly answered it. "Hello," she said with the phone to her left ear. She immediately recognized the voice on the call as that of Leo Forrester and the realization that he was calling at that moment created butterflies in her stomach, but she had no idea why.

"Hello, Ale?" he began.

"Yes?" she answered as though she had not recognized his voice.

"Leo Forrester here, how are you?"

"Oh hi," she said being careful to disguise the identity of the caller from Terry. Responding to his question she continued, "I guess I'm okay."

"Ale, I am genuinely sorry about the accident, and I know that you must be just coming from the funeral, so I am not calling for a business reason. I am calling to see how you are. I am concerned about you personally. Could we perhaps get together tomorrow for lunch and talk?"

Ale wasn't sure how to respond to this kind, although unusual overture. She thought for a moment and then said, "Sure but I'll call you back a little later this afternoon and we can firm up the details. How's that?"

"Good," replied Leo, "I'll wait to hear from you."

"Who was that?" asked Terry.

"That was," Ale paused for just a fraction of a second, "my mom," she said cautiously.

Her mom, thought Terry. *We can firm up the details? That wasn't her mom!* He wasn't accustomed to thinking that Ale was lying to him, but he was quite sure she was now. *Not important*, he thought, *just let it go.*

Ale quickly changed the subject. "Are you coming to Johan's birthday party this afternoon?" she asked.

"Wouldn't miss it for the world!" Terry demonstrated an obvious relief that the stresses of the past few days seemed to be easing for each of them, at least a little. But he was still more than a little curious about that phone call.

* * * * *

What a difference a few hours can make in one's frame of mind, thought Terry as he watched the mayhem unfold before his eyes that afternoon.

"Johan German has got to be the cutest little four-year old boy on the face of this planet!" Terry made this comment to a woman standing next to him at Johan's birthday party just before he realized that she was obviously the mother of one of Johan's party guests. "Except for your son, of course," he quickly added. *Too late, it didn't work*, he thought as she turned her back to him and walked to the other side of a room full of screaming kids at this Chuck-E-Cheese restaurant in the northern suburbs of Washington, DC. As Ale was busy taking care of her youngest son's celebration and his dozen or so guests in the arcade section of the restaurant, Terry couldn't help but stare at Johan's long, curly, dark chestnut hair and his mesmerizing cherubic smile that literally begged everyone within sight to bend down and give him a loving hug. And it was in his nature to hug everyone back, that is, when he wasn't running between the basketball and race car games with his pockets bulging with gold tokens.

When Terry suddenly realized that, for one fleeting moment, he had allowed his mind to wander away from work in order to enjoy the laughter and excitement of the children around him he almost felt embarrassed. He caught himself looking sheepishly at some adults to his left as if to say, "I'm sorry, I must have lost my head!" Just then he overheard a brief conversation between two women standing to his left. He assumed they were mothers of some of the children and also assumed that they were friends, or at least acquaintances, of Ale's.

"Where is Franco?" the first woman asked of the second.

"I don't know," came the reply. "I asked Ale earlier, and she just shrugged her shoulders and told me that he is busy."

The first of the twosome commented, "Too busy to attend his own son's fourth birthday party? She's been putting up with this kind of thing for way too long!"

"Well, he is studying to be a doctor after all."

"But everything in the family seems to fall on Ale. It just isn't fair to her!" claimed the first woman as the two walked away from where Terry was standing. He did not want to be obvious and follow the women so that he could hear more, but the prospect that all might not be well in the German household did not set well with him at all. *Terrific*, he thought, *one more thing to worry about*!

One of the advantages of having a birthday party for a bunch of four-year old children at a Chuck-E-Cheese restaurant is that the parent of the birthday child doesn't have to worry much about the planning of events at the party. Immediately after the children arrive they distance themselves from any possible connection with parental control and form small segregated boy/girl groups. Each group promptly proceeds directly to the game of their choice armed with paper cups filled with small gold tokens used to start each game. The scene is a paradise, or nightmare as the case may be for any serious student of organizational dynamics! About a dozen children who have barely accomplished the art of speaking in full sentences self-organize into task-groups of three or four children each. The first child in each group who succeeds in getting the attention of the others in the group and convinces them to run to a specific game in the arcade becomes the de-facto leader of his or her group and the others obediently follow.

The group leader is usually the first to arrive at the selected game and to place a token into the slot with the big red arrow pointing to it. The others in the group watch excitedly as the leader plays the first game to its inevitable conclusion. This is where the dynamics get fascinating. The stronger the leader the longer he or she will dominate and monopolize the game without giving someone else in their group a turn. If another child in the group has a stronger personality, he or she will literally nudge the leader from the primary playing position in front of the game and insert a token before the newly defrocked leader can do so. A bloodless revolution of sorts. The original leader usually moves to another game coercing as many of the original group to follow him or her, instead of watching the new leader play the first game of choice. And so goes the ritual dance of leader/follower roles for four-year old groups in a marginally controlled environment of group dynamics. The ironic similarity of the group ritual unfolding in front of his eyes to that of the formulation and extension of committees for every minute detail of the management of business enterprises by adults was not lost on Terry. He watched with a subtle pleasure as the children created their own little chaotic dysfunctional organization in the game room during a birthday party at Chuck-E-Cheese.

After about an hour, it was time for the genuine authority figures to regain control of the scene. Ale, who had been standing in the background talking with parents and staff of the restaurant, was clapping her hands attracting the attention of the children and instructing them to sit at picnic-bench style tables in the cake and ice cream room near the rear of the facility. It took a few minutes, but after everyone was seated in a reasonably orderly fashion a decorated cake with four burning candles was placed by a staff member in the middle of the table, and Ale began singing "Happy Birthday," soon to be joined by all. Small paper plates loaded with cake and ice cream and accompanied by plastic forks and spoons were passed to all in the room, which once again was filled with the shouts and laughter of small children having a marvelous time. Many of the parents, on the other hand, were restlessly looking at their watches and their cell phones in an obvious attempt to stay in touch with reality.

As the children were finishing their treats Ale quietly carried a large, oddly shaped and gift-wrapped package to Johan who was sitting at the head of one of the tables. With a squeal of joy he stood and began ripping the ribbons and paper from the object, which immediately revealed itself as a brand new bicycle. It was a blue two-wheeler with white trim and training wheels and blue and white plastic streamers flowing from its handlebars. Johan stared in disbelief at his very own bike before turning and giving Ale a giant hug and saying, "Thank you, Mom" over and over again.

Tears formed in Terry's eyes as he watched a moment that Ale and Johan would undoubtedly remember for the rest of their lives. And as he watched, the birthday guests each grabbed a balloon in one hand and the hand of a parent in the other and said their "Good-byes" to the birthday boy. As they did so, they made their way to the door and then out onto the sunlit parking lot in front of the building. Terry then helped Ale and her boys with the gifts and balloons and the remaining cake as they walked to her car. While he waved, they drove away for what he hoped would be the quietest and most civilized part of the afternoon for a deservedly weary mom. As they disappeared from sight Terry was thinking of Johan's new bike with its training wheels. He couldn't help drawing an analogy between the training wheels and the process of successfully managing a new business enterprise.

Terry squinted as the setting evening sun nearly blinded him through the windshield of his car. It was all that he could do to keep the car in the proper lane, and he almost decided to let his cell phone keep ringing to avoid an accident. He glanced down at the screen on the phone just long enough to see that it was Greg calling and, against his better judgment, he took the call.

"Hi Greg, what's up?"

"I was just thinking about you, Terry," said Greg. "We haven't talked since the accident, and I just wanted to see how you're doing."

Terry struggled to keep from returning to the feeling of sadness he had experienced during the previous five days. "Doing better, Greg. Of course, the funeral this morning was almost more than we could handle, but we're ready now to move ahead and leave this behind us."

"Do you want to meet somewhere and talk?" asked Greg.

"Sure, as long as we don't talk about the accident or anything having to do with it. Where do you want to meet?"

Greg answered quickly as though he had already planned for the affirmative answer from Terry. "Starbucks—the one in Columbia near your offices."

"Okay," Terry said, "I'll see you there in fifteen minutes."

Terry wasn't in much of a mood to extend this already physically and emotionally draining day, but Greg had restricted their contact to more formal office visits since the change of operating control at Camber, and the informal meeting over a cup of coffee certainly couldn't hurt anything.

The Starbucks was almost empty with the exception of Greg sitting at a small, round table nestled into a corner as far from the front door as possible. He was sipping on a Venti Coffee that was obviously still extremely hot, and he pointed to a large paper cup on the table across from him with the strings of tea bags hanging over its top.

"I figured you might be in the mood for a nice relaxing cup of tea after a trying day," he said with an uncharacteristic smile.

"Thanks," said Terry, "you were right on target. Anything in particular on your mind, Greg?"

Greg thought for a moment and then said, "Yeah, there is."

Terry braced for what he feared might be yet another problem to cap off a day that began with a funeral and also included a strong desire from Ale to chuck this whole project. "What's on your mind, Greg?"

"I've been thinking," he began. "I've told you that I'm not interested in getting any more involved in the day-to-day operation of Camber while you and Ale are taking over and I still feel that way. But I have been watching the two of you, and I am curious about the approach that you are taking with the business, especially on the financial side. I was wondering if you would take just a little bit of time to explain the nuts and bolts of how you are going about this to me."

Terry couldn't have been more surprised at himself when he said, "Sure Greg, where would you like for me to begin?"

"At the beginning. I do have an undergraduate degree in business, but it was a long time ago and, frankly, I will admit that I didn't pay a whole lot of attention in class, especially the few finance classes I took. I want you to explain to me in the simplest manner possible the basics of the financial model you will be developing at Camber and don't be afraid of insulting my intelligence."

Terry sat across from Greg at the small round table and explained all of the intricacies of financial statements and the financial management process for nearly three hours. Greg never once appeared bored or overwhelmed by the technical jargon and Terry, although he was tired, viewed it as a bonding opportunity with the possibility of turning a passive doubter into an active ally in the Camber turn-around. Terry was the first to suggest that perhaps they should call it a night and Greg agreed, but not before thanking Terry for the personal instruction and explaining that it had been helpful to the wealthy but ill-informed partial owner.

FOURTEEN

THE NEXT DAY was an exceptionally busy one on everyone's schedules. Terry, Ale, and Greg were to meet in the morning to discuss the details of the transition of power at Camber, and then Ale had made plans, without Terry's knowledge, to meet Leo for lunch in Annapolis. During the evening, the first company-wide meeting was scheduled, and all were more than just a little anxious about how it might turn out.

Alejandra German was an enigma and her first weeks on the job at Camber clearly demonstrated to all of the employees that an air of mystery surrounded her actions, but not her intentions. Her infectious smile and friendly demeanor captivated all who came into contact with her, but they quickly learned that she was all business and would accept nothing less than a complete effort and stellar results from each person on the company payroll. A few members of the workforce, especially the pilots, didn't seem to take Ale or the nature of her management role with the company as seriously as they should have, and the result was the surprise of their professional lives.

One of the first actions taken by the new management team was to schedule a mandatory company meeting on the second evening following their assumption of full management responsibility for the company. There had been few meetings prior to this time requiring the attendance of all employees, but none had been scheduled during the evening hours, and most turned out to be a complete waste of everyone's time because they were poorly executed by the managers running them. Greg made certain that he thoroughly briefed Terry and Ale on the individual personalities of the staff and their previous experiences with the company in general, and management in particular, so the dissatisfaction of the group with the change in leadership and the requirement that they attend this meeting came as no surprise to either of them.

There was one surprise, however, for Greg and Ale that occurred in a meeting with Terry that took place almost immediately after Ale first reported for work at the Camber offices. The purpose of the meeting was to review and edit, if necessary, the memo that Greg had written to the employees informing them of the changes taking place with the company. It had been obvious to Terry that Greg was under the impression that Ale would be performing some sort of clerical duties with the firm reporting directly to Terry and having little, if any, formal management responsibility within the company. Ale, on the other hand, knew that she would have a strong role on the business side of the enterprise, but she had expressed to Terry on more than one occasion her impression that her position would shadow his when it came to the overall operation of the company. At the beginning of the short meeting Greg distributed his draft of the memo. There was silence in the closed conference room at the end of the hallway in the Camber office suite while all three read the four paragraphs on the neatly typed page. Terry was the first to speak.

"Ale?" he said as though she could read his mind and needed no further prompting from him.

"It's too long! Way too wordy!" she said immediately. "Greg, rewrite it so that it says that the company is under new management. In the second sentence identify the roles that you, Terry, and I will individually be executing under the new arrangement. And in the third and last sentence tell them that if they have any questions or problems with these changes they should make an appointment to speak with Terry."

Greg quietly stared at Ale with a look of dazed surprise. His mouth was open only slightly, not as if he were about to say something, but as though he had forgotten to close it all the way.

"Something wrong, Greg?" she said with just a slight amount of determination in her voice.

"Why does it have to be so short? It's just so cold that way," he said.

"Management communications are most effective when they are as short as possible," instructed Ale. "Blue plus yellow equals green, Greg. That's it! If someone needs to know after reading a memo what color blue must be combined with what color yellow to yield a certain color of green, they can ask."

Greg didn't know whether to laugh at Ale or to admonish her for being so direct with him. He decided to do neither when Terry joined the conversation with an announcement.

"And while you're rewriting the memo, Greg," stated Terry, "it must be clear that Ale is totally in charge of the day-to-day operations of this company."

"What do you mean she's in charge?" Now Greg's tone was a startled one rather than just the surprise he had demonstrated a few moments before with Ale. "If she's running the company what are you going to do?"

Ale was just as surprised as Greg at Terry's pronouncement. She was sitting at the end of the table with Terry at her left and Greg at her right, and her head was going back and forth as though she had been watching a tennis tournament.

"I'll be functioning as the chief executive officer and Ale will perform the duties of chief operating officer," continued Terry.

"But," said Greg, "this is just a little piss-ant company. It's not large enough for a CEO and a COO. What will you be doing, Terry, while she's being the boss?"

Terry did not want to get into an argument with Greg over this issue, so he decided to attempt to put an end to it quickly. "I'll be explaining that to you, Greg, as I teach you more about our approach to the financial strategies of the company. If you'll just be patient with me, I think you will see the wisdom of what we're doing soon enough. Now, let's adjourn so that Ale can prepare properly for her first meeting with all of the employees."

Greg left the conference room fairly abruptly.

"I don't think he's happy with your structural direction," said Ale.

"That's too bad," said Terry. "We're going to make this work, and I'm not going to lose any sleep over how Greg feels about the steps we're taking to do just that! He'll come around."

"You know I don't like surprises, Terry," said Ale. "Why didn't you tell me that you were going to make me the COO?"

"Didn't think about doing that until we were sitting there with Greg! You have to admit though, it's a pretty good idea, right?"

"Sometimes you scare me Terry Longbow. I guess we'll find out whether it's a good idea. Won't we?"

* * * * *

Ale parked her Nissan Pathfinder on the third level of a garage in downtown Annapolis and walked briskly down Main Street toward the harbor and the historic Middleton Tavern where she was to have met Leo fifteen minutes earlier. The Middleton was a plain brick building located near the harbor and dating back to the Revolutionary War. The Tavern served as a stopping place for notable Americans traveling between Annapolis, and the Eastern Shore across the Chesapeake Bay and it is said that George Washington and Benjamin Franklin were among its early guests. Ale did not expect anything as grandiose as the history of this meeting place to come of this appointment, in fact, she had no idea what to expect. *Leo said that he wanted to meet with me but that it had nothing to do with business,* she thought. *What could he possibly want to talk to me about? I don't even know the man.*

Ale entered the front door of the large building and was immediately greeted by a young man standing behind a polished wooden lectern that appeared to be an antique perhaps as old as the building.

"May I help you?" asked the young man with impeccable manners.

"Yes," answered Ale, "I am meeting…" she was not able to complete her sentence when she was interrupted by the host.

"You are meeting Lieutenant Forrester by chance?"

"Why yes I am."

"Please follow me," said the young man walking rather majestically into the main dining room.

As Ale approached the table where Leo was sitting he stood to greet her as soon as she came into view and, with a single smooth gesture of chivalry he pulled a chair from under the table next to him and then slid it under her as she sat. *I haven't had a man stand and then take care of my chair since, uh, actually I don't think I have ever had a man do that*, she thought as she smiled at Leo and thanked him.

"Thank you for accepting my invitation, Ale. I am sure you are wondering why I asked you to join me today," he said without taking his eyes from hers.

"Yes, Leo, I am very curious."

Leo was dressed in his khaki service uniform which seemed to Ale to be much more comfortable and informal than the white dress uniform he was wearing when she first met him in the Orion conference room. Nevertheless, he was sitting at attention next to her and the only thing informal thus far about the meeting was the warm and supportive tone of his voice.

"First, Ale, let me assure you that I debated with myself long and hard about whether I should have this conversation with you and I sincerely hope that you won't consider me out of line for doing so."

Ale sat quietly and focused on Leo as she wondered what could be coming next.

Leo continued, "As you probably know I have two combat tours in Iraq behind me, and along with those experiences comes the inevitable exposure to losing people one has become close to. When I heard of the tragic accident involving people from your operation I felt badly for them, but also for you. I pride myself to be a reasonably good judge of character, and my first impression of you was that you are a tough business woman on the outside but that you are a sensitive and caring person on the inside. I learned early on that the only way to deal effectively with life's unexpected calamities is to talk about them with someone who has experienced similar events and who will genuinely listen and care. I don't know what your personal situation is like so if you have this base covered then we can just have a nice lunch together and then go our separate ways. But if you do not have someone in whom you can confide and off-load some of the emotions stemming from the crash then I would like for you to know that I am volunteering to be that person for you."

Ale was shocked that he, a total stranger, and a man at that would have the audacity to think that she would be comfortable sharing her personal feelings with him. But, on the other hand, she immediately recognized as a result of this suggestion that she indeed had not had anyone who had even come close to fulfilling that role in her life for years. She thought about Franco, who had not said a word to her about the accident or its possible effects on her since she told him about it the day it happened. And she thought about Terry, who was anything but objective because of his irrationally exuberant outlook on Camber and its future. *Maybe it is time*, she thought, *to drop the tough-girl business veneer and to explore the possibility that this is someone I can talk to and who will actually listen and express an interest in me as a person. But I'll be careful in case Leo has other than acceptable intentions.*

"Leo, you do know that I am married don't you?"

"Yes," was his immediate and pointed response, "and I am not in any way trying to come-on to you. But I am also acutely aware that being married doesn't necessarily provide one with the type of emotional outlet that I am suggesting for you. In fact, sometimes it is quite the opposite. If you have any doubts regarding the sincerity or motives of my offer, then I think we should abandon the conversation altogether."

"No, Leo! I just wanted to make sure I took off the table any sort of relationship that might compromise my marital situation right at the beginning," said Ale with an inflection of emphasis.

"I understand, and I wouldn't want it any other way," he replied.

Ale and Leo ordered lunch and then talked for hours at the table afterward. She shared her strong sense of guilt that four people, three of them teenagers lost their lives in an aircraft rented from a company that she owned. And that led to her confiding that she had never been in favor of the Camber project from the beginning but that she felt an obligation to Terry to give it a try since he was so enthusiastic about it. Ale was very surprised at the intensity of Leo's interest in her descriptions of things she had never taken the time to discuss with anyone else. She carefully stayed away from her frustrations with Franco and her marriage and intended to continue doing so regardless of where her new friendship with Leo might go.

Ale glanced at her watch for the first time and realized how the time had gotten away from her. "Wow," she said, "it's 3:30 already. I totally lost track of the time, Leo."

"Me too," he replied. "Do you have to go?"

"Yes, I have a company meeting this evening, and I have a lot of things to do beforehand."

Leo walked Ale back to her car in the garage a few blocks west on Main Street. They said their good-byes, and as Leo extended his hand for Ale to shake she instead gave him a brief hug, something exceptionally out of character for her, and thanked him for a pleasant lunch.

On the drive back to BWI, Ale could not help but think of everything they had discussed and how good she felt about the experience. But she was also surprised at how easy it was for her to talk to Leo and how much she comfortably divulged before even realizing it. She had never encountered such a good listener. She found herself looking forward to the next time they could sit and talk again, but she also warned herself not to let her guard down—just in case!

* * * * *

The company-wide meeting was scheduled to begin at 7:00 p.m. The large conference room in the Elite Services facility was reserved for the occasion so that there would be enough room for all of the employees to be seated at the oversized conference table and around the outer perimeter of the room. Ale was sitting at the head of the table with Terry and

Greg sitting in chairs in the back of the room. This was her show, and Terry didn't want any of her thunder to be overshadowed by his or Greg's presence at the table with her. Greg had accepted the seating arrangement when informed by Terry just as he seemed to be accepting the firm's newly announced management structure.

At precisely 7:00 Ale said, "Let's get started. For those of you whom I have not yet had the pleasure of meeting I am Alejandra German, the new chief operating officer of Camber Flight Training, Incorporated. It is a pleasure for me to be here with you this evening."

The room was silent. Ale noticed before she began that only half of the employees had appeared for the meeting on time, and the ones who were in the room were not at all happy about it. Most were dressed in old tee-shirts and cut-off pants, and the rest were just downright sloppy. Suddenly the solitude was pierced.

"How long is this going to take?" came a voice from her immediate left. "I have something important I have to do this evening."

Her reply was swift and direct. "I can't imagine that any of you have anything more urgent to do with your evening than to discuss the future of your employer. But to answer your question, Mr. Fadely, it will take less than an hour. I have an agenda for you if you will take one and pass the rest on."

Joel Fadely was clearly startled that Ale knew his name since they had not yet met. He sat quietly for a few moments and then he made a statement while looking at the others in the room and not directly at Ale. "Well I'm going to have to leave in a half-hour, so I suggest you cover the important points early in the meeting!"

Again Ale's response was swift and direct. "Mr. Fadely, if you or anyone else plans on leaving this meeting before I adjourn it, you can leave your keys and badges here because you won't be needing them to work at Camber any longer. Is that clear to everyone?"

Walk softly and carry a big stick, one of Ale's favorite lines, kept going through her head. She hadn't come into this meeting looking for a fight, but if a fight is what some of these people wanted then they had no idea what was in store for them.

The first fifteen minutes of the meeting were devoted to introductions around the table. Considering the unexpected nature of the change in management and the poor attitudes of many of the employees, Ale thought that this would be a good way to try to break the ice. Each employee introduced him or herself briefly with little or no attempt to be friendly or talkative. One stated his name and refused to say anymore about himself. It was a classic example of a group passive-aggressive confrontation with little hope of changing the mood in the short-term.

At 7:18 three more employees entered the conference room, and as they did they were talking loudly to each other and interrupting any semblance of a meeting that might already have been taking place in the room. "Sorry we're late," one of them said sarcastically as all three sat at the table. "We had something important to take care of, and it took longer than we expected."

Ale sat quietly and stared at the three for several moments. "Gentlemen," she finally said, "I was born at night, but I wasn't born last night! The three of you finished flying students at 5:00 p.m. when you left Camber and met down the street at Jason's Bar. That was the 'important matter' that you had to take care of." The entire room was silent, but Ale could almost read the thoughts of her employees from their facial expressions and the look in their eyes. *How in the world did she know this soon about the local bar where most of us hang out when we're not working? And how did she know that Tom, Dave, and Steve were at Jason's for the past two hours?*

"Here's what we're going to do." Ale was formal and deliberate with these remarks. She spoke with a soft but demanding tone as she looked each employee straight in the eye. She moved from one to the next, from her left to her right as she delivered her words succinctly and with authority. "I am going to adjourn this meeting in three minutes. We will meet again at 7:00 tomorrow evening in this same room. Every employee of this company will be seated at this table and ready for business so that we may begin right at seven. If you cannot attend the meeting, or if you will not be here on time, you are to make arrangements to have your keys and your badges delivered to me not later than seven o'clock tomorrow, and you will consider yourself immediately dismissed from employment with Camber.

This is a business, ladies and gentlemen. From now on it will be managed as a business and you will behave as dedicated employees of this business. There will be no exceptions! Are there any questions? Oh and one more thing. You will appear for this meeting tomorrow dressed in acceptable attire for a business meeting, and, effective immediately, you will dress for work in clothing that reflects the seriousness of your profession until we can issue proper uniforms to you. Is that understood?"

Everyone around the table nodded, some with obvious disdain as Ale continued to focus her eyes on them.

"That will be all for this evening."

The room emptied quickly, and Ale walked over to Terry and Greg still sitting in the far corner. They stood as she approached, and Terry asked her, "Feel like going somewhere and talking?"

"Sure," said Ale, "anywhere but Jason's!"

The trio each drove separately to a nearby Ruby Tuesday's restaurant so that they could be on their way home after their meeting without having to return to Camber. After ordering appetizers, the conversation quickly turned to the meeting and Ale's performance.

"Greg," said Terry, "I'm anxious to hear your take on the events of this evening."

Greg was playing with the salt and pepper shakers and moving them between his hands on the table in front of him. He never looked up from the shakers focusing intently on their movement from one hand to the other. He did not acknowledge the question for nearly a minute causing both Terry and Ale to think that his review of the meeting would be critical. He abruptly stopped fidgeting with the objects in front of him and said, "I'm beginning to understand what you are doing and why you are doing it. I realize now that I have allowed the company to operate as a sort of club where the flight instructors could come and go as they please, regardless of the impact that routine has had on the bottom line of the firm. I didn't mean for that to happen, but it's obvious now that the employees have been running the company and not the management. Ale, I thought at the beginning of the meeting that you were unnecessarily heavy-handed with the group even to the point where I was thinking that I had made a serious mistake by bringing the two of you into the company. But when I saw how some of the employees were treating you, and therefore the company, I realized that they had been treating me the same way. I became your biggest cheerleader quickly. I think you handled things in exactly the manner necessary under the circumstances. I am very curious to see if anyone shows up tomorrow evening."

"They'll be there," said Ale, "and I'm betting that they will be singing a different tune after they've had some time to discuss and think about their options."

The three finished their sparse meal and moved out onto the parking lot together. Just before walking separately to their cars Greg stopped and asked Ale, "How is it that you know so much about people?"

Ale donned a wry sort of smile, glanced at Terry, and said, "I am a people, Greg!"

Terry and Greg chuckled as Ale gave them a playful wink and walked to her car.

During the thirty minute ride home Ale thought about the meeting and how she would be handling the employees the next night. Greg's comments about her approach earlier that evening were helpful, but she had intended to be firm and direct during the follow-up meeting even if he had not approved. Her thoughts quickly turned from Camber to her lunch with Leo earlier in the day. As she carefully reviewed the conversation in her mind, she couldn't help but wonder whether Franco would greet her upon her arrival home or whether he would, as usual, be too occupied with his own life to acknowledge her presence. *This is dangerous*, she thought. *I can't allow myself to compare the interest that Leo demonstrated in my well-being with the disinterest regularly demonstrated by Franco. I have to treat these two situations as totally separate if for no other reason than the preservation of my own sanity.* When Ale arrived home the house was dark and quiet and she walked directly upstairs to kiss her boys goodnight and then retire for the night. It took her an unusually long time to drift off to sleep but just before she did a lone tear slowly made its way from the corner of her left eye across her cheek and onto the pillow below.

FIFTEEN

THE NEXT DAY passed quickly for Terry and Ale as they carefully reviewed the financial records of Camber in detail behind closed doors in the company's small conference room. Their goal was to execute the hundred-day plan as soon as possible. In order to achieve that each of the new owners would have to become intimately familiar with the company's books. Terry had long since ceased to be surprised at how quickly Ale was able to assess the financial condition of a firm despite her lack of formal training and experience in the field of corporate finance. The two were approaching the end of their comprehensive analysis when Greg opened the door and reminded them of the company meeting set to begin in thirty minutes.

At 6:45 p.m. Ale was seated at the head of the table in the Elite Services conference room, and Terry and Greg had taken the same seats they occupied the night before. Some employees had arrived and were already seated when the trio of owners entered the room, and Ale made a mental note of those who had made the effort to be early. By 6:55 the seats surrounding the table were all filled, and every employee on the Camber payroll was in the room. Everyone wore reasonable business attire—with the exception of Joel Fadely, whose frayed cut-off shorts, old and dirty tennis shoes without socks, and tee shirt exclaiming "Life Sucks" across the front looked conspicuously out of place. Ale decided to subtly acknowledge the flight instructor's obvious attempt to undermine her authority at the beginning of the meeting, and she would deal directly and more thoroughly with Mr. Fadely in a private setting later.

At 7:00 Ale began the meeting. "Good evening," she said with a smile but also an authoritative tone. "There are additional copies of the meeting agenda on the table for those who may not have been here last night. I would like to thank all of you for being on time and, with one exception, for wearing business attire appropriate for the occasion. Mr. Fadely, you and I will have a career conference in private tomorrow." Everyone in the room focused their attention on the poorly dressed employee, and it was clear by the expression on his face that his attempt to challenge the directive of the new boss had backfired. Instead, he had provided her with an opportunity to exercise her new authority in front of all of the employees and at his expense.

During the first fifteen minutes of the meeting each employee delivered a brief introduction followed by the same from Terry, Ale, and Greg. The general attitude in the room had changed considerably from that of outward displeasure to one of conservative cooperation. At the end of the introductions, Ale thanked everyone for their comments and for keeping them brief.

"I will be using the next half-hour or so to summarize for you my opinion of the current state of the company followed by a short presentation of the goals which we all will be working to achieve together during the next one hundred days. If you have any questions about anything that I am covering, it would be in the best interest of time if you would make notes of them, and we can discuss them at the end of my remarks."

"Camber Flight Training Incorporated is, and has been throughout its history, performing exceptionally poorly by virtually any business standard available. The company has never had a profitable quarter and the reason for this is quite simple. The first and one of the most crucial steps to profitability is the effective utilization of all of the assets of any firm, and there are two primary assets in this firm, aircraft and flight instructors. Let me define the word asset as I am using it here. An asset is anything used by the management and employees of the company in order to generate revenue. This is not necessarily the technical accounting definition of the word, but it is the operating manager's definition."

Ale paused to take a sip from the bottle of Deer Park water she had brought with her, then continued. "I have reviewed all of the data with regard to revenue generating flight operations for the past two years. The average aircraft utilization for the entire fleet over that two year period is slightly less than seventeen percent. And the average utilization for the flight instructors is twelve percent. This means that, of all of the hours each day, week, month, and year, that aircraft could have and should have been flying and earning revenues for the company they actually have been doing so only seventeen percent of the time. The same applies to flight instructors, only that utilization rate is twelve percent. We could triple these numbers, and they would still be low by just about any standard."

Stacey McCoy, one of the three chief flight instructors raised his hand to catch Ale's attention.

"Yes Stacey," she said. Ale spent several hours studying the personnel files of all of the employees the first evening that she was on the site. She made a concerted effort to match identification pictures in the files with names.

"I'm sorry, I know you said we should wait to ask questions, but I really think that this one would clarify something and is appropriate here."

"Okay Stacey, I'll tell you if it should wait until later. What is it?" she asked.

"You mentioned in your introduction a few minutes ago that your background is in business, and you don't have any experience in aviation. I think a large part of the low numbers you are generating comes from the fact that we don't fly students at night and when the weather is bad. These situations significantly decrease the average amount of time that we could fly."

"That's an excellent point, Stacey. But we have adjusted our worksheets to account for those factors. We used standard daily sunrise-sunset tables to identify how many hours of daylight were actually available for flying during the period that we researched. We also found data from the United States Weather Service which we used to determine exactly which days the weather in the BWI area prevented normal flight operations. We also factored in the average amount of down time due to maintenance for each aircraft during the two year period. After accounting for all of these periods when flight operations would not have been expected we were left with the total amount of time that the planes should have been in the air and generating revenues. The aircraft were only doing so a little less than seventeen percent of the time. We ran the same exercise with the number of hours the instructors had committed to being available to fly versus how many they actually flew. That number turned out to be twelve percent."

Several of the flight instructors in the room shot glances of surprise at each other after Ale explained the methodology used to determine the asset utilization of the company. At no time, either in company meetings or outside of them, had the management of the firm shared information like this about the business with the employees.

"Let's move on," said Ale after another gulp of water.

"As far as I can determine there are two reasons for the consistently unacceptable utilization rates. It appears that the Midshipmen at the Academy should be flying much more frequently than they are. It is a scheduling challenge that we are going to have to address and correct immediately."

"Good luck," came a muffled comment from the other end of the table and to Ale's right.

"What was that?" she asked, turning her head in the direction of the remark.

Joel Fadely was the chief flight instructor selected by Greg to be directly responsible for the coordination of the Naval Academy flight operations. The irony that Fadely, of all of the flight instructors in the company, had been selected to manage a military program requiring a high degree of discipline and precision had not escaped Ale's attention when he entered the room dressed so unprofessionally.

"Mr. Fadely," Ale persisted, "did you have a comment to add to my analysis?"

Fadely paused for a few moments and made eye contact with as many of his colleagues as he could in the brief time before saying, "Yes, I do.

The Midshipmen generally don't fly as often as they should because they have several priorities that are higher on their list than flight training. They cancel a large proportion of their scheduled lessons usually at the last minute leaving us standing here with no student and no income for that three hour period. If you can solve that problem, then you'll see your aircraft and flight instructor utilization increase dramatically."

Ale smiled and replied with an obvious tone of gratitude. "Well thank you, Mr. Fadely. Obviously I have a lot to learn about the intricacies of the Navy program. I look forward to your help with it." Fadely quickly adopted a facial expression that could best be described as a smirk as he looked around the room seeking the silent approval of his fellow employees.

"That brings me to the second reason that we are severely underutilized in this firm. Our primary focus until now has been on the delivery of flight training almost exclusively to The United States Naval Academy. Effective immediately we are implementing a comprehensive marketing campaign designed to attract civilian students. We are forming a civilian division and each of you will be assigned these students, in addition to your Navy student load."

The room suddenly became alive with loud discussion between all of the flight instructors around and across the table. This appeared to be the first miscalculation of Ale's in an otherwise civilized company meeting. She had assumed that the instructors would welcome the opportunity for a broader range of students and, therefore, a significant increase in their earning potential. But what she was witnessing after her pronouncement appeared to be the beginning of a full-fledged revolt.

The room was bristling with chatter. The employees who weren't talking excitedly to each other were talking simultaneously and directly at Ale. The level of emotion in the room soared from one of near lethargy to one of collective anger in a matter of seconds and Ale allowed the venting to continue for less than a minute when she raised both of her hands, palms toward the meeting participants, with her elbows still resting on the table in front of her. Everyone, with the exception of Joel Fadely, fell silent immediately and in unison. Fadely had been complaining the loudest, and his head was turned away from Ale when she raised her hands signaling that she wanted quiet in the room. Suddenly he was the only one in the room talking, and he finished the sentence which he had started before realizing that he was the only one left speaking.

"...and if she thinks I'm going to fly civilians, in addition to the Navy students, then I'll just quit!" At the end of his statement, he turned toward Ale and lowered his voice slightly as he noticed that he was heard by all including her.

Ale exhibited no change in facial expression as she stared directly at Fadely and lowered her hands in front of her. After several seconds of silence, with all eyes at the table moving from her to the defiant co-chief flight instructor, she spoke in a stern but controlled tone.

"Mr. Fadely, I now have a desk back in the Camber offices and this space on that desk will remain empty and is reserved for your written resignation any time you wish to quit your employment with us. I don't take threats like that lightly!" As she spoke her two index fingers traced a space roughly the size of a piece of standard Stationery on the table slightly to the left and in front of her. As she looked intently at each of the employees around the table she continued, "And that goes for anyone who would rather move on than to accept the changes that will have to be made in this company in both the short and long-term future."

The tension in the room was nearly overwhelming as everyone waited for the inevitable smart-aleck reply from Joel Fadely. None came as he sat quietly and stared at the table in front of him.

Alejandra German knew people. During her relatively short career in the Human Resources field, she had been an astute observer of human behavior. While many in that discipline focused on corporate policy development and on navigating through the organizational bureaucratic constipation that evolves with company size and the interaction of massive egos, Ale had successfully taken the fundamentals of human resources to the next level. Her training and experience had instilled within her a quasi sixth sense, which allowed her to recognize the personality of an individual with whom she had come into contact almost immediately. Mr. Fadely demonstrated virtually all of the characteristics of a highly dominant personality profile, but in Fadely's case it was decidedly in the extreme. Ale knew that when the dominant personality significantly exceeded the level of all of the other personality traits in any individual the result is almost always a person who is consistently confrontational at best, and many times outwardly defiant when dealing with authority. She had identified Fadely as the latter early in her dealings with him and consequently considered him easily expendable for Camber, and the sooner the better.

Ale glanced at her watch and said, "We have nearly exhausted the time set aside for this meeting. I will summarize by stating once again that the very survival of this company depends entirely on several changes that will need to be made in short order. I understand that there is serious opposition to the strategy of opening training avenues for civilians but, frankly, we have no alternative. We also must significantly and immediately improve the utilization of all of the assets of the firm. This means that aircraft and flight instructors must be generating far more revenue than they are at the present time. In order to provide an incentive for the flight instructors to be more productive, we will be changing the structure of your compensation. I am not interested in giving you any details at this moment, but you can expect that the calculation of your pay will be changed so that you will earn a higher rate of pay for each hour that is worked beyond a set minimum in any given month. In other words, the more revenue you create for the company the more money you will earn."

A guarded smile crossed the faces of some around the table. Joel Fadely scribbled something on the back of the agenda laying on the table in front of him and then passed the paper across the table to Stacey McCoy. Ale continued her summation but noticed that Stacey read the note and immediately rolled his eyes at Joel and smirked sarcastically.

"In addition, effective as soon as we can implement it, there will be full scheduling of students throughout every weekend. We can devise a scheduling process that will allow for perhaps a weekend a month off on a rotating basis, but all of the assets of this firm will work, and will work hard seven days a week. And finally, within the next sixty days the company will be providing all employees with work uniforms and company policy will require that every employee wear the uniform at all times while on company property. Employees will be involved in the selection of uniform styles and colors. Until that time, all employees will wear dark blue polo-style shirts with khaki pants at all times while on the premises. There will be no exceptions. Oh, and no sandals or tennis shoes. Informal dress shoes are to be worn by all. Are there any questions?"

The silence, as quiet as a tomb, was the best indicator of the mood.

"Oh, and one final thing," she stated emphatically and then paused long enough to look into the eyes of each employee from her left around to her right. "I met with the people at our friendly local FAA FSDO recently, and they informed me that there have been some illegal and dangerous incidents in the area involving aircraft of the type Camber uses for training." She paused again, briefly, but long enough to notice quick glances from all present in the direction of Joel Fadely. Once again she continued, but now looking in Fadely's direction. "I have two strong messages for each of you as we adjourn this evening. If I learn of anyone using Camber's aircraft for any purposes other than those legal and necessary for the safe and efficient operation of this company, I will personally turn that individual, or those individuals in to the FAA, and I will urge the feds myself to punish those involved to the full extent of federal law. Also, and just as importantly, I will not tolerate the use of any asset of this company for purposes other than official business, which includes, but is not limited to computers, phones, offices or other facilities, or any other company property. If I find that any of these assets have been abused, I will immediately terminate the employment of any and all offenders. Have a pleasant evening!"

Ale adjourned the meeting and watched as everyone in attendance, with the exception of Terry and Greg, quietly exited through the door directly behind Ale's chair. It was quite obvious to Ale that an informal meeting of the employees of Camber Flight Training, Inc. would be continuing well into the late night hours at Jason's and that the conversation was not likely to be supportive of the new management of the firm.

Terry and Greg approached Ale from the far side of the conference room. The expression on Terry's face was one of obvious approval while Greg's face clearly reflected a serious concern about what had just transpired. But Ale wasn't in the mood for a debriefing from either of them.

"Gentlemen," she said before they could say anything, "would you mind leaving me here alone for awhile? I've got some thinking to do."

The two men didn't even have a chance to slow down, and they continued walking until they left the room and closed the door behind them. Ale, now alone in the large and formally furnished conference room, formed a mental picture of the employees as they were sitting at the table in front of her. As she imagined she was looking at each, she reinforced her belief that the most critical and immediate element for success for this company will be the way she interacts with each employee and whether these people will accept her and the changes that must be implemented. She found herself searching this group for examples of other personality types that, along with Joel's dominant style, comprised all of the styles in her arsenal of tools for effectively managing people. It was easier to identify the personalities of each of the employees than she first thought it would be and Ale sat in deep thought as she assessed each in her own definitive terms.

The peaceful quiet of the Elite Services conference room, which was located on the ramp side of the terminal serving all general aviation aircraft at BWI airport, was suddenly broken by the loud whine of jet engines just outside of the window on the far side of the room. She turned toward the window in time to see a large corporate jet taxiing away from the building. Her train of thought about employees and personalities was broken briefly when she caught herself wondering where that aircraft was going and who was in it. She was deeply fearful of flying in any type of aircraft but at the same time she was always intrigued by the ease with which people, especially those in private aircraft could travel between any two cities in the country in a matter of hours. She imagined herself sitting in a plush leather seat on the departing corporate jet headed to vital business meetings in San Diego, perhaps talking on the plane's phone as she watched the Elite building disappear from sight. Her curiosity got the best of her as she wondered if she would ever be a corporate tycoon and deal-maker, and it was the thought of this professional quest in her life that brought her immediately back to reality. Once again her general lack of self confidence derailed a dream as she chuckled and thought to herself how unlikely it would be that a female immigrant from Uruguay might ever become a captain of industry in the United States in her lifetime. Her attention then returned to the imaginary employees sitting at the table around her.

As Ale sat quietly in the empty Elite Services conference room, she was confronted with the irony and the magnitude of the challenges facing the new management of Camber on several different levels. Terry's focus on the financial hurdles was paramount in his eyes, and she was unable to forget the importance of that factor mostly because he would not let her forget about it. Greg's approach to the business was almost identical to Terry's because of the sizable financial risk he was shouldering, and his trepidation about the strategies being implemented by the new management was overshadowed only by his skepticism about the long-term potential of the enterprise based on his experience with it. But Ale's concerns centered on the people of Camber. Her experience with several businesses had taught her that while the success or failure of an enterprise depends squarely on the integrity of its financial stability and the viability of its product in the marketplace, more times than not companies fail due to an inability of the people within the firm to work effectively together. She decided that her involvement in this project would support the financial and technical challenges identified by Terry but that her primary commitment at Camber would be to the development of the people in the company and their working relationships with her and each other. After all, it wouldn't serve anyone's interests if the financial foundation of the firm is secured only to have the company fall apart because the different types of people within it fail to pull together in the same direction. Ale decided to keep this aspect of her turn-around strategy to herself, at least for now. As she stood and walked to the door she abruptly stopped, turned toward the large window looking out over the vast BWI acreage, and she smiled as she saw another private jet lift from a runway in front of the building. She turned the lights in the room off and left the Elite building walking slowly across the parking lot to the Camber offices.

Ale found Terry waiting in his makeshift office area. It appeared that everyone else had gone for the evening which was something that Ale was anxious to do as well.

"I know you want to get home to the boys," said Terry, "but can we talk for just a few minutes before you pack up and leave?"

"Sure, what's on your mind?" She was prepared for the inevitable lecture on how she had been too harsh with the employees in the company meeting which had ended a little less than an hour before but was surprised when the subject was not even mentioned as Terry continued.

"I've been thoroughly reviewing Camber's present numbers, and the projections that we'll use for our long-range planning process and I have some concerns that I think we should discuss right away."

"Okay," Ale said, "but let's try to keep it to about ten minutes so that we can both get out of here. It's been a long day, and I'm anxious to get into a hugs and kisses environment for a change!"

Terry smiled at her and said, "I don't have any hugs and kisses to go home to but I'll make it as quick as possible because you do. Camber isn't going to be generating enough cash to pay either one of us any kind of salary for at least two years and probably longer." He paused for a moment and then continued, "When we proposed to Greg that we will not receive any compensation for the Camber project it was when we had other paying clients. But now we have none, and there obviously will not be any cash from Camber to fill that void."

Ale stared at Terry with that look that only she was capable of delivering. "But we developed all of the numbers together for both the hundred day and the long-term plans. We put enough in each to cover the salaries and benefits that we are paying ourselves from Orion. I was frustrated enough that we wouldn't be getting any increases for some time to come, but I certainly can't afford to go for a month without a salary, let alone a couple of years. What happened? Where did the projections that included our income go?"

"I've reworked the projections at least a half-dozen times in the past twenty-four hours. The market in the Baltimore-Washington metroplex is solid, but Camber's expansion into a first-class business with a strong balance sheet is going to take the reinvestment of every penny that we can scrape from the income statement for some time to come. We're going to have to expand the facilities, buy or lease aircraft, and pay for a lot of marketing and advertising to be able to attract the civilian population necessary for the expansion. We grossly underestimated all of those costs the first time around."

Ale reached to her right for the arm of a chair that she had been standing next to and she sat down. After a few moments, she asked, "What do you propose, Terry?"

"I've given it a lot of thought today Ale, and I have decided that I will personally invest the necessary cash into Orion to keep you going until Camber can produce enough cash to cover your salary and benefits. I'll have to live off of what is left in my savings until Camber can support me as well."

Ale thought for several seconds and then said, "Terry, we've never talked about how much you are worth because I never felt it was any of my business." She took a long breath and then continued. "But I have to assume that the only way you can do what you are suggesting is to wipe out any retirement fund that you've been able to accumulate over the years. I just can't let you do that—especially for me. That's way too much of a risk for you to take just so that I can survive until Camber pays off. We don't even know if it will pay off."

"Like I said, Ale," Terry reiterated, "I've made my decision. We have made a commitment to this project, and this is the only way it will work. I need for you to accept it. It's not as though I'll be giving you charity. After Camber is producing enough cash to carry us both, we will work out a repayment plan from the firm to Orion to replenish the cash and Orion will then reimburse me. Strictly a loan from me to the company which will be repaid in full."

"Still one hell-of-a-risk, Terry! I have always supported you, and I have all the faith in the world in your judgment. But what if something goes wrong? What if Camber fails?"

"Then we'll pick ourselves up, dust ourselves off, and we'll move ahead—together. But we're not going to let that happen, are we? Now go home to those hugs and kisses and let's not talk about this anymore. We're in agreement, and we will work out the details tomorrow."

Ale stood and walked toward the door. Just before walking out of the office she turned and said, "You know Terry, your favorite interview question that I have watched you ask high-level management candidates for years suddenly makes a lot more sense to me now than ever before. Do you know which question I'm talking about?"

"Yeah," said Terry with a slight grin.

Ale continued, "You would stare right into the soul of the person you were interviewing and you would ask, 'Have you ever had to bet everything on your own ability to succeed? Tell me about it.' I never understood the full meaning of that question. But now I do. It goes right to the heart of what a person is all about. It strikes right in the center of the bulls eye. It's all about the power of people. And that's the position we now find ourselves in. This is no longer just a job, it's a struggle for survival. We are actually now facing that challenge confronting every entrepreneur every day. It's all or nothing isn't it?"

"I guess it is, Ale. Have a good night. I'll see you in the morning."

As Ale departed, Terry turned and slowly scanned the darkened lobby behind him. In barely a whisper, he repeated, "I guess it is!"

SIXTEEN

DURING THE MONTH that passed since Ale first met Leo for lunch the two enjoyed breakfast, lunch, or dinner at least once each week and rarely a day went by without a phone call and several e-mails between them. Their conversations were always intense for Ale, usually centering on her trepidation about the future of Camber and her quest to cultivate a fulfilling career in a multinational corporation. Sometimes she talked at length about her sons and how much she missed spending the kind of time with them that they deserve. Leo shared many of his Navy aerial combat experiences with her that she found mesmerizing since she had no prior exposure to military life or the cold and calculating process of combat decision-making. As a direct result of listening to Leo's exploits Ale drew a number of similarities between her own managerial decision-making style and those required in the cockpit of a fighter aircraft engaging the enemy. In each of their meetings to this point, they skillfully avoided any discussion of Leo's personal life and likewise of Ale's relationship with Franco, but it had occurred to her that their friendship was becoming so strong that these subjects were probably not going to be off limits for long.

Breakfast with Leo on this early morning in May was every bit as pleasant for Ale as all of the times they had spent together during the previous weeks. They had decided a few weeks earlier that it would be wise for them to meet at locations where it would be unlikely for them to be seen by anyone associated with Camber. Both were well aware of the potential that their frequent contact might be misinterpreted by employees, and especially by Terry, as inappropriate or unethical. On this particular morning, they met at a restaurant near Grasonville, a small town just beyond the eastern side of the Chesapeake Bay Bridge on the Eastern Shore of Maryland. They traveled to the restaurant separately, a drive of about forty-five minutes for each of them. Ale was pleased with the secretive meeting arrangements because, although she was doing nothing wrong, it made the prospect of having to explain her friendship to Franco less likely. *Not that it would have mattered to him anyway,* she'd thought when it first occurred to her.

After breakfast, the two reluctantly parted with a long hug. The drive west across the bridge to BWI was a pleasant one for Ale. The weather was clear, and the traffic light as she thought about how quickly the time always passed when she was with Leo, and how refreshed she always felt after the cathartic effect of sharing things with him that she never felt comfortable talking about with anyone else. On this beautiful May morning, she actually smiled as she pulled onto the Camber parking lot and entered the flight school building.

✻ ✻ ✻ ✻ ✻

Elmer Maurer was harnessed snuggly in his seat on the instructor side of the DA20 trainer aircraft as it cruised at 3,500 feet heading east across the Chesapeake Bay toward the Eastern Shore of Maryland. This heading would take him into the airspace used by Camber flight instructors and their students for training and the practice of fundamental flight maneuvers. The sight of the sun slowly rising from the flat and seemingly lifeless terrain in front of him nearly lulled him back to sleep on this clear and windless Wednesday morning in May. The vibration and the low drone of the 125 horsepower engine in front of him produced a similar effect. Elmer's student, Allison, was a senior at the Naval Academy and in the process of completing her fifth flight lesson of the Navy's tightly controlled and monitored syllabus. It required a total of twenty hours of dual instruction and seven hours of solo flight. Their mission was to proceed due east using visual navigation skills, known as VFR, from BWI to a point just northwest of the city of Easton, Maryland. When they arrive, Allison will spend an hour reviewing and practicing the gentle climbs, descents, and turns from her last lesson and then will be introduced to slow flight and stalls. These maneuvers are all demonstrated and practiced in a sequence, with the goal of mastering the skills necessary for a safe approach and landing.

Allison was a good pilot overall but had been progressing a bit more slowly than the average Academy student. She seemed to lack confidence and tended to become nauseated during some of the turning maneuvers. Elmer had long since learned that he must always keep a small bag, known as a sic-sac, at the ready for this kind of student. He had learned the hard way that nothing ruins an otherwise pleasant training flight faster than projectile vomit in the cockpit.

Elmer was pleased with Allison's progress as she demonstrated shallow and medium turns to predetermined headings and gentle climbs and descents to predetermined altitudes.

"That was really good, Allison," he said through his headset microphone. The Naval student nodded and smiled only slightly, never taking her eyes off of some point straight out in front of them.

"Okay Allison," he said, "now what makes this airplane fly?"

"Sir?" she said.

"As succinctly as possible," he repeated, "what makes this airplane fly?"

"Why, the lift created on the topside of the wings sir."

"And what happens if that lift is disrupted?"

"The aircraft will stall and rapidly lose altitude, sir."

"Right Allison, and that's just what we're going to simulate right now. But there's no danger because we are at 3,500 feet, right?"

"Yes sir," said the midshipman, as the crack in her voice conveyed her anxiety.

Elmer began to instruct Allison in a step-by-step fashion through the sequence of initiating a midair stall and then recovering from it. "Relax and follow my directions and you will see how easy this is to execute. But before we start show me your hands." For the first time since they arrived in the practice area, Allison stopped staring out of the windshield in front of her as she looked directly at Elmer.

"Do what, sir?"

"Show me your hands," he repeated with slightly more emphasis.

She complied first removing her left hand from the stick and exposing her palm to his view. Then she quickly moved it back onto the stick and removed her right hand from the throttle and showed him that palm.

"They're red and very sweaty," he said. "You are applying a death grip to the stick and the throttle! You're going to have to relax. Don't apply any more pressure with your hands and your feet than is necessary to control the aircraft. Watch this—I have the controls," he said.

"Your aircraft sir," she said.

Elmer skillfully took command of the plane, placing his hands and feet on the controls. He steadied the plane in an attitude known as straight-and-level flight, which means that it was maintaining a constant altitude and was not turning in any direction, by applying slight adjustments to controls called trim tabs located between their seats. These trim controls moved small tabs on the plane's aileron and elevator surfaces and served to keep them in a fixed position as the air streamed rapidly over them.

"An aerodynamically stable aircraft, when trimmed properly, will continue to fly in the desired direction and at the desired altitude indefinitely without the application of any additional pressure on any of the controls." As soon as Elmer made that statement he removed his hands and feet from the controls of the plane and it continued in straight-and-level flight without any help from him.

He then placed the plane into a 30° bank to the left, trimmed it slightly, let go of the controls, and it continued to turn at the desired rate and at a constant altitude again without any additional help from him.

"Okay Allison, it's your aircraft again. Don't press, just relax!"

"Yes sir, I have control," she said placing her hands and feet back onto the controls.

"Now," Elmer continued, "pick another spot, relax, and follow my directions. Ease the power back all the way and maintain your altitude by continually applying back pressure to the stick. That's good! Use your rudder pedals to keep the nose on the spot you picked. Good! Now, when you can no longer pull the stick back any further, you will feel a shuddering and hear what sounds like someone rippling a light piece of aluminum. The nose will want to drop to the left a little. When this happens gently ease the nose forward still keeping it straight in line with the point and smoothly and fully apply full power until we have assumed straight-and-level flight once again. Okay now."

Allison's first reaction was to release a muffled and brief groan as the nose of the aircraft dropped and swung sharply to the left. She overreacted by moving the stick and pushing the right rudder pedal abruptly to the right simultaneously. Elmer forcefully but calmly called for power to which she responded by shoving the throttle into the console as fast and hard as she could. A situation that seemed to Allison as an aircraft wildly out of control was rapidly corrected by smooth and immediate adjustments to the stick, rudder pedals, and throttle by Elmer. "I've got the aircraft," he said.

"Roger, sir," she replied.

"Not bad for a first try," he said. But before he could even complete his statement his student groaned and proceeded to plaster the console and windshield with a generous coating of a partially digested breakfast burrito and coffee that had been itching to escape for the better part of an hour.

"I am so sorry!" exclaimed Allison as the DA20 proceeded westbound at 3,500 feet toward the Chesapeake Bay and, just beyond, BWI airport.

"Wish I could say that it is the first time, Midshipman," was the reply as Elmer cleaned the last speckles from his aviator sunglasses. "You've got the aircraft, Allison, while I try to clean up some of this mess. Just maintain 3,500 feet and a heading of 270 for awhile."

"Roger, sir."

Elmer's attention was focused on cleaning the instrument glass on the panel in front of them and on trying to find another container of handi-wipes that was supposed to be located behind the seats for just such unfortunate occasions. He glanced toward the altimeter and artificial horizon to ascertain that Allison was maintaining the proper aircraft flight characteristics, and then he once again stuck his head in the rear compartment searching for anything that would help to reduce the mess and the awful smell. At one point, he thought he heard Allison crying which was a definite reportable offense in the Academy student flight regulations. It would be severe enough for her that he had to write her up for puking in flight but an F-18 fighter pilot sobbing uncontrollably in a difficult situation was something that the Navy would never stand for. After all, one of the two primary purposes of the Academy training program was to screen-out unfit flight applicants before they ever had a chance to get to a training slot in Pensacola.

Elmer reached under a tarp located in the very back of the compartment behind their seats and retrieved a plastic canister of scented handi-wipes when suddenly the plane lurched slightly to the right with a loud thump and then the nose pitched slightly up with another loud thump.

"What the hell was that?" he asked as he quickly turned straight-forward in his seat and instinctively took control of the aircraft.

"I don't know," said Allison, "I… I…I didn't do anything!"

"I've got the plane," Elmer said as he scanned outside from the left wingtip to the nose and then…

"Roger sir, you've got it!"

There on the leading edge of the right wing about three feet from the fuselage was what appeared to be an area of blood and feathers and a dent in the surface of the wing about the size of a basketball. Elmer knew immediately that the extent of damage visible to him was not serious enough to place the aircraft in imminent danger, but what he couldn't figure out was why the plane's controls were suddenly sluggish and only partially responsive to his touch. Unless…

"Allison," he said emphatically, "listen up!"

"Sir?" Allison was in the process of deciding that she had just experienced every bit of a Naval aviation career that she ever intended to experience. And she was busy making all kinds of deals with her God if He would just extricate her from this situation alive and in one piece.

"I need you to look directly behind us, Allison! Can you see the tail of the aircraft?"

"No sir, I can't."

The Plexiglas canopy was clear in the front and on all sides but a sunscreen shade was built into the canopy directly over the pilots' heads extending all the way to the rear. It was designed to better protect the occupants from the effects of the heat in the enclosed cockpit, especially on hot summer days.

"Disengage your seat belt and lean as far as you can around me to see if you can get a vantage point that will allow a visual on the tail," he said with just slightly more urgency in his voice.

"Can't see it, sir. It is totally obscured by the sunscreen material. What do you suspect?"

"We obviously have a bird strike on our right wing. But it is possible that the wash from our prop threw the bird into our tail section causing damage to the vertical and/or the horizontal stabilizers. I can control this thing, but we have to get it down as fast as possible."

They were ten miles due east of BWI airport directly over the Chesapeake Bay. There was no option of landing at another airport as BWI was the closest and was straight ahead, a critical factor for a plane that was obviously in difficulty with its control surfaces. The only option for the crew was to proceed directly to BWI and to land as soon as possible.

Elmer selected the BWI approach control frequency into communication radio number one. He chose to avoid the prescribed emergency frequency because they were so close to BWI that he could save the time it would take for the emergency personnel to switch him back to BWI approach anyway.

"BWI approach control this is November 635 Delta Charlie declaring an emergency – this is a Mayday," was Elmer's first transmission.

"November 635 Delta Charlie this is BWI approach control. What is your location and the nature of your emergency?" came the immediate reply.

"BWI, we are eight miles east squawking 7700. We have sustained a bird strike and are unable to determine the extent of damage. We have control of the aircraft, but it is sloppy at best."

Modern aircraft, even small trainers are equipped with radios known as transponders which are actually small radar transmitters constantly producing signals that are received and decoded by air traffic control operators. The 7700 transponder code signifies an emergency and immediately allows all controllers in the area to segregate the aircraft in trouble from all other aircraft on their radar screens. The initial response of the controllers is to clear all air traffic away from the endangered plane as quickly as possible.

"November 635 Delta Charlie radar identification established. What do you want to do?"

"What do I want to do? I want to get this damn thing on the ground right now!" Elmer was a patient man, but his patience wore a little thin when he thought his primary desire should have been obvious at this point.

Terry had just entered the lobby of Camber Flight Training when he noticed Ale and several other employees huddled around the front counter listening intently to the conversation between the tower and N635DC on the communication system speakers located just behind the counter surface.

"What's going on?" he asked in a worried tone.

"One of ours on final approach after a bird strike," said Ale without taking her eyes from the speaker.

"Who's in it?" asked Terry, now himself staring blankly at the object of attention.

"Elmer and a Mid."

"How bad is it?" inquired Terry from any of the instructors who might be distracted long enough to answer his question.

"Elmer reports that he has control of the aircraft but that it is very sluggish," said Stacey. "They're about three miles from the end of the runway," added Stacey.

"Terrific!" exclaimed Terry. "Just when I was thinking today couldn't get any worse!"

Ale leaned over to Terry and whispered in his ear, "Fasten your seat belt because when this is over we're going to fire half of our employees!"

Terry just looked at her in amazement.

"November 635 Delta Charlie, Baltimore approach, switch now to Baltimore Tower on frequency 118.5, and..." there was a slight pause, and then the approach controller finished his sentence with something that neither Elmer nor Allison needed to hear.

"Good luck!"

Runway 28 at BWI airport is almost exactly two miles long, and 200 feet wide providing more than enough asphalt surface to accommodate an emergency landing by a loaded Boeing 757. The emergency and rescue services available exclusively for the airport operations are extensive as well, and when an inbound aircraft declares an emergency of any kind the fire and rescue equipment and personnel are immediately dispatched to the runway. When the alarm is sounded everything and everyone rolls in a precisely coordinated and orchestrated parade, and they position themselves on each side of the runway exactly as they have in countless drills. To say that the six massive fire trucks might be overkill for a small, two-seat training aircraft in trouble might be a natural conclusion for the untrained civilian observer. But professionals take no chances, and they were not about to skimp on this imminent emergency landing. In addition to the six fire trucks, two fully-equipped rescue vehicles, two ambulances, and two command vans were stationed and at the ready at strategic points along the runway. The decision was made early to eliminate the costly and time-consuming process of covering the runway with fire-retardant foam because the stricken aircraft did not report any malfunction of, or damage to its landing gear. The occupants of N635DC were in good hands once they touched down at BWI. That is, of course, assuming they could make it to the runway at all.

"November 635 Delta Charlie this is the Baltimore/Washington tower, do you read?"

"Affirmative," was the immediate reply from Elmer.

"635 Delta Charlie you are two miles from the end of Runway 28. Please confirm your altitude."

"635 Delta Charlie is at 3,100 feet, over."

"Roger, Delta Charlie. We have visual surveillance of your aircraft through binoculars. Be advised that you have a large protrusion extending forward from your right horizontal stabilizer. It appears to be the carcass of a large bird, but you are still too far away for us to get anything more definitive."

"Roger, tower—that's what we were afraid of!"

Allison had never been so scared in her life. She knew that Elmer was a more than competent flight instructor and that she could trust him to get them both out of this situation alive. But she felt that she had to say something to ease the tension in the cockpit.

"Sir, maybe if we execute a maneuver to dislodge the bird's body from the flight surface. Maybe that would…"

Elmer gave her no opportunity to complete her thought. "Thanks Allison, but we don't have time for maybes. We don't have the altitude or enough control of the aircraft for such a risky maneuver. And," there was a brief pause while Elmer reached in the cabin side pocket for the aircraft checklist booklet, "just maybe that damned bird carcass is the only thing still connecting the tail of this bucket to our rear-ends!"

It took most of Elmer's strength to keep the aircraft in flight with his right hand firmly on the stick and his left hand on the throttle. "We have to make sure we stay as high and as fast as possible until we get over the threshold of the runway, Allison," he said with authority. "If this piece of crap is going to stall and fall out of the sky I want it to happen right in between all of those flashing lights on both sides of that runway."

Elmer motioned to Allison with the bottom of his chin toward the booklet now resting in his lap. "Open the checklist book and find the emergency landing checklist," he said. "You're going to have to read off every item and then make any adjustments necessary for landing yourself. It's everything I can do to keep this thing in the air as we get lower and slower."

Allison flipped the pages over the top of the booklet until she located the proper checklist. She then read every item on the list in a forceful and clear voice and reached to touch each control with her hand after reading its respective item.

"Mixture full rich," she began while touching the knob on the mixture control next to the throttle.

Ale suddenly lurched from her position at the counter in the lobby of the Camber Flight School, and she shouted over to Stacey whose attention was glued to the speakers. "Stacey," she barked, "grab a portable handset and we'll all take the ramp van out to the edge of the tarmac to watch Elmer bring this to a happy ending."

Stacey complied with her orders and within one minute Ale, Terry, and three flight instructors, with Stacey behind the wheel, were loaded into a 2001 Chrysler minivan displaying the proper security placards and on their way to the far edge of the ramp between the Camber building and the closest active taxiway. That would be the nearest accessible vantage point for observing the action about to unfold.

"November 635 Delta Charlie, Baltimore Tower, you are cleared to land on runway 28. Winds are two-niner-zero at four knots."

"There's virtually no cross-wind to have to fight, Allison, so we've got that going for us!"

"Roger, tower, 635 Delta Charlie cleared to land."

"Good luck."

"Again with the good luck!" Elmer exclaimed with a calmer and more focused tone in his voice. "If you or I or that damned bird had any luck at all none of us would be in this predicament in the first place!" There was no mirth discernible in the comment.

Allison had completed the reading and securing of the items on the aircraft emergency landing checklist. "What can I do?" she asked Elmer in the most confident tone he had heard from her all morning.

Elmer replied immediately, "Slide your seat forward as though you are going to fly the aircraft. Place both hands lightly on the stick and be ready to help me if this thing gets sluggish as we near the runway surface. I'm not going to bleed much speed off of it until we're a few feet from touchdown. I'm going to fly it right into the runway so that we don't lose control too high up. I'm not going to take my eyes off of my planned point of touchdown. You're going to have to read-off the airspeed and altitude to me about every ten seconds or so until we're down." There was silence until he barked, "Got that, Midshipman?"

"Yes sir," was her crisp reply.

"Five-hundred feet and one-hundred knots, sir."

"Let's drop the sir for now, Allison. We're in this together as equals right now!"

Ten seconds later, "Four-hundred fifty feet and one-hundred knots."

The normal procedure for landing this aircraft would have called for decreasing power and the slowing of the airspeed at this point, but Elmer was fixated on slowly increasing the power for aircraft stability while maintaining a constant airspeed well above the stall speed in a landing configuration. This also decreased the plane's rate of descent, which is a positive outcome for this type of situation.

"Four-hundred feet and one-hundred knots." Allison was rapidly focusing her eyes outside of the cockpit and then back inside onto the face of the airspeed indicator and altimeter. Back-and-forth, back-and-forth.

"Three-hundred feet and ninety-five knots."

"More power!" exclaimed Elmer as if he were talking to himself. But the throttle was in the full position with the knob of the plunger-like device resting against the panel.

"Two-hundred fifty feet and eighty knots."

"Okay Allison we just crossed the threshold of the runway. I'm going to lower the nose to lose the remaining altitude. Then, just before we hit the runway, I'm going to kill all of the power and apply consistent back-pressure to the stick. The plane will stall, but we should be just inches off the ground when it does. You need to help me with the back-pressure when I say now."

"Roger, sir."

All eyes were riveted on the little plane. There was a small gasp from the people in each location when they first noticed the size and delicate location of the Canadian Goose on the horizontal stabilizer of the small trainer.

"They're damned lucky that thing didn't rip that little tail right off the airframe!" exclaimed a fire truck driver. "If it had they'd both be floating in the bay right now!"

"Now," shouted Elmer as he swiftly pulled the power to idle and he and Allison both applied maximum pressure on both of the sticks to a nearly painful position deep in each of their belt buckles.

Ale, Terry, and all of the other spectators watched in awe as the nose of the little DA20 moved away from the runway surface and the two main landing gear touched down with two plumes of smoke rising into the air. The excessive airspeed caused the plane to rise again off the runway, but Elmer and Allison maintained full back-pressure on the sticks and the craft quickly settled onto the runway for a final time. The nose-wheel gently glided back to the runway just a few moments later, and Elmer allowed the plane to roll to a stop without applying an excessive amount of braking. He was too drained to force his toes to apply pressure to the brakes located at the top of the rudder pedals under his feet.

After the plane came to a full stop in the middle of the runway with a dozen or so emergency vehicles and a hundred rescue workers surrounding it Elmer unlatched and raised the canopy. He and Allison now got their first look at the twenty-pound Canadian Goose impaled firmly onto the right side of the horizontal stabilizer. As Elmer had suspected early in the emergency situation, the bird first hit and damaged the leading edge of the right wing and then, probably already dead from the first impact, lodged itself into the composite plastic structure of the tail. Elmer and Allison looked at the plane then exchanged glances, and both simultaneously shook their heads.

"Sir," said Allison.

"Yeah," replied Elmer after a brief moment.

"Let me see your hands," she said in the first lighthearted moment the two had been able to share all morning.

Stacey drove the ramp van back to the Camber building, and they all filed into the lobby to await the arrival of the flight instructor and his student.

After the paramedics determined that both Elmer and Allison were healthy, aside from a strong case of trauma-induced stress, they were driven from the aircraft to the Camber ramp entrance. Spontaneous applause greeted them at the flight school lobby. Elmer walked slowly from the doorway to join Ale and Terry on the other side of the room. He looked as though he was searching for the right words, but he had decided when 635 Delta Charlie was at an altitude of about 500 feet exactly what his message to them would be if he actually survived the ordeal.

"Terry, Ale," he began looking them in the eye alternately, "I mean no disrespect whatsoever, but you can take this job and shove it where the sun never shines. I quit!" Whereupon Elmer pivoted on one heel and exited the lobby of The Camber Flight School never to be seen again.

Terry and Ale understood the stress that Elmer had just experienced, or at least they could imagine it. Ale, the most seriously flight-impaired person Terry had ever encountered had an especially frightful reaction to the incident swearing up-and-down for days afterward that she "wouldn't be caught dead in one of those little planes," asserting that if she did fly in one she would certainly wind up dead! But neither of them expected that Elmer would just up-and-quit.

Once again Ale was faced with the immense safety risks inherent in the ownership of a flight school. *How many of these accidents or potential accidents are going to occur before I just walk out of here too?* she thought.

SEVENTEEN

THE REMAINDER OF the morning was quiet and uneventful for Ale. It had been a month since the company meeting where she attempted to communicate her seriousness to all employees, but now she noticed an almost inconsequential improvement in their working habits and attitudes in general and the flight instructors in particular. This had become increasingly disturbing to Ale especially since she had been so adamant with Terry about the necessity of her role as the team builder and human performance enhancer in this attempted turn-around. It was becoming obvious to Ale that her attempts to bring about a significant change in Camber's corporate culture via a positive motivational methodology would not succeed. She was spending the early part of this morning closed off in her office working on her list of potential candidates for employment termination and her rationale for doing so.

The termination of someone's employment is a matter that should never be taken lightly by any manager and should always be considered only as a last resort. The effects of this action on the employees directly involved are obvious, but there is also a lingering negative effect on the remaining employees for quite a while afterward. Ale was acutely aware that this alternative was even direr in Camber's current state because there was a serious shortage of available flight instructors in the area and an even more serious shortage of instructors with the experience and maturity required for the challenges facing the flight school. It struck Ale as no coincidence that the flight staff at Camber was demonstrating an attitude of quasi defiance at a time when securing replacements for them would be particularly difficult. This was especially true for the function of chief flight instructor. Greg had appointed three different instructors as chiefs and had divided the responsibilities of the job among them because no individual instructor possessed all of the FAA required qualifications to hold the single position alone. Locating a qualified individual to be a chief instructor of the entire school and providing incentives for this person to take the job was going to be a daunting task and Ale knew it. To make matters worse, the FAA regulations require that a certified flight school must fill a vacant chief instructor position within 180 calendar days of the vacancy or face a shut-down of the entire operation. The decision that Ale had made and was about to execute was one of no less than life-and-death for Camber as a certified flight school and as a company.

Ale somberly completed her plan of action for culling Camber's staff of less than dedicated and productive workers as she vaguely remembered a quote that she believed to be attributed to the revered Vince Lombardi. "If you're not fired with enthusiasm, you will be fired—with enthusiasm." *Clever,* she thought, *but how do we go about replacing these lethargic employees with ones who will be fired-up with enthusiasm?* Filling a job with a qualified employee had never before been a particularly difficult challenge for Ale, but this situation just seemed different. The question that was haunting her was *do I pull the trigger now and risk not finding anyone to better serve our needs in this difficult turn-around, or do I settle for what we have because it is likely to be the best that we'll be able to do?* But as soon as the question presented itself to her an answer appeared. *Never settle for second best. Search hard enough and we'll find the right people to make this a success,* was the obvious answer.

Back in the conference room and behind closed doors, Terry and Ale sat down to discuss Ale's poorly timed announcement to Terry that she intended to fire a large proportion of Camber's employees. But Terry started the conversation with a less than savory comment considering the circumstances.

"Well," he said, "Elmer's gone, there's one flight instructor you don't have to fire."

Terry's attempt to be cute didn't work with Ale.

"What are you talking about, Terry?" she said with that visceral revulsion she was so good at demonstrating when she wanted to. "Elmer was the only flight instructor we had, including the three who are masquerading as chief flight instructors, whom we could count on. He was the only responsible and reliable one out of the whole bunch!"

Ale had an acerbic edge to her strongly sovereign personality that she was able to control most of the time but which she would occasionally allow to escape from its cage squarely located within the recesses of her subconscious.

"Okay," Terry said defensively, "I didn't mean to strike a nerve! I was just trying to lighten things up a bit. It's only mid-morning, and we've already experienced more than a year's worth of stress. Tell me about the conclusions you have drawn regarding the staff and your plans to attempt to rectify the situation."

Ale quietly regained her composure, retrieved a manila file folder from her briefcase, opened it and shuffled some papers that obviously were not priorities at that particular moment. And then she spoke. "I'll begin with the three employees to whom we are paying a premium to perform the duties of a single chief flight instructor. Joel Fadely was appointed by Greg Holland over a year ago to perform the duties of Chief of the Naval Academy program and, according to Greg, he was to be the Chief of the civilian Private Pilot Program as well. As you have witnessed Terry, Joel consistently demonstrates a strong personality style in the form of an infantile defiance toward any authority figure and he can be expected to go off and do whatever he damned well pleases even after being directly instructed to do otherwise. He is not just a weak link in the organization, he is a loose cannon just itching to go off in an organization that requires the highest level of discipline and professionalism from its flight instructors and especially its chief flight instructors! Feel free to chime in at any time, Terry."

"That's okay, Ale, I'll wait until you need a break."

"Alright," Ale said, "let's look at Stacey McCoy. Stacey was selected by Greg as our Chief of the Instrument Training Program, which, as you know, is the most complicated and demanding learning challenge that we offer here at Camber. Again this position demands the highest level of discipline and professionalism in that the chief must set the example for students and instructors alike. Stacey is a very nice guy, but the bottom line with him is that he doesn't want to fly. I don't even know why he became a flight instructor in the first place. He is always canceling flights with the flimsiest of excuses, and he has told me more than once that he would rather stay on the ground and get paid to perform administrative duties than to fly with students. Stacey's personality style is one where he's far more comfortable socializing and creating friendships with the students than focusing on the intricate and complicated responsibilities associated with teaching these students how to fly an aircraft in instrument conditions. He's a bad fit, Terry, and we can't afford a bad fit! Are you still with me?"

"Yes I am," he said. "Go on."

"And to complete our little trio of misfit chiefs we have Daryll, who was given the title of Chief of the Commercial Pilot training program by Greg under the same circumstances as the other two, that is, there just wasn't anyone else who was qualified on paper and available. But Daryll is a flake! He's clumsy and forgetful. You constantly have to go behind him and double-check to make sure that he has actually done what he has been assigned to do. His students have complained more than once that he has neglected to enter flights into their pilot logbooks, and you know how crucial that task is to keep up with in a school like this one. And last week when he was walking away from an aircraft after a flight, he tripped over a wheel chock in clear sight, in front of him on the ramp, and he sprained his ankle. He missed three days of work, and we had to file a Worker's Comp claim, which will cost us precious cash even though indirectly. This isn't a professional flight school, Terry. Judging by the people that we have in crucial positions it is a reform school for wayward wannabes that never will be. If I were forced to rename our three chiefs, I would call them bewitched, bothered, and bewildered. We have to do something, and we have to do it now! And I haven't even scratched the surface. The instructors reporting to these guys are still worse. Okay, it's time for you to react."

Terry knew that Ale was right. And he also knew that she was not one to exaggerate or to exhibit alarmist behavior. He had seen her resolve more difficult personnel problems than this one without resorting to firing everyone in sight, so he recognized that his challenge was to convince her that patience and training might buy them the time they so desperately needed to find a competent staff of employees. But he would have to choose his words carefully.

"Okay Ale, to quote a phrase from one of my favorite M.A.S.H. episodes, 'let me give you the poop on the overall situation status-wise'!"

Ale looked at him with an expression of confusion. "What?" she asked.

"Never mind. Let me summarize our big picture situation here and then we can discuss your frustrations with our personnel. First I want to say that I totally agree with you. The employees that we have inherited are not now equipped nor are they prepared to undertake the challenge that lies ahead for this company. But I want to introduce some other mitigating factors that we had better be ready to deal with, factors that could well mean life and death for Camber in both the short- and long-terms."

Terry waited a moment for some sort of response from Ale. Witnessing none he continued. "As you know the good news is that all of the major and regional airlines in this country and several others are aggressively pursuing licensed pilots with little logged flight time to hire and train as flight crew members. That's good because we can practically guarantee prospective civilian students in our marketing campaigns that they will be hired by an airline soon after completing our program. It's bad because the airlines are hiring every flight instructor in sight, and flight instructors don't want to be flight instructors—they want to be airline pilots. This means that although we should easily be able to fill our new civilian commercial pilot courses with paying customers, hiring new flight instructors to expand our operation will be a serious challenge for us. Not to mention finding replacements for the ones you want to fire. Envision our predicament if we fire the flight staff we now have while at the same time, we are enrolling perhaps dozens of new students expecting to be trained in the shortest amount of time possible. And introduce into that vision the probability that we will not be able to hire and train anywhere near the number of flight instructors we will need to fulfill our promises to the enrolled students. Not a pleasant thought is it?"

"So it's a chicken-or-egg problem isn't it?" said Ale. "We've got a bunch of inferior flight instructors who basically don't want to fly as instructors in the first place and whom we are going to have to try to whip into shape in order to train a large number of students who want to complete the program quickly."

"That's about the size of it, Ale."

Ale thought for a moment and then she snickered quietly.

"What?" said Terry.

"In the words of an old economics professor of mine what we have here is a very strong demand for a service that we know from the get-go we have a marginal or poor supply of."

"That about sums it up!" said Terry. He continued, "Now, are you ready to identify the second level of personnel and staffing problems we are facing?"

"Do I have a choice?"

"Okay," he said, "we currently have a demanding Navy training program under contract. I have completed a detailed analysis of this contract and Camber is consistently losing a substantial amount of money on it. Not necessarily because the pricing is not sufficient but more because there is no set of standard operating procedures governing how efficiently or inefficiently the instructors are teaching while in the aircraft, how and where they are refueling the aircraft, and how they are logging the time they are spending which, in turn, generates their own pay."

Terry continued, "Don't misunderstand, the pricing of the current contract is way too low for us to continue it at this level, but the lack of standardized procedures is aggravating the financial losses even more."

"So this becomes a major strategy issue for us doesn't it?" asked Ale.

"Yes it does."

"Okay," said Ale, "let me take a shot at a strategy to attempt to solve a number of problems. You can tell me when I'm done if you agree or not."

"Alright, shoot!" said Terry.

"Right now the Navy contract represents approximately eighty percent of our annual revenues, right?"

"Yes," said Terry, "maybe even more."

"So let's do everything we can to keep that part of the business going, at least for awhile, even though we may be taking it on the chin with the current pricing. What we must do is to build other market segments of business around the current Navy core. So is it realistic to assume that we can build a commercial pilot training program and that, at some point in the next two years, it will provide the same gross revenues to Camber that the Navy is now producing?"

"Sure," said Terry, "but you want to replace the Navy contract with the commercial program?"

"Not necessarily now but perhaps down the road if they don't agree to increase their pricing of the contract. But in the meantime the strategy is that we will grow three separate service divisions of this business. One will serve the Navy contract, another will attract and train airline-ready pilot candidates, and the third will focus on the smaller but potentially more lucrative civilian private pilot market in the Baltimore/Washington marketplace. We can initially plan a revenue segmentation of 40% from the Navy, 40% from the commercial airline training division, and 20% from the civilian market training."

"That sounds very good and doable, Ale," said Terry thoughtfully. "But how do we address the personnel problem that started this whole conversation?"

"Well," she said, "from your previous comments it is obvious that we're going to have to try to make do with the talent that we now have even though it is pretty inferior. So we'll have to train them to do what we want the way we want it done. They won't respond positively to the training unless they are motivated to make the changes that will have to be made. So we'll use the unveiling of our new multi-purpose flight school concept as a motivational tool. We will hire someone to create all of the standardized documentation necessary to make Camber a first class learning environment. And we will use the new format as a recruiting mechanism to attempt to lure flight instructors to come to work for us. As we are recruiting some new blood into the organization, we will also be formally evaluating the training progress of the instructors we now have. Those who are not progressing satisfactorily will be leaving us, and we will be replacing them with the new hires who will have agreed to work the way we want them to work."

"That makes a lot of sense!" Terry's mind was operating at full speed now. "We establish ourselves as a premier provider of civilian flight training, which will not only attract students but instructors as well."

"Right, Terry. We know that the demand is there, but what we must do is to provide the supply side of the equation."

Ale was busily jotting some notes on a pad in front of her. She paused and said, "You know, Terry, we have the hundred day plan well behind us, but we haven't yet replaced it with a full long-term strategic plan. We can no longer afford the excuse that we are too busy to do that."

"You're right! Let's clear our schedules and get it done," said Terry.

Ale and Terry opened their laptops, logged in to their schedules, and then proceeded to earmark heavy amounts of time in the upcoming weeks to create and finalize Camber's Five-year Strategic Plan which will serve as their roadmap for the success of this now promising enterprise.

* * * * *

Later that evening Terry was sitting at his dining room table in the home that he had occupied for nearly thirty years. He was shaking his head as he reviewed his personal financial situation over and over again. *I have enough cash sitting in my checking and savings accounts,* he thought, *to cover Ale's salary and benefits for another couple of months. But then what do I do? I just know that Camber is going to pay off for us—I just know it! I am going to have to find a way to keep Ale and me financially afloat until it does!*

EIGHTEEN

SHORTLY AFTER EARNING his MBA a few decades ago Terry Longbow was hired by The American Management Association, an international provider of management training and education headquartered in New York City. Terry still describes his three years traveling throughout America and Canada teaching for AMA as enlightening and life-changing. He began as an instructor teaching three-day seminars in the fundamentals of management and finance to entry-level supervisors usually in hotel meeting rooms in the largest cities on the continent. He fared extremely well earning exceptionally high marks from his audiences on the evaluation forms that they submitted at the end of each seminar. Although the constant travel quickly became hard on him and his young family, he enjoyed every minute of time in front of dozens, and sometimes hundreds of people, and he soon was promoted into the AMA President's Association program. This division of the giant purveyor of management wisdom was dedicated to delivering seminars and workshops exclusively to chief executive and chief operating officers of some of the largest corporations in the world.

Terry rapidly became a regular facilitator at President's Association conferences around the globe, which was a positive turn for him in three ways. First he was delivering a single workshop in a three-hour time period rather than having to hold the attention of a group of adults for three full days. In addition to the shorter delivery time, the high concentration of corporate presidents and top decision-makers in each session significantly broadened his networking contacts and capabilities, a factor that would become crucial for his career only a few years later. Finally, Terry was groomed by the vast production talent at AMA to be a specialist in strategic planning, a skill that endeared him to his high-level audiences. This paved the way for him to lead the development of strategic plans for large corporations at AMA's Strategic Planning Center at Lake Hamilton, New York. He has often said that the education he received from his AMA experience was far more valuable to his career than all of the courses he took from undergraduate school through his MBA and his later doctoral work at Stanford. Just three years after beginning his work with AMA the chairman of a large corporation in Memphis offered Terry an opportunity to turn-around a company subsidiary and Terry's career as a turn-around specialist was launched.

Although Terry was good at what he did for AMA and the corporations that he worked with, one of the reasons for his rapid success in the field was the popularity of his specialty. During the last half of the Twentieth Century, a number of concepts were popularized primarily by the mass marketing of books by the publishing arm of AMA, and the terms used to describe them became industry buzzwords virtually overnight. Zero Based Budgeting, Management by Objectives, Leadership, and of course, Strategic Planning were successfully marketed to willing and wealthy company decision-makers who cumulatively turned the management training process into a multibillion dollar empire. Although Terry himself did not become a millionaire as a result of his work with the popular strategic planning trend he did well for himself and he was able to lay the groundwork for a multi-decade career running companies and returning them into productive and profitable enterprises.

Much to Terry's dismay the last half of the final decade of the Twentieth Century signaled an ominous change for the way corporate strategic plans were viewed and constructed, especially in the hi-tech industries and in the start-up arena. From the mid- to late 1990s the Internet and Internet related companies were emerging and growing as rapidly as employees could be hired and trained to support the growth. These fledgling companies were awash in cash as eager and greedy venture capitalists, angel investors, and even common investors literally stood in line to hand over large sums of capital to the new elite entrepreneurs to fund their .com ventures of grandeur and promise. Many would later call this time of unbridled enthusiasm for the Internet boom the era of the .con, rather than .com, and for good reason.

Most of the young tycoons-to-be had strong engineering backgrounds and skills and remarkably little business training or acumen. And they soon learned after tossing their technical hats into the corporate ring that the arduous process associated with the traditional development and implementation of comprehensive company long-term strategic plans was not necessary in order to secure the venture capital required to launch their ideas and inventions into a profitable enterprise. It rapidly became an accepted practice among the wealthy potential investors to sign a large check over to the sure thing du jour after viewing a protracted and colorful PowerPoint presentation and skimming an extensive, yet mostly contrived, set of financial projections for the future of the start-up presented in an extensive Excel format. The investors were generally blinded to the overwhelming business and management naiveté of the entrepreneurs by the prospect of returns on their investments beyond their wildest dreams resulting from buying into a piece of the .com gravy train.

Terry quickly learned during this decade of irrational exuberance that most potential clients seeking his services were not looking for his comprehensive approach to corporate strategic planning. Instead, they were seeking someone to prepare a quick-and-dirty PowerPoint presentation and an accompanying set of Excel financial spreadsheets that would dazzle an unsuspecting quiescent investor or customer into submission. He also discovered that the .com bubble that burst with disastrous consequences around the turn of the century did not eradicate the notion that quick-and-dirty was still the best way to approach corporate strategic planning. His frequent attempts to dispel this notion yielded only frustration and disappointment as he courted potential clients during the first decade of this millennium. Convinced that his approach to planning was still the most viable and productive, Terry confined his and Ale's focus on enterprises in distress. The owners and creditors of these turn-around challenges were usually not in a position to haggle over the techniques required to save them.

The project resulting in the creation of a strategic plan for Camber Flight Training, Inc. was a daunting one, not because of unfamiliarity with the work involved, but more due to the time away from the day-to-day operation of the company that would be necessary to develop the plan. This is a serious disadvantage of a planning process in any growing enterprise, but it was particularly difficult for Terry and Ale because they could not rely on any of their employees to run the company effectively in their absence. It was for this reason that Terry insisted that Ale complete the financial and operations sections of the strategic plan for Camber while he would address the less time consuming facets of the plan leaving him time to be on-site at BWI to manage the daily operations. Ale balked at first claiming that she did not possess the expertise necessary to develop the plan on her own, but then she eventually caved to his better judgment and agreed to finish the bulk of the document.

"I have something else very important to discuss with you, Terry and now seems as good a time as any." Ale closed the folder in front of her and looked Terry right in the eyes.

"Sounds serious," he said.

"It is. I need to get my MBA and things aren't going to lighten up any for me in the next few years, so I think I better get it done now."

Terry thought for a moment never breaking his stare at Ale. "I have always tried to support you, Ale."

"No, you haven't just tried. You have always supported me, and that's the only reason that I feel so strongly that I should get this done now. I know that you know how valuable this missing piece is to my career no matter what the future may bring."

Ale made sure that she did not communicate any doubt on her part about the future of Camber, Orion, or her working relationship with Terry when she chose those words to use in this setting. But the reality was that she was getting more and more uncomfortable with the direction that the companies were taking and with the cost of her salary and benefits that Terry was having to shoulder on his own.

"Will you major in human resources?" he asked her.

"No, I already have a strong background in HR, and I have my Senior Professional in Human Resources certification. I have found a program that offers an MBA in finance in one year, and I can take most of my classes online. That means no driving to a campus, sitting in classrooms, and no scheduling conflicts."

"When do you start?" Terry asked with a smile.

"This month," she said. "So you're with me on this?" she asked sheepishly.

"One hundred percent, kid. You just be sure to let me know what I can do to help."

"I'll need a lot of encouragement," then she paused and smiled, "and maybe a lot of babysitting."

"You've got it—and anything else you need." Terry stared at Ale for a few moments and then said, "You're going to do just great, Ale!"

* * * * *

A strategic planning document for a company is the creation of a detailed road map for the firm's management to follow. Usually the strongest result of the exercise is the process itself, which should include all of the employees in the company contributing to each of the elements of the plan. This inclusive approach to planning can serve to reinforce the motivation of each employee toward the successful implementation of the plan and the ultimate success of the company. But in this case time was of the essence, and if the two turn-around specialists were to achieve success in as short a time as possible they would have to eliminate the time-consuming involvement of all but a few chosen employees. The fact that Ale's level of confidence in the majority of the employees was as low as it could be was not at all lost in this decision.

Ale was most anxious to create the current and projected financial spreadsheets due to her lack of confidence in her own ability to do so. She would first have to finalize a set of assumptions that would serve as a solid foundation for the entire plan as well as the financial section. A group of well thought-out and reasonable assumptions serves as the cornerstone of any credible strategic plan and is the key difference between a solid business plan and the feeble attempts contrived by the remaining veterans of the failed .com era. Ale would build this set of assumptions for the Camber plan from the pieces of the puzzle that were already in place at the small and unstable company. The Navy program was firmly established, and she and Terry had already decided that they wanted it to represent 40% of the total revenues of the company at some point in the future. That meant that Ale could use all of the elements of the Navy business as a platform for building the expansion of the enterprise into the commercial and civilian markets. So based on her earlier conversations with Terry she endeavored to create a set of reasonable working assumptions that would establish the future Navy work as 40% of the firm's total revenues while building the commercial training division into another 40%. This while growing the private civilian market segment into a 20% share of total sales.

Ale was off and running. She had established her starting point, and she had identified her growth goals. Now it was just a matter of fitting the pieces of the complex but manageable plan together into an integrated and meaningful whole.

Terry had busily covered the four walls of his Orion office in Columbia, Maryland, with large pieces of flip chart paper upon which he had scribbled the notes of his work on the company's due diligence results. Meanwhile, Ale had set up shop in the conference room across the hall and was fully engrossed in the task of creating a solid foundation for the development of a comprehensive mission statement and then a complete assemblage of financial and operations planning materials.

To any objective outside observer of this joint creative process the stark contrast in working styles between the two executives would have immediately been obvious. But to Terry and Ale it was business as usual. Terry, having been entrenched for some forty years in the "old school" of project management was frantically jotting notes and ideas on large pieces of paper fastened to an easel in one corner of his office. As quickly as he would fill a piece of the paper he would tear it across the top and fasten it to an empty section of the wall with strips of masking tape. His office was cluttered with paper strewn across his desk, his credenza, and even on the floor. The only recognizable artifact in this disaster area of an office was a small, black, thirty-year old Hewlett-Packard financial calculator sitting on top of some papers on his desk.

Unlike Terry, Ale appeared to be in calm and total control of the development of her parts of the plan. She was sitting at a clean and freshly waxed conference table with only her laptop open in front of her. Ideas were obviously flowing freely from her mind, through her fingers and onto the pages of the Word and Excel software illuminated on the screen in front of her. The conference room was totally quiet, a serene tribute to the Twenty-First Century approach to executive creativity and documentation in stark contrast to the disorganized activity occurring in the office just across the hall. This unfettered approach by Ale to the creation of a complex and vital document that would control the future of a vibrant corporation was not being exercised because she had less work to do than Terry. It demonstrated the working Modus Operandi of the new generation of managers in the United States and around the globe. They are inextricably tethered to the immediacy of a worldwide information systems network and infinitely more responsive to the demanding, integrated needs of organizations and humans. And it was no coincidence that it was Ale who occupied the conference room, soon to become the command center for this critical project, rather than Terry, who was much more comfortable working within the confines of his spacious yet delineated office. An objective outside observer might be inclined to ask at what point does the student actually become the teacher?

For five straight days, the two owner executives labored over the creation of different parts of the strategic plan that would serve as the roadmap for Camber Flight Training during the ensuing five years. Ale arrived at the Orion offices early in the morning and worked uninterrupted until late in the afternoon taking short breaks only to stretch her legs. Terry spent the mornings at BWI and arrived at the Columbia office shortly after lunch-time. Late each afternoon Terry and Ale would meet together in the conference room to review the details of the work they had accomplished individually to that point. They would challenge each other with detailed questions and they would discuss at length how all of the separate pieces of the plan that was taking shape would be merged seamlessly into one cohesive and well-structured planning document. This was not an unusual methodology for these two executives to follow. They had often found themselves thousands of miles apart on different job sites while attempting to coordinate the documentation of yet a third project in order to meet an impending deadline.

Ale often likened this fragmented approach to the building of a sizable bridge. She had always been amazed by the intricacies involved in the design and building of the San Francisco Bay Bridge. One time when she and Terry were on a flight out of San Francisco climbing out over the bay, the bridge was clearly visible through the window below. Ale pointed to the bridge and began to explain her fascination with its creation to Terry.

"Have you ever taken the time to look at pictures of the construction of the Golden Gate Bridge?" she asked and then continued without waiting for an answer. "They didn't start at one end and keep building until they wound up somewhere on the other side. They started on both sides and built to the center of the bay. The planning for the construction of this bridge took years of painstaking precision. There was just no room for anyone on the planning or the construction teams to have any less than absolute commitment and accountability for every single thing that they did on the job. What if someone had experienced a 'bad hair day' and the result was that the two halves of the span suddenly did not meet exactly in the middle? There are no do-over's when something like this happens. It must be exact, or they've just wasted millions of tons of steel and hundreds of thousands of worker-hours on a gigantic tribute to human ineptitude."

Although Terry did not exactly share her excitement with the description of that gigantic project, he appreciated the point that she was making. From the time of that brief discussion, they both worked closely on weaving the separate parts of any project that they created independently with the challenges faced in the building of that bridge clearly in their minds.

The Camber plan began to take on a life of its own during those five intense days. Ale had initially invested a substantial amount of time and energy in the crafting of a mission statement that would succinctly identify the primary business purpose of the Camber enterprise while also placing an adequate amount of emphasis on satisfying the interests of the various people associated with the firm. Although still a little skeptical about the wording of the statement she had created, she presented it to Terry during one of their first afternoon review meetings together.

"The mission of Camber Flight Training, Inc. is to provide the most comprehensive, highest quality flight training experience to our customers consistently delivered in the most efficient and respectful manner possible. We will be outstanding corporate citizens and neighbors to all who come into contact with us and we will continually strive to provide a high quality work environment for all of our employees while creating a profit and adding a maximal level of value to the investment of our stockholders."

Terry was acutely aware that the business people who were less than impressed with the whole idea of the value of a strategic plan were especially critical of the usefulness of a mission statement. In fact, many considered it little more than a flowery testimonial to meaningless prose. But through the years he had become a staunch believer in the organizational utility of the concept. He would often preach to whoever would listen that a strong and internally respected mission statement could prevent a company from straying into a marriage made in hell such as the Time-Warner/AOL debacle. It could also possibly help to prevent the collapse of a business altogether as happened with several airlines in recent decades.

Terry warmly received the mission statement proposed by Ale and commented that it embodied both the spirit and functional purpose of the enterprise while placing just the right amount of emphasis upon the interests of investors and stockholders. He was particularly pleased with the latter portion of the statement since he and Ale were not receiving any direct compensation for their efforts on this project. They would have to rely on a significant increase in the total value of the company in order to make the venture eventually worth their while.

   Ale had invested an enormous amount of time and energy concentrating on the financial spreadsheets that would appear in the plan. There were two basic reasons for this amount of focus on just one section of the document. This was not her forte, and therefore, she had to work twice as hard and long as Terry would have in order to be comfortable with the results. The second reason for her fixation on the numbers was that she believed strongly that if the financial weaknesses of any company could be identified and subsequently strengthened everything else that might be weak about the company would be much easier to fix. In the case of Camber, she zeroed-in on the firm's seriously anemic capitalization and its resulting shortage of cash.

   Ale's approach to the creation of corporate financial projections was disarmingly simple. She started with what she knew to be fact from past and present documentation, then applied a list of working assumptions about future operations to those facts. The result was a series of detailed portraits of what the months and years of future operations should yield in the format of the company's financial statements. But as simple as this process sounds the underlying basis for her assumptions was far more complicated.

   Ale had shared Terry's frustration from the very beginning of their work at Camber by the excessive amount of time that the flight school's aircraft sat dormant on the ground when the weather and other conditions were more than acceptable for safe flying. When developing her underlying assumptions and projections for the scheduling of aircraft for training missions Ale took a page out of Southwest Airlines' book of profit-making tips. The airline began its operations in Texas in the mid-1960s and faced stiff competition in the early years from Braniff Airlines and others in the region. Chairman Herb Kelleher, the spirited chain-smoking founder of Southwest learned early in the game that commercial aircraft that sit on the ground not only do not make any profits, but they actually cost the company money. So he and his management team initiated a revolutionary policy at the fledgling airline requiring that aircraft landing at any particular airport would spend an extremely short amount of time in turn-around, that is, unloading passengers and baggage, cleaning the cabin, then reloading passengers and baggage. The new policy was so successful that Southwest became profitable for the next sixty years, and Braniff went out of business only a few years later.

Of course, there were many other reasons that Southwest Airlines became a legend of profitability in the airline industry and Ale knew that several of the others were applicable to Camber as well. But for the purpose of developing an aircraft scheduling strategy for the company the Southwest turn-around model served her needs quite well.

Ale's diagnosis of the primary scheduling problem at Camber was that there was literally no discipline involved in the system that had been in place since the company began operations a few years earlier. The schedule for each aircraft available to fly was essentially a blank sheet. There were no specific time slots to be filled, but rather a student would agree to a time for a flight that was convenient to both the student and an instructor and the instructor would enter the agreed upon time onto the schedule of an available aircraft. Often the time period reserved was much longer than required for the flight lesson to be completed, and just as often flights would exceed the time period scheduled simply because the student and instructor decided during the lesson to land at an airport and grab a soft drink. This haphazard and undisciplined approach to scheduling either left a significant amount of aircraft idle time in between the lessons on the schedule, or left students and instructors waiting for an hour or more for an aircraft that they had scheduled but was late returning to the school. Either way the scheduling process was frustrating for many students and extraordinarily costly to the company. The solution was relatively uncomplicated to identify but would prove difficult to implement.

Ale had alluded to a more streamlined scheduling system in an earlier company meeting, and it was met with significant resistance from instructors and Midshipmen alike. Nevertheless, she used the Internet to research the sunrise and sunset times for every day of the year at BWI. She established a standard lesson duration for each aircraft of three hours which gave the student and instructor approximately thirty minutes to get out to the plane, pre-flight and start it, taxi to the active runway, and take-off. The allotted time also allowed for another fifteen minutes for the aircraft to reach the practice area over the Eastern Shore of Maryland. The student-instructor team would then have a full hour-and-a-half for the actual lesson, another fifteen minutes to make their way back to the airport, and thirty minutes to deplane and walk to the Camber offices. In addition to being a much more streamlined and disciplined system of scheduling flight lessons, it was a blueprint for potential profits.

Camber earned its revenues primarily from two sources with both tied directly to the clock. The company charged students by the hour for the amount of time recorded that they spent with an instructor on the ground and in the air, and also by the hour for the amount of time that an aircraft's engine was actually running. The latter was recorded by a clock-like instrument, called a Hobbs meter, in the aircraft that displayed the time that the engine was actually running in hours and tenths of an hour. Ale's strategy with this new scheduling system was that every three-hour block of time on the schedule would be filled with a student lesson which would yield three hours of guaranteed revenue for the instructor's time and also nearly three hours of additional revenue for the aircraft. Of course, she would constantly remind the instructors that they must get to the plane and start it as soon as possible, and leave it running at the end of the time block as long as possible, in order to maximize the revenues for that particular lesson.

The new scheduling system devised by Ale and incorporated into software to be made available to all company computers was the cornerstone of the entire financial structure of the firm's new strategic plan. Although the official title of the program was the "Camber Flight Schedule," Ale had designed her own financial reporting system tied directly to the scheduling program which she called her "Asset Utilization" program. From this control program, she could access data at any time of the day or night that would immediately tell her the billing experience for any aircraft and any instructor. She programmed the system to account for the times and/or days that a particular aircraft was unavailable for flights due to maintenance requirements. And she designed into the system the capability of identifying exactly when the weather was unacceptable for safe flight and how many night hours there were in a given day. Flight instruction was generally not conducted during the night hours.

Ale was pleased with the result. From the data about maintenance, weather, and night hours consistently being fed into her system, she was now able to view the exact number of hours billed for instructors and for aircraft compared to the number of hours that could have, or should have been billed. It was a productivity control system sorely needed by the struggling company.

In a sort of "road test" of her new invention, she entered all of the historical data from a recent month in which revenues were particularly low and then the data from a month with relatively high revenues. The results startled her. Ale had expected the aircraft and instructor utilization rates to be low, but she had a difficult time believing the actual numbers. During the slow month tested the billed hours, and therefore dollars, for Camber's aircraft was a dismal 6% of the hours that were actually available and acceptable to have been billed. The instructor hours were not much better, with only 8% of those available having actually generated revenue. The month with the highest activity level which was tested showed that the aircraft generated 17% of the revenue they were actually capable of producing and the instructors slightly less than 20% of their potential. Ale was appalled and excited at the same time.

Every successful business incorporates a strong and effective system for controlling the productivity of all of its assets and human resources. Camber now had one as well. And Ale was enormously proud that she had designed it independently.

NINETEEN

Leo was sitting quietly at his desk in the early morning hours of what he had expected to be a routine spring day at the Academy when his cell phone rang startling him slightly. "Lieutenant Forrester," he answered formally.

"Let's play hooky today," he heard from the other end of the call.

"Ale?" he asked inquisitively.

"How many other women do you have calling you early in the morning and asking you if you want to spend the day with them?" she replied.

"Well, uh, none," he said obviously still trying to recover from the surprise of her call.

"Okay," Ale continued, "are we on or not?"

"What did you have in mind?" Leo asked.

"No," she stated firmly. "No planning—I'm sick of planning everything. Meet me at The Deck when you can. We're just going to see where this day takes us, okay?"

"I'll be there as soon as I can," came Leo's reply.

Ale made the call from home just before she would have left for the office. She returned to her bedroom and changed into a more comfortable combination of jeans and a tee shirt and quickly slipped out the front door. She was glad that her mother left a few minutes earlier to drop the boys off at school so that she would not have to explain the sudden change of clothing. Before getting into her car for the trip to the Eastern Shore, she sent a brief e-mail to Terry explaining that something had come up and that she would not be at the office or available by phone for the entire day. She knew that this would make him worry, so she made sure to say in the message that it was nothing urgent. Terry and Ale had developed an extraordinary working relationship over the years. It was extremely unusual that either of them would miss a day of work, but when it was necessary neither would ask any questions. Ale didn't expect any now.

The Deck was a relatively small restaurant on the Eastern Shore approximately six miles east of the Chesapeake Bay Bridge in an area known as the Kent Narrows. There were several restaurants in this area, most situated on scenic waterfront property and catering to tourists traveling from the Baltimore-Washington-Annapolis corridor to a vacation in Ocean City, Maryland, or just to spend a day in the area feasting on crab dishes and other plentiful seafood fare. But unlike most of these other popular eating establishments, The Deck was nestled into a remote cove area which was difficult for the typical tourist to find. It was perfect, however, for the local Kent Island residents looking to escape the noisy and crowded venues positioned near the off-ramps of the heavily traveled Route 50/301 extending from the Bay Bridge through Kent Narrows to the seashore points to the east. Due to the heavy morning traffic it took Ale nearly an hour and a half to make the trip. When she arrived at around mid-morning Leo was already sitting at an outside table overlooking to the south the serene body of water known as Wells Cove. Seeing her appear through the glass doors separating the indoor restaurant from the outside deck, he immediately rose from his chair and walked toward her. There was no one else sitting at the tables on the deck, which was exactly the kind of solitude that both sought frequently during the months that they had been meeting. Ale gave Leo a brief hug and extended her left cheek inviting a friendly peck as was her customary greeting ritual for any number of people whom she considered friends. Leo happily obliged. He pulled a chair from the table and slid it back under Ale until she was comfortably seated.

"So what possessed you to invite me to play hooky with you today, Ale?" he asked with a broad grin.

"Well let's see," she replied. "I've had my fill of Camber and the challenges there, and I figured I could use a little time away from Terry as well. I haven't spent more than a few hours or so each week with you since we met and I got to thinking that maybe it's time we have some fun together. And I am developing a new philosophy requiring that every once in a while I am just going to have to say 'oh what the hell' and do something crazy. That enough reasons for you?"

"More than enough," he answered. "I'm just glad you called!"

Ale sat quietly as Leo described the kinds of daily activities that had been on his calendar prior to her call. She attempted to demonstrate a polite interest in what he was saying, but she was more focused on the quiet nature of her surroundings and the gradually warming sun that was causing her face to tingle slightly. She watched over the side of the deck as small to medium-sized fish lazily moved in wide circles in the water below. Ducks gently glided in groups on the surface as if to convince anyone watching that they were en route to some predetermined destination, yet all the while knowing that they had nowhere to go. She occasionally nodded in agreement with something Leo was saying while thinking that this was precisely where she needed to be at this particular time. *Why haven't I done this kind of thing more often?* she wondered. *Day after day, week after week I am consumed with the responsibility of taking care of the needs of others. My family, Terry, and Camber all make demands on me and my time constantly, and working hard to satisfy all of those needs leaves me no time for myself. I am here in the equivalent of a quiet paradise with someone who has demonstrated that he cares very much about me and my welfare and happiness. I am going to make the most of this day—my day!*

"Look at me," said Leo. "I'm talking your ear off about stuff I'm sure you have no interest in."

"No, Leo that's OK. I'm just enjoying being here. This is a terrific spot, and I am just soaking it all in."

The two finally ordered an early lunch from the waitress who had patiently visited their table several times earlier only to be told that they wanted to sit and talk for awhile before having something to eat. Leo informed the server that he would have a broiled crab cake while telling Ale that the crab cakes at The Deck were superior to any he had ever enjoyed anywhere else. Ale, with a polite deference to Leo's culinary suggestion, ordered a lightly broiled rockfish with the locally famous Old Bay seasoning sprinkled on top. Both had been sipping on iced tea, which was being regularly replenished without either of them even noticing. While they ate they talked about the things that meant so much in their individual lives. Ale spoke at length about Stefan's and Johan's interests in sports, especially soccer and basketball, and Leo described in detail his achievements as a competitive swimmer from his childhood years through high school. And then about his adoption of football as his primary sport in his freshman year of high school and then through his four years at the Academy. They traded stories about the years when they were growing up, Leo on Lake Minnetonka in Minnesota and Ale in Montevideo, Uruguay. The time flew by, and Ale felt a warmth and comfort both with her surroundings and with the company she was keeping that she had not experienced for many years.

When they had finished lunch and realized they had been sitting for hours in the same place, they stood and walked away from the table.

"What would you like to do now, Ale?" asked Leo.

"I don't know. What do you suggest?" was her reply.

"I think we should rent a small boat and explore this incredible place by water for the rest of the afternoon."

"Oh I don't know, Leo. I'm not much of a small boat person."

"Tell you what," he continued. "We'll get the boat and give it a try just in this area for awhile. If you don't like it, we'll come right back and that will be that. What do you say?"

"Okay Leo, I guess I did say that I wanted to see where the day takes us. I'm game!"

They walked to a pier not far from The Deck where there was a small shack and some rowboats and canoes tied to wooden pilings adjacent to the pier. Leo decided to rent a rowboat with a small outboard motor so that they could return quickly in case of sudden bad weather or if Ale did not like the experience. The rowboat had two wooden seats situated from the center and back toward the motor and a large cushion extending from the floor to the bow so that an occupant could more comfortably relax in a semi-lying position while enjoying the ride. Ale chose to sit facing forward on the wooden seat farthest from the engine while Leo sat on the one closest to it.

"Ready to go, Ale?" asked Leo with a large grin.

"I guess so. You're not going to do anything crazy with this thing are you, Leo?"

"Smooth, quiet sailing all the way me lady," came Leo's reply.

Leo started the engine, which turned out to be quieter than Ale had expected. He untied the ropes attached to the pilings, increased the power from the engine, and they were off.

"Where are we going?" Ale asked without turning her head back toward Leo.

"Wherever the day takes us," replied Leo. "That's what you said isn't it?"

The small boat proceeded slowly down the eastern side of Wells Cove toward a point of land jutting from the east containing a relatively new community called Oyster Cove.

"How are you doing, Ale?" asked Leo.

"I'm fine," she answered. "Why?"

"Because if you don't like it now is the time to turn back—before we get too far from the Narrows."

"No, I like it! I'm in for the long haul."

Traveling south past the Oyster Cove point they crossed the mouth of a body of water to their left known as Marshy Creek and proceeded toward a larger piece of land, which Leo explained contained the Horsehead Farm Wildlife Sanctuary. He was careful not to spoil the tranquility that Ale seemed to be savoring, but Leo told her about the many times that he and some friends from the Academy while he was a student there, would rent a sailboat and sail this same route for the better part of a day until they reached a farm owned by an Academy alumnus. He said they would camp on the property of the generous naval officer and then the next morning set out to sail the route back to where they had rented the boat. Ale was quietly listening to Leo's stories of his days at the Academy. She could not help but wonder how much of a normal life she had missed by immigrating from Uruguay, working so hard to support herself and her mother here in the States, and then marrying so young. She was captivated by the adventures of Leo Forrester and his Midshipmen friends from over a decade ago. She never once thought about the cell phone she had left in her car or about the e-mails she might be missing while on this little journey. She just sat and watched as the land passed by and listened as Leo quietly narrated the trip.

Leo steered the boat on a course parallel to the shoreline on their left. As they passed by the Prospect Bay Country Club and then the mouth of Shaw Bay, Ale had taken the lead in the storytelling. She described memories of her early childhood including the difficulties created by her parents divorcing when she was only four years old. She then recalled her days as a student at an all girls boarding school in Argentina. Every once in a while she would stop talking and ask Leo if he was truly interested in hearing these stories of her past, and he would assure her that he was hanging on her every word. Nearly two hours after leaving Kent Narrows, Leo changed to a southwesterly course and announced to Ale that they would be stopping to explore a small town that he thought she would like. A short time later they entered St. Michaels Harbor and tied-up their little boat between two enormous pleasure yachts at the town dock, and then walked past the old St. Michaels Light House toward the center of town. Ale was thrilled as they visited shops along Main Street that appeared as they might have over a century earlier. She had never been particularly interested in antiques and old stuff in general, but there was something about this little old town that captivated her imagination. After an hour of exploring they had dinner at The Crab Claw, another waterfront restaurant serving seafood specialties and once again they sat on an outdoor deck overlooking the quiet harbor.

During dinner, it seemed as though they could never run out of stories to tell and Ale observed a side of Leo that had not previously revealed itself. A dry wit, masquerading as a funny series of one-liners permeated the discussion throughout an appetizer and main course and left Ale laughing so hard that her sides hurt and she had difficulty catching her breath. She wondered why she had not spotted this entertaining side of Leo before.

Later, as they finished fueling the boat and began to pull away from the St. Michaels pier she realized that he was now the most relaxed she had ever seen him and that he too must be enjoying their day together enormously. For the trip north and back to the Narrows, she decided to sit on the bottom of the boat with her back and head resting on the large cushion leading up to the bow. She figured that this position would be more relaxing and easier on her back. It would also have her facing Leo steering from the back of the boat making conversation a bit more direct. Her calves were raised and resting comfortably on the wooden seat between her and Leo. *Now this is the life!* she thought as the boat departed St. Michaels Harbor. She watched the small quaint town disappear behind Leo as she continued her thought, *I hope I get to come back here soon, and I hope it is with Leo again!*

The sun was still warm and was focusing its rays on the right side of her face as it occupied its early evening position in the southwestern sky. The trip back up the shoreline seemed to Ale to be shorter than the one earlier in the day, although she knew that it was just an illusion. The two friends continued their conversation from dinner pausing frequently to enjoy the peaceful signs of nature all around them. When they were once again passing the Horsehead Farm Wildlife Sanctuary they saw dozens of birds of all types flying over the shoreline and as Leo steered closer they could easily observe more wildlife on the shore in the evening sun.

"Want to stop here and watch for awhile?" asked Leo.

"Sure," responded Ale.

When Leo shut the engine down there was a peaceful serenity about this spot that overwhelmed her. She watched quietly as a large group of deer worked on their evening meal near the waterline.

"You know, Leo," she was the first to break the almost eerie silence, "this reminds me of a place that I used to love in Uruguay. I would go there with my mother and brother and my mother would get so angry with me because I just walked away from them to be alone with nature. And when I was alone I would dream about my future. Of course at that age the dream of a quest for happiness and fulfillment included white knights and castles. But the solitude of places like this one and the one in Uruguay just carries me into a totally different world."

Leo did not respond right away. But a few moments later he said, "And what is your dream now, Ale?"

"What?" she said as though the spell upon her had been interrupted. "Oh, I don't dream anymore, Leo. At least I don't dream about myself or my future. I do dream about the future of my sons though."

"Okay that's understandable I guess. But I want you to dream right now—about yourself. What do you most want out of life? What do you want your future to be? What is going to make Alejandra German happy and fulfilled?"

Ale sat up with her weight on her left arm and entered into what must have appeared to Leo to be a few moments of deep introspection.

"I guess I want what everyone else wants out of life," she began. "I want to be a terrific mom. But in order for that dream to come true I have to be there for my sons. I want to be a successful businessperson preferably at the top of a large multinational corporation. But those two dreams are seriously conflicting, aren't they? How can I always be there for my sons if I'm spending all of my time working and on the road for a large corporation? I guess it all confuses me and frustrates me, and that's why I try not to think about it. Ever."

"Are you happy with your life now?" asked Leo.

Ale knew all along that this conversation with Leo was inevitable. He was so easy to talk to, and he had become such a close friend that assuming she would never have to disclose to him her frustrations at home and with Franco was just not a realistic assumption.

"Not really," she responded.

"When you were that little girl in Uruguay what is it that you would have dreamed for your happiness today? Just one thing that you don't have now that you would have dreamed back then for yourself at this point in your life?"

"Remember," she said, "I was dreaming that I would be a princess surrounded by white knights and living in a castle. I think that was my way of portraying an adult life filled with the love and the devotion of a husband who clearly demonstrates his unconditional caring for my happiness."

"Obviously you are saying that you do not have that now," Leo said with a cautious tone.

"It's complicated, Leo. Franco is a wonderful father to the boys, and he works extremely hard eighteen hours a day to become a doctor. He's not a bad person by any stretch of the imagination."

"But he is fulfilling his dream for himself, right? He's not fulfilling your dream for the two of you is he?" Leo seemed to be trying to be particularly careful. He was apparently hoping to turn this conversation into one with a positive outcome for Ale, not one that turned a beautiful day uncomfortable at the very end.

"I guess," responded Ale. "I could never in a million years leave him, Leo! I experienced what it was like to be a young child of divorce, and I would never subject my sons to that nightmare under any circumstances!"

"I would never even hint at the suggestion that you should leave him, Ale. We're just talking here."

"I know. But he's never going to change. Now all of his attention is focused on becoming a doctor. Later it will all be focused on being a doctor. That's why I don't dream for myself anymore, Leo. It's a frustrating exercise in futility. He is never anywhere near as attentive to my needs as I would like and he never will be. But I am stuck with it. My boys come first, always. I would never do anything to hurt them. So I am just stuck. It's that simple." She paused for several moments and then said, "I guess you think I'm the most selfish woman in the world, don't you?"

"Not at all, Ale. We all have needs, and we all dream that those needs will be satisfied in our lives one way or another. But you can't stop dreaming for yourself. You can *never* stop dreaming for yourself."

The next few minutes were quiet ones. The two friends sat and watched the wildlife show being played out in front of them. And then Leo said, "We have to go."

Ale was afraid that perhaps she had said too much, that maybe Leo was suddenly anxious to bring this day to an end after her revelation.

"Is something wrong, Leo?" she asked hesitantly.

"No," he replied quickly as he started the engine. "There might be some weather moving in, and I don't want to get stuck out here if it hits."

"But the sky is blue, how do you know there might be bad weather?" she asked.

Leo pointed to the far western horizon and said, "See that one high cloud out there on the horizon?"

"Yes."

"That's the leading edge of an anvil-head belonging to a thunderstorm below and behind it. I don't know whether it is moving directly at us. It may pass to our north or south, but I'm not going to take any chances especially with you aboard!"

"Okay," said Ale, "it's getting kind of late anyway. I just don't want this day to end anytime soon."

"Me either, Ale. Me either!"

During the next forty-five minutes, the small boat completed the trip to the Kent Narrows pier where Ale and Leo's day-long adventure had begun. And in the same amount of time the thunderstorm Leo had spotted earlier was in full view just to the west of them. They had enough time to complete the boat rental transaction with the old man in the shack at the pier and to walk briskly to their cars.

Ale opened her car door and turned to Leo to thank him for a wonderful day. But before she could say anything he placed his right hand on the small of her back and leaned down and gently kissed her. The lack of intensity of the kiss conveyed to her that it was not necessarily one of passion. But the duration of it convinced her that it was not one of mere friendship. Suddenly she slowly eased him away with her hands on his chest, and she turned her head to the side.

"I'm sorry, Ale. I don't know what made me do that—it just came about naturally."

Before he could say another word Ale turned back toward him and placed her arms around his neck, and kissed him with a clearly unmistakable meaning. It began to rain hard as the two continued the embrace. Ale loosened her arms and ended the kiss and stared at him for a moment before getting into her car without saying a word. *What the hell did I just do?* she thought. *What the hell did I just do?*

During the long ride home, the rain pelted her car as vivid lightning lit up the late evening sky and loud thunder bombarded her from all sides. It was all that Ale could do to focus on the road ahead as tears rolled down her cheeks and onto her already soaked tee shirt. She couldn't decide whether she was crying because she felt that Leo had betrayed her trust by kissing her the way he did, or whether it was from the happiness she was feeling after one of the most incredible days of her life. Either way she was confronting the sudden realization that the kiss initiated by Leo, and then reinforced by another from her, immediately transformed a milestone day in their friendship into a decision point in their relationship. *What am I going to do now?* she thought. *I should have known that this could never work as just an innocent friendship. What was I thinking? What am I going to do now?*

Ale pulled the Pathfinder into her driveway, exited and locked it, and then entered the house through the front door. The boys were still up as her mother cleaned the kitchen from dinner and Franco was obviously out for the evening. She skillfully deflected questions from her mother who could tell that she had been crying as she walked her mom to the front door and attempted to reassure her that nothing was wrong. After tucking the boys comfortably in their beds, Ale took a much-needed shower and retired to her own bed. But she was unable to sleep throughout the entire night. At one point, she suddenly felt ill and ran to the bathroom fearing a surge of vomiting that never materialized.

TWENTY

It was the perfect afternoon for flying. Not even the slightest breeze stirred, and the cloudless, deep and brilliant blue sky was breathtaking on this late spring day.

The small two seat training aircraft was heading east in level flight at 2,000 feet having just passed over the Chesapeake Bay Bridge. The pilot, Joel Fadely was on a routine maintenance test flight, usually denoted in a pilot's flight logbook as Mx, meaning that the aircraft had just undergone some sort of engine or airframe repair. Immediately after such work a short test flight conducted by one of the flight school's instructors was customary. Flight instructors had little opportunity to fly alone so they would gladly accept a rare Mx flight to do so. Fadely had requested to be assigned to this flight, and had no intention of making it as short as possible as Ale had directed.

The Diamond DA20 featured a fuselage and wings constructed mostly of glass and carbon reinforced plastic composite materials and a 125 horsepower engine. The nose of the aircraft was pointed directly at the town of Easton in the middle of the Eastern Shore's lush farmland.

The young but experienced flight instructor was feeling particularly feisty on this beautiful afternoon. He intended to exorcise some of the demons of frustration that had haunted him recently after numerous major airlines declined to offer him a real pilot's job.

Fadely was keenly aware that the FAA did not allow the DA 20 to perform any sort of aerobatic maneuvers because the plane's airframe wasn't built for the stress. But the young flight instructor had been exposed to weeks of excruciatingly mundane flying with his students handling the controls most of the time and little opportunity for him to utilize his own skills. *Now*, he thought, *is the time to do some real flying! After all, the main ingredient of excitement in the air is danger now isn't it?*

The frustrated pilot climbed to an altitude of 4,000 feet and made a shallow turn to the left looking intently for any other aircraft in the area, then he did the same to the right. Seeing none he returned the attitude of the plane to straight-and-level, meaning a constant altitude with no turning. Then, in a single smooth coordination of movement between his left hand on the stick, his right hand on the throttle, and his feet squarely on the rudder pedals, he increased the power. He raised the aircraft's nose thirty degrees and initiated full sideways pressure on the stick, first to the left, then after the plane was totally upside down he began easing the pressure slowly. Fadely had successfully completed a barrel roll rotating the aircraft a full 360 degrees around from side to side. A wry smile of contentment appeared on his face as he exhaled and ignored the empty plastic soda bottles and gum wrappers that suddenly became airborne during a moment of weightlessness at the halfway point in the maneuver. It did not even faze him that, had he performed the roll properly, the trash carelessly left on the floor would never have moved. He wasn't looking for perfection, however, he was having too much fun just being free.

Still at 4,000 feet and now pumped with boyish enthusiasm he lowered the plane's nose to increase the airspeed then eased the throttle to the full power position and simultaneously applied steady backward pressure to the stick until his left hand was firmly planted into his stomach. As he held the stick tightly into his gut, he was careful to keep the wings perfectly level. The aircraft progressed steadily upward into the dark blue sky until it was perpendicular with the ground and its nose was pointed straight up. The small engine could not provide enough power to take the plane all the way over the top of the loop and Fadely could feel the small trainer slipping backwards. He immediately recognized this as a potentially perilous situation that could easily lead to the aircraft stalling, entering a spin, and plummeting earthward. But he remained calm drawing upon his many hours of training designed to recognize and recover from stalls and spins as he continued to hold the stick firmly against his body. He patiently waited for the nose and propeller to pass over top of him, and when they did he slowly brought the power back to idle. At the very top of the loop, the lack of power caused a weightless condition for an even longer time than if he were looping a high powered aircraft. Once again empty plastic soda bottles, gum and candy wrappers, and even his flight jacket dropped from the floor of the cockpit to the inside of the Plexiglas canopy over his head, and then back again to the floor as the aircraft completed the loop maneuver. The instructor's skillful hands returned it to a straight-and-level attitude in the sky over the quiet countryside.

Fadely was exhilarated. Just a couple of the simplest aerobatic maneuvers and he felt a sense of serenity that he couldn't remember experiencing in a long while. But the jubilant solitude that he was so enjoying was abruptly interrupted by a colleague's voice in his headset earphones.

He had one of his two communication radios set to a general frequency, called a unicom, that was regularly used by most of the other local flight instructors to communicate with each other in flight. There was nothing official about any of these communications, but the pilots were aware that the FAA occasionally monitored these frequencies which motivated all of them to "keep it clean" when talking to each other. They had adopted a "secret" informal communications code to use with each other on this frequency and also, having grown up as *Top Gun* aficionados, each instructor had his or her own "call sign" or nickname. Fadely was known as "Ripple" because of his father's predilection for the cheap wine.

"Ripple, this is D-Day, over," announced the voice that had so rudely awakened Fadely from his airborne fantasy.

D-Day was Scott McCoy's call sign. He chose that particular nickname because it was also the nickname of his favorite character in one of his most-watched classic movies, *Animal House*.

"D-Day, this is Ripple, over."

"Ripple, you alone on a maintenance flight?" asked McCoy.

"Affirmative," came Fadely's reply.

"Me too, what's your position?" asked McCoy.

"D-Day, this is Ripple. I'm five miles due east of Easton airport, over."

McCoy said, "Ripple, want to link up?"

"Affirmative," replied Fadely, "you coming to me?"

"Affirmative, do some lazy-eights, and I'll join you in seven minutes," McCoy said.

Lazy eights is a name of a common non-aerobatic maneuver, but McCoy was just using it to relay to Fadely that he should stay where he is. Fadley did, however, take advantage of the waiting time to perform two more loops and two more rolls.

"Ripple, I'm closing in on your position. What's your altitude? I don't see you."

"4,000, D-Day," responded Fadely.

"Oh," said McCoy, "I know what you were doing!"

"No you don't!" emphasized Fadely. Both men were careful not to say anything over the frequency that could get them in trouble with the FAA or with anyone else.

"Ripple, drop to 2,000," advised McCoy.

Fadely reduced the throttle with his right hand and with his other hand he eased the stick slightly forward and to the left placing the aircraft in a gentle left turn and descending at a rate of 1,000 feet per minute. Two minutes later he leveled off at 2,000 feet and had D-Day's aircraft in sight.

McCoy said, "I'll come around on your right and be your wingman."

"Good because it's time for a Choptank run!"

"Oh no man—not the Choptank run," said McCoy.

"Yessir, D-Day, we're doin' the Choptank run." He continued, "I've been having a good time up here and the afternoon just wouldn't be complete without a Choptank run."

The Choptank River is 71 miles long and runs from a point in Delaware through the heart of the Eastern Shore of Maryland from northeast to southwest and ends a few miles beyond Cambridge, Maryland where it meets the Chesapeake Bay. There are portions of the river that are quite wide and others, especially in the tributaries and smaller rivers that feed the Choptank that are fairly narrow. Some of these are spanned by old two lane bridges. One of these bridges only a few miles southeast of the town of Easton is a favorite fishing spot for the locals who occupy both sides of the bridge with their fishing lines descending into the water. This narrow span that sits low over the water was referred to by some of his colleagues as Fadely's folly.

The two small and sleek white training aircraft were flying at 2,000 feet in close formation over the town of Easton with Ripple in the lead and D-Day as wingman to his right and slightly behind and below the leader. The two planes were cruising at an airspeed of 140 miles per hour. From this point on D-Day would duplicate Ripple's direction, speed, and altitude. Wherever Ripple would go, and whatever he would do D-Day would neatly follow. McCoy tried not to think about an accident that occurred involving the United States Thunderbirds a few years earlier over their practice area near Las Vegas. Four of the F-16 jets were performing a tight formation loop when the lead aircraft's control system failed just after completing the top of the maneuver. The lead pilot was no longer able to control the plane, which flew straight into the ground at a speed exceeding 400 miles per hour. The three other planes each maintaining the tight formation followed the leader into the ground as well. McCoy dismissed the recollection by making a commitment to himself to stay aware of his surroundings as they neared the ground.

Both pilots knew full well that what they were about to do was a gross violation of federal regulations that could result in the loss of their pilot licenses. It was critical that they maintain radio silence from this point on.

Fadely was calm and unruffled. His pulse began to accelerate with the adrenaline rush. His lips separated slightly just barely revealing a mischievous smile. He turned his head to the left as he applied a gentle pressure to the stick in the same direction and eased the power to idle. The aircraft smoothly followed his lead and began a slow descent in a shallow bank to the left.

McCoy was a nervous wreck. He had never done this before, but he had heard the stories and couldn't help but wonder what would possess a man to take such a foolish risk. Now he was about to do it himself. *Why am I doing this*, he asked himself. *Am I that desperate for Fadely's approval*? But as D-Day saw Ripple's aircraft start to drop to the left he followed, carefully maintaining a constant distance between the nose of his plane and the tail and right wing of his leader.

Fadely's folly traversed a narrow yet relatively deep section of a tributary that lazily flowed from east to west. A mile to the east of the span both sides of the water were flanked by thick stands of trees rising up forty feet from the shore. Moving from east to west just above the water between these trees and moving toward the bridge, one eerily experiences the sensation of passing through a narrowing tunnel. The horizontal space steadily constricts until it opens up as the trees end on both sides about 100 yards before the bridge.

Ripple descended at cruise speed to an altitude of 1,000 feet over a barren field just one mile north of the flowing tributary. D-Day was skillfully maintaining his wingman position slightly to the right and behind his leader. As the two aircraft approached the eastern edge of the tall trees, Ripple descended to 100 feet, and then to 50 feet, and then to 30 feet, with his wingman as his shadow. Both planes made a tight right turn to the west around the trees and rolled out on a course that had them flying straight toward the bridge just ahead. At a speed of 140 miles per hour, the DA20s would be on top of the bridge in less than thirty seconds. They were flying directly into the sun. This timing was critical to the success of the mission because after passing over the bridge, they would be flying right into the sun and no one on the ground would be able to identify them. On a Choptank run survival was paramount, but anonymity was a very close second.

McCoy was gripping the controls so tightly that his hands were wet and red. Beads of sweat were streaming down his forehead and into his eyes. But as soon as his plane entered the cavernous area over the water and between the trees his fear subsided and the only thing that raced through his mind, over and over, was—*this is so cool!*

The thirty-second race to the bridge seemed much faster. Ripple dropped even closer to the surface of the water, and D-Day followed. And then the one thing happened that always seemed to happen when Fadely performed this stunt, and it was the one thing that he loved more than the danger of the flying itself. The locals fishing from the bridge suddenly became aware of the two planes closing in on them with great speed and the pilots could almost see the eyes of these people widen with stark terror. All had been calm only a few moments before, almost boring, on this pleasant spring day. But now fishing poles dropped in unison from the hands that had held them and into the water below. And then, just as swiftly, most of the people on the east side of the bridge jumped over the short railing in front of them and dropped into the water just a few feet below. The pilots smoothly extracted full power from their engines and raised the noses of their aircraft to climb directly over the bridge. Ripple made a sudden and sharp climbing turn to the left and D-Day made an equally steep climbing turn to the right. Neither pilot said a word to each other on the radio during the entire flight back to BWI airport in Baltimore. But each was hooting and hollering like cowboys at a rodeo in the privacy of his own cockpit. D-Day was especially excited as he began to plot his next visit to Fadely's folly.

Jason's Bar was about a mile down the road from the entrance to Camber Flight Training, Inc. Fadely and McCoy entered Jason's together after their daring flights and ordered two cold beers. When the drinks arrived they were joined by Daryll Flint, another of Camber's twenty-two flight instructors. He made a space for himself at the bar between the two, signaled to the bartender that the two beers just served were on him, and then he raised his glass as if to toast Ripple and D-Day. He smiled after they raised their drinks in return and quietly said, "You are both serious mental cases!" Fadely and McCoy smiled at each other coyly as the three gently tapped their glasses in unison. As Flint turned and walked away from them, it was obvious that the two renegade pilots had taken his toast as a compliment.

Just then the front door to the bar opened and almost immediately the loud talking and laughing suddenly stopped. Fadely and McCoy turned their attention from the bar toward the door where they saw Ale German flanked by two FAA inspectors dressed in suits walking toward them. The inspectors each showed their badges and identification to the two flight instructors as they ordered the duo to leave the bar with them. Ale displayed no facial expression as she slowly followed the four outside.

TWENTY-ONE

NEARING THE END of the spring months Camber's 100-day plan had been completed, and the management team was well into the execution of the firm's strategic plan. But surprises continued to appear on a daily basis. From the middle of May through the second week of June all of the Midshipmen who had neglected to schedule training flights earlier in the spring as required by the Navy contract and those who had also failed to appear for scheduled flights, suddenly descended upon Camber with a vengeance. They wanted to squeeze all of their flight training into the extremely short amount of time before they were due to report to Pensacola to begin their careers as Naval aviators. Lieutenant Leo Forrester was getting an inordinate amount of pressure from the brass in Pensacola to get all of these students through the program rapidly, and he, in turn, was channeling as much of that pressure directly through to Terry and Ale. This created an awkward situation for him because of his personal, and secret relationship with Ale which had blossomed into far more than just an incidental friendship. As a result, Forrester bypassed Ale and focused all of the unpleasantness associated with the inability of Camber to accommodate the unrealistic demands of the situation directly onto Terry. At this point, Forrester was not about to threaten his perceived future with Ale by antagonizing her with this nonsense.

It was obvious to all that Camber was unable to satisfy the sudden demands of all of the Midshipmen desiring to complete what amounted to hundreds of hours of instruction in a time frame that would have required three times the aircraft and instructors available at Camber. It was decided that the only way to resolve the problem was for the officers in Pensacola to postpone the start dates of a dozen or more of the affected newly graduated Ensigns for several weeks into the summer, in order for them to be able to complete their training at Camber. Pensacola made no secret of the fact that they all considered this problem the fault of Camber's poor management and vowed to conduct an investigative meeting in Annapolis as soon as all of the Ensigns had completed their instruction with Camber.

The meeting was scheduled for the first week in August in a conference room near Lieutenant Forrester's office in Luce Hall on the grounds of "The Yard."

✳ ✳ ✳ ✳ ✳

The United States Naval Academy is an impressive place to visit. It is located on a point of land at the intersection of the Severn River and Chesapeake Bay on a 338-acre site. Within its hallowed halls, *honor duty country* is not just a slogan but a sacred vow to be lived every day.

Its 4,400 male and female students all live in one building, Bancroft Hall, the largest dormitory of its kind in the nation, and they are all served meals at the same time in one dining hall in that same building. Terry has often wondered over the years when he has come into contact with the Academy and its personnel how any organization could achieve the logistical results demonstrated daily here at The Yard. *Surely*, he thought during this visit, *the brass would be able to understand that changes must be made to the Navy-induced scheduling nightmare that is creating serious problems for Camber and its delivery of the Midshipman flight training program there.*

The two civilians entered Luce Hall, and it was similar to entering any other building at The Yard. The hallways were wide, the ceilings were seemingly limitless, there was an abundance of marble throughout, and everything was spotlessly clean. *Amazing what you can do when the taxpayers' money is no object*, thought Terry.

Upstairs they found the conference room Lieutenant Forrester had assigned earlier. The room was open and the lights were on, but there was no one else nearby. Terry and Ale were conspicuously early for the meeting out of respect. They sat in two chairs located at the long oak conference table on the farthest side from the door. A few moments later two uniformed lieutenants entered the room and proceeded to chairs directly across the table from them. Before sitting they both looked at Ale and crisply said, "Ma'am," and then looked at Terry and said, "Sir," and then sat down without saying another word. Ale couldn't help but admire the impeccably uniformed men sitting at attention and staring straight forward with no facial expression whatsoever. *We could sure use some discipline like this at Camber*, she thought as she opened her briefcase and extracted some papers.

Suddenly the door of the conference room opened forcefully and was being held by Lieutenant Forrester as two uniformed and generously decorated Naval officers entered the room. Upon seeing Leo in his full-dress uniform Ale's throat got dry, and her palms began to sweat. One of the officers sat at the head of the table on the end farthest from the civilians. The other sat immediately to the right of the first as Forrester closed the door behind him and sat to the left of the ranking brass.

"Good morning," said the senior officer, "I am Commander Hollister. This," he said pointing to his right, "is Lieutenant Commander Finch. We are the commanding officers of the Navy's IFS program in Pensacola. I believe you already know Lieutenant Forrester," he added as he offhandedly motioned to him. Upon that introduction, Ale glanced quickly at Leo and made every attempt to keep from revealing any expression that might betray the butterflies in her stomach

Forrester spoke up and introduced Ale and Terry. He explained to the officers that the two were new to the flight training program at Annapolis.

"That's one of the two reasons we are here," stated the Commander.

"We like to personally meet the civilians running the flight schools with whom we are doing business." Ale noticed that the expressionless remarks being made by this officer were clearly directed toward Terry even though she sat closer to the speaker. She decided to ignore his apparent rudeness, at least for now.

"The second reason we are here is to deliver a message to you," continued the Commander in what was now clearly his dispassionate style.

"Excuse me, Commander," interrupted Terry.

"Yes?" He sounded slightly annoyed.

Terry continued, "You seem to be addressing your remarks directly to me and I think you should know that Ms. German is the ranking member of Camber's management team at this table."

The Commander stared at Terry as though he had just been told that his fly was down. He was obviously embarrassed by this brash revelation. The Commander looked to his right at the Lieutenant Commander and gathered himself before continuing. "I sincerely apologize, Ms. German was it? It was not my intention to slight you in any way."

"Thank you, Commander," she replied, careful not to break the established formality. A slight guttural sound came from Leo which he swiftly disguised as a cough just before taking a sip from the bottle of water on the table in front of him. He could not help his almost imperceptible smile as his eyes met Ale's for less than a moment.

"As I was saying," the officer continued and now delivering his remarks solely to Ale. He locked eyes with her. "There have been some serious scheduling problems at Camber within the past few months, and we are here to inform you that if you are interested in continuing to contract with the Navy as a flight training facility these types of problems must not repeat themselves in the future. Is that understood?"

Ale remained silent for effect before she responded to the obviously condescending question. "Listen Commander, Lieutenant Commander," she said looking directly at each officer as she addressed them separately. "I can understand and appreciate this whole formal pomp and circumstance thing you've got going here." She paused for the proper effect. "But we are civilian business people, and when it is obvious to me that the person I am dealing with has not been given the courtesy by his own people of hearing both sides of a difficult set of circumstances then I am going to take the opportunity to present my side."

The Commander sat back in his chair and motioned to Ale when he said, "By all means, Ms. German, please continue."

Ale leaned forward, picked up a pile of papers sitting on the table in front of her and said, "It is simple, sir. I have in my hand just a few of the dozens of reports documenting the failure on the part of the Academy to honor the contracts that Camber entered in good faith. There have been a totally unacceptable number of instances where Midshipmen failed to schedule flights as promised, and failed to show up for flights that they actually did schedule. Then once the pressure was on them from Pensacola to complete their training just before graduation they descended upon Camber in hordes expecting us to produce aircraft and instructors in an effort to rectify a situation caused by their own irresponsibility and lack of discipline. I won't bore you with any of the details, but I have all of them if you wish to review them." Ale sat back in her chair and waited for a response.

The Commander turned to the Lieutenant sitting to his left and asked, "Is this true, Forrester?"

"Well, sir, uh, you see, uh, we tried to…"

The stuttering Lieutenant was interrupted in mid-sentence. "You fix this problem here at The Yard immediately, do you understand, Forrester? I never want to hear again that a problem with one of our contractors is actually our fault or you'll be sitting in a barroom with some of your buddies telling war stories all day. Got it, mister?"

"Yes sir."

"Ms. German, Mr. Longbow it has been a pleasure. Please let me assure you that Lieutenant Forrester will resolve all of the scheduling issues here at The Yard before you receive your next group of Midshipmen in the fall." The Commander stood and turned toward the door. The Lieutenant Commander followed as Leo held the door for them. The two Lieutenants across from Ale and Terry stood at attention immediately as the Commander arose from his seat. They walked to the door in unison and held it open for Forrester as he left.

Ale and Terry packed their papers into their briefcases and walked through the conference room door into the hallway making sure they turned off the lights in the room as they departed.

On the ride back to Camber, Terry was ecstatic, laughing and recounting how Ale had reduced a Navy Commander to putty in her hands and had strategically turned the tables of guilt right back on Forrester where the guilt obviously belonged. Ale sat in the passenger's seat quietly during Terry's celebratory ranting wondering if she had just ruined a relationship that she considered the best thing to happen to her in the last decade.

＊ ＊ ＊ ＊ ＊

Almost twenty-four hours after the meeting in Annapolis, Ale had not heard from Leo, and she was more concerned than ever that she had offended him with her critical comments. She had managed to get little sleep during the night, and she decided that she should call Leo to discuss the matter.

"Forrester," he answered after one ring of his cell phone.

"Hey," she said softly. "Are you angry with me?" Ale was not at all accustomed to playing a subservient role with any man, including her husband. But this was different. She was afraid that Leo would exit her life as quickly as he had entered it and she would admit only to herself that he was a shining light in an otherwise dismal emotional world for her lately.

"Angry?" he answered incredulously. "Why on earth would I be angry with you?"

"Because I got you in trouble with the brass from Pensacola yesterday."

"You didn't get me in trouble," he explained. "Hell, even if you had, I care immensely more about you and us than I do about what those blowhards think of me or the job I'm doing. I can't believe you thought I would be upset with you!"

"Well I haven't heard from you," she continued, "and they were pretty nasty with you when the meeting ended."

"Hey," he added, "just don't give it another thought. I have to go, but I'll call you tonight, okay?"

"Leo," she spoke up as he was about to hang up.

"Yeah?"

"Thank you."

"For what?"

"For being you."

※ ※ ※ ※ ※

Ale and Terry sat down together at the table in the Orion conference room at their Columbia, Maryland location for their routinely scheduled weekly management meeting. On the agenda was the resolution of one of the most pressing issues confronting them and the location of this particular type of meeting was always away from the Camber offices due to the highly confidential nature of matters to be addressed. Ale assumed the role of chair of the meeting and conducted it according to an agenda prepared and given to Terry at least a day in advance.

"Our first order of business is Camber's cash position," she began.

For decades Terry had been in the habit of carefully checking the cash position of each company he was working with first thing every morning. This routine has been made infinitely easier with the Internet access of banking records, as opposed to having to retrieve the information via telephone with bank officials. Ale immediately adopted the same habit with her first corporate turn-around project with Orion.

"Dangerously anemic," she added as they both inspected printed versions of the Camber checking register in front of them.

"Yes it is!" added Terry.

"I don't get it," said Ale. "I thought you used the Camber bank records to project the cash flows in the Strategic Plan on a month-to-month basis. We haven't had a new class of Midshipmen since the beginning of April and, therefore, we haven't had any revenue since that time. How did we miss this timing?"

"I'm not going to make any excuses, Ale. I know exactly how it happened. Pressed for time I used the information Greg gave me as exact. I assumed that we would receive twenty new Mids each month of the year and I based our cash flow projections on that anticipated routine. I have gone back and reviewed all of the receipt records, and I find that there are no new students during the summer months and also between the first week of November and the first week of February each year. I should have double-checked something this critical in detail."

"Okay," said Ale, "so we have only $20,000 available in cash right now and no payment from the Navy anticipated for a couple of months, right?"

"Right," said Terry with a strained look on his face. "That's if they don't fire us!"

Ale did not want to appear too cavalier about the seriousness of the meeting, so she responded to Terry's observation with a light hearted, "Well if they fire us that solves a lot of problems doesn't it?"

"But let's assume they don't fire us," she said, "how do we survive this cash drought until our next payment?"

"Easy, we put our 'cash-is-king' system into action. We treat Camber for the next few months exactly as we do our most cash-strapped turn-arounds when we first start working with them. We make the payroll first and on time, and we stretch all of our payables to sixty, maybe even ninety days before they get paid. We have the full line of credit to fall back on as we need it. And we work our butts off to get paying civilian customers over the transom as quickly as possible."

"Alright Terry, 'cash-is-king' it is!"

* * * * *

Christian Foster was the founder and owner of SafeFlight Maintenance, Inc., which had been based at BWI for over ten years. Their corporate offices were located directly across the lobby from Camber's in the same building. The aircraft maintenance company leased half of a large hangar from Elite Services, and since Elite had been unable to find a tenant for the other half of the hangar, Foster had utilized the entire space for his work for years. The majority of SafeFlight's revenues were generated from airline contracts for maintenance usually performed at the gates of the terminals at the three major airports in the Baltimore/Washington area. The hangar facility adjacent to Camber, however, was not used for that work. Ale had noticed that this hangar area was frequently not busy, leading her to believe that Foster could use some general aviation business in order to utilize this rather expensive space more efficiently. At least that was what Ale was hoping as she met with her fellow entrepreneur a few days before Thanksgiving.

"Thank you for meeting with me, Christian," Ale said as she entered the office of the six-foot-four, two-hundred-eighty pound black gentleman who looked more like a linebacker for the Baltimore Ravens than a businessman.

"My pleasure," came the reply. Ale sat in a comfortable chair directly in front of an expansive desk covered with piles of files and papers, and she couldn't help but notice that the entire floor surrounding Christian's side of the desk was also covered with stacks of paper. *A rather unusual filing system* she thought.

"Christian, we presently operate over two dozen aircraft. We are looking to expand our fleet significantly over the next few years. You are in the business of providing aircraft maintenance services to clients. I think our companies should do business together. What do you think?"

Ale intentionally worded her introductory remarks so as to elicit a positive response from her colleague. She knew that if Christian's response was an affirmative one, there would exist more of a commitment from the other side of the desk than if the two entrepreneurs had simply danced around the main issue for a while.

"Of course, Ale, I am always open to new and exciting business relationships. Have you spoken with Greg about this?"

Ale wasn't sure why this question appeared so soon but she decided to take full advantage of the opportunity to share Greg's primary concern about Christian's operation with him.

"Yes," she said, "we discussed it at a board meeting a few weeks ago. Greg is a fan of your operation, but he is concerned that your first priority is your contractual obligation to your airline clients and that we would be stuck waiting for our planes to be completed. He also conveyed his opinion that your rates are too high."

Christian laughed mildly in a deep sonorous way. "I am very familiar with Greg's concerns," he said. After a short pause and with a more serious expression he added, "Suppose I can create a contract with Camber that assures you that I will have a division of my operation devoted solely to general aviation work. Next, suppose we can negotiate a pricing arrangement that is competitive with the prices you are now paying?"

"If you can do that, Christian, then SafeFlight will have an exclusive new client."

"Good," said Christian with a broad smile, "I'll prepare a draft of the contract, but I'm going to ask for a copy of all of your aircraft maintenance bills for the past year so that I have a basis for my proposed pricing. Will that be a problem?"

"Not at all. When could I expect to see a draft of the agreement?"

"Late next week."

Both stood, shook hands, and Ale left being careful not to disclose her delight with this potentially lucrative agreement for Camber.

TWENTY-TWO

THE STAFF OF Camber was rapidly outgrowing even the large conference room in the Elite facility. The twenty-eight flight instructors, both full- and part-time, and four clerical employees, plus Terry and Ale, created a standing room only event when they all gathered there for the mandatory monthly company meetings. Ale liked the idea that the meetings would be crowded because she believed that the more uncomfortable the attendees the less they would be inclined to extend the length of a meeting with useless discussion about irrelevant topics. A lifelong hater of frequent and worthless meetings, she had been known during her career to hold necessary meetings in rooms without any chairs or a table, just to keep the conversation during the meeting to a minimum and to ensure the shortest discussion possible.

Ale began the meeting at precisely 10:00 a.m. which was the scheduled starting time. The staff was acutely aware of her disdain for employees who arrived late so all were careful to be present a few minutes before the event was to begin.

"Good morning everyone," she said followed by a chorus of identical greetings from the group. "Each of you has an agenda, and as you can see this will be another short meeting. We'll begin with some quick announcements. As you know our fleet has grown to thirty aircraft, which includes twenty DA20s for introductory training and ten high-speed, complex planes. We have noticed that some instructors are attempting to influence the scheduling staff to assign the advanced students to them, rather than the introductory students so that they can log more time in the complex aircraft. I will be reviewing student assignments personally to ensure that the distribution of both introductory and advanced students is accomplished equitably among all instructors. Are there any questions or concerns about this?"

There were none, so she continued. "I do have two items that I think everyone will consider good news. First, we have five new airline pilot training candidates who will be starting with us next month. This is exciting because our corporate strategic plan has established the penetration of the airline training target market as one of our primary goals for this year. Each of these students will be entering our fast-track commercial training program and some of you will be selected to form our airline instructional program team. Matt Foreman, our new chief, will be selecting the instructor candidates for this separate division of our company during this next week. The second piece of good news is that we will be traveling to Florida soon to explore a partnership with an established jet training school. This new arrangement will provide jet training for all of our airline pilot students after they have completed their program with us."

There was a sudden change in the mood of the employees as soon as Ale made this announcement. Ale and Terry were both pleased with the reaction of the staff to these positive developments at the company. They gave each other a small smile as they looked around them at a group of employees who seemed to appreciate all of the hard work and energy that had been invested in Camber so far. Ale then proceeded to deliver the corporate focus for this particular meeting. The two entrepreneurs had decided when they began holding monthly company meetings that they would end each with a brief presentation of a concept, or issue, or story that management considered beneficial for the staff to use as a focal point for their work as the company grows.

"When we first became involved with Camber the customer base was almost entirely comprised of students from the Naval Academy. While we still serve this vital market segment, we are now nurturing a sizable civilian clientele. The topic of today's focus segment is the critical importance of exceptional customer service. Please don't misunderstand my segmentation of our customers into the separate groups of Navy and civilian because every student, regardless of their reason for learning to fly, deserves a customer experience well beyond their highest expectations. Does everyone agree?"

Ale was remarkably accomplished as a group presenter, and she knew that the best way to keep an audience from feeling as though they were being *talked at* was to involve them in the presentation in some way. Everyone nodded and agreed after hearing her question, so she continued.

"Frances and William (Pop) Haussner were extremely young when they immigrated from their homeland in Germany in the early part of the Twentieth Century. The history of Pop and Frances Haussner and of Haussner's famous restaurant provides enough material to fill a book. So we will have to settle for describing just a little piece of the Haussner legacy, which was a large part of the success of the restaurant for three-quarters of a century."

"Pop Haussner died early in the odyssey which delivered the restaurant from one of local neighborhood notoriety to an internationally known tourist draw for an excellent meal at a modest price. Frances was left to carry on with the day-to-day management of the enterprise as a single owner-operator, and it was she who engineered the metamorphosis that resulted in the overwhelming success of the large dining establishment. She was a tall attractive woman who spoke the English language well but with a heavy German accent. Her smile and soft spoken manner intrigued the patrons at the front door long before they even saw the menu or had an opportunity to taste the food. And that is one of the many things that Frances Haussner did to distinguish herself, at least in my mind, as a successful businessperson. If she could not personally greet each of the hundreds of daily customers at the front door, she would certainly visit them at their tableside to inquire about their dining experience. Often, if she was certain that she was not being intrusive, she would sit at an open chair at a table of guests and engage in a conversation with them, usually answering all of their questions about the unique characteristics of her thriving business. Then, as quietly as she had arrived, she would leave the table for another. She would especially make sure that she visited with uniformed men and women of our armed services to express her thanks and admiration for their service to the nation."

"Once, during the Second World War, she was visiting at the table of a young serviceman and a young lady that Frances assumed was his girlfriend. She soon learned that he had just proposed to her and that he had waited for many months while fighting in Europe just to be able to propose to his true love at Haussner's restaurant. When Frances asked his fiancé if she could see her ring the girl looked bashfully down at the table as the soldier explained that he could not yet afford one but that he would have enough money upon his next return from the war. Frances asked the two to join her for lunch the next afternoon to celebrate the occasion when the restaurant would not be so crowded and noisy. Early the next morning she visited a local pawn shop, picked out an engagement and wedding ring set that was elegant in its simplicity, bought it and presented it, nicely wrapped, to the serviceman and his soon-to-be bride at lunch. For years after that, she trolled local pawn shops and purchased ring sets that she could have on hand in case members of the United States Military on leave, or just back from a war, chose Haussner's as that special spot to pop the question. Legend has it, although her acts of kindness were never publicized, that she had a part in getting many a marriage off to a good start over the decades."

"A colleague of ours recently shared a story with us about an experience that he had at Haussner's many years ago. He took his small family to the restaurant for a celebration of some sort because he had been there once before and was quite pleased, not only with the meal, but with the fact that the owner had taken the time to visit with him briefly at his table. On this visit with his family, he was amazed that Frances not only recognized him from his earlier visit but remembered his first name as well. She had a knack for doing that. Once again she sat with him and his family but after a few minutes into their conversation she placed her index finger into the air toward the group as if to say, 'Excuse me for just one moment.' She leaned back in her chair and gently touched the elbow of a young lady on her staff who was clearing the dishes from a table that had just been vacated. When the young lady turned to Frances she looked surprised, and all Frances did was to shake her head back-and-forth, slowly but sternly, a couple of times and point to the tray in which the bus girl was placing the dishes. The bus girl nodded, and Frances returned to the table conversation with our colleague. She explained that she had just disciplined the young lady because she was making too much noise while clearing the table. She said that there is already too much noise, and there are too many distractions in a restaurant of that size and that diners deserve an environment where the serving of food and the clearing of tables does not contribute to the noise. Frances Haussner for decades had a strict policy regarding the clearing of tables. She spent a considerable amount of money on the purchase and laundering of table linens that were to be used to separate every plate, glass, and article of silverware when they were placed in the soiled dish tray so that the clearing of the tables would be a silent process. The trays were then wheeled into the kitchen where the dishes could be handled without adding in any way to the decibel-level already existing in a large room full of people dining. Her training of the staff on this particular issue was absolute. To this day that story has destroyed for me what would otherwise have been delightful restaurant dining experiences which were marred only by the noisy clatter of dirty dishes at a nearby table!"

"One more quick example of superior customer service. Haussner's became so popular that the line to get into the restaurant for dinner many evenings formed on a sidewalk and stretched all the way around most of the building. As you know, winters in the Baltimore area can be quite cold, so Frances invested in the installation of heaters with fans above the sidewalks so that her clientele might be a little less uncomfortable while they waited to get in. She certainly did not have to endure this capital expense, diners would have stood in line for hours in freezing temperatures whether the sidewalks were heated or not."

Ale paused for a moment before she concluded her focal point for this company meeting. She was pleased that everyone appeared to be hanging on her every word. There were no yawns. No one was looking at their watch to see what time it was. She was particularly happy to note that there were no apparent negative attitudes like the ones when she and Terry first arrived at Camber. This made her feel remarkably positive. She now began to feel that this company was finally on the right track.

"I know that you think this is a story about a restaurant, but it's not. It's a story about how people should treat people. Please remember Frances Haussner whenever you come into contact with one of our customers. Whether you realize it or not students are every bit as anxious to have a positive and reinforcing experience with their flight instructor during every lesson as they are to experience the excitement of flying a plane. Make their experience an incredible one. Exceed their highest expectations. The company will be much more successful if you do and you will be too!"

And then something happened that neither Ale nor Terry ever expected in their wildest dreams. The employees of Camber Fight Training, Inc. all stood and clapped in unison as the two exited the conference room.

TWENTY-THREE

THE NEXT MORNING while waiting to board their 7:00 a.m. non-stop Air Tran flight to Ft. Lauderdale from BWI Terry and Ale witnessed something they had never seen before. From where they were standing they could see straight down the jetway, and they noticed the Captain of the flight that they were about to board walking up the jetway toward them. He was clearly an experienced Captain with gray hair and meticulous grooming, and as he exited the jetway into the waiting area he turned to his right and walked over to the ticket counter where agents were preparing to begin the boarding process. After reading some papers and talking with the agents, the Captain walked over to an elderly woman sitting in a wheelchair and waiting patiently for a skycap to wheel her down the jetway to the aircraft. The Captain smiled at the woman and leaned forward toward her just slightly and said, "Are you ready to go flying today, honey?" She nodded, and he walked to the back of her wheelchair, unlocked it, and began wheeling her toward the door of the jetway. When he got to the door he turned the wheelchair around with great care, and he pulled her down the jetway instead of pushing her, obviously so that there would be no chance of her falling forward out of the chair. They saw him pull her all the way down the jetway and around the corner at the end and onto the aircraft. The entrepreneurial duo had never seen the Captain of an airliner personally assist a handicapped passenger onto the plane before.

A few minutes later while they were still waiting for the agents to make the boarding call the Captain again walked toward them up the jetway. By this time, Ale could not resist the urge to say something to him. She walked up to him and said, "Excuse me Captain but I noticed that you helped that handicapped woman onto the aircraft. I've never seen a Captain do that before, and I am curious as to why you did."

He smiled at her and said, "I always do that for two reasons. First, handicapped passengers feel particularly vulnerable and tend to worry that if something should happen aboard the aircraft no one will remember that they are there. What better way to let them know that they are in good hands than for the Captain himself to make sure that they get onto the aircraft and safely settled in." He continued, "You are about to board this flight. Just imagine yourself sitting here in a wheelchair having to depend on others to take care of your needs instead of being able to look out for yourself. Under those circumstances, you would feel far more comfortable if I were to take you to your seat and make certain that you are safely buckled in."

The Captain went on to explain that the second reason that he personally cares for handicapped passengers is because of the example that it sets for the rest of his crew during the upcoming flight. He said, "It has been my experience that when the crew on my flight sees me treating people with such care before the flight begins they also tend to be much more considerate of each other and of the passengers during the flight."

"There's your next corporate focus story about excellent customer service, Ale!" quipped Terry. They would later observe firsthand that the Captain's philosophy for motivating people to treat others well actually worked, for the customer service provided by the flight attendants on that flight was far superior to any that they had ever experienced on any airline.

Although the flight to Ft. Lauderdale-Hollywood International Airport was smooth and uneventful Ale white-knuckled both arms of her seat the entire time. Terry had long since abandoned any attempt to convince her that flying is statistically much safer than driving a car, and he surmised over the years that she would rather he just ignored her discomfort flying in any kind of aircraft and to any destination. Once they deplaned she headed straight for the nearest ladies room, and a few moments later she rejoined him as though nothing frightening had ruffled her.

The ride to the Ft. Lauderdale Executive Airport took them only about fifteen minutes once they secured their car at the less-than-convenient offsite car rental facility and merged onto I-95 North toward the city of Ft. Lauderdale. Ale insisted on driving. She didn't say anything to Terry, but she wasn't about to endure his cat-and-mouse footwork between the brake and the gas pedals after just surviving two hours in a crowd-killer no matter how short the drive. In the meantime, Terry was fiddling with his trusty portable GPS and giving Ale directions at every turn simultaneous with the lady's voice from the GPS saying the same thing. Upon arrival at one of the many fixed-base operations on the grounds of the Executive Airport, they were cheerily greeted by Dwight Philips, the Diamond Aircraft Regional Sales Director for the Mid-Atlantic Region.

The lobby and hallways of AvTech Jet Training were bustling with student activity. All students and instructors were required to wear uniforms similar to those worn by crew members of regional airlines around the country, so identifying the clientele was not a challenge at all. Although this flight school specialized in the training of licensed commercial pilots, in jet simulators, preparing them for a smooth transition into a regional airline jet cockpit, the owner of the enterprise, sixty-year-old Howard Young, recently expanded the operation to include exactly the same type of training performed by Camber. A student with no flight time whatsoever could now begin training with AvTech, and about a year later expect to be hired by an airline as a first-officer, also known as a co-pilot, immediately. The price tag for the full training package was a hefty $150,000 which included dormitory-type room and board at the AvTech facility. The company had a long waiting list due to the regional airline demand for qualified pilots nationally. In fact, Young realized early on in the growth of his company that he could advertise a guarantee that every graduate would be hired immediately after graduation. He had no problem living up to that guarantee during the recent airline scramble for crew member candidates.

The AvTech facility was extremely clean and modern, looking as though it had just been renovated throughout. Dwight escorted Ale and Terry into a spacious conference room on the first floor of the building adjacent to the sprawling lobby. The Camber management team sat on the side of a large oak conference table which allowed them to observe all of the activity on the lobby side of a glass wall separating the two spaces. Dwight asked the two if they would like coffee and Ale quickly declined but Terry requested a cup of hot tea, inquiring as to whether it would be too much trouble. At that point, the three were joined by Howard Young, a partner in the business named Louis Schatz, and the firm's Chief Financial Officer, a young woman named Carolyn Mann.

"Good morning," began Young, "and welcome to AvTech."

After introductions around the table, the power in the room seemed to shift rapidly from Young to Schatz as the latter suggested they all begin a tour of the facility and everyone nodded in agreement.

For the next hour, the five executives and the salesman walked through the halls and training rooms of the AvTech building. Young, Schatz, Dwight, and Terry walked ahead with Schatz delivering what appeared to be a scripted but detailed description of how the company works and what they do in each of the meticulously designed rooms. Ale and Carolyn walked together at the same pace as the others, but a few steps behind, and were deep in discussion about the financial, administrative, and personnel issues facing AvTech and its management team. Terry was most impressed with the three full-movement CRJ-200 simulators which Louis assured him were in constant use 24 hours a day. The Canadian built CRJ-200 was the backbone of many regional airline fleets, accommodating between forty and fifty passengers somewhat comfortably on short-haul flights, usually connecting large hub airports around the country with smaller municipal jetports. Terry couldn't help but be extremely impressed with the way AvTech had designed and was utilizing the facilities in what appeared to be an exceptionally efficient instructional manner. Ale had been informed by Carolyn that the flight school now had 150 registered and paid airline students and the latter appeared to be boasting when she assured Ale that the company had a significant cash balance on hand.

The last stop on the tour was a walk out onto the ramp where about a half dozen small Diamond trainers were awaiting the first wave of the day's introductory students as a part of AvTech's newly formed novice pilot training program. Terry and the two principals from the jet training school were engrossed in a discussion comparing the way AvTech runs its initial pilot programs and the way that Camber was doing the same thing. After an hour of touring and talking all returned to the glass-sided conference room.

Louis was the first to speak. "Ale, Terry, we have enjoyed showing you around our operation, but there is a reason we asked Dwight to invite you down here and introduce us to you."

Ale and Terry exchanged quick glances. "What would that be, Louis?" asked Ale coyly.

"I think AvTech and Camber would make a really good team," stated Young. "You are looking for a jet training school where you can send your graduates who are ready for the last stage of their airline prep training. That's what we do here at AvTech. So we are anxious to join forces with you in that respect. But there's another dimension that we think will be equally beneficial for both our firms," said Young. "We are extremely anxious to expand our student market to an international scope, but we can't."

"Why not?" asked Ale.

"Because we are not an FAA part 141 flight school like Camber is. In order to accept students from other countries legally a school must be formally approved by SEVIS, and in order to be approved by SEVIS, a school must first be approved by the FAA as a Part 141 operation."

"What's SEVIS?" asked Ale sheepishly.

"It stands for the Student and Exchange Visitor Information System and is administered by the Department of Homeland Security as a result of 911," said Louis.

"Why don't you just apply for and get the Part 141 approval from the FAA and then apply for the SEVIS approval?" asked Terry.

"Great question, Terry," said Howard. "The FAA has frozen all Part

141 application activity in the South Florida region indefinitely because their backlog is way too large. Right now it is taking several years to get approved in this region."

Terry was beginning to piece this whole thing together. "So you want to partner with us on our 141 certificate," Terry began.

Howard finished his sentence for him, "And then you apply for the SEVIS approval with us as your partners." Howard grinned, "and everybody wins!"

"I think the only way that the FAA will agree to this is if we declare AvTech as a satellite of the Camber operation in Baltimore. They aren't the most progressive group of people as you must know, Howard," offered Terry. He continued, "How long do you think it would take for us to secure the SEVIS approval?"

Before Louis could gather his thoughts Howard said, "Officially the SEVIS website says that it takes sixteen weeks from the time of application until approval but being located as close as Camber is to Washington, D.C. I'm sure you can work with them to take some shortcuts for us, Terry."

"Maybe so, Louis, but if we proceed with this everyone should expect at least a sixteen week project. Like I said earlier, the feds aren't accustomed to rushing things!" Howard and Louis looked at each other with a degree of concern and then returned their attention to the other side of the table.

"Well," added Terry, "let's cross that bridge when we get to it."

Then Ale motioned with her left hand to attract the attention of the AvTech managers. She asked, "So what are you offering us to entice us to consider moving forward with this arrangement with AvTech?"

Louis and Howard sat back in their seats and just stared at Ale with an expression of amazement on their faces. Then Howard asked, "What do you mean, what are we offering?"

Ale paused, glanced at Terry, and then said, "This is the way I see it. You are offering us this opportunity to send our students to you for their jet training. But we could choose any number of schools around the country. You are asking us to adopt you in a partnership on our FAA 141 certificate which will take a significant amount of effort on our part within the federal bureaucracy, and then you want us to secure the SEVIS approval so that

AvTech can attract what will probably be large numbers of foreign students. It just seems to me that you are suggesting an arrangement where Camber will be undertaking an enormous amount of effort and risk only to have AvTech ultimately benefit."

"What do you have in mind, Ale?" asked Louis.

"Right off the top of my head I think $250,000 would be a fair monetary consideration," she proposed.

"You've got to be out of your mind!" bellowed Howard.

"Now wait a minute, Howard," Ale said, "what you are suggesting will cause us to hire additional technical staff, increase our legal expenses considerably, and create the need for a sizable amount of travel between Baltimore and Ft. Lauderdale on a long-term basis. It wouldn't be difficult at all for us to spend $250,000 while attempting to pull this off. And there's no guarantee that this will even work. Are you suggesting that we front all of this costly labor intensive work and then eat the losses if it fails?"

Terry smiled as he listened to Ale negotiate.

Howard and Louis huddled for a moment and then turned their attention back to Ale across the table. "Here's what we're willing to offer," said Louis. "We'll give Camber $100,000, and we'll hire a good friend of ours to assist you with the undertaking. He can be your technical expert, and we'll pay all of his salary and expenses. His name is Jerry Schuler, and he is a retired Pan American Airways and Air Tran Captain. We can arrange for you to meet with him today before you travel back to Baltimore."

Ale carefully placed her right thumb and index finger studiously on the bottom of her chin as she continued to stare at the pair across the table. She never once made any effort to consult with Terry, and he never once indicated the need for her to do so. Finally, she said, "The hundred thousand is all up front. We'll take a check with us today."

Howard chuckled and looked directly at Terry. "Where in the hell did you get her?" he asked. "No," he continued directing the answer at Ale. "We'll give you a check for twenty-five thousand now, one for an equal amount in thirty days, and the remaining fifty-thousand sixty days from today. That's the best we can do."

Terry felt compelled to answer the question just posed, "I didn't get her, Howard—she got me!"

Ale reached her right hand across the table in a gesture to shake Howard's and then Louis' hand to seal the deal. Everyone stayed in the conference room for another two hours discussing the new partnership. Howard placed a call to Jerry Schuler who agreed immediately to the employment arrangement for him, and he suggested that Terry and Ale meet him at Bubba Gump's restaurant on the A-1 highway and the beach.

With the meeting over and back in the car, Terry smiled at Ale. "You are amazing, Ale!" he exclaimed.

"Nah," she said as she shifted the small SUV into drive and began to leave the parking lot, "I should have pressed them for $175,000. I think they would have gone for it."

TWENTY-FOUR

THE MOST ALLURING quality of Bubba Gump's of Ft. Lauderdale is not its disgustingly tempting array of deep fried foods powerful enough to induce serious arterial damage to even the fittest of patrons. Rather it is the spring vacation all year 'round atmosphere of its location immediately across the highway from the beach and the turquoise ocean. One can sit on any of several wooden picnic benches gracing the restaurant's outdoor concrete patio area and have an unobstructed view of skateboarders, beach volleyball games, surfers, and scantily clad coeds at just about any time between sun up and sundown. It's an upscale beach bum's paradise, and sometimes it's not so upscale. Terry ordered an unsweetened iced tea and Ale her usual Diet Coke with a little ice and a lemon wedge while they awaited the arrival of Jerry Schuler.

Terry, who was obviously more taken with the human scenery than Ale and for obvious reasons, mumbled, "Boy, could I get used to this in a hurry!"

Ale ignored the comment as though she hadn't heard it and continued to expose her face to the sun as much as possible so that she could return to Baltimore with at least a hint of a tan. *Like I said before*, she thought, *he's still just a boy at heart!*

Her ringing cell phone rudely interrupted her brief and comfortable moment in the sun. She plucked it out of her handbag, looked at its screen and immediately noticed that the call was from Leo. "I'll be back in a moment," she said to Terry, who gave her a surprised look.

"Leo," she said trying to keep her voice from sounding anxious, "how are you?"

"Hi Ale," he responded, "I'm good. Are you still in Florida?"

"Yes," she paused for a moment looking over her shoulder and making sure that she had moved far enough away from Terry that he would not be able to hear her conversation. "We'll be finishing up in a few hours and then flying home."

"I was just thinking about you," he said eagerly, "I've been doing that a lot lately. You have been so busy we haven't had any time to get together."

"I know, Leo, and I am truly sorry about that. I've been swamped and then I had to rush right down here. It's been crazy!"

After an awkward pause Leo said, "You're not upset with me for any reason are you, Ale?"

"No, of course not, Leo," came her reply. "Like I said it has just been crazy."

"What time do you think you will be back in Baltimore?"

Ale thought for a moment and then said, "We should be there by around six, why?"

"How about driving straight from the airport and meeting me for dinner?"

Her reply was delayed by the thought that she had not been home earlier than midnight for four straight days before the overnight here, and she should not extend her absence any longer. But she also wanted to spend some time with Leo. Her decision was almost made for her when she remembered that Franco was not expecting her until late that night anyway, and it would be easy for her to have dinner with Leo without even having to make an excuse for getting home late. Franco would be none the wiser. "Okay," she said, "where should we meet?"

"Tersiguel's in Ellicott City," said Leo. "I'll text you the address for your GPS."

"Okay, I should be able to be there by seven at the latest," she quipped cheerfully, "gotta go now, see you soon!"

Just then a thin man probably in his late sixties approached their table and introduced himself as Jerry Schuler. The typical pleasantries ensued with introductions and then comments about the ideal weather and scenery. Ale was the first to bring the boys back to reality and to get down to business.

"Jerry," she said, "what do you know and what do you want to know?"

"Howard and Louis are not real effective communicators," he began. *That's good to know*, thought Ale. Jerry continued, "So all I know is that Camber is a flight school up North, and you all have agreed to join forces and attract a whole mess of foreign students into AvTech in the not-too-distant future. Howard and Louis want me to help make it happen. Now you are up-to-date with the entire sum of my knowledge about the project."

"Well Jerry, there are some fairly critical details about the challenge that you should be aware of right up front," advised Terry. He continued, "Are you aware that AvTech is not an FAA approved Part 141 flight operation?"

"No, I'm not. I worked with these guys in an earlier life at a different company in Miami. I recently ran into Howard at a restaurant downtown, and that's probably why he decided to call me about this project. I know little about AvTech other than the fact that it appears to be a cash cow right now." Jerry seemed to be willing to be highly transparent with Ale and Terry, a quality admired if not demanded by both.

"Okay," said Ale, "let's get to work."

During the next three hours, the Camber management brought Jerry entirely up-to-speed with the history and present capabilities of their company. They also briefed him thoroughly on the details of the meeting that had occurred earlier in the day at AvTech, including the exact nature of their understanding of the agreement reached between the two firms. Terry showed Jerry the AvTech check in the amount of $25,000 and Jerry was duly impressed with the negotiating skills of the twosome from Baltimore. Then the newcomer asked a particularly pointed question.

"Who do I work for?"

"Good question, Jerry," said Ale, "until you hear otherwise you report to me."

"I can live with that."

Ale continued, "You'll spend the next week at Camber working with Matt Foreman, our Chief Flight Instructor. You will learn our operation inside and out during that week—you only have the one week so don't waste a minute of it. Then you'll return to learn everything possible about the new AvTech initial flight training program. Here's your assignment." Ale waited a moment to make sure that Jerry was following her. "You must create an exact duplicate of the Camber flight training operation down here at AvTech. When the FAA comes to inspect for the approval of AvTech as a satellite operation of Camber they will expect to see exactly the same operation that exists in Baltimore. There can't be so much as a different cost for the Cokes from the soft drink machine down here, understand?"

"Sure," Jerry said, "but what if I get flack from someone about the changes I have to make?"

"Then you inform me immediately, and I'll set whoever has a problem straight. There is a darned good reason why we'll be sitting on $100,000 of their cash, Jerry!" stated Ale with that wry smile of hers.

The meeting adjourned, and Ale and Terry caught their flight home an hour later.

* * * * *

The Nineteenth-Century three story white house that has been Tersiguel's Restaurant for decades sat majestically on a hill on Main Street in Ellicott City, Maryland. A little more formal than most restaurants in the area, and also more expensive, they specialized in elegant, always fresh French cuisine delivered unobtrusively to the table by wait staff dressed impeccably in tuxedos and with manners as formal as their attire. This particular dining experience had been a favorite for memorable occasions with repeat patrons from near and far and Leo, having been introduced to the superb cuisine and service by a fellow Naval officer a year earlier, decided that it was just what his deepening relationship with Ale needed.

Ale was not sure how she was able to predict her arrival time at Tersiguel's as accurately as she had earlier on the phone with Leo, but she laughed as she climbed the four stone steps to the restaurant's front door and noticed on her watch that it was precisely seven. Leo had texted her that he was already seated and awaiting her arrival and as she proceeded through a small vestibule and a second entrance door the maître d' swiftly escorted her to his table. As she walked behind the older gentleman through a narrow hallway, she noticed that there were two smaller rooms with tables of varying sizes, one to her left and one to the right as they continued beyond both into a larger and brighter dining room at the end of the hall. At first she wondered why Leo had not chosen one of the more private settings for their dinner together until she noticed him sitting at a table to her far right after she entered the larger room. The intimate table for two was nestled into a small nook just large enough for the two of them and was privately removed from the dining activity in the adjoining salle à manger.

Leo immediately rose from his chair when he saw Ale enter the room and walked around the tiny table in the cramped space so that he could hold her chair for her as she sat. She never tired of the thoughtful and chivalrous gestures that she had not experienced prior to meeting him.

"Hello Ale," he said with a broad smile as he placed a gentle kiss on the cheek she offered to him.

"Hi Leo. Have you been waiting long?"

"About an hour," he replied without altering his smile.

"An hour?" she exclaimed. "But I said I would be here at about seven."

"I know, but I wanted to be sure to get this table for us. It is a special one for our special dinner together."

The evening passed without either noticing how swiftly as they were engrossed in the depth of their conversation and the grandeur of their meal. Leo laughed when Ale excitedly exclaimed that one of her favorite foods from her native Uruguay, figs, was being offered on the menu as an appetizer. They shared a single order as she described her childhood in a land over five thousand miles away. The only brief interruption to their intense conversation occurred upon the arrival of their main course, a Chateaubriand prepared exquisitely at the side of their table. Just when Ale thought that the evening could not possibly get any better, and before they ordered a Crème Brûlée, which they would share, Leo presented her with a small rectangular box with an equally small envelope attached. The expression on Ale's face quickly changed from one of startled surprise to warm gratitude as she read the words hand-written by Leo on the card. It said, *You are the light of my life. Thank you!* After a brief moment of silent but obvious astonishment, Ale slowly opened the hinged lid of the dark blue box resting in her left hand. Inside the lid, gold letters elegantly announced that the gift was from Tiffany's, and in the box lay a strikingly simple, white gold necklace consisting of a small linked chain and six silhouetted hearts. At first Ale was speechless, then she stood, leaned across the table and gently but briefly kissed Leo on his left cheek before saying, "It's beautiful, Leo. Thank you!"

After dinner, Leo walked Ale to her car, which was parked in a public lot adjacent to the rear of the restaurant. They walked slowly and passed across a wooden bridge traversing the narrow Tiber River which flowed gently between the restaurant and the parking lot. Leo commented on the inconsistency of the name of the "river" when it was actually more of a rippling stream. Ale smiled and continued to walk lazily toward the lot and her car.

"Do you have to rush right home?" Leo asked as they approached the Nissan Pathfinder, and Ale fumbled through her handbag for her keys.

"I really should get home," she replied. "I've been away a lot, and it's getting late."

"I understand," he said quietly.

As Ale unlocked the door and slid into the driver's seat she looked up at Leo and said, "Come on and get in, we'll sit and talk for a little while longer." Leo smiled as he walked around the car to the front passenger door, opened it and got in. Ale activated the CD player which was set to play some of her favorite gentle songs and she adjusted it to a low background volume. The two sat privately in the dark parking lot for over an hour, first talking, and then embracing.

"I have to go, Leo," she finally said as she realized that their amorous activity was beginning something that she was afraid she would not be able to discipline herself to bring to an end.

"Are you sure?" he asked in a disappointed tone.

"No," she quickly replied, "that's exactly why I have to go!"

They wished each other a good night, and Ale drove from the lot to an adjoining road as she simultaneously programmed her GPS to guide her home.

It was a delightful evening, she thought. *Why did I allow it to evolve into a physical encounter?* Once again she was struggling with the internal conflict of passion and guilt. *I'm going to have to do something about this, and soon!* A lone tear slid down her cheek as she pulled into her driveway and she noticed that the house was dark. *He didn't even leave the porch light on for me,* was her final thought as she attempted several times to find the door handle in the dark. Upon entering the foyer Ale did not bother to turn on a light as she closed and locked the front door behind her. She wiped the tears from her face and slowly climbed the steps to her bedroom as she had done alone so many times before.

TWENTY-FIVE

HAVE YOU EVER had to risk everything on your own ability to succeed? That was the final interview question that Terry had rather cavalierly asked so many candidates for senior management positions in the past, and now that same challenge kept racing through his mind over and over again as he stared blankly at the four-inch high stack of paper sitting on the table in front of him. His mouth was dry, his palms sweaty. He could feel a nearly imperceptibly small bead of perspiration slide lazily across his left temple and down past his cheek as the young mortgage settlement clerk standing over his right shoulder was speaking in a low, guttural tone and pointing to the signature page of yet another stapled grouping of papers she had just pulled from the top of the ever-so-slowly shrinking stack.

Terry knew that he should be focusing on the papers that he was signing. *This is really important*, he thought. But all that he could bring to mind on that cold and windy day in January, 2008, was the events of the past few months since that first meeting at AvTech Jet Training in Ft. Lauderdale. He thought about all of the encouraging accomplishments at Camber during that time. Although the management at AvTech dragged their feet with the remaining cash installments of the agreed upon consideration for the satellite partnership born at that meeting, they finally kept their word. The cash infusion resulting from this payment dramatically helped the Baltimore flight school survive a few dire shortages of cash experienced between two large infusions from the Navy for new training classes in the late summer and mid-fall months. The number of civilian airline pilot students had grown to over twenty and this division of the company, which was so critical to the long-term strength of the enterprise, was growing as rapidly as predicted. The U.S. airlines showed no signs of slowing their hiring plans for years to come assuring Camber of a steady stream of new commercial students. Jerry Schuler had turned out to be an invaluable asset to the management team at Camber. Not only with the addition of the AvTech program to Camber's FAA Part 141 certificate, but with the redesign and implementation of the new Advanced Aviation Training Devices, or simulators, into all of the programs delivered by Camber, including the Navy. Jerry was a knowledgeable, amiable, and productive member of the team both in Baltimore and in Florida. And then there was the eventual approval of Camber's application for a SEVIS status that would pave the way for marketing to international students at both locations. Although the management at AvTech had been both impatient and unhappy with the amount of time it took the Camber staff to secure this approval, it did indeed take exactly sixteen weeks just as the federal website had promised.

There was also an encouraging turn-of-events while Camber was waiting for the final SEVIS approval. An Indian gentleman by the name of Aman Chopra approached Terry about a month before the approval and had submitted a proposal from his company, with its headquarters in New Delhi, that the two enterprises partner to bring dozens of Indian students to America for airline pilot training and then to eventually establish four brand new, full aviation training facilities in India. Terry was most excited about the potential of this new venture, and he smiled broadly as the young lady to his right continued to place papers in front of him to sign.

The papers kept on coming and his thoughts kept on flowing. But now his mind was consumed with thoughts of the discouraging aspects of the business to date. The shortage of cash was still a significant threat to its survival, and it was getting worse. Camber aircraft had suffered three prop strikes in a period of four months. A prop strike occurs when the propeller of a plane unintentionally strikes any object while in motion. It can happen when the plane assumes an attitude whereby the tip of the propeller descends lower than the nose wheel, usually during landing, and it strikes the ground. Two of the Camber strikes occurred during landings, but the other one was particularly disturbing to the management team. The incident happened as an exceptionally negligent flight instructor, with a Navy student on board, taxied a DA20 from its parking spot on the BWI ramp and within a short twenty-feet from that parking spot he struck a bright orange traffic cone. No one was injured in any of these incidents and the company's aircraft insurance covered all of the expenses of totally dismantling the engines, referred to as "tear-downs," except the $2,000 deductible in each case. The consequences of these accidents, however, were serious for Camber. The additional $6,000 took its toll on the company's cash position, the loss of the three aircraft for nearly two months each for the repairs played havoc with an already full training schedule, and the Navy was furious that all three occurred with Midshipmen aboard. The fact that the two landing prop strikes occurred during solo landings by Midshipmen magnified Pensacola's displeasure with Camber's management maintaining that the discipline of the flight school toward safety precautions was obviously too lax.

Exacerbating the company's financial woes, two full-motion simulators recently added to its programs were acquired on long-term leases that were eating nearly a half-million dollars a year combined. Moreover, additional space had to be rented in a new industrial building across the street from Camber for the simulators costing another $36,000 a year. The use of these simulators would provide an enormous increase in the company's profits but only after it fully digested the up-front costs, which was estimated to take as long as two years. Although the intricate planning conducted by Terry and Ale accounted for most of these sources of cash drain, the cash was still not coming into the company as rapidly as it was going out.

As Terry mentally reviewed all of the discouraging developments presenting themselves during the previous months, he couldn't help but recall a favorite phrase of his grandmother's in situations like this. She would say, "Sonny boy, when it rains it pours!" Aside from being a trademark for a popular manufacturer of table salt his grandmother's pronouncement meant that when things go bad they *really* go bad. And thus Terry brought to mind probably the most threatening turn-of-events to the firm yet. During the previous year, the cost of aviation fuel mirrored the drastic escalations in the price of automobile fuel rising to nearly five dollars per gallon. Ale frequently lamented that filling the tank of a DA20 training aircraft with five dollar a gallon fuel was like putting an extraordinarily expensive cologne on a pig. Just during the most recent six months Camber was paying nearly twice the price for fuel and oil-related products that it had paid earlier in the year. The danger was multiplied by the fact that the students in the airline pilot program had contractually locked-in the prices for their flight training as had the Navy for its program with Camber. The company was being forced to eat the mounting losses caused by the longer-term spike in the cost of a barrel of oil.

Nearly an hour had passed, and Terry was still signing the papers being placed in front of him from a pile that was now almost depleted. But his thoughts were still rampant. *This situation with Camber reminds me of a children's song that Ale told me about from her native Uruguay*, he thought. *It was from her childhood years. The song was about elephants balancing on a string and repeated a verse several times, each time adding another elephant to the string until in the final line of the song:*

> *"All of a sudden the piece of string broke*
> *And down came all the elephant folk"*

I wonder how many Camber elephants it will take before our string will break! Will we be able to dump the Navy contract before it buries us? Stop obsessing on the negative, Terry, he admonished himself, *this new deal with the Indians will turn everything around, and that's on top of all of the potential that this partnership with AvTech has in store for us.* He smiled generously, *we'll be swimming in cash by this time next year!*

"This is the last of the documents you must sign, Mr. Longbow," said the young clerk.

Terry looked at the signature page in front of him and just before he placed his pen to the paper he had one more thought. It was more of a vow actually. *I will never under any circumstances allow Ale to know that I mortgaged my home to the maximum so that Camber could continue to pay her salary and benefits. She must never know!*

While gently biting his lower lip, he signed his name and was handed a cashier's check in the amount of $300,000. As he left the Legg Mason Building in downtown Baltimore and walked briskly in the cold wind across Pratt Street toward the Food Pavilion of Harborplace these words kept going through his head, more as though he was attempting to convince himself of their truth. *Everything is going to be fine, Ale. You and the boys will be much more secure once we turn the corner. And that's going to happen real soon. The string just got a lot stronger under the elephants!*

❋ ❋ ❋ ❋ ❋

The months since the intimate dinner and even more intimate time that Ale and Leo spent together in the car afterward passed quickly, but her thoughts about the events of that evening continued to weigh heavily on her. She found it difficult to sleep through the night due to a haunting realization that she was embarking on a double life that she feared would be impossible to justify. The relationship that Ale had welcomed as a close and fulfilling friendship had turned into a potential nightmare of internal conflict. As the dark of the night turned into the light of dawn one morning in January Ale knew, after thinking about her feelings for Leo over and over, that she desperately wanted him in her life but that she could never justify the potential costs associated with having what she wanted. She got out of bed and opened her laptop to craft an e-mail to Leo. Once again tears streamed down her cheeks.

Leo,

I've been up all night struggling with one of the most difficult decisions of my life. While I want so much for us to continue to nurture our developing relationship I fear that it will lead to my having to accept the adoption of a secret double life, and that is a life that I simply cannot see myself living. You will never fully comprehend how sorry I am to have to make this decision. I am asking that you do not try to contact me or to change my mind by any means. When we see each other for Camber business, we must perform as professionals, as though our personal relationship never existed. I can assure you that this will be every bit as difficult for me as it will for you. Thank you for the times that I will remember for the rest of my life and for a friendship just as memorable. I am truly sorry!

Ale

* * * * *

Christian Foster had not only become a strong ally as a business colleague, he had become a good friend to all at Camber as well. He and Terry were particularly close and, although they never socialized away from work, they could often be seen together in the offices and the hangar during working hours. So when Christian asked for a meeting between himself, Ale, and Terry the two Camber executives thought little of it.

Terry and Ale made themselves as comfortable as they could in Christian's massively cluttered office. They sat in two chairs that faced the SafeFlight CEO's desk. Christian turned toward them while seated behind the desk and began the meeting.

"Ale, Terry, I'm in trouble!" he began. "You see this pile here?" Christian pointed to a stack of brown expandable file folders to his immediate right that each contained about three inches of paper. "These are all unpaid bills owed to me by United Airlines for maintenance we've performed on their aircraft going back almost five months." His voice began to crack as he continued. "This represents over $80,000 in unpaid revenue for SafeFlight and I have to meet a payroll one week from today, and I don't have enough cash to cover it." Christian had been short the cash needed to cover payrolls before but only by a few thousand dollars that he managed to scrape together at the last minute each time. "But now," he continued, "I'm $25,000 short. I don't know what I'm going to do!"

Ale asked, "Have you tried everything to collect it?"

"Sure," he said, "for weeks I've been calling them. Every time they assure me that I will be paid. They keep saying that they are looking into it and they'll get back to me. But they never do."

"What do you think the problem is on their end, Christian?" asked Terry.

The giant of a man sat back in his chair, and it squeaked and groaned as he did. "The bills go from here to a local office that United has on the other side of the field." He pointed out the expansive window to his right that looked out on the entire BWI airport. "People there must approve it, then it goes to a district office located in D.C., and from there to St. Louis, and then to Denver, and finally to their maintenance headquarters in San Francisco. Each bill has to be approved and signed-off at every one of those locations. Then, once approved in San Francisco, the bills go to United's main headquarters in Chicago. Once approved by the accounting and finance people there a check will be cut and mailed—within thirty days."

Terry wasn't trying to make light of an obviously serious situation, but he did want to try to ease some of the stress showing on Christian's face when he said, "Ale and I often refer to what you're describing as typical bureaucratic constipation."

"Well," lamented Christian, "whatever you call it, it's killing SafeFlight!"

Terry looked straight at Christian and said, "You've been extremely good for Camber, and we appreciate that immensely. And I think you know that if we had any spare cash we would happily lend it to you to get you through this difficult stretch. But we're not much healthier in that department than SafeFlight. I just don't know what we could do to help you."

Christian began to say that he wasn't asking for a loan when Ale interrupted him. "Now wait a minute, Terry, maybe there is something we can do."

Suddenly Terry looked puzzled. "What do you mean, Ale?" he asked pointedly.

"I've handled a few situations like this in the past. I have found that the most effective course of action is the direct route to the top." Ale was scratching her head and squinting while she was talking. "Sometimes it has worked and sometimes it hasn't. But if you have tried everything else to no avail I will give it a try."

"What do you have in mind?" asked Christian.

Terry was now smiling a bit as Ale continued, "You make a copy of everything in that pile for me. Give me the name of the maintenance boss-of-which-there-ain't but one—I assume he or she is in San Francisco?"

"Yes," said Christian, "but what are you going to do?"

"I wouldn't do this for anyone else right now but you, Christian, but I'm going to San Francisco."

"What?" came the astounded response.

"It's Friday afternoon," said Ale, "I'll be at the United Airlines maintenance offices at San Francisco Airport first thing Monday morning. I can't make any promises, but I'll do my best to get you paid before payday!"

"You're crazy!" exclaimed Christian. "I'm not gonna argue with you, Ale, but you are one crazy person."

Ale stood as did Terry, and they both walked out of Christian's office toward their own.

"You are crazy, you know!" said Terry.

"Yeah." Ale smiled as she said, "I know!"

At precisely 7:00 the following Monday morning Ale German entered the front door of the office complex attached to the enormous maintenance facility of United Airlines located on the eastern side of the San Francisco International Airport. The lobby was small and narrow with a reception counter to the right and a long sofa opposite it along a windowed wall. There was one receptionist behind the counter when Ale entered, and she immediately greeted her with a smile.

"Good morning," she said, "how can I help you?"

"Good morning," Ale said, "my name is Ale German, and I'm here to see Mr. James McPherson."

Ale fielded the obvious response which the receptionist was trained to deliver, "Do you have an appointment with Mr. McPherson?"

"No, I don't, but I have traveled all the way here from Baltimore to discuss a matter of extreme urgency with him."

Ale had not called ahead to find out if McPherson was even going to be in the office on this Monday morning. For all she knew, the Executive Vice President for Maintenance of United Airlines might have been on the other side of the world. But she did know that the fact that she was asking for the EVP and that she had traveled thousands of miles would most likely draw some serious attention to her presence.

"Why don't you have a seat and I will do everything I can to locate Mr. McPherson for you," said the perky young woman.

Ale sat on the sofa facing the receptionist counter directly in front of her and stared blankly ahead. From time-to-time, the young lady would inform her that she was still unable to reach Mr. McPherson but that she would keep trying. Once, about two hours into her camp-out she was asked if she would like to make an appointment and return. Ale declined, saying that she had to catch a plane back to Baltimore as soon as possible and that she would just wait. She continued to sit in silence. She brought no laptop to work on, and she did not browse through any of the magazines neatly piled on the coffee table in front of her. When asked by the receptionist if she would like anything to drink she politely smiled as she declined. Her demeanor was focused and intense, and she did not want anyone to assume that she was willing to occupy her attention with anything except the purpose of this mission.

The door to Ale's left, obviously the entrance to the office area, was securely locked, and anyone entering the lobby had to sign-in, and then they were escorted through the door by a badged employee. A security guard stood near the door and checked the credentials of all who gained entrance whether they were badged employees or escorted guests. It was clear to Ale that she would not be sneaking through that door undetected at any time during this visit. At noon, another young woman relieved the receptionist who had been facing Ale all morning as she obviously was leaving for her lunch hour. She explained to her replacement before leaving why Ale was waiting patiently and the newcomer immediately placed a call which was followed by the now familiar announcement that Mr. McPherson was not yet available.

When the first receptionist returned from lunch, she tucked her pocketbook securely behind the counter and then placed a telephone call. She spoke in muffled tones for about a minute and then she walked from behind the counter around to the front. She addressed Ale directly. "Ms. German, you have been waiting so patiently for so long to see Mr. McPherson and I am terribly sorry for the wait." She paused, and Ale thought she had probably been instructed by someone to get rid of her tactfully when she continued. "I had lunch with Mr. McPherson's assistant just now and she said that anyone willing to be patient this long deserves the meeting you came for. I just spoke with her and Mr. McPherson is on his way down to greet you."

A few moments later the secured door opened and a tall man dressed in an expensive tailored suit walked toward Ale with his right hand extended. "Ms. German?" he asked with gusto.

"Yes, thank you for taking the time to see me, Mr. McPherson."

"Nonsense, I hear you've come a long way." He paused as he led Ale over to the counter and handed her a pen to sign in, "And please call me Jim."

"Okay, Jim," said Ale as she signed her name in a large bound book on top of the counter.

"Come with me, Ale, there is a small conference room on the other side of this door."

The two sat at a smaller round table as another attractive young lady came to the door and asked if either of them wanted coffee or something else to drink. Ale declined, and Jim said he would have his usual. She seemed to know exactly what he was talking about.

"Now Ale what can I do for you?"

"Jim, when is the next payday at United Airlines?"

The Executive Vice President gave her a bit of a bewildered look and then said, "Well next Friday. Why?"

Ale said, "Jim, all of the employees of United Airlines will get a paycheck next Friday but none of the fine employees of SafeFlight Maintenance, Inc. in Baltimore will be getting one thanks to United Airlines." Ale continued to fill Jim McPherson in on the situation for about a half hour. She explained about Christian and how United had been stalling the payment of all of the invoices that were then placed on the table for the United executive to see first-hand.

When Ale was done McPherson apologized profusely, and he explained that he was escorting her upstairs to the Accounts Payable Department where he would give Betsy, the assistant manager of the department, instructions to take care of the situation. And he did just that. Betsy made copies of every page of the large stack of invoices. She thanked Ale and then escorted her down to the lobby where she then expressed her undying gratitude to the receptionist she had first met about seven hours earlier. Ale got into her rental car and drove to the small hotel where she had spent the night before and would be staying for one more night. At approximately seven that evening her cell phone rang, and when she answered she heard the voice of Jim McPherson. "Ale?" he said on the other end of the call, "I just want you to know that every one of SafeFlight's invoices is on its way to Chicago aboard one of our flights right this minute. I have instructed our staff there to process a full payment tomorrow via wire transfer. Your friend Christian will have every cent of his money before you land back home. Again, please accept my sincerest apologies and extend them to Christian as well."

Ale pressed the "end" button on her phone and said to herself softly, *well what do you know? It worked again!*

TWENTY-SIX

THE STORY OF ALE's success in San Francisco quickly became a legend among all who had any contact with SafeFlight, Camber, and Elite Services. It seemed to her as though everyone wanted the story from her first-hand during the months that followed. She was careful to explain to all who inquired about it, however, that the outcome could have gone either way. Furthermore, it actually wasn't that much of a gamble when you compare the cost of a round-trip coach plane ticket and a couple of nights in a hotel against the possibility of collecting $80,000 for a company desperately in need of cash. Nevertheless, Ale was the hero of the day to many and this one happenstance incident seemed to change the entire mood of the employees and customers of Camber to a much brighter one than had existed before her trip to the West Coast. The euphoria was short-lived, however, as the events of the following six months gradually overshadowed it.

The late winter and early spring months of that year were particularly brutal for a growing yet financially struggling flight school in the Baltimore area. If it wasn't snowing or raining then the winds were blowing constantly at twenty knots or higher, and Terry marked the calendar sitting on his desk at Camber for each day that the planes could not fly due to the weather. By the first of April his calendar revealed that of the 90 days since the first of the year, many had been totally unflyable, and the financial toll this trend had taken on the company was nearly catastrophic. Every Camber student, regardless of their program, had long since used every simulator hour they were allowed for their respective training curriculum, so nobody was flying anything until the weather subsided. Instructors and other hourly employees were starving for lack of income, the owners of the planes leased to Camber were forced to pay all of the fixed expenses for their aircraft without the benefit of any revenue to offset them whatsoever, and the management team at Camber was scrambling to cut costs to the bone and stretch payments to vendors and creditors to well beyond acceptable dates. It had become commonplace for Terry to remark to Ale that things would change for the better as soon as they could finalize the Indian deal. But that potential relief seemed to be moving much too slowly for anyone's comfort.

In mid-March, about two-thirds of the way into the weather related shut down of Camber's flight operations, Terry received a call from the less-than-pleased Lieutenant Commander in Pensacola. He was complaining about the exceptionally low number of flying hours accumulated by Naval students in the previous months and accusing Camber of slighting the Navy program in favor of the civilian programs that the flight school was developing. Terry was as calm and reserved as he could be while explaining that the weather must be just as bad outside the windows at the Academy as it was just twenty miles up the road at BWI and that there would not be any resumption of flying for anyone until the weather improved significantly. Terry was then informed that there had been a change in command at Pensacola and that the new commanding officer of the Navy's flight indoctrination program would be visiting Annapolis the following week. The Pensacola second-in-command told Terry that he and Lieutenant Moultry, the new C.O., would be inspecting Camber on Monday morning of the following week and that a formal meeting at the flight school would follow the inspection. Terry agreed to be prepared, but after hanging up he wondered aloud why the Navy would place a lowly Lieutenant in charge of the entire training program in Pensacola. There had never been an officer ranking lower than a Lieutenant Commander in the position since the training initiative began decades earlier.

The inspection of the facilities and fleet went as well as could be expected on a cold, rainy, and windy Monday morning at BWI. Lieutenant Moultry, a rather formal and quiet officer obviously in his early forties, with Lieutenant Forester in tow led Terry, Ale, and Matt through a regimented inspection routine. During the hour-long walk through the Camber facilities and out on the tarmac Ale and Leo remained carefully separated by the others, so as not to come into direct contact with each other. Following the site inspection the group walked to the Elite building for the scheduled meeting in one of the available conference rooms. Ale and Leo seated themselves on opposite sides of the conference table, but it was difficult for each of them to avoid eye contact with the other. Immediately after sitting, Leo caught Ale's attention while looking at her and she gave him a restrained, business-like smile which was promptly returned. Moultry got right down to business.

"Some changes are being made with my new command in Pensacola," he began, "and I want to go over them with you while I am here. First, Camber's record of completion of students in a timely manner is abysmal."

Ale interrupted him immediately. "Excuse me, Lieutenant," she said sternly, "but I have here in my hand a series of regular reports that we get from the staff at Pensacola that all state that Camber has the best record of any Naval indoctrination school in the country." Leo couldn't help but grin when she went on the offensive with the upstart from Pensacola so quickly. He placed the fingers of his right hand over his mouth so that no one else would notice.

"Doesn't matter," replied the unrelenting junior officer. "None of the schools in the system is meeting even the minimum standards so being the best of the worst is not acceptable!" He turned his attention away from Ale's eyes and toward Terry as he continued, "Effective immediately there will be a financial penalty charged for every day that every student is extended in the program beyond the 100 days allowed for the completion of that student's training."

Terry looked at Ale in disbelief.

Ale reached down into her pocketbook, which was sitting on the floor by her left foot under the table, and removed her cell phone. She kept the phone in her lap so that no one else could see what she was doing. While the Lieutenant from Pensacola was continuing his impression of Napoleon, she tapped a text message onto the Blackberry's keyboard.

"Leo—meet me somewhere after the meeting?"

"We are also changing the amount that will be paid for each student's training. It is being reduced from $5,500 to $4,675 per student effective immediately. And we will no longer be paying for training in advance. Each school will submit an invoice for the full amount of training for each student immediately after he or she completes the program. The invoices will be audited and processed in Pensacola after they have been approved by the Lieutenant's staff in Annapolis, and then payment will be processed via the same credit card system we now use. Any invoice submitted incorrectly or with inaccurate or incomplete information will be rejected, and you will have to start the process all over again. Any questions?"

Ale stared at Moultry for several moments. Then she spoke in a controlled and deliberate tone of voice. "Lieutenant, you do realize that these changes in the Navy program will put most if not all of the flight school contractors out of business don't you?"

"We're not concerned about propping-up a bunch of private businesses that are in poor financial shape with our liberal cash-up-front policies any longer, Ms. German," he replied in as stern a manner as his earlier remarks. "We have a military job to do, and we are going to do it in an efficient and effective military way."

The officer looked around the room for just a few seconds and then said, "Hearing no further questions this meeting is adjourned." He and Forester stood, then turned and quickly exited the conference room.

"Well Terry," said Ale with a reserved smile on her face. "As I see it, we could have told them to stick their changes where the sun don't shine, or we could have just quietly sat there and listened. Openly fighting them would have put us out of business immediately. At least this way we buy ourselves a little bit of time to follow through with our original plan to replace the Navy business with another source of revenue. But whatever we do we'd better do it real soon!"

Ale stood, reached down for her pocketbook, and began to walk to the door of the conference room. She turned toward Terry who was following behind her.

"I'm going to disappear for awhile, Terry. Can you hold down the fort?"

Terry responded, "Sure. Everything okay?"

"Yeah I just need to get away for a little while. I'll be back in a few hours."

She walked into Elite's lobby and once again removed her Blackberry from her bag. When she powered it up, she saw a response from Leo.

"Of course, where do you want to meet?"

Ale knew that they should stay away from Annapolis and from the vicinity of Camber and the Orion offices, and she thought for a few moments.

"At the park—at the end of Runway 33 Left—where everybody goes to watch the planes land. Know where I'm talking about?"

A few minutes passed as Ale walked the few hundred yards across the parking lot to her car. As she opened the door and slid into the driver's seat, she heard the familiar sound from her phone indicating an incoming text.

"Proceeding there now."

*****

The Thomas A Dixon Observation Area was located almost immediately adjacent to the end of one of BWI's busiest runways and was a part of a 12.5 mile paved jogging and bike trail providing a circumference for the expansive BWI airport property. The Observation Area contained a free parking lot for about a hundred cars and next to the lot was a playground. Children divided their time there between the jungle gym and sliding boards and then shouting and pointing every time a large jet would lumber overhead at a low altitude just seconds before touching down on the nearby runway. Ale pulled onto the lot and parked in one of the only remaining spots and just after exiting her car she saw Leo waiting near the playground. She waved and smiled at him as she closed the distance between them and he did the same.

"Thanks for meeting me here, Leo," she said as she gave him a hug and extended her left cheek.

"Are you kidding?" he responded with a subtle chuckle. "I was convinced that I would never have this opportunity again. I don't know what you want to talk about, Ale, but I want to start off by saying that this has been one hell of a bad few months for me! But I'm guessing you just want to discuss what happened back there in the conference room."

"No, not at all!" she replied rapidly. "In fact, I don't want to talk business with you. I want to talk about us."

"Okay," Leo said sheepishly, "let's talk."

"Do you mind if we walk and talk at the same time," she asked.

"No, I'd prefer it."

"Leo," she paused and looked to the ground in front of her while still walking at a moderate pace. "A part of me wants to apologize to you for the way I reacted to the end of our last meeting, but the other part of me is convinced that I shouldn't have to. That will give you a good idea of how confused I am."

"That's easy," said Leo when she paused again. "There is no reason in the world that you should feel the need to apologize to me!"

"I know," Ale continued, "but we had a good thing going and I just suddenly cut it off. I'm afraid I hurt you real badly, and I am sorry for that, but I just got scared and, at the time, ending our relationship just seemed like the only alternative available to me." She stopped talking for a moment, looked up at Leo, and waited for him to say something.

"Ale, I made a mistake. I shouldn't have compromised the trust that you had built in me by trying to take our relationship to the next level. Your reaction is more than justifiable and understandable and I've been kicking myself every day for months for being so stupid."

Ale chuckled and said, "Well you're still being kinda stupid."

"What do you mean?" he responded.

"I wasn't upset, Leo, about what happened in the car after dinner that evening. I was upset, and scared to death because I enjoyed it. I was up many nights terrified that I was allowing myself to fall into a relationship that I might deeply regret later on. I imagined what until that day was the unimaginable, that I was taking the first step toward leaving Franco and exposing my sons to a life after divorce that I have solemnly sworn all my life I would never allow to happen. While I was laying in bed and all of these thoughts kept racing through my mind I felt like the walls and the ceiling were closing in on me. Believe me, Leo, the last thing in the world I wanted to do was to write that e-mail to you. But," she hesitated as though she was not sure that she wanted to divulge what was coming, "my life has been one gigantic empty for the past six months without seeing you or talking to you. And today when I saw you again, especially when you were trying to hide that stupid little grin behind your hand at the conference table, I knew that we had to meet as soon as possible to see if we can talk this thing through."

Leo walked quietly for several yards and because of his silence Ale was beginning to think that he was having second thoughts about meeting her at all. And then he stopped, turned toward her, and took both of her hands into his.

"Ale," he spoke softly and slowly, "I've never been a big lady's man. I don't date much, and I really never have. I like to think that the reason is because I'm just not cut out for all of the games that people play in dating relationships. So I'm not going to play any games here with you. As corny as it may sound to you, I've known from the moment I first saw you in the Orion conference room that I truly want to have an extraordinarily special relationship with you. I'm going to ask you not to laugh, and please don't run away, but I love you."

Ale started to say something, but Leo gently placed the index finger of his right hand on her mouth before any words could be spoken.

"Let me finish please," he said. "But I have known since that first time that I will never be able to have you as my own. That's why I feel so foolish for allowing our time together in the car go in the direction that it did. That was exactly what you didn't need at that time or any other. I want you to know that if you will just allow this relationship to continue I will never do anything that you may feel is inappropriate. Again, I hope you don't think this is silly, but if the only way that I can continue to see you and be a part of your life is for our relationship to be a purely platonic one then my love for you is strong enough to accept that condition—for the long haul."

"Leo, I don't think you are silly, and I didn't run away, did I? In fact, I feel the same way about you. This past month has taught me that although I thought I couldn't live with you in my life, I honestly don't want to live without you in it. I believe now that you not only know about my situation but that you respect it and will continue to respect it. That's all I ask. Let's just see where this life takes us, okay?"

Without even consciously realizing it, the two had completed the smaller circular path back to the parking lot and were standing by Ale's car.

"Okay," said Leo warmly and with a smile.

Ale gave him a firm hug and then stood on her toes to kiss him on the right cheek.

"Hey," he said almost as a post-script. "How about if you are the one to always call me? That way I won't be catching you at any inopportune times."

"Okay Leo," she responded with a smile, "I'll call you!"

Ale got into the Pathfinder, started it, and began to pull from the parking spot, and she never took her eyes off of Leo.

* * * * *

A few weeks into April all was returning to normal at Camber. The skies had turned sunny, and the winds died down. Flight operations were running at full schedule once again with students in all of the programs attempting to make up for the time they lost during months of being idled by the inclement weather. Jerry Schuler was racking up some serious frequent flyer miles commuting between Ft. Lauderdale and Baltimore, especially since the FAA approved the Florida operation as a satellite of

Camber Flight Training, Inc. The approval was not without its challenges and delays, however. The FAA's representative designated as responsible for approving or rejecting the Ft. Lauderdale proposed site was none other than Mark Ingram, the Baltimore FSDO agent best known for splitting hairs and going by the book. Just when the time consuming process was nearing an end, the inspector placed a serious obstacle in the way of the completion of the deal. It was his opinion that Camber could not establish the AvTech flight training operation as a satellite because the former company did not own the latter. Terry and Ale argued long and hard that there was nothing in any of the FAA Regulations that would require ownership by Camber in order for the Satellite to be established, but Ingram wouldn't budge. After a few months of appeals during the winter to the FAA regional offices Ale's arguments prevailed and the FAA reluctantly approved the arrangement in early April. But the damage of the inordinate delay had taken its toll on the relationship between the ownership of Camber and that of AvTech as Jerry was about to inform Terry and Ale in his regular weekly meeting with them.

"What do you mean Howard Young is playing games in Ft. Lauderdale, Jerry?" Ale asked as she, Terry, and Jerry were meeting in one of their favorite spots in Ellicott City not far from their offices in Columbia. Jerry made every attempt not to appear defensive as he was reporting the latest turn-of-events at the Florida operation.

"Young has transferred all of AvTech's aircraft and instructors over to another Part 141 school located right next to them at the Executive Airport. He has dismantled almost everything I worked so hard to establish to mirror our Baltimore program, and he has begun delivering jet training to international students using the 141 certificate of the other school without formally becoming a satellite approved by the FAA. He says you guys just took too long to pull it off. And," Jerry sheepishly paused, "by the way, Young says he wants his $100,000 back!"

Ale chuckled as she stirred some Splenda into her skim cappuccino and took a sip. "I don't think so, scooter!" she said. "We worked far harder and spent far more money making those SEVIS and FAA certifications happen than we ever expected. If Young wants to pull out of the deal then fine, but he's not going to see a dime of that money from me!" The other two nodded in complete agreement as they sipped on their coffee and tea. Terry and Ale would often meet at The Old Mill Bakery because of its charm and location on the eastern side of historic Ellicott City. It was situated just across from the old B&O Railroad trestle that was part of the legendary Tom Thumb race between a steam locomotive and a horse drawn carriage on August 28, 1830. The two Camber executives usually sat on a comfortable sofa around the corner and to the right from the entrance. Ale motioned to Jerry with her half empty cup and said, "Can you find us another jet training school that will be more anxious to partner with us, Jerry?"

"I know just whom I'll talk to! Harvey Crouse owns National Flight Training, Inc. in Miami. The company is ten times larger than AvTech and has many more full-motion simulators for all kinds of air transport aircraft. I think he would jump at the chance to do business with us!" Jerry exclaimed.

Ale looked squarely at Jerry and asked, "Who do you work for, Jerry?"

"I work for you Ale, and Camber. I have no allegiance to anyone else!" replied Jerry immediately.

"Okay then," she said in return, "make it happen with Crouse and National Flight Training!"

Jerry left the Camber duo a few minutes after their meeting had concluded. Ale was telling Terry how this new setback would have to be overcome quickly because of the Navy time bomb that was still ticking away, when her cell phone rang and interrupted her. She looked at the screen, and before she answered it, she excused herself from the vicinity of Terry's ears. "I'm sorry, Terry, I have to take this." She walked outside and spoke privately on the call for several minutes. Terry watched her through the window as he thought, *that's odd, she's never excluded me from hearing one of her phone conversations, even some extremely private ones since we started working together. I wonder what's going on?*

* * * * *

Terry, Aman Chopra, and his partner Todd Zanti spent nearly the entire month of May negotiating a partnership contract between Camber and Chiva Pria Corporation of India. The effort was so time consuming that Ale remained at BWI and managed the day-to-day operations of the flight school while Terry was occupied in their Columbia offices with the negotiations. The two agents of the large Indian investment holding company were extremely excited about the opportunity and were nothing short of animated in their presentations of the outstanding opportunities for each company involved. Chopra was the primary spokesman of the two and he eloquently made several PowerPoint presentations emphasizing the phenomenal growth potential of India as a rising financial power in the world while at the same time graphically portraying the antiquated, and in many cases non-existent state of the infrastructure of the entire nation, especially the country's primitive aviation industry. The presentations highlighted the Indian firm's desire to create a sophisticated airline network throughout the emerging society and their desire to begin with four flight academies located strategically near large population centers. Zanti pointed out that the government of India had already ruled that expatriates, or foreign airline pilots, were to be slowly reduced in number by the nation's airlines and replaced by qualified Indian Nationals in an organized and deliberate manner. The number of pilot positions projected to be opened by this directive was enormous, and Chiva Pria planned to be on the profitable side of this cultural transition.

The meetings were long and the discussions detailed and technical, but they were never once contentious in any way. The three executives got along famously, and the final contract that was taking shape promised to be a lucrative deal all the way around. Toward the end of the month of negotiations, there were frequent telephone conference calls between Baltimore and New Delhi, which required several late night sessions in Columbia. Terry did not mind the long hours, but the timing of many of the meetings made it virtually impossible to spend much time helping Ale run the business. He was more than confident in her ability to handle everything by herself, but he felt guilty that it required her to work some long hours as well, placing additional stress on her responsibilities as a mother. On several occasions, Terry promised her that as soon as the Indian deal was a reality he would ship her and the boys off on a long and well deserved vacation together, perhaps to her native Uruguay, which she hadn't visited in over a decade.

Everything Terry and Jesse heard from the two representatives in the conference room and by phone from the executives in New Delhi was extremely encouraging. At one point, Terry brought Jerry Schuler directly into the negotiations because he had expressed a strong interest in traveling to India to manage the foreign flight school development on behalf of Camber. When the agreement was completed it provided that Chiva Pria would own thirty percent of Camber Flight Training, Inc. In return for their ownership share of the corporate stock, they would invest $3 million in cash in the business, payable in equal six month increments beginning with the first $1 million delivered when the contracts were signed. The Chairman of the Indian holding company agreed to travel to Baltimore with two other high-level executives for the contract signing and that he would take a tour of the Camber facility while in town. The agreement stated that the initial payment would be wire transferred immediately upon the document signing and the exchange of the stock certificates. The consummation of the partnership was tentatively scheduled for the week of July 21st, which would give the partners-to-be plenty of time to obtain the approval of their respective boards halfway around the world from each other.

During the arduous and sometimes difficult negotiations due to the language barrier, Terry forged an intriguing friendship with a group of Americans of Indian descent not far from his home. The owner of a Seven-Eleven located at the intersection of Maryland Routes 103 and 104 in Ellicott City became a crucial and trustworthy advisor to Terry regarding the Indian culture and what the Camber owner should and should not say or do that might be offensive to his new partners. Rupen Parikh, the owner, and his employees Jignesh, Jessica, and Shyam, frequently met with Terry late at night in the back room of their store and tutored him on all matters crucial to the success of his negotiations with the Chiva Pria group. Rupen had already proven to be an excellent example of how to succeed as an entrepreneur in an inventory intensive retail business after Terry's many visits to his Seven-Eleven, and now he and his employees provided critical information in his role as an international negotiator.

Once the negotiations were completed Jerry returned to Florida to continue to work on the partnership with Crouse and National Flight Training in Miami. Terry got some much-needed rest and then immediately returned to Camber to help Ale with a busy schedule there. He took the time to brief her on his first day back, and although she seemed relieved that the meetings were over, she still appeared to Terry to be a little skeptical about the whole Indian partnership.

The summer months passed slowly as Terry shuttled back-and-forth between Baltimore and Miami tending to all of the meetings and decisions involved in forging a partnership with the management of the jet training center there. The NFT facility was immense, and the company's clientele was predominantly international. This served to convince Terry that even though the deal with AvTech collapsed all of the work involved in securing the SEVIS approval would still pay off when the Indians started arriving in Baltimore in large numbers.

By mid-July Camber was serving nearly fifty airline pilot students, all on a part-time basis, however, and over one-hundred civilian pleasure students. The Navy flying was bleeding the company dry of cash. The invoices submitted to the Academy for Midshipmen who had completed the program got lost immediately in bureaucratic constipation worse than Terry had ever experienced before. Ale had set up a tracking system so that she would know where any invoice submitted to the Navy should be at any time in the approval process. The average time from invoice submission to payment was taking nearly three months with the Navy claiming that many of the bills Ale was attempting to collect on had never actually been submitted by her. Camber had to hire an additional clerical employee just to handle the paperwork created by the changes recently instituted by the Pensacola brass. Complaints from Terry to Lieutenant Forrester fell on deaf ears and the officers in Pensacola rarely returned any of Terry's calls demanding payment.

No one but Ale seemed particularly discouraged when the week of

July 21st came and went with no visit from the Indians and no million dollar cash injection into the business. Aman Chopra and Todd Zanti both stopped by Camber every day to reassure the management personally that there was nothing to worry about. And they continued to visit the flight school on a daily basis and meet with Terry and Ale, reinforcing the strength of the agreement during the months of August and September. In the meantime, Camber was faltering. The schedule was full and students in the civilian programs were flying regularly, but cash was becoming more and more scarce.

At the regular Camber board meeting on Thursday, October 30th, the mood was one of near despair. Despite the cheerleading of the two primary contacts for the belated Indian partnership, the delegation from India had not yet presented themselves or their money. The only thing they had presented was an excuse each month why they couldn't yet make the trip. Chopra and Zanti were at the meeting, and they swore that they would personally travel to India to secure the funds and bring them back to America if there were any more delays. Then just when the board was prepared to move on to discuss the Miami deal Chopra spoke up.

"We have a very big surprise for you!" he exclaimed in his own style of broken English. He placed his cell phone on the conference table in front of everyone and he said, "Hello, go ahead."

"Hello?" came a male voice from the speaker of the phone, "are you there, America?"

Terry was the first to speak up, "Yes, we're here, who is this?"

"I am Venygopal Rao, Chairman of Chiva Pria in New Delhi, and I have with me Raj Kapoor, Vice Chairman. We want to assure you that we are sincere about our agreement, and we will tomorrow purchase our plane tickets to come to America next month to sign the contracts."

Understanding the broken English was difficult enough but having it transmitted to you over thousands of miles via a cell phone on each end was nearly impossible. But everyone around the table knew what was said nevertheless. And everyone, or almost everyone, was visibly relieved. When the call had ended the two Indian representatives left the room and Jerry proceeded to inform the board that Terry, Ale, and he would be traveling the next week to Miami to conduct the final negotiations with National Flight Training, Inc. It finally appeared that the two deals that meant life or death to Camber would indeed be coming to fruition.

When Terry left the meeting and got into his car, he was exhausted. In addition to all of the full days at Camber and all of the stress of recent activities, he had gotten into the habit of waking up at 3:00 a.m. to watch the CNBC coverage of the Indian Sensex, their stock market, to see if they were doing any better than the Dow Jones. Terry was a finance man first and foremost, so it was not unusual that he kept a close eye on the American economy in general, and the stock markets specifically. During the previous year, he had been worried about the Camber cash position and the personnel problems as well as all of the potential good things that might happen to make this foray into the world of aviation a smart move. But what he worried most about during that year was the American economy. The Dow finished at 14,164 in October of 2007; then down to 11,740 in April of 2008, and it was diving toward 8,500 on the day of this board meeting. And he knew from his consistent late night review of the Indian stock market that it was in even worse shape than the Dow. He knew full well that he would be terribly worried until the moment he sees that first million dollars in the Camber cash account. But he also knew that he could not let on to Ale or anyone else about his serious worry regarding the situation. And then while driving home in the dark from the board meeting he heard a familiar song on the radio. He turned the radio up so that he could hear the words clearly. It was a song from a couple of decades earlier written by Terri Sharp and the version he was listening to was being sung by Don McLean. Suddenly the Camber executive sat up straight, and he felt a cold chill run down his spine as he listened closely to the song's familiar lyrics. It cautioned that if you ignore all of the warning signals at a railroad crossing, and attempt to cross the tracks in spite of them, *"well then you can't blame the wreck on the train."*

TWENTY-SEVEN

AT PRECISELY 6:00 on Monday morning, November 17th Ale was startled by the ring of her cell phone located on her night table and close to her ear. She had forgotten to lower the ring volume on the phone before she turned-in as was her custom and the shrill sound imitating the ring of a Twentieth-Century land-line phone snapped her to consciousness immediately.

"Hello," she barely uttered in a sleepy guttural tone.

"Good morning, Ale," came the quick reply from the caller.

"Leo?" she said not even attempting to hide the surprise in her now clear voice. "What the…"

She was sharply interrupted by Leo's deep voice. "I'm sorry to call you at this hour, Ale," he continued, "but we may have a serious problem."

"What's wrong?"

Leo's tone was somber but urgent. "I just got a call from Moultry in Pensacola and he wants Terry and me down there in his office as soon as possible today. This isn't good, Ale."

"Uh," Ale paused for a moment as she thought of her response. "Terry is leaving for Miami, and he's going to be tied up for at least two days with our airline training contractors down there. I have to be in Atlanta tomorrow, so I'll have to get on the first flight to Pensacola, stay there tonight and then leave for Atlanta first thing tomorrow morning."

"Moultry specifically said that he wants Terry there," said Leo.

"Well then he's just going to have to be disappointed, isn't he? I'm just as much an owner of Camber as Terry, and I'm not going to tolerate any of Moultry's chauvinistic bullshit about wanting to deal with Terry instead of me!"

"Whoa Ale!" answered Leo. "Don't kill the messenger! I'm just telling you what he said."

"I know, and I'm just telling you that I'll be in Pensacola later this afternoon and if Moultry tries to intimidate me in any way, directly or indirectly, he'll wish he was a steward on the Good Ship Lollipop scrubbing the deck all day with rust solvent and a toothbrush."

Leo astutely decided that he would end this conversation with Ale as quickly as possible since his early unplanned wake-up call was probably the cause of her acerbic attitude. "What time do you want to leave BWI? I'll make the airline reservations for us."

"Leo, I would like for you to make a reservation for me, but I want to be on a different flight, actually, a different airline. I don't think it would be wise for us to arrive together."

"Okay," said Leo, "I'll text you with your flight information. Want me to make a hotel reservation for you? I assume you'll want separate hotels for us as well."

"Yes Leo, please make a room reservation for me. But the same hotel is OK with me—just rooms on different floors if you don't mind."

"Got it, Ale. I'll see you in Pensacola," he said immediately before hanging up.

Ale was angry that Moultry had summoned a Camber owner to Pensacola without any prior notice whatsoever. And she was even angrier that he specifically preferred Terry over her for the meeting. But she was also excited about being able to see Leo in a distant environment without having to rush home early. *It will be nice to have a quiet dinner with Leo*, she thought. *We haven't had any quiet time together since the day we agreed to continue our relationship. Uh-oh,"* her thought process continued, *what if…?* She caught herself for a moment, smiled ever so slightly, and then thought, *let's just see where the day takes us.*

＊＊＊＊＊

The Airtran Boeing 717 jet aircraft gently touched down on Runway 17 at Pensacola Airport on time at 2:37 p.m. The flight was uneventful in clear weather all along the route although there were slightly turbulent moments at times. Ale was delighted to be back on the ground, and she fumbled for her cell phone to catch up on texts and messages while the plane taxied for a few minutes to the arrival gate.

The cab ride to Moultry's office complex took less than five minutes, and the meeting was scheduled to begin as soon as Ale could arrive on the site. She entered the front door of the building and was greeted by a Lieutenant JG who looked to Ale to be too young to be enrolled at the Academy, let alone an officer. She smiled and received one in return and was unceremoniously escorted to the conference room where Leo and two other Navy officers, whom Ale did not recognize were waiting. Leo was obviously being careful to discreetly avoid eye contact with her as she sat in a chair on the side of a large oak conference table opposite where everyone else was sitting. Ale was hoping that the silence for the ten minutes that it took Moultry to arrive was as awkward for the others as it was for her.

The door to the large conference room opened immediately following a loud click from the electronic security lock, and Moultry's impressive six-foot-two presence seemed to fill the doorway with little room to spare. The three officers rose to salute and then shake hands with him, but Ale decided to remain seated and maintain as formal a posture as possible.

"Good morning," said Moultry sternly appearing to be careful that he address all without focusing on any one individual. He continued as he sat in the largest chair at the head of the table, "Welcome Ms. German," he said with more of a sneer than a smile. "Are we awaiting the arrival of Mr. Longbow?" He made no attempt to shake hands with Ale nor did he offer her any sort of refreshments, which she might have welcomed after her flight from Baltimore.

Ale could feel the hair on the back of her neck bristle at the sound of his question as she fought to contain a visceral revulsion brought on by Moultry's arrogant and condescending attitude toward her. "Terry won't be joining us, he had some important business to attend to," she said with only the slightest tone of scorn in her voice.

"Oh," replied the Lieutenant. He stared at her for a moment as if in deep thought and then continued. "Well then I guess everyone necessary is present. Let's get started."

Moultry looked at each of the officers sitting to his left one at a time before addressing Ale. She was sure that she noticed an almost imperceptible smile of hubris on his face as he began his remarks to her. "When we met at BWI back in March I informed Terry that Camber was not meeting its contractual obligations to the Navy and that the company's performance would have to improve dramatically and very quickly to avoid inevitable punitive consequences."

"You didn't just inform Mr. Longbow, Lieutenant. I was there as well, and I am an equal owner of the business with him." *Keep your cool,* she thought. *If you lose it then you lose period! Don't give him the benefit of knowing that he got to you!*

"Of course you are," said Moultry in a patronizing manner. "Anyway, I'll continue. Unfortunately, Camber's performance has not improved. Your firm has continued to deliver sub-standard training and still is completing students well after their respective deadlines required in the contract."

"I'm going to interrupt you here, Lieutenant."

"No, Ms. German. You can wait until I ask you to speak," he admonished.

Ale German could be as patient a business person as any other, but she also steadfastly adhered to the philosophy of the mid-Twentieth-Century rock singer named Janis Joplin who sang, *freedom is having nothing left to lose.*

"Lieutenant," she said in a stern but still professional tone as she rose from her seat and applied her weight to the knuckles of both of her hands resting as fists on the table in front of her. "Nobody informs me in a condescending manner when I can and cannot speak; you got it, Mister?"

Still speaking in a volume only slightly higher than that of a pleasant conversation she did not give the startled junior officer a chance to get a word in as she continued. "As I explained to you in March the Academy refuses to exercise any authority or discipline over your future pilots and, therefore, we have an alarming record of no-shows for scheduled students, and many give numerous excuses for failing to even schedule in the first place. We had abysmal weather this last spring, and an enormous number of flights had to be cancelled as a consequence. As for the quality of our instruction, these current reports from your own people prove that you don't have the foggiest idea what you are talking about. Camber continues to deliver the highest quality pilots to Pensacola of all of the civilian contractor flight schools in the country." Ale began to rise from her knuckles and she reached to her right for her pocketbook without ever pausing from her soliloquy. Standing straight up with her pocketbook in her right hand and motioning to the Lieutenant with the index finger of her left hand she continued. "Your information is wrong, and it always has been. And your attitude toward me and Camber is wrong, and it always has been. You can take your Navy flight training contract and stick it where the sun don't shine, Lieutenant. Camber is terminating our working relationship with you effective immediately!" As she walked in a most dignified manner to the conference room door, everyone could hear her say in a quasi respectful manner, "Good day, gentlemen."

At the curb in front of the small office building, Ale was able to hail a cab almost immediately. She gave the cab driver the name of the hotel texted to her earlier by Leo and, upon her arrival, she registered in the lobby then proceeded directly to her room. *My next conversations with Terry and Leo are going to be extremely interesting,* she thought.

✶ ✶ ✶ ✶ ✶

"That was nothing short of amazing," exclaimed Leo for the fourth time during his dinner with Ale at The Fish House restaurant located just off of East Main Street and right on the harbor. Their table on the wharf deck overlooking the docked pleasure craft and the open water that, somewhere out there, joined the Gulf of Mexico was perfect for a quiet and relatively secluded conversation. The weather was clear and warm, but Ale noticed the tops of some high clouds way out on the horizon over the water that reminded her of the ones they saw during the last leg of their St. Michaels boat trip.

"Looks as though we may be in for a storm tonight," she said as she nodded her head toward the distant clouds and took another bite of the fish sampler in front of her.

"Not unusual at all," Leo replied as he also continued to eat. "Have you told Terry yet?" he asked a little sheepishly.

"No. I figured I would wait and call him when I land in Atlanta tomorrow morning. No sense in spoiling his night, and frankly I don't feel like going into it with him right now."

There was a short period of silence as the two finished their dinner and enjoyed the scenery and then Leo asked, "What's in Atlanta?"

Ale did not answer right away using a sip of her water, with only a little ice and a twist of lemon as usual, as a decoy to stall her response. Then she said, "I just have some business to take care of and then I'll be meeting Terry in Miami so that we can finalize the deal with National Flight Training for the jet side of our airline pilot program."

Leo decided not to push for anymore answers about her visit to Atlanta as he slid his chair from the table, turned to one side and crossed his legs comfortably. It was obvious to him that Ale had something on her mind, and he could not determine whether she was just preoccupied with the events of earlier that afternoon, or whether something else was bothering her, but he figured it best to be quiet and let her take the lead if any conversation was forthcoming. Occasionally she caught him admiring her striking features in the light of the sun which was setting just to the south of the thunderstorms which appeared to be getting closer to the shore. When he got caught he smiled, and she smiled back, and then her eyes wandered out to sea once more.

"I'm sorry that I am not much of a conversationalist this evening, Leo," she said with a warm look straight into his eyes. "It's not you, I just have an awful lot on my mind right now."

"Are you uncomfortable being here with me twelve-hundred miles from home?"

"No, not at all!" After a short pause, she added, "I think I'm more comfortable than I've been in years."

Once again he yielded to her silence and watched the storms approach from the southwest. Thunderstorms had always mesmerized Leo. He would sit for hours on the deck of the USS *Nimitz* in the Persian Gulf watching them move slowly across the water in the pre-dawn hours before climbing into the business end of an F-18 Hornet to deliver a few tons of ordinance to surgically selected targets in Iraq.

"What are you thinking about?" Ale finally asked him.

"You," he replied quietly.

She smiled at him as she gently touched the tips of the fingers on his left hand with those of her right hand and then withdrew her hand across the table as cryptically as she had advanced it a few seconds earlier.

"Are you ready to go?" he asked. "The storms will be hitting soon, and I'd like to get you back so that you don't get too wet."

"Yes," she replied. "And I want to call the boys before it gets too late. Thank you for a very nice dinner, Leo. Again, I'm sorry I wasn't much company."

"I would have enjoyed every minute even if you hadn't said a single word."

The ride in Leo's rented Ford Taurus from the restaurant to the hotel was about ten short minutes and already it had started to rain. He pulled the car under the carport roof at the hotel's entrance so that Ale could get into the lobby without getting wet and then parked as close as possible to the front door, but still far enough that he got soaked making his way across the parking lot. The lightning was vivid and frequent and the thunder shattered the otherwise tranquil night air at times setting off car alarms in the vicinity of the hotel. Leo was pleased to see Ale waiting for him just inside the entrance.

"You're drenched," she said as she laughed along with him while they entered the lobby and walked toward the elevators. As the elevator doors closed she was the closest to the control panel, and she asked, "What floor, Lieutenant?"

"Uh let's see," he said as he removed a small paper envelope containing his plastic room key and he looked at the writing on the outside. "624—the sixth floor please, Ma'am," he said jokingly. Ale pushed the button labeled six and then the one labeled eight, and then gave Leo a tight hug as the doors opened on the sixth floor.

"Thank you, Ale," he said as he began to exit the elevator. "Call me when you get settled-in so that I know you're okay."

"I will," she said with a smile. "Good night, Leo."

An hour later Leo was sitting in a chair near the window of his room in his sweatpants and a tee shirt after having taken a warm shower, when his cell phone rang.

"Hey, are you all tucked in for the night?" he said having seen Ale's name on the screen.

"Not exactly," she answered.

"Why, what's wrong?" he asked.

"Nothing, I'm not in my room," was her reply.

"Where are you?" he asked with some concern in his voice.

"Open the door and you'll see."

The night hours passed all too quickly for Ale and Leo. The curtains were left open, and the dark room frequently lit up brightly as lightning bedazzled the sky outside the windows that stretched across the full length of the room. The wind driven rain relentlessly pounded against the windows with a din punctuated frequently by the explosive roar of thunder. But the occupants of Room 624 were oblivious to the sounds outside. They treasured the brief time they had together before the first light of the morning, and their inevitable and imminent parting which would relegate this night to a mere memory, albeit a cherished one for each of them.

During the early morning cab ride from the hotel to the airport Ale was consumed in deep thought. *Of course, I feel guilty, but I'm not ashamed! This wasn't some tawdry one-night-stand! Leo loves me very much, and I have the same feelings for him. Never in my wildest dreams did I envision the fulfillment that I experienced last night. Why should I have to give that up? Why can't I have the best of both worlds? Besides,* she rationalized, *my marriage will be stronger now that I won't be angry because of Franco's insensitivity to my needs!* She stared out the window to her right and was fixated on a drop of rain that was slowly proceeding down the outside of the glass. The drop was meeting another drop, and the two formed a single larger drop which then met another and joined it, again making yet a larger one until this drop got so large that it raced to the bottom and disappeared. *I can have both, and I will. I deserve it, and no one will ever get hurt! Now,* she paused, *now on to Atlanta and perhaps another new chapter in my life—our lives.*

TWENTY-EIGHT

THE SUN ROSE low and late in the mid-November Florida sky. Terry never set the alarm in his hotel rooms on the road because he had long since learned that they are never as reliable as is the rising sun. He had intentionally left the curtains open as he had done so many times before, and he awoke immediately at first light. On this particular morning and in this particular hotel room, he awoke with a start because the strong rays of the sun were reflected into his eyes from a large mirror on the wall directly opposite him. This rather rude awakening had no ill effect on the start of his day, however, for he expected that this was destined to be a day he would remember for many years to come.

Moving immediately and directly from the bed to a desk in a far corner of the room Terry sat in the chair, opened his laptop and pressed the small round power button. As was his first-thing-in-the-morning ritual every day, he logged onto the Camber corporate checking account site and reviewed the cash position of the company as of midnight. His primary concern on this Tuesday morning was the sizable payroll deposit that would have to be made the next day in order to cover the impending payday on Friday. He knew that he would need at least fifty thousand dollars for the payroll, the payroll taxes, and the accompanying benefits payments and was relieved to see a cash balance in the account of fifty-five thousand dollars. *Man,* he thought, *I sure am glad that the Indians will be here with their million dollars on Thursday! Things could have gotten downright ugly real fast if it weren't for that deal!*

Terry had spent quite a few nights in the Ft. Lauderdale Embassy Suites hotel during the past several months so it was no surprise that he was greeted with a smile and a hearty, "Good morning" from every hotel staff member in his path to the front door. *How can we instill this same level of customer service in our employees?* he thought. After handing the claim check for his rented Nissan Pathfinder to the bellman at the valet parking stand, he couldn't help but notice what a beautiful morning it was in sunny South Florida. His morning weather check for the Baltimore area on his laptop had revealed that a cold rain, low ceilings, and a stiff wind from the east would preclude any student from flying out of BWI today. The irony was not lost on him that he would be conducting the final negotiations on a contract to provide jet training to Camber career students in Miami today, and those same students would be sitting idly at a window somewhere watching it rain and unable to fly in Baltimore. *Maybe*, he thought, *they should just move the entire flight school to Ft. Lauderdale to reduce the flight time lost to weather in the mid-Atlantic region.*

The trip by car from Ft. Lauderdale to Miami is only about twenty-seven miles and normally at the non-rush hour times takes about a half-hour. But at 9:00 on this Tuesday morning, Terry was stuck in bumper-to-bumper traffic on I-95 South moving at less than ten miles per hour, and he was anticipating that the trip to Miami International Airport to pick up Ale would take nearly an hour and a half. *Why didn't I stay in Miami last night instead of Ft. Lauderdale? It would have saved so much time this morning*, he thought. Then he remembered that this was not a planned trip and that he had been summoned to attend this final negotiation meeting just twenty-four hours earlier, and all of the flights last night into Miami from Baltimore were over-sold. Ale, on the other hand, was flying into Miami this morning from Atlanta, and the seating on these available flights was much more forgiving. *No matter*, he thought, *I gave myself more than enough time to make the trip this morning so I'll just sit back and enjoy the warm breeze flowing through the car.*

But as promising as he thought the results of this day would be, and as comfortable as he was in this tropical paradise, there was still this unknown factor about Ale that kept nagging at him. He had come to learn the hard way over the years about her relentless protection of her privacy so it shouldn't have come as a surprise that she had been as secretive about her business in Atlanta over the past few days. *But still*, he thought, *she usually doesn't keep secrets from me. I've been her confidant, her rock. It must be something intensely personal for her to leave me out of it as she has done. Or maybe,* he paused with a shocked look on his face, to be viewed only by the occupants of the cars stuck in the traffic around him. *Could it be? Is she thinking about defecting? Na—she wouldn't look for another job now,* he thought. *We're just now finalizing our work with Camber. We're about to go international with this one. We've waited for such a long time without any payback, and now it is all about to pay off.* But there was this little nagging thought that kept appearing from his subconscious and then disappearing again. *What if she leaves? What would I do? She's been my inspiration, my motivation to keep this dream going. Oh this is silly,* he thought, *she isn't going anywhere. She would never leave me and what we've created together!*

An electronic sign perched across the road ahead of him spelled out the words in small white lights on a black background, *Miami International Airport 8 miles*, and just to the right of the distance it said *8 minutes. Terrific*, Terry thought, *nobody is paying attention to what is going on. We're moving at six miles an hour, but the brain surgeons in the Miami transportation department think we can still cover the next 8 miles in 8 minutes. Why do they even bother putting those signs up?* he ranted to himself. *That sign must have cost a couple hundred thousand dollars to erect, and it is giving people the wrong information. Even if it was correct, how difficult is it to calculate in one's head how long it will take to travel a known distance at the speed registered on one's speedometer? A couple hundred thousand dollars of taxpayers' money and all it's doing is pissing everyone off!*

What just happened here? Terry thought, *I just went from being extremely happy to thoroughly aggravated in a very short time. Damned Ale, it's all her fault!*

Once Terry was able to exit from I-95 South onto the Miami

International Airport entrance road the traffic thinned out considerably. A quick glance at his watch confirmed that he was right on time to meet Ale after her arrival. He pulled into the cell phone waiting lot, turned off the car's engine and began glancing through a magazine he had purchased the night before upon his arrival in Ft. Lauderdale.

In less than ten minutes, the cell phone sitting on the console between the seats chimed indicating the receipt of a text message. *Under the Air Tran sign on the departure level—pink blouse,* was all that it said. Terry and Ale had learned after years of experience as air travelers that the quickest way to pick up an arriving passenger at a busy airport was usually to retrieve them on the departure rather than the arrival level. In spite of numerous warnings threatening those who are inclined to sit and wait in the arrivals area with fines or worse the artery feeding that arrivals path tends to clog much more frequently than the one leading to the departures roadway.

Terry drove the Pathfinder slowly around cars in front of him that were stopping and then pulling to the right to drop passengers off below the signs of the various airlines. United, American, Delta, finally he saw the Air Tran sign and maneuvered the car between the others that were also inching their way toward the same crowded real estate. *It's astounding,* he thought. *They can design an aircraft to fly hundreds of passengers at six-hundred miles per hour from here to California in less than six hours, but we are still moving those same people from the curb in front of the airport to the plane in the same antiquated manner that was used in the 1950s.* Just then he recognized the top of Ale's head and her pink blouse and he pulled the large SUV in front of her and popped open the rear door for her to stow her bags.

"Why such a big rental car?" she asked as she hopped into the passenger's seat and slammed the door closed behind her.

"Nice to see you too, Ale!" exclaimed Terry. "It was the only thing they had in Ft. Lauderdale at the last minute."

"How was your visit in Atlanta?" he prodded knowing full well that his feeble attempt to get her to explain why she was there in the first place would be ignored.

"Fine," she said as she casually stared out of the passenger side window. "What does our day in Miami look like?"

Terry gave her a quick glance, which immediately defeated his desire to appear uninterested in Ale's purpose for being in Atlanta without an explanation. *Let it go*, he thought, *I'll find out sooner or later.*

"We have a noon meeting at the National Flight Training facility. We need to finalize this career training contract so that when we meet with our new Indian partners on Thursday back in Baltimore we can fold this deal into our final contract with them. This whole thing is coming together quite nicely."

"What do you mean?" Ale asked offhandedly.

"The timing is just perfect. Our Indian investors will be meeting with us on Thursday with their first million-dollar portion of their investment in Camber in hand. We are going to finalize the only missing link in our product, the jet training component, today at NFT. And Jerry is in Mumbai as we speak scouting locations for our first India based flight training facility. It couldn't be more perfect."

"Sure it could," said Ale in an almost self-righteous tone.

"What do you mean?" asked Terry.

"Look Terry, I'm genuinely excited about the prospects here. We have worked hard to get Camber to this point, and we certainly deserve to have this thing come together as we have planned. But we are about to sign a contract with NFT that requires an up-front payment from us of one hundred thousand dollars. And that's money that we don't have!"

"But we will have it on Thursday when the Indians come across with our first million-dollar payment," Terry replied.

"That's just what I'm talking about, Terry. You're betting on them coming here. You're treating this Indian component as though it's a sure thing. You're about to commit to a payment of one hundred thousand dollars based on a promised investment by a group of people we've never met and who are right now eight thousand miles away from us. I would feel a lot more comfortable if we were walking into this meeting only if, or when the check from the Indians clears!"

"If or when?" Terry asked. "You know, Ale, we've been partners for a long time now. You have done a remarkably good job of accepting my idiosyncrasies, and I have tried hard to do the same with yours. But I'm finding it more and more difficult to be patient with this skeptical attitude you have demonstrated since the beginning of the Camber project. I just don't understand why you always seem to be so negative lately."

Ale thought for a moment and then she said, "Terry, first of all I'm not negative—I'm cautious. There's a big difference between the two. And second, I watched you for years before this Camber project came along being about as conservative as anyone could be when we have dealt with difficult turn-arounds. Now we are deeply involved in a project which has literally sapped the life out of us, as well as almost all of the money out of your savings, and I am watching you turn reckless with what little we have left between us."

Ale was carefully watching Terry's facial expression as he was focused on the road in front of them. She was intent on delivering her message to him without becoming too emotionally invested and thus risking accidentally and prematurely divulging the secret that she must keep from him at least for a few more days.

She continued. "During the first year of this project the economy was booming, and the airlines were hiring pilot candidates as fast as they could be sent to them. Camber's balance sheet was becoming solider each day, and our students could actually visualize the prospect that they would soon be hired to be the airline pilots they had always dreamed they would be. But in the past six months the global economy has gone into the tank, especially the Sensex in India, and late last month the United States economy nearly collapsed. We still don't know what's going to happen with that. The airlines in this country are not hiring anymore. In fact, they are engaged in the wholesale furloughing of pilots. And we have pinned all of our hopes for the growth, no actually the sheer survival of Camber on the promise of a group of investors from India who have held us at bay for over three months and whom we are supposed to meet for the first time on Thursday. This is why I'm not sitting over here painting rainbows about our situation. We're sitting on top of a house of cards here, Terry, and you act like the road ahead is paved with gold."

Terry was clearly upset with the direction in which this conversation was going. His fingers were tapping nervously on the top of the steering wheel, and a thin layer of sweat was now visible across his forehead just above the eyebrows. Although it was warm in the car with the midday Florida sun piercing the windshield, Ale noted that Terry had not appeared to be sweating before she delivered her brief but pointed state-of-the-company address to him. She wisely decided not to say anymore until he reacted to her comments.

A few minutes that seemed like an eternity to both of them passed before Terry spoke. "What do you want from me, Ale? Are we just supposed to throw our hands up in the air and give up because the economy and the U.S. airline industry have both weakened? We have an opportunity here with the Indians to keep this thing going. They have the money to invest not only in us but simultaneously in the aviation infrastructure of their own country. The growth potential of India's airline industry over the next dozen years is gigantic even if the industry here in the States retrenches. This is our only hope to salvage all of the endless energy and all of the money we have invested in this project. I can't afford to be pessimistic in the least about the future of this deal. And frankly," Terry paused for a moment to weigh his words, "neither can you."

"You have always taught me, Terry, time and time again, to have a back-up plan. What is our back up plan? What if we can't consummate this deal with NFT today? What if the Indians want more in return for their investment or want to invest less than we need to survive? What then, Terry?"

"We don't have a back-up plan this time, Ale. If any of those things happen, then we are going to have to beat the bushes quickly to find another investor. We will be out of cash by the end of the month if we don't. This whole situation with the economy and the contraction of the airline industry was so sudden. It just caught us totally by surprise. I have been so careful for so many years to manage every business as conservatively as possible in an attempt to ward off the inevitable wolf at the door. But this time it all looked so good. Everything has fallen together so well during the past few years. I guess I let my guard down. I guess I just didn't anticipate a wolf this time."

"So that's it," replied Ale. "If this all happens to fall apart, the lesson that we have learned from all of our work and money and dreams is that you can never let your guard down." Ale paused as she watched a flock of beautiful flamingos glide to a safe landing near a lake to her right, then she added, "because the wolf is always at the door!"

"Com'on, Ale!" exclaimed Terry with a new vigor in his voice. "Let's not allow our morale to sink before this important meeting with NFT. We're going to go there and close this deal. And then we're going back to Baltimore tonight to prepare for our new partners from India. And nothing is going to stand in our way. We just have to believe in ourselves and everything will be okay. You still have that kind of faith in us don't you, Ale?"

Ale dug down deep and tried to muster all of the convincing conviction she could locate within her before uttering her response to Terry. "Yes Terry, I do. But each of us should have a back-up plan." And as she gazed out the passenger side window she added almost in a whisper, "There should always be a back-up plan. Shouldn't there?"

The National Flight Training building looked especially impressive to Terry on this sunny and warm morning. He and Ale entered the lobby where they were greeted by Cynthia working behind the front desk. They signed the visitors' book, obtained and donned their visitor's badges, and were escorted to a medium-sized conference room to the left and just inside the first set of security controlled double doors from the lobby. It was only a few minutes before noon, and Harvey Crouse, the president of NFT had not yet entered the room. Ale was the first to extract file folders and her laptop from her travel valise followed swiftly by Terry doing the same. A mahogany mantle clock sitting on a credenza centered evenly in front of the wall farthest from the entrance struck twelve, and before it completed its twelve separate and distinct bass-tone gongs the door to the room opened, and Harvey entered with his chief financial officer Todd in tow. The multitude of hours spent together by these four corporate executives hammering out the agreement that they were about to consummate set the stage for the warm greetings with everyone on their feet and hands extended for shaking, exchanged by all. An outside observer of the dynamics in the room might easily mistake the gathering for a reunion of old friends rather than the beginning of a final meeting to complete the negotiations for a multi-million dollar jet training contract.

Once the pleasantries were completed the four sat at the long polished conference table with Harvey and Todd sitting together on one side directly opposite Terry and Ale on the other. Harvey began the meeting.

"Ale, Terry," he began, "our board met last night to vote on the final acceptance of the contract that we are here today to sign. I asked you to be here on such short notice because I had a hunch that a couple of our board members may want us to do some more work on the agreement before we can accept it. Turns out I was right."

Terry shot a quick look of concern over to Ale to his right and then asked, "What's the problem, Harvey?"

"I don't think it's anything insurmountable, or even unreasonable for that matter, but our board wants some more assurances against the risk that we are being asked to assume on a longer term basis," said Harvey.

There was a pointed pause that for a brief moment appeared to be created because no one was sure who should speak next.

"Harvey," said Ale with her hands open and outstretched toward both NFT executives in an apparent gesture of good will, "we have discussed the importance of both companies sharing equally in the risk involved in this project. Are you now saying, at the very last minute, that your board wants to shift more of the risk onto our plate?"

Ale had a way of addressing sensitive and potentially hazardous negotiations that clearly states the most critical issue to be addressed without upsetting the balance of the negotiations themselves. Had Terry used exactly the same words that Ale just spoke, with exactly the same inflections, facial expressions, and body language they all would have been interpreted on the other side of the table as threatening to the stability of the relationship between the two companies. Ale's talent, however, allowed the issue to be placed directly and clearly on the table in a far more constructive manner. It also opened the door for Todd to enter the conversation.

"We have worked together for months now putting this partnership together," said Todd, "so you are more than familiar with the up-front cash which we must invest in order to be ready to accommodate the training needs of the students coming to us from Camber. The hundred thousand dollars that we originally thought would be adequate to make these preparations is just not enough in the eyes of the board."

Terry shifted the weight of his body in his chair. Once to the left and then again to the right. If this did not betray his discomfort with the direction of the conversation the beads of sweat forming on his forehead and the nervous movement of the fingers on his right hand, from his little finger around to his thumb in sequence, certainly would. Ale, on the other hand, remained motionless with her eyes fixed intently on Todd.

Ale responded to Todd's revelation, "Just how much does the board now want up front, Todd?"

It was Todd's turn to shift the weight of his body in his chair. "Remember the total amount that Camber invests in the project now is just a deposit and will be prorated across the first year of operations so that Camber breaks even on the deal by the end of that year."

"How much, Todd?" repeated Ale just a little more sternly.

Todd paused, glanced once at Harvey, and then said, "Two hundred and fifty thousand."

Ale remained focused on Todd as Terry looked at her and then looked back at Harvey in disbelief.

"You mean to tell us that your board, at the very last minute, wants a hundred and fifty percent more in deposit than we have agreed all along was sufficient at one hundred thousand?" asked Terry.

Harvey felt that it was time he entered the discussion again. "The board feels strongly that the environment has changed significantly since we first began our negotiations."

"What environment?" asked Terry.

"Come on, Terry," said Harvey, "the national economy is suddenly in the tank, the airlines are furloughing instead of hiring and the availability of credit is going to be drying up rapidly during the next year and perhaps for years to come. Our risk associated with restricting our foreign business to make room for your students has quadrupled in just sixty days. We have a very savvy board especially when it comes to corporate finance. Two hundred and fifty thousand dollars is approximately the amount of profit that NFT would realize during the first year on the foreign students that we must displace to make room for Camber's students. The board wants the assurance that we have that margin in the bank should an external influence cause Camber to be unable to supply the promised students."

"You do realize, Harvey," said Ale in a rather cold tone, "that if what you are saying about the economy weren't accurate this would look very much as though your board is trying to pry more cash out of us when we just do not have the time to begin negotiating a new contract with someone else!"

Harvey scowled at the remark, his thick black eyebrows scrunching toward each other causing deep wrinkles to form at the top of his already oversized nose. "But our assessment of the economy is accurate, Ms. German and frankly if your level of trust in us were actually that low you certainly would have abandoned these negotiations a long time ago."

There was an uncomfortable silence around the table, like when someone raises the stakes in a poker game.

Terry broke the silence. "We can't make that kind of commitment immediately. We'll have to discuss it and present it to our board and then get back to you."

"We totally expected that, Terry," said Harvey. "If there is anything we can do to help you through the next few days please call on us."

"You could drop the cash requirement back down to a hundred," quipped Terry then he continued, "but I guess that isn't going to happen."

"No, it isn't," said Harvey.

Harvey and Todd then rose, shook hands and left. The door closed gently behind them, and the room was eerily quiet.

Ale opened her laptop, which had remained on, but closed on the table in front of her for the duration of the meeting. As was her habit, she immediately logged into her e-mail account to catch up on the correspondence.

Terry was silent at first then he said, "Man, this day began with such great promise and now things aren't looking so good are they?"

Ale did not respond. Her eyes were glued to the screen of her laptop, and the expression on her face was one of disbelief. Terry at once noticed her silence and looked at her. The sinking feeling in the pit of his stomach as a result of the meeting became even more pronounced as he observed and began to interpret the silent terror written all over her face.

"What is it, Ale?"

Ale looked at Terry without saying a word or even attempting to mask the desperation conveyed through her eyes. She just moved the laptop toward him and sank back in her chair in quiet exhaustion. Terry watched her for a moment and then turned to the screen to read the words of an e-mail received just a few minutes earlier.

Ale and Terry, we regret to inform you that the recent events in the global economy in general, and in India specifically, leave us no choice but to cancel our plans to invest in Camber Flight Training, Inc. at this time. Best wishes, Aman Chopra

TWENTY-NINE

THIS TURN OF events that was so devastating for Camber might make it a little easier for Ale to explain to Terry her recent life-changing decision, but in many other ways it would make it infinitely more difficult. As she sat quietly in the car on the ride from the NFT building to the Miami airport, she wondered if what transpired during the past couple of hours was a painful demonstration of what Terry had been saying all along. That fate plays a role in everything, both personal and business.

Surely, she thought, they had done everything possible with Camber during the past two years to stabilize the company and turn it into a winner. Yet, in spite of all of their efforts and all of the positive steps taken, it was something totally out of their control, something they didn't even have any influence over that reared its ugly head and may destroy the enterprise they had worked so hard to build.

She was concentrating so intensely on her own thoughts that she wasn't hearing a word that Terry was saying as he drove them to the airport. Terry was right this morning, she continued to ponder, when he said that they had not considered the potentially fatal impact of a severe downturn in the economy on the ability of a flight school to survive. They failed to create a backup plan for such a contingency, a weakness they had both witnessed many times in businesses run by novices, but one that they'd never envisioned experiencing themselves. This "mortal sin" was supposed to be indigenous only to naive entrepreneurs and reckless investors. They'd put all of their eggs into one basket. And like the tragic flaw of a character in one of those English literature stories Ale read as a college freshman, this oversight of monumental proportion was about to destroy something precious to her, Terry, and a number of innocent and unsuspecting people back in Baltimore. Worst of all, the cause was stupidity rather than fate.

"I'm sorry, Terry, my mind drifted away for a few minutes. What were you saying?"

"I said," his tone more melodic than sardonic, "that this is just a case of last minute cold feet on the part of our Indian friends. As soon as we get to the airport I'm going to call Chopra and set up a meeting for first thing tomorrow morning. It will be evening in New Delhi, so we will get everyone together on an international conference call, and we'll be able to straighten this out in short order." Terry paused for a moment, and then said, "I'm sure we will be able to make this right." Another pause, and then, in almost a whisper, "We have to, for everyone's sake."

Ale didn't have the heart to ask him if he were trying to convince her or himself, but she knew that he knew that these efforts to save the Indian investment surely would be futile.

In the terminal, the normal security rituals seemed even more preposterous than usual. Ale placed all of her metal objects into the Ziploc bag she reserved in her valise for just this purpose. She paused, however, and stared blankly at the necklace that Leo had given her at Tersiguel's before placing it into the bag.

The nonstop flight from Ft. Lauderdale to BWI was smooth and uneventful, just the way Ale liked them. Terry seemed anxious to talk incessantly about how he would turn this situation around in the meeting with Chopra, now scheduled for 8:00 the next morning in their Columbia office. But Ale told him just after takeoff that she was tired and just wanted to listen to some music on her Ipod with her Bose earphones. She'd purchased the earphones a few years ago for the express purpose of being able to ignore people politely, especially men, sitting next to her on airplanes, but she never imagined that she would use them to avoid talking with Terry. *Interesting*, she thought, *how things in life change.*

The sleek Boeing 737-800 landed on Runway 33Left at BWI exactly on time. Terry and Ale deplaned, walked silently together through the terminal to the arrivals curb, caught separate shuttles to different parking lots, he to the short-term parking facility and her to long-term. As they drove to their homes from the airport, each had a feeling of impending doom. But Ale was also experiencing a sense of closure and almost a feeling of vindication. It was apparent to her now that she no longer had to worry as much about Terry perceiving her decision as a personal betrayal. She decided that tomorrow will be the day that she will tell him, and that, under the circumstances, he should perceive it as a brilliant backup plan.

Katie, Orion's newly hired receptionist ushered Aman Chopra into the conference room at precisely 8:00 a.m. The casually clad Indian national extended his hand, first to Ale and then to Terry, in a formal, respectful manner. His expression and body language clearly communicated the remorse that he felt for having to send the poisonous e-mail to them the day before. Once seated, it became obvious to him from the silence on the other side of the table that he should be the one to speak first.

"I am so sorry," he said with his now familiar thick accent. "Our board in New Delhi decided in their meeting the night before last that the investment of three million dollars to a relatively risky project such as this would not be prudent given their recent, huge losses in both their Sensex and real estate portfolios. They have decided to postpone any further new investment projects until after the global financial markets stabilize. They extend their deepest regrets to you and your board."

"Chopra," replied Terry, who never quite understood which of the gentleman's two names was his first or last, or which one he should use to address him, but he was assured early in the relationship that referring to him as Chopra would be more than acceptable. "Surely your board understands that we have a signed contract."

"Yes, that was discussed at length at the meeting, and it was decided that, although an unfortunate remedy indeed, our firm is much better off reneging on the deal now and risking an international lawsuit than it would be to invest such a large sum of money in this project. We are acutely aware of the immense cost to you of filing such an international suit, and we also know that you do not have that kind of cash available to you."

"So it's checkmate," said Terry in a somber tone.

"I am afraid so, my friends," replied Chopra.

The three exchanged some brief pleasantries, wished each other well in future endeavors, and then Terry escorted Chopra out of the conference room and to the front door of the Orion offices after just twenty short minutes. Terry returned to the conference room where Ale was still sitting at the table with a half-emptied Starbucks cup of low fat cappuccino in her left hand. He sat in a chair, this time directly across from her, and waited for her to say something. But she did not.

After a real deep breath and a sigh apropos for this moment, Terry said, "We can start making phone calls. We'll contact anybody we know who is anybody. We don't need the full three million right now. Two hundred thousand will get us by until we can get a handle on this thing and recover. I think we have enough cash to cover Friday's payroll, and we'll just have to hold off on all of the other payables until we can scrape up the necessary cash to pay them. We can do this, Ale, I know we can."

Ale stared blankly at Terry, listening to his every word and slowly finishing the suddenly bitter tasting remains of what was once a pleasant drink. After nearly three minutes of terrifying silence, she spoke. "Terry, I'm going to take a walk outside, alone. I need to think about all of this. When I return we can talk some more. In the meantime, I think you should go ahead and authorize the transfer of funds to cover Friday's payroll. Regardless of what we decide we are going to pay our employees. We have never missed or been late with a payroll, and we're not about to start now. I'll let you know when I have returned."

Ale stood, packed her laptop and papers into her valise, and closed the conference room door quietly behind her, leaving Terry sitting at the table staring at the empty chair across from him.

She left the building and walked toward the lake. The cold rain that fell most of the day before left in its wake a clear but breezy and chilly fall day. She zipped the front of her brown, leather jacket up to her neck, wound her scarf tightly below her chin, and walked to a black, macadam path that she would follow all the way around the lake and back to the building's entrance. The wind and cold made her want to walk briskly, but her somber mood dictated a slower and more thoughtful pace.

Ale's first thoughts were about the entrepreneurs with whom she had come into contact during the past eight years. She focused on an irony that had attracted her attention many times but had never been quite as clear as it was in her mind at that moment. The greatest strength that American entrepreneurs have going for them in their quest for success is a blinding perseverance, a relentless tenacity that compels them to get up every morning set to overcome all of the challenges and obstacles which they will confront that day, and never to give up. But, as Ale had witnessed first-hand, this can also be the ultimate Achilles heel of many of these entrepreneurs. The most valuable advice that she had been able to give to a number of small business pioneers? To make sure they knew exactly where to draw the line between forging ahead against all odds and throwing in the towel because it just wasn't worth it anymore. She thought about at least a dozen of these entrepreneurs whom she had observed and with whom she has worked. Each of these hard working professionals had devoted his or her entire life, including the investment of every penny of their own personal life savings, into a business idea that had yet to lead to anything other than total frustration for them. And when these good people were confronted with the reality portraying the desperation of their situations they would launch into a rousing chorus of how they were right on the edge of success. Each would convincingly describe the latest investor or opportunity that would soon lift them from the abyss and into that elite club of wildly successful start-up pioneers. That success was just around the corner, they chanted. Just a little bit longer and it would all pay off. But, it just never seemed to happen for them. Ale thought as she walked, a little more briskly now, that she didn't want Terry to fall into this trap. It is a black hole of cockeyed optimism that sucks the life out of people without the realization of what is happening to them. That's it, she thought, I have to convince him to throw in the towel on this one.

Ale walked around the wide semicircle of paved pathway on the side of the lake directly opposite the point where she began this short journey of introspective analysis. She was now headed back toward the Orion offices.

She began to think about her own situation. *Am I doing the right thing?* she wondered. *I have my sons to think about, how will they adjust? What about the house? And, what about Terry?* And then she remembered a time several years ago when she and Terry were having dinner in Minneapolis. The topic of conversation was happiness, and she'd asked Terry to describe his definition of happiness. She smiled to herself as she recalled his explanation and the smile on his face as he spoke.

"Ale," he said, "did you ever see the movie *City Slickers*?"

"Sure," she replied.

"Do you remember the scene where Billy Crystal's character asked Curley what he thought the secret to life is? Jack Palance was sitting on top of this big black horse with a cigarette hanging from his lips, and he stared right through the slicker as he held up the index finger on his right hand and said, 'one thing.' When Crystal asked him what that one thing is, Palance answered, 'that's for you to decide!'"

"Okay," asked Ale inquisitively, "what's your one thing, Terry?"

"Well," he said, "I don't have just one thing, I have three extremely powerful things that must exist in order for me to be happy, each with its own reason for being important. First, I have to wake up every morning in a place that I totally want to be that day because way too many people wake up in a place where they just wound up being."

Ale's smile was getting so big as she remembered Terry's words that she suddenly had to attempt to hide it so that others walking the path in the opposite direction wouldn't think she was goofy.

"And second," she recalled him saying, "is that I have to look forward every day to doing exactly what I want to do that particular day because far too many people have to do what they wound up doing every day. And third, I have to wake up every morning next to the one person that I most want to spend the rest of my life with, even if that is nobody because far too many people wake up next to the person they just wound up with."

As Ale neared the entrance to the building she felt fresh and invigorated. *Nothing helps clear your head like a brisk walk around a lake*, she thought. As she climbed the three steps toward the door, she caught herself flashing a bright and happy smile at a young girl leaving the building, even though she had never seen this person before in her life.

Terry sat in the same chair staring blankly with the same expression on his face as the moment Ale had left the conference room nearly an hour earlier. He looked up at her as she entered the room and sat in the chair right next to his. She had never seen him this down before, and she waited for a moment for him to say something to her. Finally, he broke the ice.

"Well kid, what are we going to do?"

She didn't want to appear happy, so a broad smile wasn't going to work here, but she also wanted to convey to her old friend, her mentor, and her father figure that all was not lost either. So she just broke out that warm, caring, beautiful grin that kind of said, *Terry, this is going to hurt me more than it's going to hurt you.*

"Terry," she began, "we're going to call Jerry and tell him to return from India immediately. Then we're going to call a meeting of all Camber employees in the Elite conference room at 2:00 p.m. this afternoon. That's when we will announce that we are shutting the company down effective immediately. It just wouldn't be ethical for us to incur one more cent in expense or liability knowing what we know now."

Terry sat quietly and listened to his former student, and now his teacher, as she made more sense of the situation than his emotions might ever have allowed him to.

"And in the meantime, we're going to compose an e-mail to all of our students and one to all of our creditors explaining what we are doing and why. We're not going to shut this thing down and slither out of town in the middle of the night. The best defense is a strong offense, and we will just tell everyone now that we did our best."

"You're right, Ale, and we will just pick up the pieces together and move on to the next project…"

Ale was unsuccessful at interrupting his newfound enthusiasm.

"I was talking to Ben Layton last week, remember him? And he said that he knows of a company…"

"Terry," Ale interrupted forcefully, "I'm moving to Atlanta."

Terry's mouth kept moving for a few moments, but no sound was heard. His eyes glazed over as he looked straight into hers. "You're leaving?" he asked in a quivering whisper.

"Yes, Terry, I have accepted a senior management position with Coca-Cola."

Careful not to betray the smile she had so carefully placed on her face and even more careful not to allow herself the luxury of breaking down in tears, Ale slowly placed her arms around Terry's shoulders and squeezed with the firmness of undying respect, and yet the softness of an enduring love. Terry wept openly as he returned his young protégé's affection.

At 2:00 p.m. Camber employees were assembling in the largest of the two conference rooms located in the Elite building. Some sat around the expansive, well-polished board table, and the rest sat in seats around the perimeter of the room. It was highly unusual for the management of the company to call an unplanned mandatory company meeting, let alone one with only two hours notice, so the majority of the employees were on time and talking briskly among themselves before Ale and Terry arrived. Greg walked into the room first and sat in a chair in a corner by the window that overlooked the tarmac. Terry was next to arrive, followed closely by Ale. Terry made his way to the open chair farthest from the one at the end of the table that Ale unceremoniously occupied, signaling to everyone that she would be in charge of the meeting. The chatter that had been more of a din only moments earlier quickly quieted to near silence as Ale appeared ready to address the group.

"Good afternoon," she said in a formal businesslike tone. "You are all aware of our plans to contract with NFT in Miami for the provision of jet training for our career students, and of our contract with an Indian investment group which provided for the expansion of Camber into an international flight training entity. Yesterday, Terry and I were in Miami to finalize the NFT deal when we were informed by their management that their board is demanding 150% more up-front cash than originally negotiated to move forward with the contract."

Faces around the table began to look dead serious as the employees looked to those sitting to one side and then to the other. No one said a word, and the attention once again became riveted on Ale.

"Almost immediately after receiving that news, which we might have been able to accommodate with the imminent Indian investment, we opened an e-mail sent from the American representative of our friends in India, which informed us that there will be no investment forthcoming due to the suddenly unstable global economy. This morning Terry and I met with Mr. Chopra and he confirmed that there is no hope of reviving the Indian deal anytime soon. I am afraid we are here this afternoon to announce to you that Camber Flight Training, Inc. simply cannot survive without these critical pieces of our strategic puzzle, and we are forced to close the company effective immediately. There will be no severance for anyone, but this Friday's payroll will be distributed in full as usual. We profoundly appreciate the loyalty and hard work of everyone in this room, and we sincerely regret having to terminate the business in this manner. It is anticipated that we will be vacating the premises next door as soon as possible, so we ask that you take all of your belongings with you today when you leave. We wish each and every one of you the very best."

Ale rose and turned to exit with Terry and Greg walking closely behind her. The employees remained in the room for several minutes, appearing to be in shock from the surprise announcement.

Ale thanked Greg for joining them in this difficult meeting, knowing full well that he too stood to lose a significant amount of money that he had invested in the company. Then she advised both of her male counterparts as they walked from the Elite building across the parking lot to the Camber facility that the three of them should wait in the lobby until all employees had cleaned out their desks and departed. Earlier in the afternoon Ale informed the Elite management that they would have to change all of the locks to doors accessing the Camber portion of the building at approximately 3:00 p.m.

History has proven that companies experiencing shut downs like this one at times have been hit by vandalism, and all precautions must always be taken to avoid the destruction of company property. Greg asked if the security steps weren't a little draconian and Ale responded immediately stating that they weren't taking any chances.

Within an hour of the adjournment of the meeting, all Camber employees had recovered their personal effects from the premises and driven from the parking lot to wherever it was that they would be meeting to drown their sorrows. Greg departed about a half-hour earlier, and Terry and Ale were sitting in what two hours before had been a bustling flight school lobby. They were both silent as they watched three maintenance workers move from door to door changing locks and then checking them with the newly tooled keys.

"Come on, Terry, let's get out of here," said Ale as she searched in her purse for her car keys.

"Na, Ale, you go ahead. I'm going to stick around for awhile."

"You're not doing yourself any good by staying here now, Terry," she said. "Go home and do something to get your mind off of these two very dismal days."

"I'm okay. You go home to those beautiful kids and give them a whopping big hug from Uncle Terry."

Ale gave him a hug and a kiss on his leathery cheek and then she walked toward the front door of the lobby. Just as she was about to go through the door, Terry called to her. "Ale," he said, and then paused. She stopped and turned. "I'm tremendously proud of you, kid! Someday I'll be able to say that I once worked with the CEO of Coca-Cola."

"Thanks, Terry, but that'll never happen," she chuckled.

"Why? Because you're a woman? Because you're Hispanic? Whatsa matter, you never heard of Indra Nooyi? If you can dream it, kid, you can do it! Don't you ever forget that I told you that!"

"I won't Terry, my friend."

Ale walked in the brisk late afternoon air to her car, one of two remaining in the parking lot. *Interesting*, she thought, *that Terry would mention the woman from Calcutta who, just a year earlier was named CEO of Pepsi Corporation. Maybe? You think?* She laughed out loud as she opened the door to her car and climbed in. *First things first, girl*, she mused, *first things first!*

❄ ❄ ❄ ❄ ❄

Ale arrived home from the office earlier than she had in months. She entered the front door, and as she closed it behind her she placed her keys and handbag on an antique table to her left. She checked on the boys who were in their rooms doing homework, and proceeded directly down the stairs to the finished basement area that Franco had been calling home ever since he began pursuing his medical degree. Armed with an informally memorized script of sorts she approached Franco, who was sitting at his desk facing away from her with earphones on his head and staring at the oversized computer monitor as always. Ale was determined that she would not acquiesce to any attempt on his part to postpone the conversation she had planned. She gently tapped him on the shoulder to capture his attention, and when he turned toward her she motioned to him to remove the earphones. She could hear from the earpieces now resting on his lap that he had been listening to another online medical lecture, and she almost felt guilty about the interruption.

"We have to talk, Franco," she said without smiling and in her more serious tone of voice.

"Ale," he said as he smiled and began to rise from his chair to greet her. "I didn't expect you so early."

"I know," she replied, "sit back down, we have to talk." She sat on a steel folding chair beside the desk and to Franco's right as she began her prepared delivery. *Keep it short and without emotion*, she thought as she said, "Franco, the Indian and Florida deals have suddenly gone sour and we just had to close Camber permanently."

"Oh baby, I'm sorry to hear that," he said as he quickly glanced back at the computer monitor that was continuing with the lecture he had been watching earlier, "you and Terry will just have to get some more clients and move on, right?"

"Not this time, Franco," she replied, now getting seriously annoyed with the ongoing lecture distracting him. "Turn that thing off for a few minutes, please," she said, allowing her impatience to show. Franco shut the computer down and turned back toward Ale with the slightest expression of annoyance on his face.

"Before I met Terry in Miami yesterday for the most crucial of our meetings I was in Atlanta for two days for the final negotiations for the position of Senior Vice President of Human Resources for Coca-Cola. At the end of those negotiations, I accepted the job, and I begin next month."

"Coca-Cola?" he asked, now expressing a higher level of interest. "How are you going to do that?"

Now Ale was visibly angry. Upon first hearing of the single most exciting thing that had happened in her career since she began working with Terry years before, her husband had no congratulations for her. There was no sign whatsoever of happiness as a result of this major bit of news for the family as well as for her personally. His only reaction was to ask how she was going to pull it off, referring of course to his roots, which were firmly planted here on the East Coast.

"I'll tell you how I'm going to do that!" she said communicating her extreme disappointment in his selfish and thoughtless response. "I'm moving to Atlanta with the boys as soon as possible, and I'm asking you now if you will be moving with us." She hadn't wanted this conversation to become contentious or emotional, but Franco's obvious indifference once again to her and her needs triggered all of the emotions of her long-standing disappointment in him and their marriage and brought them immediately to the surface.

"Wait a minute," he said, standing and walking slowly away from her. He turned and asked, "You mean you've made the decision without even discussing it with me? You applied for the job, traveled to Atlanta, probably on several occasions, and now, when you are giving me an ultimatum, is the first I am hearing of it?" Franco now demonstrated a level of displeasure equal to Ale's.

"I didn't tell you about it because I was certain I wouldn't get an offer and besides," she said after a brief pause, "frankly I didn't think you would be all that interested." *There, I said it,* she thought, *you just don't care anymore about me, or my needs.*

"I can't leave here now, Ale! I'm in my last year of medical school. I have already been accepted at Georgetown to begin my internship in the spring. How can you be so self-centered that you accept a job hundreds of miles away just when you know I can't leave now?"

Ale struggled to contain her anger, and she made every attempt to disregard his description of her as self-centered. She quickly decided that an escalation of this emotional confrontation would serve no purpose. "So I guess you are saying that you're not coming with us, is that right?"

"I can't, Ale," he replied in a much more subdued voice, "you know that! Please reconsider the job with Coke. I promise I'll make it up to you once I have my own practice."

"I can't do that, Franco, you know that. Then I guess it is settled. The boys and I will be leaving for Atlanta immediately. We'll discuss the details when you have the time. You can get back to your lecture now, Franco."

Ale stood, turned to her left toward the steps without looking further at Franco, and climbed to the floor above. Franco placed the headphones around his ears, powered up the computer, and resumed the lecture that Ale had interrupted.

❊ ❊ ❊ ❊ ❊

Two days later, at 7:00 a.m., Terry drove the largest capacity truck available for rent from Ryder up to the front door of the Camber offices. He began to pack all of the files, furniture, computers, and ground school supplies into the truck. By 5:00 p.m. he had loaded all of the assets of the now defunct flight school into the truck by himself, and then he drove the only remaining remnants of the previous two years of his life to his home. He spent the rest of the night and most of the next day unloading the truck and delivering its contents into the mostly empty rooms of his modest abode.

THIRTY

IN MANY WAYS this Monday morning, December 1, 2008, started out like any other morning in Ale's recent life. But in some ways it was dramatically different—and would be for years to come. She got herself out of bed at the same time as usual, got the boys up and moving, and fixed some breakfast for all of them. But on this crisp, bright morning on the outer edges of Washington, D.C., in suburban Maryland, Ale German would not be dropping her sons off at school and then driving on to her office in Columbia or to Camber Flight Training, Inc. Her bags were packed, as were those of her sons and were piled snuggly in the back of her Pathfinder. On this particular morning, Ale German's life was about to change, forever.

One of the extraordinarily unusual differences about this morning was that Franco joined Ale and the boys at the breakfast table, something that had not occurred for many months. The meal was a quick and quiet one, with all sitting around the circular glass kitchen table exchanging rapid glances at each other more as though they were strangers than family members.

"Okay boys, time to go," said Ale as she rose from the table and began to clear the dishes to be placed in the dishwasher.

"I'll do that after you leave, Ale," said Franco, with a strained smile.

Everyone walked slowly through the living room to the front door and then stopped just after Ale opened the door. She turned to Franco, and put her arms around him in a way that she hadn't in years. She hugged him tightly, and he returned the hug with even more intensity.

"I never in a million years thought you would decide not to come with us," she said with a lump in her throat that seemed the size of a baseball.

"I never in a million years thought you would even consider going without me," he replied.

Still hugging, but now looking each other straight in the eye, Ale said, "You know, Franco, you can change your mind anytime. You can join us in Atlanta anytime," she paused for a few moments. "You do know that, right?"

Franco did not answer. He gave Ale a gentle kiss on her forehead, released her from the hug they had shared, and turned toward Stefan while in one motion slowly dropping to his left knee. "Take care of yourself, sport," he said with tears now visible in his eyes. "And take care of your mom and your little brother. You're going to be the man of the house now, so make me really proud of you, okay?"

"I don't want us to leave you, Daddy!" exclaimed Stefan, now failing to hold back the sobs.

"Don't cry, son, we'll all be together again soon, you'll see. In the meantime, you have to be a man about this, okay?"

"Okay, Daddy," a long hug and a pause followed, and then Stefan said, "I love you Daddy!"

"I love you too, son!" said Franco as he turned toward Johan, who was by this time crying uncontrollably. They hugged, and Johan would not let go of Franco's neck until his father gently removed his hands one at a time. He lifted Johan and handed him to Ale. With a kiss on his left cheek, he said, "I love you, Johan—don't you ever forget that."

Franco looked deeply into Ale's eyes one more time. Then he turned and walked away from all three of them, and he did not look back as he disappeared through the basement door, which closed quietly behind him. Ale steered the boys, still sobbing, through the front door, and closed and locked it behind her.

She could hardly keep from bursting into tears as she got the boys settled in the car. For two brief, separate moments, she almost convinced herself that she should go back into the house and into the basement and drag Franco with them, even though it would be against his will. *Maybe I wouldn't drag him,* she thought, *but perhaps I should beg him to go with us. No, it is what it is. Time to move on with our lives!*

In the car, the boys were sitting quietly, an unusual occurrence in itself, and listening to music through their individual earphone sets. As she drove north on I-95 toward Baltimore, she began to think about that day, ten years earlier, when she decided to get her college degree. She remembered the exact moment that she made her decision as though it had happened just yesterday. There were so many terrifying questions in her head wrestling for attention back then. *How will I get the money to pay for college? How will I make the time to study with a full time job and children to care for? Am I smart enough to pass the courses? Will all of the hard work, money spent, and sacrifices that I am going to have to make pay off in the form of a better job, and better pay than I have now? Is it the right thing to do for my boys and for me? What if I fail?*

Ale had discussed her desire to start working on a college degree with friends and family members during the weeks before that day when she actually made her decision. Everyone meant well in these discussions, but no one gave her any encouragement whatsoever. Some even criticized her desire to attempt to achieve such a lofty goal, given her job and family circumstances. "Raise your family," she was told emphatically. "Save the money you will need for college, and when the boys are grown maybe you can go to a community college part-time." One of her closer friends advised her, again with all of the best of intentions, "You are an immigrant, and you are still learning English as a second language. What makes you think you could ever write papers and pass college courses even if you are able to fit it into your hectic schedule? Wise up and take care of the kids and forget this nonsense. Save yourself the heartache that will come with failure!" That was the exact moment when she decided to move full speed ahead with her quest for a college degree. Her thought process in making the decision was clear and devoid of emotion. In effect, she was making her first executive, business decision. But it was a life-changing one. And now she had just completed her MBA as well.

I appreciate the importance of the level of caution contained in the advice of my friends and family, she thought at the time. And I fully understand that I am not exactly the strongest candidate for this kind of a step toward higher education, given my background and less-than-perfect language skills. But then something struck her. It became as vivid and convincing as any thought that had come to her at any time in her life. If I succumb to all of the reasons that people tell me that this will not work, as well-meaning as they may be, then I will never know. I am going to do it, she thought with conviction. But I'm not going to do it to prove to anyone else that they are wrong. I am going to do it to prove to myself that I am right. I know that I have what it takes to succeed at whatever I set out to do. I will dig down deep, and I will make it happen. Life never moves forward, she thought, when you are looking back. I must never look back. I am moving forward with my life and those of my sons. Everything will be just fine! And it was fine. She graduated with high honors, and she learned a lot of lessons, the most significant of which was to set her goals and to achieve them, even in the face of others who may not support her in her efforts.

Ale's concentration was abruptly broken by a large truck suddenly cutting in front of her on I-95, causing her to step on the brake swiftly and swerve to the left in the path of cars approaching her from behind in the faster lane.

"Mom," exclaimed Johan from the back, "what happened?"

"Nothing, Johan," said Ale in a less-than-convincing tone. "Everything will be just fine!" she said with a smile.

Her mind wandered again as she used a napkin from between the seats to wipe the sweat from her hands and the steering wheel. This time she thought about her first night of class as a freshman at Loyola. She was so nervous about being there that she feared those around her and her instructor, Terry Longbow would be able to see her trembling uncontrollably. When she submitted the first paper required for that class, which she had written and rewritten a dozen times in the middle of the night, she was certain that she would receive a failing grade on it. So fearful and lacking in self-confidence was she, that she could remember sitting in the parking lot of the building where her second night of class of this course was to be held. She was just sitting there trying to convince herself that if she just went home and forgot about this college thing everything would be alright. Fortunately, she thought now, she wasn't terribly convincing. When she sat at her table in the classroom, Terry placed her graded first paper in front of her, face down. She looked at him with terror in her eyes as she turned the paper over. On top, in red pen, clear as day, was the letter grade "A." Ale remembered repeatedly looking at the name on the top because she was certain that he had handed her someone else's assignment. She couldn't decide whether to scream or cry, so she did neither. Instead, she looked up at her instructor with an expression of strong will and assurance, and said, "Thank you."

Terry smiled and responded with a quiet, but clearly discernible, "Don't thank me, you earned every bit of that "A!"

As she turned the Pathfinder to bear right onto State Highway 100, driving toward BWI airport, Ale thought, *and that's how Alejandra German first learned that there truly was a chance that she could accomplish what she had set out to do.* She laughed when she recalled that the first thing she wanted to do after that class was over was to go to all of her friends and family who doubted her, and show them that Ale is an "A" student. But instead, she folded the paper and slipped it into her briefcase as she opened the Course Syllabus to take a quick look at assignment number two.

"Mom," said Johan, "listen to this song on my earphones."

"Not right now, son, Mommy has to concentrate on driving safely in this traffic. I'll listen to it on the plane."

On the plane, she thought, *I cannot believe this is happening to us!*

Her thoughts drifted once again, this time to her Loyola graduation day. It was June, 2004. The Meyerhoff Symphony Hall in downtown Baltimore, the venue rented for the occasion was packed with graduates and their guests. She remembered that the air conditioning for the building was not up to the task of adequately cooling the cavernous theater. It was hot, the ceremony seemed to take forever, and the crowd was noisily screaming every time the name of a graduate was announced. But Ale was oblivious to her surroundings. The only thing she actually heard was exactly what she had come to hear. "Alejandra German, Bachelor of Science in Business—with honors!" There it was—with honors. All "As" and one lousy "B" in a statistics course. And she only missed an "A" in that course by two stinking points. It didn't matter. "With honors" still resonated in her head to this day, especially when she would begin to doubt herself—like she was now.

The traffic slowed to a crawl as Ale merged onto Maryland Route 3, just a few minutes away from the Elite Flight Support Services terminal. *It seems odd*, she thought, *that today I will be arriving at the Elite general aviation terminal, just as I have so many times in the past two years. But this time I will be a passenger boarding a private jet instead of conducting a meeting with Camber employees, potential investors, or prospective customers.* She was apprehensive about her first trip on a sleek corporate aircraft, and she was dreading the farewell that Terry had planned for her at Elite just before she boards the plane. Terry had insisted during their phone conversation the night before that he wanted to say goodbye to Ale and the boys as they embarked on their new life in Atlanta. As uncomfortable as Ale was with the prospect of a tearful goodbye, she could hardly refuse Terry's request after all they had been through together.

Maybe I should have said no, she thought.

Ale continued her conversation with herself. The boys were quiet in the seat behind her and the traffic was tedious, so, what else was there to do? She could not help but to reflect on her relationship with Terry. The one person who had enough faith in her when she graduated from Loyola to hire her and then make her a full partner in his business. I wonder, she thought, what his real reaction is to my abrupt decision to make this move. Does he think I am a rat deserting a sinking ship? That's silly, she mused with a muffled snicker and a wry sort of smile. The ship sank straight to the bottom of the sea two weeks ago. If anyone totally understands my decision to accept the professional opportunity of a lifetime, it's Terry. In fact, she rationalized, it would have been a much more difficult split if Camber had succeeded. Then I certainly would have been abandoning

Terry and Orion and leaving them in an extremely difficult situation. Yes, she thought, it's easier and better this way. Her only regret with the way things have turned out is that Terry is now alone and he has lost just about everything. *I just wish there was something, anything, that I could do to help him,* she thought.

Ale made the left turn from Aviation Boulevard and accelerated onto Aronson Drive toward the Elite terminal. She could not control her urge to turn her head to the right and look at the building that once housed the offices and people of the now defunct Camber Flight Training, Inc. There was only one car in the parking lot in front of the building—Terry's. The lot that she and Terry had fought so hard to reserve exclusively for the Camber students now was barren. The sign on the front of the building, which once so proudly announced in blue and gold letters and a logo that here stood the Camber flight school, had been covered with what looked like black plastic trash bags loosely fastened to it. How ironic, Ale thought, that I would be seeing the skeleton of what was once a center of my life, just before I depart for a new job—and a new life. Her earlier enthusiasm and excitement surrounding the trip she was about to take was suddenly punctuated with sadness injected by the sight she had tried so hard to ignore. She caught herself worrying about Terry and what he would do now that the project they had worked so hard to bring back to life had indeed died. And even more distressing to her was the thought of what Terry would do now, without her. Maybe I should have turned this offer down, she thought, so that I could stay and help Terry pick up the pieces and start over. Not to mention that if I had turned it down the boys would not be leaving their father behind. The doubts and fears, similar to ones that had always plagued Ale before a major change in her life, were starting to eat away at the strong confidence and enthusiasm she'd felt earlier that morning. Am I doing the right thing—for my boys, and for me? What about Terry? Don't I have a responsibility to stand by him?

Ale parked on the far side of the Elite customer parking lot. She knew that she would be back several weekends through the winter and spring to sell the house and clean up other business, and having it handy at the airport gave her one less thing to have to worry about during her transition.

She got the boys out of the car, and while they were walking toward the front of the Elite building Terry appeared, walking toward them from behind the automatic doors.

"Uncle Terry," shouted Johan as he broke from his mother's hand and ran toward the man who had done so much for their family.

"Johan, my little man," said Terry as he knelt on the cold concrete with his arms fully extended.

Terry looked much older and more exhausted than Ale had ever noticed before. She turned slightly away from them when she saw tears beginning to form in her mentor's weary eyes. The old man and the young boy hugged each other an especially long time in the cold, winter air. It was clear to anyone who saw them that they were either seeing each other for the first time in a long while, or they anticipated that it would be a long time before they would see each other again.

Finally, the silence and the bear hug were broken.

"Johan," said Terry, "go inside and pick out an ice cream cone for yourself. I'll be along in a few minutes. I want to talk to your mom."

"Okay Uncle Terry, I'll see you inside."

Terry lived in dread fear of this day since the first day he started working with Ale. He hadn't slept for at least seventy-two hours, and most of that time he spent quietly, in the darkest room of his home, thinking about her, them, the empire that they tried to build, and the empire they surely lost. Although happy that she had been able to land on her feet quickly, he was devastated that this chapter in his life, certainly the happiest and most fulfilling years of his entire life, were now coming to an end. I just assumed all along, he thought, that Ale and I would be working together until the day that I die. Shouldn't take things for granted! Should never take anything for granted!

He watched her as she gave the keys to one of the Elite porters so that her bags could be transferred directly to the plane. He smiled as he thought about all of the times that they had laughed about all of the big stuff that just makes you laugh. And about all of the little stuff that just makes you laugh. Ale had a bright, contagious smile and a haunting laugh that just begs everyone around her to join in and laugh with her—even if no one knew what she was laughing about.

Ale turned from the porter and walked straight toward Terry. Her smile was more subdued now, delivering a combination of affection, respect, and a warm happiness to see the man on whom she had relied so many times to make things that went wrong turn out right.

But the serenity in her smile was instantly betrayed by the morose message sent by her eyes.

Terry was the first to break the awkward silence. "Well," he said with the slightest quiver of his bottom lip, "I guess this is it, kid."

"Hey," said Ale, "I don't want any of this sad goodbye stuff—you understand? I'm only going to Atlanta—it's just an hour-and-a-half away. And besides," she was having a tough time keeping her emotions under control, but she was pleased that she seemed to be hiding it well, "I plan on bugging the ever-loving hell out of you by phone. D'ya think I'm going to be able to pull this off all by myself?"

"Yeah, Ale, that's exactly what I think."

"Well, you're wrong, Terry! You are a tremendously vital part of our lives," she pointed toward the boys waiting for her in the lobby, "and I'm not about to let that end anytime soon. Okay?"

Terry put his arms around Ale and squeezed. It wasn't a bear hug, although it could have been with the overcoats they were both wearing. Each of them looked straight out above the other's shoulder because each knew that any eye contact at this moment would have resulted in both breaking down and crying.

Terry could hardly whisper his desperate response, "Okay."

As he eased back from her and turned toward the lobby, he pointed through the expansive windows on the other side of the room.

"There's a plane out on the ramp that's waiting for you. I figure it's costing somebody about six thousand dollars an hour to sit there. So—you better get going."

Ale stooped to pick up a small travel bag, and walked briskly through the automatic doors into Elite's well appointed lobby. Terry followed her in.

"Mom, look at this ice cream!" Johan squealed.

"Johan, it's nine o'clock in the morning! You know better than to eat ice cream this early!"

Johan instinctively knew that she was kidding as he walked away with the chocolate ice cream cone dripping over his fingers.

"Ms. German," came a voice from over her left shoulder.

She turned toward the sound and replied, "Yes?"

"My name is Cynthia Stewart. I will be your Captain on the flight to Atlanta this morning." A young woman standing to the Captain's right smiled and said, "And I am Kaelyn Capobianco, your First Officer."

Ale was immediately embarrassed. Her first instinct when she turned and saw the two women, dressed in matching, crisp white shirts and dark slacks, was to assume that they might be the flight attendants for the ride south. She immediately suppressed her surprised expression and replaced it with that disarming smile of hers.

"It is a pleasure to meet you," she said. "Are we ready to go?"

"Whenever you are, Ms. German," said the Captain, with the appropriate degree of formality.

Ale, her sons, and Terry followed the flight crew through the ramp door onto the tarmac, walking toward a sleek, gleaming white Grumman G-5 corporate jet parked in the closest spot to the Elite terminal.

The steps of the aircraft extended down from the body of the plane and would fold up into the doorway when all were on board and ready to depart. Ale sent the boys up the steps with instructions to find a seat.

"What seat numbers do we have?" asked Stefan.

"Any seat you want, son," was Ale's reply. "We're the only passengers on this flight!"

To say that the majestic G-5 was impressive would serve as a massive understatement. Elite ramp attendants were busy completing the refueling with long hoses attached to the underside of the wings. Kaelyn, the First Officer, was slowly walking around the aircraft carefully executing a mandatory visual inspection of every part of the plane that could be seen and touched from the ground.

Ale stood silently by Terry's side at the base of the steps as she looked at the large and majestic vehicle that would carry her family to a brand new challenge in her life. She was impressed by the plane, and its crew, and with the fact that her new employer sent this expensive symbol of corporate success to fetch her from the familiarity of her past, and carry her to the curiously exotic vision that she had conjured of her future. But she was most impressed with the large tail of the aircraft. There it was, this solid white structure protruding into the dark blue sky, announcing to the world that Ale German was now a member of the senior management team of Coca-Cola, USA.

"Look at you, Ale!" exclaimed Terry. "Senior Vice President of Human Resources for one of the largest manufacturing and marketing corporations in the world."

Ale turned, put her arms around Terry one last time and said, "I'll always love you, Terry Longbow! How can I ever repay you for what you have done for us?"

Terry hugged back and didn't skip a beat with his reply. "You just did, Ale! Take real good care of yourself and those future executives of yours."

Ale turned and climbed the steps to the plane. She sat in a plush leather seat at a window looking out onto the ramp toward the Elite terminal. As she watched Terry walk slowly with a slight limp to the terminal door, she broke down and cried for the first time on this emotionally charged morning.

Stop it, she admonished herself. *You never cry. Is it because I'm leaving Terry? Is it because we're leaving Franco behind? Or because I'm leaving everything that is known to me for everything that is unknown? Maybe it's because I'm scared of this plane ride? Or maybe because I'm afraid I'm going to fail in Atlanta? Whatever it is—stop it! You never cry—do you?*

The phone in the console rang and it startled Ale back into her surreal surroundings. She heard the voice of the Captain ask, "Are you ready to leave, Ms. German?"

"Yes," said Ale, "let's go to Atlanta!"

But then she almost shouted, "Wait! Not yet—just a few more minutes!"

What she saw out the large oval window shocked her. It scared her and yet excited her at the same time. She quickly wiped what was left of some stray tears from her eyes to make certain that what she was seeing was real. But in an instant she knew that it was. Running toward the plane at full speed from the doors of the Elite lobby with a large duffel bag over his right shoulder was Franco, waving his arms and shouting, "Wait!" He leapt onto the steps of the aircraft and climbed them two at a time until he appeared in the front of the cabin. Ale had not said a word to the boys when she saw Franco running across the ramp, so the screams and squeals from them when they saw their father were the result of genuine surprise and excitement. They immediately left their seats and ran to him with arms outstretched as he picked them both up into the air in one single motion.

Franco walked over to Ale who had just stood to greet him and said, "My internship is with you and the boys in Atlanta! I know that now."

Ale gave Franco a hug while he was still holding the boys and then said, "I never in a million years thought you would decide not to come with us!"

He replied looking her straight in the eye, "I never in a million years thought you would ever consider going without me."

They both laughed as Ale sat back down, lifted the phone from the console and said to the Captain, "Now we're ready to depart!"

"Yes, Ms. German," was the reply from the flight deck.

A member of the Elite ground crew was standing directly in front of the Coca-Cola corporate aircraft and facing it with his arms straight upward, and his hands pointed to the sky. It was his responsibility to make sure that the plane taxied safely from its parking spot without striking anything in its path. The two Rolls Royce engines were screaming now as Coca-Cola Four, cleared by BWI Ground Control to Runway 10, taxied toward the ground crew member and then made a ninety-degree turn to the right.

No turning back now, Ale thought as she made sure her sons had strapped themselves into their seats securely.

I wonder why they're taking us all the way out to Runway 10 for takeoff, she thought. *That's almost the farthest runway from the general aviation ramp. Oh God,* she thought, *I'm thinking like an aviator!*

As Coca-Cola Four taxied slowly to the active runway, Ale thought again about her decision and about her past. She knew that the decision to join Coke should eliminate a lot of risk in her life. After all, there will always be a Coca-Cola, and there will always be a need for a Senior Vice President of Human Resources at that company. But the turns in her short life that led her to this auspicious moment once again flashed before her eyes in rapid sequence. Once again she remembered the doubts she'd constantly had about her own ability to succeed in a country that just seventeen years earlier was totally foreign to her. The discouraging advice that she'd received when she wanted to earn a college degree. The intimidation that she'd quietly absorbed from the experience of being a woman in a man's world.

And then she chuckled when the irony of an all-female flight crew sitting in the front seats of this multi-million dollar aircraft sank in for her.

Ale heard the intercom click, and she smiled when she heard the Captain say, "We've been cleared for take-off, Ms. German."

She was surprised at how quiet it was on the inside as the wheels of the plane separated from the runway below. And out of her window she saw the Camber building shrinking in size as the G-5 climbed rapidly into the sky. *That's why we were sent to Runway 10*, she thought. *I was supposed to get one last look at the past.*

Just then the chime sounded from her cell phone indicating that she had just received a text. With the phone in her left hand, she opened the text with her thumb, and she was surprised to see that it was from Leo. "I'll be visiting you soon and often in Atlanta! Love, Leo."

A warm narrow smile appeared on her face behind the index finger of her right hand as she read the text several more times and then looked at her sons sitting in the seats across the aisle from hers. *I think I understand now*, she thought. *Happiness is a fickle illusion. I've been desperately pursuing an illusion—something that will always be just a little bit beyond my grasp. I now know that my tenacious quest for happiness will always result in self-*

doubt and frustration. I will achieve a much greater fulfillment in my life if I ignore the long-term end, which is happiness and simply pursue the short-term means, which are satisfaction and contentment. Steve Jobs was right—the journey IS the reward!

Ale sat back in her plush leather seat and closed her eyes. She thought about the dream for her future that she had so many times when she was a child. The one where she was a princess and there was a castle. And the one where there was also a knight. For the first time in her adult life, she was comfortably content. And as the powerful jet made a graceful climbing turn to the right in the direction of Atlanta, Ale smiled and thought, *I can't wait to see where tomorrow takes us!*

THE END